The Codex Rebellion

Shield of Silence, Book 1

A.D. Tenebris

RWCM, LLC

Contents

An Atlas of the Story

Chapter 1: The Book Burn

The morning sun cracked open the day with a slab of dirty gold across the public square, throwing long, cold shadows that seemed to shiver as much as the citizens assembled. The square—once a place of midday commerce and midnight flings—stands repurposed, stripped of color and sound, save for the metallic whir of drone-cameras and the click of boot heels on tile. Every shopfront is shuttered; the fountains run dry, filled now with nothing but stagnant, green-tinted rainwater and a slurry of torn paper.

Kaia stands near the front of the crowd, hands jammed into the pockets of her over sized coat, shoulders hunched in a way that makes her look younger than eighteen, though the cut of her jaw betrays something old and unyielding. She's not tall, but what she lacks in height she makes up for in a kind of coiled tension, the kind of posture that says she's here on her own terms. Her eyes—deep brown, almost black in this light—never left the center of the square, where scaffolding formed a crooked ring around the largest bonfire pit Kaia had ever seen. At the pit's base, books pile up in a gluttonous heap: textbooks, prayer scrolls, hand bound diaries, popular science rags, cheap adventure serials, and, scattered among them like trampled flowers, children's picture books with covers as bright as bruises.

She clutches her copy of "The Girl with the Silver Thread" under her coat, pressed hard against the heat of her sternum. In her fist, hidden and palmed with professional sleight, is a scrap of aged vellum: her mother's bookmark token, a blue-ribboned slip embossed with a feather. The paper is soft at the edges from years of nervous fiddling. Kaia tasted metal at the back of her tongue, not unlike the blood that slicked your teeth after a fall. She swallows, but it stays.

The square fills slowly, a thickening crowd of silent citizens—mothers, scholars, children, shoulders brushing as they press closer to the pyre. The crowd—two hundred strong, maybe more—packed in tighter as more citizens were herded from adjoining streets by the blocky silhouettes of government Censors. The Censors' uniforms are new this season, the kind of precise tailoring that screams confidence and coin, though every inch of it is designed to be anonymous: matte olive-green, zero insignia, zero humanity. Their faces are rendered as featureless slabs behind polarized visors. Each carries a long baton and a sidearm. It would be comical if it wasn't so perfectly calculated. Kaia wonders if that was the point.

A mother with a tangled bun and a stained utility apron pulls her two boys close, pressing their faces into her hips as the eldest—barely seven, thin arms wrapped around a battered comic book—tries not to cry. An old man in a scholar's cap stands ramrod straight, bookless, eyes fixed on the ground as if studying the subtle cracks between flagstones. Further down, a woman in a patched-up windbreaker hugs a stack of handwritten ledgers to her chest. Her nails are bitten to the quick. There is a low current of conversation, all of it conducted in a language of glances and barely-audible whispers.

At exactly six minutes past dawn, a siren blared—a reedy, unpleasant wail designed to get under the skin and stay there. It does its job. The crowd jolts as one. Kaia's knuckles went white around the book's spine.

Censors line the perimeter of the square, some standing sentinel, others prowling the edges like wolves denied the kill. At the head of the pyre, a raised dais has been constructed—temporary, but well built. A woman stands atop it: not tall, but every inch a commander, her hair hidden beneath the standard-issue cap, her posture radiating authority. She holds a voice amplifier in one hand and a tablet in the other. When she speaks, the sound fills every crack in the square.

"Attention, citizens of New Vahlien," the woman's voice rings. "By executive order of the League of Security and Censorship, all unauthorized written materials are to be surrendered immediately. Compliance ensures your safety and the safety of those around you."

In her voice resonates not anger, but a profound certainty honed through countless repetitions in a thousand towns, with the promise of a thousand more to come. The very words reverberate from the speakers perched on high scaffolding, underscoring the omnipresence of surveillance beyond mere human sight.

Censors moved into the crowd, arms outstretched. "Books. Now. No exceptions," they repeated, each word a bludgeon. A few people in the back resist at first, clutching their volumes like life preservers, but the press of bodies and the hard eyes behind the visors make protest evaporate. One by one, citizens pass forward their stories.

Kaia sees the little boy with the comic. His mother kneels and pries the book from his hands, gently, like removing a splinter. The boy's lips quiver, but he does not make a sound. When the Censor reaches him, he merely holds out his arms, empty, eyes wide and dry. The Censor snatches the book, its cover a riot of reds and yellows, and tosses it toward the pyre. The boy's mother keeps her hands on his shoulders. He stands very straight, like he's learned that from someone important.

Rows ahead, a girl not much older than Kaia surrenders a collection of poetry, its spine shot through with duct tape. She kisses the cover once, quick, then hands it over without meeting the Censor's gaze.

Kaia's turn comes. The Censor in front of her is tall, genderless behind the armor, but the movement of his gloved fingers suggests impatience. "Book. Now."

She pulls "The Girl with the Silver Thread" from her coat, her thumb lingering on the embossed title. The Censor's hand closes over the cover, but Kaia doesn't let go.

"Please," she said, voice tight. "This was my mother's."

The Censor tilts his head. "No exceptions," he repeated. But his grip doesn't tighten. For half a heartbeat, Kaia thinks he might hesitate.

He does not. With a practiced jerk, he yanks the book free, leaving Kaia's fingers gripping nothing but the air. For a moment, she is nine years old again, crouched behind a couch as men in identical uniforms smashed the glass of her childhood bookshelf, taking everything that wasn't stamped with the right insignia. Her mother's hands, soft and strong, had shielded Kaia's face then, whispering: "Remember, stories outlive stone."

The book lands atop the pile with a flat, unimpressed thud. Kaia doesn't move. The crowd surges forward, the lost books growing into a mountain, a monument to something no one is allowed to name.

The Censor leans in, closer than necessary. Kaia meets the reflected shape of her own face in his visor. He could say a hundred things. He says nothing. She feels the words lodged tight in her throat.

She slides her hand back into her pocket, finds the bookmark token by touch, and squeezes it until the edge bites into her palm. She wills herself steady. She is a witness; she is not a victim. Her mother's voice in her head, steady as a tide: "Hold fast to what's true, no matter how the wind howls."

The Censors continue the sweep, each confiscated book a small funeral, each exchange stitched together with the same mix of resignation and desperate, failing dignity. The woman on the dais raises her amplifier again.

"All contraband is to be incinerated. Anyone found concealing or distributing forbidden literature will be detained for reeducation. Your cooperation is appreciated."

As the last of the books join the pyre, a hush rolls over the square. The Censors retreat to the perimeter, forming a solid ring. From the scaffolding above, a young Censor-in-training pours accelerant over the pile. The scent hits Kaia's nose—sharp, chemical, obliterating the residual memory of ink and old paper.

She sets her jaw, focusing on the child with the comic, on the old scholar with his empty hands, on the clutch of people who watch their private histories become state fuel. She makes herself memorize each face. Someone has to.

She will tell this story again, if only to herself.

A single match drops. The pyre erupts in a blossom of orange and black, the smoke rising like a bitter prayer against the morning sky.

Kaia does not cry. She stands with the crowd, eyes locked on the flame, the taste of iron thick in her mouth and the sharp edge of the bookmark token digging deeper into her flesh. The wind shifts, and the ashes drift. She breathes them in, lets them settle, waits for what must come next.

The child with the comic steps forward, his small hands trembling as he adds his treasure to the pile. Kaia watches as the old scholar follows suit, a resigned sigh escaping his lips. The crowd's murmurs fade into silence, their collective breath held in anticipation of the inevitable.

They come for her with a rhythm: two Censors, flanking, boots crushing gravel and cigarette butts. One—the taller, with a scar bisecting his chin—raises a hand. "You. Hands out."

Kaia feels the weight of her vulnerability pressing down on her, clutching her book protectively against her chest. Despite her efforts to diminish herself, the Censor moves with decisive swiftness. "Hand it over," comes the demand, delivered in a tone as chillingly smooth as ice freshly sculpted. This request holds no trace of personal vendetta; it is a cold and calculated necessity.

As her legs tremble with the threat of collapse, Kaia summons the strength within her by summoning memories of her mother. She recalls the comforting cadence of a story told during a fierce storm, finding solace in the warmth of a blanket and the familiar voice that once sheltered her. With steely determination, she locks eyes with the Censor through the visor, only to be met with a reflection of her own strained visage—a ghostly image, her features stretched taut and drained of color, lips forming a line of resilience.

"Please," Kaia says. Not louder than a whisper. "That's mine."

The taller Censor's glove clamps down on her wrist and pulls, exposing the book. The cover is faded, the edges chewed by years and by hands more gentle than this. The Censor rips it from her, thumb leaving a greasy print across the title.

Kaia's arm jerks, and the air is colder where the book was. She fights the urge to clutch at the empty space, to howl. Instead, she inhales, her breath catching half-way, as if her lungs aren't sure whether to fill with oxygen or despair.

The book is tossed without ceremony onto the pyre, vanishing into the heap. Someone else's diary lands next. A stack of school primers, then a glossy magazine with a smiling woman on the cover. Every story ever held close, every secret scribbled in a margin, every word some kid dared to spell out loud—all of it landing in the pit with a sound too soft for what's being done.

The Censor's hand lingers a moment, as if to ensure Kaia won't cause trouble. Her knuckles are white on the bookmark, her pulse a furious drum. She feels the slick wetness of sweat, or maybe blood, where the token's corner digs into her flesh. She keeps her hand at her side, curled, refusing to wipe her face even as her eyes threaten to leak.

The Censors move on, methodical, their collection of griefs unbroken by argument or plea. The pile grows, becomes monstrous. The old man at the front, empty-handed before, is pulled aside and frisked. They find nothing but a sheaf of blank notepaper, which the Censors take anyway. Blank pages, futureless.

When the last book is thrown, the commander on the dais gives a signal. A young woman—Censor-trainee, barely older than Kaia—walks up with a long lighter. Her hand shakes, just once, before she presses the trigger.

There's no dramatic whoosh, just a hungry sizzle as fire snakes its way up the heap. The first thing to go is a stack of coloring books, their covers curling like the petals of dying flowers. The flames move fast, an orange beast devouring its own tail. Pages blacken and shrink, then burst into dry gray flakes. The words lose meaning, burn through language, become dust.

Kaia's heartbeat thundered in her ears as the last of her mother's book disappeared into ash. The blue thread on its cover—gone. Her jaw clenched until the hinge ached, but the pain felt distant now, replaced by something colder, sharper. The sweet-sick scent of burning glue filled her lungs, no longer choking—fueling. Around her, others coughed or stared hollow-eyed at the blaze. But something inside Kaia was crystallizing.

She opened her bloodied fist. The bookmark token lay in her palm, its feather imprint pressed red into the skin.

This wasn't just witness anymore.

This was vow.

She tucked the token into her pocket with care she'd never given herself, fingers trembling, unapologetic. No one was watching now. All eyes were on the fire.

The last of the books collapsed into themselves, a slow implosion of smoke and color. The Censors remained ringed around the square, still and faceless, their job done but their presence unrelenting.

Then came the voice—mechanical and final—from the platfor m."The cleansing is complete. All citizens, disperse. Return to your homes."

No one moved at first. The crowd stayed rooted, as if expecting more. A reprieve. A rescue. Something.

But nothing came.

People began to peel away. A mother guiding her sons. The ledger woman blinking through soot. The old man in the scholar's cap, who hadn't brought a book but had lost something just the same. They slipped into alleys and avenues like ghosts leaving their own funeral.

Kaia stayed.The pyre was still smoldering, edges glowing like coals beneath a dead star. She stepped closer—not close enough to invite questions, but enough to see the shape of her book's spine among the remains. It didn't matter if it was truly hers. She decided it was.

A Censor turned her way. She didn't flinch. Just shifted her weight, made her body look compliant.

The visor held still. Then turned away.Only then did she allow herself to breathe.

She reached inside her coat, fingers brushing the inside seam she'd stitched shut last winter. With a slow, practiced motion, she tucked the token inside. Hidden. Safe. If they wanted it, they'd have to tear it from her.

The wind changed. Ash drifted sideways, soft as snow.

Smoke drapes the square, refusing to dissipate. It clings to coats and skin, gets under nails, lives in the hollows of throats. Most in the crowd turn away from the fire as soon as the first wave of heat and memory hits—eyes watering, faces shut tight, spines bent in the posture of defeat. A few, though, keep their faces turned to the flames, unblinking: the mother with her two sons, the ledger woman, the old man with the scholar's cap.

Kaia stands among them, arms folded tight across her ribs, the chill now numbed by the intensity of the blaze. She tracks the faces of those around her—how some flinch with every new book tossed into the furnace, how others stare at nothing, their thoughts folded inward. There are even a handful who watch the burning with a kind of brittle anticipation, as if waiting for the fire to render them empty enough to start over.

She catches the old man's gaze. He nods, just once—a motion so small it could be mistaken for a tic. In that second, Kaia feels a sharp, electric communion. They are both witnesses. They will both remember.

The Censors patrol the edge of the square, making a show of vigilance even as the work is already done. When the last book is nothing but a ghost of itself, the commander lifts the amplifier one more time.

"The cleansing is complete. All citizens, disperse. Return to your homes."

The crowd, once packed tight with anxiety, splits apart. Some people hurry, eager to flee, while others linger at the perimeter, unwilling or unable to leave the place where their history was unmade. Kaia does not move. She remains as the crowd thins, stands until the only company she has is the crackle of cooling paper and the occasional distant cough.

The pyre guttered down to embers, the square stripped of sound except for the wind and the faint, slow footsteps of the last departing witnesses.

Kaia's jaw worked side to side, teeth grinding against the taste of ash. Her heart still races, but the pulse is steadier now—each beat forging something harder inside her chest. She takes a deep breath through her nose, lets it fill her lungs with the acrid air, then lets it out slow and deliberate.

She uncurling her stiff fingers, looked down at the bookmark token. The ribbon is scorched at the edge, the embossed feather smudged but still visible, blue against brown and red. She wiped it clean on the inside hem of her coat, then held it up to the dying sun, letting the light filter through. It's damaged, but it's survived. She allows herself one nod of acknowledgment. Small mercies.

The ash settles like gray snow, coating her boots, her shoulders, her resolve. Kaia turns away only when the last ember dies, when even the Censors begin their methodical retreat into the gathering dusk. Their white uniforms catch the failing light, making them look like ghosts drifting through the haze.

With care, Kaia tucks the token into a secret seam in her jacket, a place no Censor will ever find unless they tear her apart to get it. She smooths the coat over, then squares her shoulders and looks again at the ashen pit.

She knows, with sudden clarity, that this is not the end. They can burn every book, every scrap of memory, but they cannot erase the hunger for story, or the things that stories plant inside those who read them.

Her steps are steady as she turns away from the pyre, leaving the square behind. Each footfall presses a line into the dust, a small act of reclamation. The taste of ash is still in her mouth, but it's fading—replaced by something sharper, something alive.

Kaia walks home alone, spine straight, the wound in her palm already clotting. She touches the spot through her coat, lets her thumb rest there, a silent promise made to nobody but herself.

Let them think they've won, she thinks. Let them think they've buried every word. They haven't met me yet.

Later, in her narrow bunk, she traces the token's edges until her fingertips go numb. Sleep won't come—hasn't come easily since that night three weeks ago when everything changed. The compound's night-cycle lights flicker their usual sickly green through her window, casting shadows that remind her of burning pages. But tonight, instead of grief, she feels something else stirring: purpose. The stories weren't just destroyed; they were entrusted to her. And she knows exactly what to do with that trust.

Chapter 2: Application Denied

She spends the wait in a windowless concrete hall, the air freezer-bright, every surface scrubbed so clean it feels less like a place for people and more like a display for how little they matter. The lighting is the sickly kind—the tubes flicker on a barely perceptible pulse, calculated to keep applicants' nerves primed and every moment measured against fatigue. Along both sides of the room, steel desks form two silent battalions, each fronted by a hunchbacked chair. She counts at least three dozen would-be recruits: some hunched in defeat before they've begun, others fidgeting with nervous kinetic energy, a handful blank and still as mannequins facing a future they refuse to contemplate.

Kaia's desk is near the end of the left row, where the drafty vent stabs at her ankles and the line of sight faces the main door—a minor mercy in the panopticon design. She cradles her application folder as if it might disintegrate, thumb stroking the cardboard edge until it turns soft. Inside: her essays (each rewritten, then recopied in careful script, then proofed again for errors), the bureaucratic forms she'd begged off a neighbor who worked maintenance in Records, and, secreted between them, her mother's bookmark token. Blue ribbon, pressed feather, still holding a faint trace of sandalwood and something indefinably home.

Every so often, an assistant in LDC livery—navy sleeves rolled and pale wrists marked with bandage ink—glides up to the next desk and deposits a numbered chit. That's the sign: approach the front panel when summoned, address the clerk only by title, answer quickly and completely, do not—under pain of rejection—ask questions back.

Her number is 41. She rehearses the script under her breath, lips barely moving. She'd spent days memorizing the current Code, cross-referencing old snippets with what leaks through the rumor-web, prepping for every trick question she can imagine. She'd also spent three sleepless nights, eyes raw and aching, certain she'd fail at the first hurdle—exposed as a fraud, a plant, or a sentimentalist and banned for life.

The scent of ash wafts in. Only the air filter recycling a poor batch, but it hits her with a whiplash—first the tang of burning paper, then the taste of iron on her tongue. She blinks, sees the square, the pyre, the Censor with a face like poured wax. She forces the image down, buries it beneath the thrum of her heartbeat and the familiar mantra: hold fast, keep going, stories outlive stone.

The speaker crackles. "Forty-one."

Kaia stands, every joint tight, and walks to the intake desk.

The intake clerk is a man who may once have been young. He has that government look, features nipped and tucked at the edges by years of routine, eyes bleached gray from the overhead bulbs. His uniform is crisp, the nameplate so polished it bounces the fluorescence straight back into Kaia's retina. His fingers—long, almost delicate—fan her packet open with the careful precision of a bird of prey landing on a carcass.

He begins to read. Not skim; read. The silence stretches, broken only by the distant cough of an applicant on the other end of the room. Kaia forces her hands behind her back. She fixes her eyes on a hairline crack in the desk's metal surface, refusing to blink.

At last, the clerk says, "Essays. Handwritten."

She nods, not sure if it's an accusation or a compliment.

"Extra forms: Redundant. Disregard those in future."

"Yes, sir."

He flips the ribboned token with a pinky and pushes it aside without a glance. "Sentimental items disallowed in application packets."

Kaia opens her mouth, but his gaze slides past her like as if she isn't there at all.

He presses a button beneath the desk. After five seconds, a narrow receipt prints from a slot near her elbow. The clerk pulls it free, snaps it flat, and stamps the top in wet red with the LDC insignia: the torqued torch.

The stamp lands hard and final in red ink: APPLICATION DE-NIED.

He passes it over. "Application rejected. Insufficient qualifications. Psychological profile: does not meet League thresholds." The words fall in a single, unbroken exhale.

She grabs the slip, skin already numb.

"There must be a mistake," Kaia says, voice less steady than she wants. "I've memorized every regulation. I know the Defense code. My test scores—"

"Next applicant." He is already reaching for another folder.

She clamps her hand on the desk, hard enough to rattle the pens in his cup. "That's it? No feedback, no recourse—?"

"Further questions must be submitted in writing to the Disputes Office." He slides her packet, mother's token and all, into a pale gray return bin.

Her fury surged, then collapsed, leaving nothing but a frozen hollow where her chest used to be. She gazes at the receipt, the words emblazoned so intensely they seep through to the other side: "APPLICATION DENIED." Raising her eyes against better judgment, she meets the clerk's indifferent gaze, already drifting to the next patron. In a fleeting moment, she detects a glint in his expression—not remorse, not compassion, but perhaps a hint of apathy or exhaustion, a man who has flattened the world and now merely shuffles its fragments.

She stands, folder pressed to her chest, she trudges back to her desk. Fellow candidates either avert their gazes or observe her with ravenous delight at her misfortune. She tries not to care.

Kaia sits in the chair, not trusting her legs to hold her just yet. She turns the LDC slip over and over, as if the words might shift, as if she could squeeze a second chance from the paper. She can't. The room feels smaller now, the lights more pitiless.

"If they won't see me, I'll make them."

Unfurling her folder, she inspects the token. Its edge is creased, the feather slightly crumpled. Still, it retains its allure. Safeguarding it in her sleeve as best she can, she rises.

With a deep breath, Kaia tucks the rejection slip into her folder. She forces herself to stand tall, refusing to let disappointment buckle her knees. Her heart pounded in her chest like a war drum as she gathered her belongings. The room seems to blur around her as she focuses on the exit, the only path left for her now.

Kaia makes it five steps from the door before the echo of "insufficient qualifications" curdles in her throat and stops her dead. She stands in the corridor, lightless except for the phosphor squares stamped every meter, and looks down at the slip. The red stamp. The finality. Her own name, spelled with that dead bureaucratic precision, as if the code has already cut out her heart and put the rest on file.

She does not move. She remembers her mother's lesson: if the world closes, you wedge a story in the crack and lever it back open. This is that moment.

Kaia returns to the hall and sits again in the cold chair, this time facing the wall, not the door. She waits for the next number to be called, for the next rejection to pass by like an untended wound. Around her, the other applicants shift in their seats, glancing up from the corners of their eyes—curious, uneasy, or just waiting for her to crack and leave for good.

She won't. She studies the room. There is a clock, but the hands don't move. A security camera tracks left to right and back again, a digital eyelid blinking in a loop. The air vent clicks on and off, adding a mechanical sigh to the room's rhythm.

At the intake desk, the clerk chews through the stack of folders, stamping denial after denial, each time with a sharp, rhythmic snap of the seal. Some applicants argue; none succeed. Every rejection is final.

When the next round of numbers comes, Kaia is ready. She waits until the line has thinned, then stands and steps back to the desk.

The clerk looks up, visibly irritated. "You were already processed."

"Yes," Kaia says, voice steady as she can manage. "But there's no reason. No specifics. How can I improve if—"

He holds up a hand. "This is not a school. It's a service. You're not qualified."

Kaia's jaw works side to side, like she might grind the words down to something sharper. "What's wrong with my profile? I met every requirement. I even—"

"Security." The clerk doesn't shout, just lifts his gaze over Kaia's shoulder.

Two guards materialize, one flanking each side of her, hands tucked casual in their belts, but eyes alert. The larger one has the kind of face that would look at home in a sculpture: unfinished, angular, with a nose left slightly askew as if no one cared to fix it.

"Let's not do this," the guard mutters, barely audible.

Kaia ignores him. She digs in her heels, not willing to budge. "I know the mission statement by heart," she says, but her voice is turning brittle, like the words could snap if she pushes too hard. "If I'm being disqualified, I have the right to know why."

The clerk sighs, not even hiding his exasperation. "If you want, I'll write it on your slip. 'Does not meet psychological profile thresholds.' There. Now it's official."

A flush rises, burning at Kaia's neck. "Based on what? You don't even know me. This is a—"

There's a bang—a door slamming open somewhere up the hall. The sound brings every face up, every body tense.

A courier in the gray-and-blue of the LDC strides into the intake room, moving like he's racing his own shadow. He looks young, too young for the uniform, but wears it with the certainty of someone who's never failed a test in his life. His boots land with a series of sharp, deliberate cracks on the tile, and the breathlessness in his gait is the only sign this isn't a scheduled event.

The guards' posture changes. The intake clerk straightens, folding his hands atop the desk in a posture of practiced subservience.

The courier speaks in a voice loud enough for the whole room to hear: "Priority override for candidate Mori, Kaia. Command Level Alpha. By order of Colonel Harada."

The room ripples—every applicant, every security, every desk drone—and Kaia feels her blood run cold, then hot. For a full second, she wonders if it's a trick, if the whole thing is an elaborate cruelty. Recognition feels dangerous, like the stamp of a target.

She pictures her mother whispering stories like secrets, an act of resistance with its own sharp edges. This moment: a crack to lever open or just another kind of control? But the courier is at the desk now, holding a sealed envelope with a wax insignia stamped so deep it has pressed through the paper. He hands it to the intake clerk, who takes it with something close to reverence.

The clerk peels back the wax seal with a shaky thumbnail, unfolds the letter, and scans its contents. Kaia's heart pounds as he scans the words on the page. The clerk's mouth moves soundlessly, then halts. His gaze meets hers, a fleeting expression of humanity crossing his features—surprise, or perhaps the faint stirrings of doubt breaking through for the first time.

He clears his throat. "Override authorization. Effective immediately, candidate is to be reconsidered and expedited for assignment."

Silence envelops the room. The pounding in Kaia's ears grows deafening. She thinks of her mother's stories, how they defied the cold precision of printouts, how her own belief in them is what matters now.

The clerk retrieves her file from the bin, placing it on the desk before reaching for the stamp once more. This time, the impression emerges clean and bold: "ACCEPTED." He adds his initials, then, as an afterthought, retrieves her mother's cherished bookmark token from within the documents, laying it gently atop the folder as if bestowing a sacred blessing.

Meeting Kaia's eyes again, he truly sees her for the first time. "You've made it."

A gasp escapes her, the tension releasing in a rush that nearly buckles her legs. The urge to scream, to laugh, to shatter something wells up within her, but instead, she simply nods, accepting the slip from his outstretched hand. Unsure how to express gratitude to a man who had attempted to erase her existence just moments ago, she remains silent.

The guards faded into the background, their duty forgotten, while murmurs of astonishment rippled through the other recruits.

"That's the girl who—"

"Level Alpha, did you see?"

"She must have done something—"

The courier gives her a look as he leaves—an up-and-down scan, as if taking inventory of her bones and skin. He doesn't speak, but there's something in his eyes: the knowledge that today's miracle is tomorrow's liability. Kaia recognizes the calculation and files it away.

As she leaves the intake desk, Kaia resists the urge to walk with pride. The room watches her, but she refuses to give them the satisfaction of seeing her gloat or falter. She just walks steady, slow, eyes fixed on the exit sign glowing dull red at the end of the corridor.

Out in the hall, she allows herself a moment to lean against the wall, the slip pressed to her chest. She reads it again, just to be sure it's real. Then she checks the letter, the override order, the wax seal—a complicated signature she doesn't recognize, a note in unfamiliar handwriting. There's a footnote at the bottom, hastily scrawled:

"Commended for recovery of contraband literature, New Vahlien. Further review recommended. Cultural Anomaly Assessment protocol: initiate."

Below that, in smaller print, a marginal scribble she almost misses: "Unwavering resolve. Recommend for pilot program. —Lt. Dojo"

She stares at the name, trying to recall it from lecture lists, public bulletins, half-forgotten stories traded over illicit cups of synth-tea. The only thing she remembers is a rumor: that once, years ago, a candidate had refused to burn their own history, and they'd made him a legend or a ghost, depending on who you asked.

The sun had already begun its descent when Kaia emerged from the government district, casting long shadows that stretched like grasping fingers across the cracked pavement. She let the cooling air wash over her flushed face, trying to still the racing drum of her thoughts. The override letter seems to pulse against her side with each step, a constant reminder of what she's just set in motion.

Above her, the massive screens that usually broadcast propaganda flicker and dim as the evening curfew approaches. Citizens hurry past, heads down, while patrol drones hum their routine patterns overhead. But tonight, even their mechanical whine sounds different to Kaia—less threatening, more like white noise in the background of her own quiet revolution. She had six hours until the meeting point. Six hours to decide if she was really ready for what the Resistance was asking of her.

The safe house lay on the other side of the industrial sector, past the defunct factories and their skeletal remains. Getting there means crossing three checkpoints, each one a test of her newly forged credentials. Kaia's hand brushes her coat pocket again, feeling the edges of her future through the fabric. The sun sinks lower, painting the smog-filled sky in shades of rust and warning. It's time to move.

Chapter 3: Initiation Day

The LDC Academy was less institution than barricade, a fortress raised not only against the world outside but the possibility of anything unknown creeping in. The exterior wall reared like the edge of a collapsed dam, slabs of poured gray stacked three stories high and capped with razor-thread and motion lights blinking in nervous sync with the wet, low-hanging sky. No banners, no domes, no ornamental gates—only the functional repetition of warning glyphs, hazard striping, and the endlessly cycling whine of perimeter alarms. At ground level, the perimeter seethed: security drones the size of severed fists skittered along the wall, their vacu-legs clinging to the cement as their single eyes flicked from red to blue and back, cataloguing the street and every face passing by. Overhead, the Central Archive Nexus arcs like the rib cage of some fossilized giant, glass and memory alloy limned in sodium lamps, its ten-story stacks wrapped around the Academy with a grip that looks almost predatory. Suspended walkways—sky-bridges threaded with mesh and reinforced by steel—spanned the narrow canyons between towers, connecting the citadel to the other floating isles beyond. At certain hours, Kaia could see the silhouettes of staff and students in transit, faces obscured by masks or visors, hunched against the wind and the watchful gaze of the towers above.

Set into the wall, the main gate is not so much an entrance as a wound. Solid iron, factory-built, coated in matte black that chews the light, it bears the stenciled warning sigils of five different security agencies. The glyphs swarm like angry script: NO UNAUTHORIZED ACCESS, LEVEL FOUR CONTAMINATION PROTOCOL, and the triple-barred hazard icon that indicts not just trespassers but anyone foolish enough to hesitate in its shadow. The gate is flanked above by twin guardhouses, each with a panoramic view port and a mounted pulse cannon. Below, the sidewalk is scored by the drag marks of countless armored boots and, less often, the tread of anti-riot vehicles. The only ornament is a single, weathered placard bolted to the right pillar, its slogan only visible up close: "Memory Is the Shield of Civilization." Someone has tried to scratch out the word 'civilization' and replace it with 'obedience,' but the attempt has been painted over so many times the result looks like a bruise.

Kaia stepped off the city tram and joined the loose trickle of new recruits funneling toward the entrance. Most walk with heads down, feet shuffling at speeds set by those in front of them. The corridor to the gate runs the length of a single football field, flanked on either side by concrete barriers. On the left: the ghosted outline of what was once a playground, now a patchwork of mud and splintered plastic. On the right: a reflecting pool, drained and littered with cigarette ends and the glassy shards of old streetlamps.

She walked steady, not too fast, not too slow, the override letter folded flat against her ribs and her mother's bookmark token wedged inside the right cuff of her jacket, held in place with a strip of medical tape. The sleeve is stiff where the tape pulls against the fabric, a minor discomfort compared to the million other ways she could get caught. She counted the steps, catalogued the distance, tried not to calculate how easily a person could be shot here and simply replaced with the next in line.

The recruits were mostly her age or younger—late teens, early twenties—the exact demographic deemed least valuable as individuals, most malleable in bulk. Some wear old league uniforms, the colors faded from repeated washes, while others show up in what looks like their best approximation of the standard-issue: black boots, gray pants, anything to blend in. Kaia is somewhere in the middle, her jacket still stained from last season's rainfall, boots patched with a strip of adhesive meant for plumbing leaks.

As she neared the gate, the sense-memory of the book pyre clawed at her—smoke and heat and the sick feeling of being watched. Here, everything is a performance of power; the burning was messy, personal, raw. This is antiseptic, impersonal—order weaponized against even the most harmless deviation.

A voice barks from the gate's PA. "STOP. PRESENT IDENTIFI-CATION."

Kaia fumbled her temp badge from an inside pocket. The plastic is warped from sweat, the barcode already smudged, but the chip still scans. The guard on the other side wears full riot armor, face shield up. His eyes are quick and dark, but he doesn't look at her, not really—he's watching her hands, her pockets, the nervous flutter at her throat.

"Remove all metal items, place in bin." The guard gestures to a plastic crate. Kaia slips the key ring from her belt, the battered coin from her shoe, the ribbon-twist that had once held her hair back during study marathons. She hesitates only a fraction before placing them in the bin. The bookmark, hidden in her sleeve, presses against the thin skin above her wrist.

She stepped through the first of three gates, each one scanning a different frequency: electromagnetic, thermal, bio. With every gate, a row of lights runs up and down her silhouette. They make no mention of the tape or the token; either the device is too small to trip the sensors, or the guards are too busy with the next hundred bodies in line. She doesn't care to question her luck.

Beyond the scanners, recruits were herded into the main intake yard. The ground here is flawless concrete, fresh-poured and still faintly reeking of lime. Along one wall, a series of metal benches lines up like pews in a secular church. The benches are filled with bodies—waiting, waiting, always waiting—while overhead, surveillance domes rotate on programmed cycles, the hiss of their servos slicing the silence into uneven ribbons.

Kaia keeps her head up, scanning the faces around her for a crack, a cue, some sign that anyone else feels what she feels. Most avert their gaze; a few stare straight ahead with an intensity that borders on self-hypnosis. One kid, maybe twelve, sits at the end of a bench, fists balled and wedged between his knees, eyes rimmed in red. Kaia recognizes the look. She almost wants to speak to him, offer something—solidarity, a joke, even just a name—but she bites it back. Nothing good comes from standing out, not here, not yet.

From the far end of the yard, another line begins to move. Two more guards, this pair less armored but more heavily armed, usher recruits forward to a series of partitioned tables. The air here feels colder still; the hum of overhead lights is so loud it almost presses against the skin. Kaia steps into line and waits her turn, fingers flexing inside her sleeves.

When she reaches the table, the intake officer—a woman with a face like a blade, her eyes rimmed in gold eyeliner—waves her forward.

"Name," the woman says, already entering data into a tablet.

"Mori. Kaia." She spells it, out of habit.

The woman's hands never stop moving. "Division?"

"LDC. Library Defense Corps. Apprentice, first class." She hopes that's the right designation; the override letter had been short on details.

The woman flicks a glance up, brief but sharp. "You're early."

"Was instructed to report at zero-eight-hundred." Kaia's voice is even, practiced, every possible permutation rehearsed and ready.

The officer checks the clock, then shrugs. "Doesn't matter. Once you're in, you're in." She scans Kaia's badge, then holds out a palm. "Any contraband? All personal effects must be declared."

Kaia places the override letter—only the letter, not the token—on the table. She's already opened it, but the envelope is still intact, the signature of Lt. Dojo visible in blue at the bottom.

The woman reads it, lips moving without sound. She looks up again, for longer this time. "You know this is classified," she says, voice soft enough that the guards wouldn't hear unless they leaned in.

Kaia nods, not trusting herself to answer.

The woman tucks the letter into a folder. "You'll be assigned a locker and a uniform. Anything else goes to storage." She slides a small plastic box across the table. "If you want it back at the end, tag it."

Kaia slips the battered coin and ribbon-twist inside, then hesitates. The bookmark token, even hidden, weighs a hundred kilos on her wrist. But she keeps it taped and silent, a risk she's willing to take.

The officer hands over a bundle: a uniform, two pairs of socks, a sheet of regulations printed on a strip of synth-paper no bigger than a finger. "You'll change in the prep hall. From there, await orientation."

Kaia takes the bundle, her fingers numb.

She moves into the prep hall—a wide room divided by accordion partitions, each labeled with a number. The air is thick with the scent of antiseptic, the kind that stings in the nostrils and leaves the tongue coated in chemical grit. The floor is smooth, recently scrubbed, but already pocked by thousands of boot marks. Kaia picks an empty cubicle and pulls the curtain.

Inside, she strips quickly, rolling her old clothes into a tight ball and shoving them into the disposal chute. The uniform fits surprisingly well, sleeves snug but not suffocating. She checks the seams, then carefully peels away the medical tape. The bookmark token slides out, feather side up. She inspects it for damage—just the same as always, the blue ribbon a little faded, the feather embossing deep and true.

She tucks it into the inner sleeve pocket, stitched for pens but perfect for something smaller, something meant to survive. She smooths the fabric, makes sure the lines are clean, then pulls on the boots. They're new, barely broken in; she wonders if anyone else got a pair that wasn't already pre-worn.

She steps out and blends into the next wave of recruits, now all dressed identical: gray-blue jackets, black trousers, boots with a red stripe at the heel. The visual effect is immediate—nobody looks like themselves, nobody looks like anyone else, either. It is the opposite of belonging—forced neutrality, a flattening.

The noise in the hall increases as more bodies are processed. Kaia joins the back of a group being led down a hallway toward what is presumably the orientation chamber. The corridor is lined with display screens showing training footage: formations, hand-to-hand, code-of-conduct statements rendered in all caps. Between the screens, the walls are perfectly blank, the absence of graffiti or even dirt a statement of its own.

Kaia's breath fogs as she walks. She watches the screens, memorizing the patterns, but lets her thoughts drift. Her mother's voice, again: "Hold fast to what's true, no matter how the wind howls." She imagines the story of herself, rewritten with every step. The girl who watched her book burn. The girl who wasn't supposed to get in. The girl who did, anyway.

The group stops at a final checkpoint: a wide metal door, reinforced with bars and a biometric scanner. A guard unlocks it with a palm print, then waves the recruits through one at a time.

Kaia steps forward. The guard's hand lands briefly on her shoulder, guiding but not hurting. The hand is warm, the touch oddly human.

"Good luck in there," he says so quietly, it might have been a mistake.

Kaia nods, then steps into the next room.

Inside: rows of seats, a raised platform, a lectern with the LDC's twisted-torch insignia. Other recruits file in behind her, some whispering, some stone silent. Kaia takes a seat near the back, where she can watch the door and the screens both.

Above her, the lights pulse. She feels the weight of the Academy pressing in, every surface engineered to erase, to overwrite, to make new. But she's here. She's inside.

She uncurls her fingers inside her sleeve, touches the bookmark, and waits.

The orientation clock blinks 09:00. Kaia straightens her spine, squares her shoulders, and prepares to learn how to survive a place that would rather she didn't.

The morning drills commence with the subtlety of a firing squad.

The orientation drags on for three hours—death by slideshow, policy manual, and carefully scripted speeches about duty and destiny. Kaia's fingers stay curled around the bookmark, its edges worn soft against her skin. She catalogs every exit, every camera angle, every face that seems too interested in their neighbors. The whole time, her mind races ahead to what comes next. The real test isn't sitting still for propaganda—it's surviving what follows.

When the final speaker steps down, they're released in controlled waves, herded through corridors that smell of industrial cleaner and fresh paint. The morning has burned away into a pewter sky that threatens rain. Kaia feels the shift in energy immediately—from the enforced stillness of orientation to something coiled and expectant. The other recruits sense it too, their whispers dying as they emerge into the cold air. Whatever comes next will strip away any illusion that this is just another academy.

Recruits are driven from the intake block onto the main quad, herded by three sergeants whose lungs seem engineered for maximum resonance. The yard is a rectangle of open sky bordered by walls of smoked glass. Directly underfoot, the concrete radiates the cold from a week of unbroken rain. Kaia is assigned to formation delta, third row, which means she has a clear view of the lectern at the far end and a slightly obstructed view of everything else. It also means she's hemmed in by strangers who still smell faintly of home, or at least the last place they called home.

As the orientation video drones on, Kaia feels a sudden chill. She glances around, taking in the identical expressions of determination and fear on the faces of her fellow recruits. The room seems to shrink, the walls closing in as the reality of her situation settles like a weight on her shoulders. She clutches at the bookmark hidden in her sleeve, a tangible reminder of who she is beneath the uniform. The video ends, plunging the room into silence.

"STAND TALL. EYES FRONT," the sergeant shouts. The recruits snap into place, ninety in all, a single block of vertebrae and uncertainty. Kaia checks the spacing, lines her boots up against the yard's laser-etched guidelines, and hopes her breath doesn't fog too visibly. There's a rhythm to being watched, and she's learning it fast.

Overhead, the digital displays flare to life, their text cycling between regulation code and aphorisms repurposed as law:

NO UNAUTHORIZED READING MATERIALS.

NO UNSUPERVISED COMMUNICATION.

NO QUESTIONING ORDERS.

The words throb in red, interspersed with the League's torch icon, which seems to wink in the low morning light. Kaia feels the threat of it, the promise that even thoughts will be monitored if they can figure out how.

A smaller, grimmer text runs beneath the main loop: REPORT ANOMALIES IMMEDIATELY. FAILURE TO DO SO WILL RESULT IN DISCIPLINARY ACTION.

Kaia's section is flanked by two recruits, both tall, both with the look of kids who'd spent their adolescence running laps in the schoolyard rather than hunched over a page. To her left, a girl with white-blonde hair cropped to the skull and eyes like silver beads. To her right, a boy with a nose flattened by old trauma and hands that fidget in the cold.

The sergeant paces the front, boots hammering out the tempo of obedience. "This is not your parents' league. This is not your old city. You are here because you are expendable, and we intend to find out just how expendable you really are." He sweeps his gaze up and down the rows, a predator sampling prey.

The air smells of bleach, rubber, and the sour tang of nervous sweat. Kaia lets her eyes flicker—never moving her head, just quick darts of vision—taking in the perimeter. At each corner, cameras track the yard, lenses blinking as if they, too, are subject to drill. There are no windows, only the slabs of smoked glass, which means whatever happens here will not be seen or remembered beyond these walls.

The sergeant changes tack. "You will speak only when spoken to. You will obey all directives instantly and without question. You will not fraternize, gossip, or indulge in nostalgia. You will make yourselves useful, or you will be recycled."

In the midst of the formation, Kaia senses a powerful surge, an unspoken command urging her to flee, to escape the pressure of being seen and accounted for. She battles against the impulse, anchoring herself firmly in place. Her boots bear the marks of time and wear from this unforgiving ground. The cold creeps through, penetrating her soles and reaching deep into her muscles.

Amid the sea of bodies, a solitary blade of grass defiantly breaks through a tiny crack in the concrete. In its small, colorless existence, it radiates undeniable strength. Kaia fixes her gaze on this resilient symbol, drawing courage from its defiance of the odds. Her thoughts turn to her mother—how even the most forbidden tales find a way to endure, whether as whispers or cherished memories.

The sergeant barks again: "When addressed by a superior, you will respond with the phrase, 'Understood, sir.' Any deviation will be logged. Any disrespect will be punished. Do you comprehend?"

A chorus: "Understood, sir."

Kaia's voice blends in with the others, but she knows hers is the only one vibrating with the memory of words not meant to be spoken here. She wonders if the sergeant can hear the difference.

From the far door, a ripple of activity signals the entrance of someone higher up the chain. The recruits, already at attention, tense further, like a net strung too tight.

Lt. Elias Dojo steps into the quad, his movements precise as a clock. He is dressed for maximum effect: crisp blue uniform, polished insignia, every line of his posture radiating the message that standards exist—and he intends to enforce every one.

He does not walk so much as advance, head up, eyes front—measuring every recruit without moving his gaze. He makes it to the lectern, pauses, and lets the moment stretch. Then: "At ease."

The recruits shift to a looser stance, hands behind backs. The sergeants cede the floor, but they do not disappear. Kaia watches as Dojo surveys the formation, his gaze landing on each face as if searching for an answer to a question only he knows.

When his eyes meet Kaia's, there's a flicker—not surprise, not quite recognition, but a challenge silently cast between two people who know the cost of standing out. Kaia lifts her chin half a degree, a reflex that's gotten her in trouble before. She feels her heart beating in her neck, a hard, insistent rhythm.

Lt. Dojo speaks. His voice is low, but it carries—every ear in the yard tilting toward him. "You are here because someone decided you might matter. That doesn't mean you do. It's up to you to prove the theory."

He begins to walk the line, slow, deliberate. As he passes, the other recruits stand straighter, shoulders drawn back, jaws set in the universal posture of people who have been told what to do their entire lives.

He stops directly in front of Kaia. The world narrows.

"Recruit Mori," he says, pronouncing it with the clipped authority of a man who learned the language from a file. "Your application required... special consideration."

He lets the words linger, each head shifting subtly, curiosity flickering with a power sharper than open defiance.

Kaia senses the gravity of the situation bearing down on her. Inhaling deeply, she masks her emotions behind a neutral facade. "Acknowledged, sir," she replies, her tone flawlessly composed.

Dojo's eyes linger a beat too long, the tension coiling in the silence.

"Let's see if that consideration was warranted," he says. Then, louder, to the rest: "You will report to the following assignments: Group One, corridor gamma. Group Two, logistics. Group Three, maintenance. Group Four—" he scans again "—special topics. Mori, you're Group Four. Report to Office C after drills."

Kaia nods, says nothing. But she marks the way he says her name, the edge in it.

The formation is breaks apart, sergeants barking new orders. The recruits disperse in ordered chaos, filing out through the quad in their designated clusters. Kaia is among the last to leave. She risks a look back at the blade of grass, still standing, still unnoticed by anyone but her.

Inside, the corridors twist and split, the routes clearly marked but designed to disorient. Kaia follows the arrow for Group Four, past closed doors and echoing stairwells. Her boots squeak on the clean surface. The bookmark token inside her sleeve is a comfort and a curse, every step a reminder of what she's holding onto.

She turns a corner, nearly collides with the boy from the intake line—the one with the broken nose. He's alone, standing by a water dispenser, eyes on the floor.

He glances up as she passes, then away again. She debates saying something, but the moment slips away.

Ignoring the boy, Kaia continues down the winding corridors, her mind focused on the task ahead. She feels a pang of nervous anticipation as she gets closer to Office C, her destination. The corridor narrows, the walls closing in around her, and she can almost taste the tension in the air.

The first day in the yard tastes of salt and ozone and the bitterness of recycled sweat. Forty recruits, all in slate-green LDC issue, line up along the cracked tarmac, forming two uneven columns bracketed by rows of red-painted pylons. The city's defensive wall looms in the near distance, casting a cold shadow that never quite leaves the training ground, no matter how high the sun claws into the sky. It's early, but already the air is alive with the anxious breath of people who know every gesture is being judged.

Kaia is number eighteen in the right line. Her boots pinch at the instep, the uniform they gave her is a half-size too long in the arms, so she rolls the cuffs and hopes no one notices. She stands with her eyes straight ahead, jaw set, sweat prickling beneath the collar. The blue-ribboned bookmark is hidden, stitched into the seam of her undershirt, a comfort more than a secret. To her left, a girl with a crow's-nest of blond hair is shaking so hard it rattles the plastic badge on her chest; to her right, a blocky boy with a round face and a nose like a battering ram stares holes through the opposite wall. No one speaks. No one moves.

At exactly 0600, a whistle shrieks—a sound so sharp Kaia feels it in the base of her skull. From the far end of the yard, the instructors arrive: three figures, boots in perfect unison, uniforms as crisp as myth. The lead is a woman built like a spear; behind her, a rangy man with a face of vertical lines; last, a shorter man face composed could pass for carved soapstone, eyes the color of old glass. The latter walks with hands folded behind his back and a kind of deliberate, predatory calm.

Kaia recognizes him immediately: Lt. Dojo. The name had run through the induction rumors like a curse or a promise, depending who you asked. He is not what Kaia expected, but he is everything she feared: compact, eyes that see but never flicker, a jaw that seems perpetually braced for the next collision. He pauses at the head of the column, sweeps his gaze across the recruits.

"You will address me as sir. Not lieutenant, not instructor, not 'hey you.' Is that clear?" His voice is smooth, measured, almost bored.

"Yes, sir," the line echoes, ragged but loud.

"Welcome to the Literary Defense Corps. For the next twelve weeks, I own you. I will break you down, rewire you, and send you out as something useful. If you're lucky, you'll get to keep your bones and your mind. If you're exceptional, you'll keep your name."

He lets the words breathe, lets the silence become a second kind of training.

"Protocol is the only difference between order and chaos," he continues. "Out there, you don't follow it, you die. Maybe you take your unit with you. Maybe you start a fire that burns the whole city down. Think about that every time you want to be clever."

His eyes flick to Kaia, then away. She feels the look, like a cold probe beneath the skin, and stands even straighter.

"First exercise: Silent Drill. No talking. No mistakes. Follow the pattern, or you run laps until you puke." He gestures, and the instructors begin issuing out the training gear: weighted packs, sand-filled canisters, rubberized batons. Every item is identical, every handoff performed with the speed and indifference of a machine.

Kaia's pack weighs twice what she expected, the straps digging hard into her clavicle. She sees the others shifting under the load, some trying to look unfazed, others already flinching with the burden.

The drill begins: march to pylon, kneel, shoulder the baton, stand, advance, reverse, repeat. It's simple on paper, but the packs shift and dig, and half the line is out of sync before the first pass. Kaia finds a rhythm and locks in, letting the repetition dull her nerves. Left, down, up, right. She scans peripheral vision, watching the pattern as much as her own steps.

On the third cycle, someone in the front line—Recruit #3, tall, dark-skinned, hands like shovels—fumbles the canister. It bounces off his knee, clatters to the pavement, and rolls in a slow, mocking arc straight toward Kaia's row. No one is supposed to break formation, but the recruit's face goes paper-white, terror blooming across his features as he realizes the mistake.

The instructors see it. They always do. The lead woman's lip curls, her eyes fixed on the trembling recruit.

Kaia's body moves before her brain can stop it. She steps out of line, one pace, and intercepts the canister with her boot. Crouches, grabs it, and, without thinking, tosses it back underhand. The action is fast and clean—a reflex, nothing heroic about it.

The yard freezes. The silence is loud enough to drown birds. Even the wind cuts out for a second.

"Recruit Mori," Lt. Dojo says, his voice as casual as a knife. "Step forward."

Kaia straightens, returns to attention, and walks forward until she stands two meters from him. She feels the eyes of every recruit burning into her back, feels the way her own heart rattles in her chest. She thinks of the boy who cried wolf and knows this is where they teach you not to help, where they make you forget how.

She says nothing. Her fists clench at her sides, knuckles bright against the skin.

Dojo paces, slow, then halts directly in front of her. She remembers the morning they burned her mother's books, how the flames erased each page as if the stories had never lived in her. He's shorter than she guessed, but every centimeter radiates authority.

"Explain your action," he says, not loud but very clear.

Kaia's mouth is dry. She stares straight ahead. "Recruit #3 dropped his load, sir. I returned it. Minimizing disruption."

Dojo's eyebrows barely move. "That's not protocol. Is it."

"No, sir."

"Then why did you do it?"

She hesitates. "Instinct, sir."

He steps closer. Kaia can see the faint freckling on his nose, the way the sun has failed to mark his skin despite hours outside. His voice drops to a private register.

"The LDC operates as a unit. Not as individuals with hero complexes. Your impulse to help is noble, but your impulsiveness is a liability. That's how operations fail. That's how people die."

Kaia's jaw tightens. "With respect, sir," she says, voice just above a whisper, "I was following the Corps motto."

"Repeat it," he snaps.

She does, loud and true: "Preserve what matters."

A ripple of attention runs down the line. The instructors go still.

Dojo's gaze sharpens. "What matters here, recruit?"

Kaia answers without flinching. "The mission. The stories. The unit, sir."

He studies her a long moment. "And yet you acted alone."

There is no right answer. Kaia knows it. She says nothing.

He turns away, then back. "Twenty laps around the perimeter," he says, voice flat. "Out loud, I want you to recite the Code of Conduct every lap. After, you will report to my office. We'll see if your conviction matches your insubordination."

Kaia doesn't move, waiting for the dismissal.

Dojo inclines his head, just enough. "Dismissed."

She runs. The perimeter is four hundred meters, the ground broken by old roots and new cracks. The pack hammers against her shoulders with every step, threatening to unseat her balance. As she passes the first pylon, she sucks in a breath and begins to recite, "Code of Conduct, Article One: Obey orders. Article Two: Protect the Archive at all costs..."

The words come out ragged, but they come—just like the forbidden nursery rhymes her mother whispered when the censors passed their block.

By lap five, her lungs sear like the day she watched them burn her copy of "The Little Prince"; by lap ten, her legs detach, running on bitter momentum while her mind recites the passage they couldn't erase: *What is essential is invisible to the eye.*

She stumbles on lap twelve, her hand instinctively reaching for the bookmark hidden in her sock—thin contraband from a world they're methodically erasing.

She hears a faint snicker from the far edge of the yard, but she can't care enough to find the source.

Every time she rounds the starting line, she sees the recruits arranged in perfect formation—bodies aligned like censored text, black bars of human obedience. Some avert their eyes, already trained to unsee deviation. Others watch with the last flickers of what the morning drills called "dangerous empathy."

The instructors never look away; their gaze is the first layer of the system designed to scrub her mind as thoroughly as they've scrubbed the library shelves.

She finishes the final lap with a shout: "Article Six: Never forget what you defend."

She comes to a halt, doubled over, arms braced on her knees. Her breath sounds like a dying animal, but she stays upright.

Dojo stands at the edge of the yard, hands still behind his back. "Report," he says, voice a touch softer now.

Kaia walks to him. Her vision swarms with red and gold. She stands at attention, but her muscles vibrate with exhaustion.

Dojo regards her, then nods once. "Next time, think before you act."

"Yes, sir."

He leans in, voice pitched for her alone. "You want to change this place, Mori, you have to learn how to survive it first. Otherwise, you'll just be another story they burn."

She meets his eyes, and for a second, she thinks she sees something there—a flicker of respect, or maybe just the mirror of her own defiance.

He steps back. "Dismissed."

Kaia heads for the bunks. The rest of the recruits form up for the next drill, some glancing at her with new calculation. She feels their eyes, the silent math they're doing—hero, liability, or just crazy enough to outlast the system. She doesn't care which.

The silence of the barracks is deafening as she falls onto her bed, the cold metal frame a stark contrast to the heat still radiating from her body. Her mind is a whirlwind of thoughts, each one more chaotic than the last. She remembers her mother's words about stories and their power, and a slow smile forms on her lips despite the pain.

Chapter 4: The Silence Drill

In the second hour before dawn, the LDC Academy's main training yard feels colder than physics should allow, like the sun is a memory no one is brave enough to invoke. Concrete underfoot. Lines and lines, laser-etched and mathematical, organizing space into something that can be measured, surveilled, and ultimately owned. High walls on every side, surface glass so perfectly black that it reflects nothing, only absorbs—light, sound, breath. Above, in the lattice of the overhead, drones thread silent circuits, their blink-codes a language designed to say: we see you, we see everything.

As the final bell tolled, the cadets filed out into the yard, their breaths misting in the frigid air. They moved with precision, each step a testament to their training, lining up along the etched lines on the concrete. The overhead drones came to life, their soft hum barely audible over the sound of shuffling feet.

The recruits are arrayed on the grid, their formation exactly parallel, bodies upright, eyes front. The only thing that separates Kaia from the other thirty-nine is her refusal to shiver, not even when the wind blows sharp enough to cut the vowels from the air. Uniforms are identical, and in the predawn, faces lose all signature. It's just posture—the little betrayals of muscle and will.

On a low riser at the north end, Lt. Dojo stands with his hands clasped behind his back, boots precisely centered on the platform, like a punctuation mark between the sky and the slab. He waits, lets the moment drag. When he finally speaks, his voice is refracted through the grid's speaker array, rendered both everywhere and nowhere at once.

"Welcome to the Silence Drill."

Some recruits twitch, expecting more. Kaia keeps her jaw set, the way her mother taught her—do not let the world see you waiting, or it will teach you to beg.

Dojo continues, voice tight and clean as piano wire. "Your assignment today is to function in the absence of information. Information deprivation is what we fight against. Today, you will experience it firsthand."

An aide in slate-gray moves down the rows, passing out bright orange earplugs. Not the cheap foam kind; these are engineered, smooth as glass, heavy for their size. Kaia palms hers, testing the weight. She suspects they'll do more than block noise. She watches as the rest of the recruits fit them in, some with the practiced efficiency of people who have done this before, others clumsy, thumb and finger betraying tremors. Kaia inserts hers last, rolling it between index and forefinger to soften the edges before pushing it deep. The sensation blooms like a pressure headache in reverse.

Sound becomes a rumor. She can still see Dojo's mouth move, but his words arrive as low, filtered burbles. The only thing she can hear clearly is her own breathing and the slow thump of her blood against the inside of her skull.

A light bar on the platform blinks red, then green, then settles on a steady blue. It's a signal. Kaia watches as Dojo raises his hand, then cuts the air with a horizontal slash. The rows move, shifting left, each recruit stepping in time. The silence is so complete it takes Kaia a second to realize that the movement is coordinated only by vision—no cadence, no command, not even the brush of a neighbor's sleeve. They execute the drill three more times: shift, reset, pivot. Kaia tracks the sequence with a calmness she didn't know she could summon. She thinks: this is easy. She thinks: this is nothing compared to the sound of books burning, to the violence of a voice that tells you don't matter.

But time gets strange in the hush. What felt precise and procedural becomes blurry at the edges. The drills compound. The light bar adds new colors, new meanings—yellow means reverse, purple means hold, green means rotate. There is no way to ask for clarification. There is only the moment and what you make of it.

Kaia adapts, reading the motion of shoulders and the set of spines, using peripheral vision to forecast the group's intent. The first fumble comes at the twenty-minute mark: a recruit two rows over pivots on the wrong foot, sending a ripple down the line. It's not much, but in this place, it's everything. The nearest instructor—she's the one with the white-blonde hair and the reflexive disdain—steps forward, plants herself in the recruit's personal space, and simply stares. In silence, the discipline is all in the eyes.

Kaia sees the recruit's jaw clench, the tremor pass through his face, and then—miracle—he doesn't break. He holds the position, absorbs the stare, and when the instructor steps back, he picks up the drill like nothing happened.

Hours fold in on itself. Kaia tries to keep track, but the only markers are the changing temperature and the endless cycle of lights. Her initial confidence begins to drain, replaced by a creeping unease. It's not the drill, it's not even the silence. It's the sense that the boundaries of her self are dissolving, that she's just another shape on the grid, no more or less real than the concrete she stands on.

She thinks of her mother's stories, the ones where heroes survived by keeping some part of themselves hidden, inviolate. She wonders, in this place, if that's even possible.

A distant bell chimes. The next phase of the drill begins. This time, the recruits must navigate the grid blindfolded, using only touch and memory to re-create the formation on the far side. Kaia feels the smooth fabric slip over her eyes, darkness blooming. The first steps are easy; she's already memorized the intervals. But by the fourth shift, she's not sure if she's moved three times or five, or if she's even on the same grid line anymore. Her left foot overlaps someone else's. She recoils, adjusting, but the contact lingers—a brief, human warmth in the chill.

When the blindfold is removed, she finds herself facing the opposite direction from the rest. The realization is a gut-punch. She tries to orient herself, but the silence is absolute now, the only movement in the yard a slow shudder of hands. She wants to laugh, to scream, or say anything—but the plug in her ear, keep her locked down.

At the end of the drill, the lights snap to white. Dojo steps forward, slow and deliberate. He raises one hand, palm open, then closes it into a fist. The recruits respond, unblinking, silent.

He surveys the yard, his gaze lingering a fraction longer on Kaia than the others. She can't tell if it's disappointment or recognition. Maybe both.

He speaks, but the words are lost to the plug and the yard and the wall. She thinks she knows what he's saying, though: information deprivation is what we fight against.

Kaia stands at attention, but inside she vibrates with the need to make a sound, any sound—to prove she's more than the silence.

The light bar dims. The squad is dismissed with a gesture. Kaia's legs ache, but she doesn't move until the rest of the formation dissolves. As she walks off the yard, the cold bites deeper. She's not sure what she's learned, only that the absence of words can sometimes be a cruelty worse than any order.

She removes the earplug. The world rushes in—the scream of a distant alarm, the staccato boots on glass, her own pulse so loud she wonders how it ever fit inside her skin.

Kaia looks back at the grid, at the ghost traces of bodies that were and now aren't.

She breathes out, then in, and finds her center again.

Tomorrow will be worse. She knows this. But for now, she lets herself remember that noise, too, is a form of resistance.

She moves through her morning routine with mechanical precision, each gesture a silent rehearsal for what's to come. The other recruits avoid eye contact in the washroom, all of them already retreating into themselves. They know, as she does, that yesterday was merely a prelude. The real test begins now, in the gray hours before dawn, when the yard will demand more than their silence—it will demand their surrender.

Many hours in, the Silence Drill has become something else—a slow-motion autopsy, each recruit peeled open by time, left to contemplate their own innards. Above the yard, a digital clock stares down with acid indifference, its red numerals locked in a countdown that makes a mockery of hope. At the edges, shadows have deepened, swallowing the lines that once demarcated the world into safe and dangerous.

Kaia stands in her box, posture immaculate but for the tremor that's crept into her right calf. She fixes her eyes on the clock, refuses to look at the other bodies slumping, wilting, fracturing. A dull, briny taste blooms at the back of her throat, equal parts dehydration and panic.

The drills have doubled in complexity: not just marching now, but coordinated gestalts—simultaneous shifts, mirrored pivots, abrupt freezes. The only guide is the pulse of the lights and the collective intuition of the squad. Every misstep multiplies, as if the silence is breeding its own currency of error.

Row five, slot three: the recruit with the sandpaper voice—Kaia can't recall his name, only the way his hands flinch when idle—has started to sob. Not loudly—no sound breaches the engineered hush. But his shoulders shake, raw and regular, the way a dog trembles when it knows the blow is coming and also knows there is nowhere to hide. Next to him, a girl with a stubborn set to her jaw keeps glancing toward Kaia, like maybe if they lock eyes, the universe will briefly acknowledge their suffering.

It's at this moment—when the group's unity is a mask that no longer fits—that Kaia spots a recruit two rows down, frozen mid-step, eyes darting. He's lost. In the strict code of the yard, to aid is to risk everything, but Kaia's own code is older and more visceral.

She risks it. Left hand, three fingers splayed—an old sign from schooldays, meaning: "Left, two paces, hold." She flares the signal just once, a flicker no longer than a blink.

It works. The lost recruit sees, corrects, falls back in line.

But the yard is not a place for miracles. There's a flicker from the far end—spotlight, blue-white and sharp, pinning Kaia in place. The sensation is as physical as a gun muzzle to the head.

Dojo's voice, crisp as the crack of a belt, slashes the silence. "Recruit Mori. Protocol violation."

The clock overhead halts, then resets, and the low hum of the yard's background noise seems to howl against the newfound tension.

Dojo strides forward, hands at his sides, his expression so unyielding it might as well have been etched in stone. His voice doesn't need volume; the stillness itself is an accusation, amplified by the way every head turns imperceptibly, every eye zeroes in on her.

"Squad will repeat sequence from the beginning," he intones. "Errors are cumulative. There will be consequences."

A ripple of unease moves through the ranks—a collective sigh, a tremor, a reluctant surrender. No one dares to look directly at Kaia, yet she's ensnared by their disapproval, a silence that grows more oppressive, more suffocating.

Her throat is parched, her skin clammy under a thin sheen of sweat, cold against the morning air. Her hands tremble so much she has to clasp them behind her back. She fights to concentrate, to hold steady, but the world around her is both deafening and eerily quiet: every breath, every heartbeat, every blink crashes like thunder in the cavernous silence.

The lights commence their sequence, and the squad follows suit. But Kaia is drifts—adrift, caught between the yard and the shadow of a memory, unsure which reality to cling to.

It comes in pieces—a melody, not even words, just the contour of sound. Her mother's voice, singing in a half-whisper as rain drummed against the roof, the lullaby curling through the air like incense. Kaia tries to grasp the words, but they slip away—slick, insubstantial, spoken in a tongue she barely remembers. She can feel the shape of the story: a girl, a feather, a promise whispered—that nothing in the world is ever truly lost if you can name it and hold it in your mouth. The memory tugs at her, warm and dangerous.

But the present yanks her back. A misstep, a flash of white-hot pain as a boot edge catches her heel. The formation stutters. The instructor with white-blonde hair is beside her in an instant, lips compressed in a hard line of judgment.

Kaia rights herself, blinks the memory away, but the echo remains—a bitterness behind her tongue, a vibration in her bones.

When the sequence ends, the squad stands again in formation, time swirling down the drain. Kaia's hands are numb. Her body aches. Sweat trickles down the curve of her spine, collects in the small of her back. She tries to remember the lullaby, the story, but all she reaches is the silence: total, implacable, as if the world itself has been smothered.

She knows now what the drill is truly for—not merely to enforce discipline, but to scrub away the parts of you that stubbornly cling to life. The relentless routine is designed to extinguish the spirit, to wear down the soul until only compliance remains. She wonders if she will endure the next grueling round, or if she will crumble like the sobbing recruit, whose tears fall like rain on parched earth. Then there's the girl who continually seeks her out, her eyes searching desperately for a glimmer of hope, a sign that this harsh existence isn't all there is.

The clock above resets again—a zeroing out of hope.

Kaia braces for the next sequence, but her mind is a blur, the world a wash of color and light and ache. She tries to recall her mother's voice, the story, the song, but the only thing left is the echo of Dojo's words: "Errors are cumulative. There will be consequences."

She wonders if she has become the mistake, the result—or perhaps both.

In the silence, she closes her eyes, her heart pounding a rhythm of desperation against her ribs. She breathes in deep, trying to find a semblance of peace in the sterile scent of sweat and metal. A memory surfaces, a fragment of a lullaby, a whisper of warmth in the cold void. It's not enough, but it's something—a spark in the darkness.

The final phase comes with no warning. The silence has calcified, every sound reduced to the private howl of blood in the head, every thought flensed by hunger and exhaustion. Kaia's world narrows to a single instruction: decode the message, and do it fast.

At each box on the grid, an aide drops a tablet—flat, black, edges sharp as regret. The display flickers: lines of redacted text, most of it blacked out, only stray words visible. The challenge is to piece together meaning before the next timer runs out. Communication is allowed, but only through the same hand signals and the frantic semaphore of eyes.

Kaia's fingers hover over the glass. She tries to focus, but her vision is swimming. Her left eye won't stop twitching. The text is gibberish—nothing but "REDACTED" and the occasional noun: "archive," "breach," "loss." The timer in the corner counts down in half-seconds, digits flipping too fast to process.

She glances at her squad: two rows up, the weeping boy is now all the way gone, face buried in his own arms. Beside him, the girl with the stubborn jaw is throwing wild, desperate signals—so many that it's impossible to tell if she's helping or drowning.

Kaia's hands move without her. She's typing, hunting, swiping left and right, but the words slip away. It's a sick joke, how the meaning is always just out of reach, how every second eats away the hope that this time she'll break through.

The timer shrieks to zero. The tablet auto-locks. Kaia blinks, tries to clear her head, but the display is already showing the next sequence.

She loses time—seconds, maybe minutes, maybe hours. Her mind cycles through the same loop: read, interpret, signal, fail. Sweat stings her eyes, and her chest burns with each breath. There is no water, no rest, only the endless, recursive nightmare of trying to make sense in a world designed to erase it.

And then, in a moment with no warning, Kaia is not in the yard.

She is nine, crouched behind the couch in the old apartment, the air thick with the smell of char and ozone. Her mother's voice is a muffled pulse, holding her tight, whispering: "Remember, stories outlive stone." There's a crash—boots in the corridor, the harsh syllables of the League dialect. The door slams open. The agents move in, black and slick, faces lost behind plastic and glass. They drag her mother up by the wrists, slam her against the wall. Kaia's mouth is open, but no sound comes out.

She watches—helpless—as the agents rip through the shelves, throwing every book, every page, every scrap into plastic sacks. She tries to memorize the titles, the covers, but her eyes fill with tears, and the words swim.

An agent grabs her mother's book, the one with the silver thread on the spine. He doesn't even look at it before snapping the cover in half, then tossing it onto the pyre they build in the center of the room.

Kaia's mother looks at her, eyes wild and bright, and mouths a word. Kaia tries to hold onto it, but the agents are shouting, the fire is roaring, and the world shatters.

She is back in the yard, body doubled over, hands shaking so hard she drops the tablet. The cold concrete bites through the fabric of her uniform. The sweat chills, clinging to her skin in salty sheets. She wants to cry, but there's no sound left in her. Only the echo of her mother's last word, the shape of it hanging in her mind like a promise or a curse.

She curls into herself, fists pressed to her sternum. The outline of her mother's bookmark token pressed sharp beneath her uniform, the ribbon's edge biting into her palm. It's the only thing real, the only thing that doesn't slip.

Above her, the clock is in freefalls, digits strobing, time itself melting.

She hears the cadence of boots—slow, measured, echoing off the walls. Dojo. He stops directly in front of her, body casting a long, predatory shadow.

"Stand, Recruit Mori," he says. His voice is clipped, but there's something else in it—something almost hidden.

Kaia tries to move, but her legs won't obey. She plants her hands on the slab, pushes up, every muscle screaming. She wobbles, nearly falls, but catches herself. Her face is streaked with tears, salt drying white on her cheeks. She blinks them away, forces her spine straight.

Dojo studies her, face unreadable. "Formation," he says.

Kaia staggers into her spot, blinking hard, her body a ruin of shudders and chills. She doesn't look at the other recruits—can't bear to see whether they pity her, or simply wish she'd disappear.

A harsh buzzer sounds. The drill is over. The silence, though, lingers—thick, sticky, impossible to wash out.

The squad was dismissed. Kaia didn't move. When she did, she stood—locking her knees, using the pain as a guide back to herself. In her head, the mantra repeated, quieter now: *"Stories outlive stone. Stories outlive—"*

She wasn't sure she believed it, not anymore. But it was the only thing left. Her heartbeat gradually slowed from its frantic pace. Each breath came a little deeper than the last, the air no longer catching in her throat. The ringing in her ears subsided to a distant hum, then faded entirely. Sensation returned to her fingertips—first pins and needles, then warmth.

As the yard emptied, she pulled the bookmark token from her sleeve, rubbed the blue ribbon between thumb and forefinger. The color was faded, but it was still blue. It was still hers. She traced the worn edge where the fabric had frayed, each thread a memory preserved. The familiar ritual steadied her, anchored her to something real amid the disorientation. She put it away, breathed in the cold, and promised herself she would remember this—not the way the League wanted her to, but the way that mattered.

As the night deepened and the moon rose high, she found herself alone in the quiet darkness of her room. The only sound was the soft rustling of pages as she opened the book lying on her bedside table. The words swirled before her eyes, carrying her back to a time when everything had been different.

She traced the lines with her finger, feeling the weight of the memories they held. The truth she had been seeking, the answers she had been searching for, seemed to be just out of reach. But she refused to give up.

Closing her eyes, she whispered a silent prayer to the universe, asking for guidance and strength. And in that moment, a sense of calm washed over her, a deep knowing that she was not alone in her journey.

With renewed determination, she tucked the bookmark back among pages—a symbol of the promise she had made to herself. Tomorrow would bring a new day, a fresh start, and she would face it with courage and conviction.

As she drifted off to sleep, she held onto the hope that her voice would be heard, that her truth would shine through the darkness, and that she would find the answers she sought. And with that thought in her heart, she let herself be carried away by dreams of a future filled with possibility.

Chapter 5: Redacted Histories

The Academy archive room is engineered to repel all but the most desperate seekers. The walls are sickly blue under institutional LEDs, every surface either plastic or steel, sanitized and forgotten by the architects of comfort. Even the floor gives nothing back; Kaia's boots tapped out a Morse of unease as she passed through the glass security vestibule, badge pressed flat to her chest by the cold sweep of internal sensors. There is a hush, but it's the hush of electricity, not peace—cameras pan in slow, expectant arcs, and the low whine of airborne drones overlays everything with a note of manufactured vigilance.

Most of the hour is self-study, but today Kaia is here by mandate, not by choice. An anomaly notice on her morning schedule: "REVIEW SUPPLEMENTAL HISTORY, ISLE BLOCK 4." The orders always capitalize what matters and erase what doesn't.

The archive's entry ranks were deserted; ahead, rows of identical workstations marched toward the far wall. Each desk is bolted to the ground, screens sunk flush and locked on a gray scale interface, the sort of interface designed to punish curiosity. At the periphery, sliding racks hold the "hard copies," shelved by decade and usage restriction. The restricted section—her destination—juts up at the far end, a glass alcove rimmed with warning glyphs and a double-locked panel. Kaia imagines, not for the first time, that the architects designed this place after a prison they themselves could not escape.

She signs in at the main console. The reader is new—installed after a rash of "incidents," rumor said—and she feels the micro-jolt as the pad checks not just her print but her oxygen saturation and stress levels. She wondered if anyone would notice her heart pounding for reasons other than civic duty.

The drone overhead paused, pivoted, then resumed its circuit. Kaia lets her eyes adjust to the room's brutal clarity, then edges toward the restricted shelf. A guard glassed-in behind a pale shield glances up, fingers drumming beside a holstered sidearm. He doesn't speak, just taps a code. The door unlatches with a hiss.

She is inside before her courage can reconsider. The air here is two degrees colder, the lighting more severe. She scans the spines, finds the designated block: "Aetherra: Contemporary Crisis and Correction, Volumes I-IV." The book she is assigned is Volume III, but her fingers linger on the older editions, the ones that look as if they might crumble at the touch.

Volume III is there, battered, its once-white cover now a patchwork of grime and pressure-wear. She pulls it loose, hefts the weight, feels the history in the looseness of the binding and the way the corners catch on her sleeve. The book's security tag flashes a brief red, then green as she logs it on the secondary terminal. She suppresses a shiver—partly cold, partly adrenaline.

The archive's main room was nearly empty; only three other bodies hunched over their screens with the posture of the overworked or the unwilling. Kaia threads the aisle, bypassing the central cluster of desks, until she finds the last seat at the corner row, half-shadowed by the tall stacks and conveniently obscured from the widest camera angle. She slides into the chair, unzips her uniform's left cuff, and slips the blue-ribboned bookmark down her wrist so only the edge peeks out. It's not for marking pages. It's for ballast.

She opens the book with a practiced flick, careful not to make the spine crack loud enough to echo. The pages are thin, grayish, printed with the matte ink favored by the League. She leafs to the index—her eyes darting, not reading, not yet—then backtracks to the title page.

"Aetherra: Contemporary Crisis and Correction, Vol. III. Compiled by the Office of Collective Memory, Isleblock 4, 21st Edition."

Beneath, in smaller type, is a revision history. Kaia's stomach twists. There are five dates listed for this edition alone, the oldest only three years past. She runs her thumb over the years, notices a smudge—a sixth date, half-scratched out, barely visible. Someone has hand-corrected the date in black biro, then whited it again, then re-inked it in a different hand. The friction of revision, visible even to the untrained eye.

Her pulse ticks higher. She flips to the first section, "The Precipitating Event." The text runs as expected: "In the second decade following the Cataclysm, the sovereign Isles of Aetherra were plagued by a crisis of information. The Great Blackout, engineered by dissident forces and exacerbated by economic failure, threatened the collective memory of the human population." A standard version, the kind recited in drills. She reads it again, slower.

But the next page betrays something. In the left margin, beside a diagram of the "old data towers," a faint indentation—like the memory of erased handwriting. Kaia tilts the book, catches the angle, and sees a line ghosted in:

"Not failure—sabotage. See: Sato doc."

Her neck prickles, hairs standing sharp as pins. She turns the page. Paragraph three—"The Office of Collective Memory, founded to safeguard the record of public truth, was empowered to redact and revise all content deemed volatile to civic order"—has been underlined. The ink is uneven, a darker stroke than the rest. Not machine. Not official.

She keeps reading, letting the peripheral details build a case: here, a sentence spliced into the paragraph, the typeface subtly askew; there, a footnote replaced by a blank bracket; whole subsections where the page numbers skip, or the text resets mid-sentence. By page 67, the text on "public resistance" reads, "Efforts to sabotage the OCM were localized and ultimately neutralized by swift and humane countermeasures." But beneath the line, she finds a pressed petal—so old it's only a memory of color—taped into place with the gentlest touch. Kaia turns it over with the edge of her thumbnail.

A petal, and beneath it, an address: "Beneath Vault. Code: 22.1A. For remembrance."

She is shaking, now, but makes no outward sign. Her gaze drifts up; the nearest drone is roving the opposite end. She folds the petal back, memorizes the address, and keeps scanning the book for more. At page 119, she finds the mother lode.

There, in the upper margin, a line in blue: "They will revise this again. Preserve what matters."

She runs her thumb along the page. The blue matches her ribbon exactly.

For a moment, she cannot breathe. She thinks of her mother's handwriting, of the way her lesson books were always annotated in blue, a different blue every year, like her mother feared that ink itself might vanish. She imagines—no, she knows—her mother left this mark. The world tilts. Kaia wants to shout, or throw the book, or run straight through the glass and out into the night. Instead, she bites the inside of her cheek, hard, and tastes blood.

She closes the book, breathing slow, and tucks her mother's bookmark inside at page 119, as if sealing the link between them.

Around her, the archive is unchanged—chill, silent, sterile as ever. But Kaia knows it's different now. The history is a battleground, and she's holding the evidence.

Her eyes scan the room for movement. The drone doubles back, hovering near the guard's alcove, as if sensing the minor deviation in her pulse. Kaia waits for it to pass, then stands, book hugged to her chest. She logs the checkout at the terminal, the screen flickering "AUTHORIZED" in its usual, unthinking font.

She walks out with careful calm, not hurrying, not lagging, her heart in her ears but her face a stone. As the glass doors hiss open, she lets her free hand drift to her sleeve, feeling for the blue ribbon, the pulse beneath it, and the promise her mother made.

Tomorrow, she will come back. She will see what they try to erase next.

But for today, she is alive with the possibility of memory, and she walks back to the dorm with the book pressed so tight to her ribs it leaves a mark.

She doesn't make it half an hour into dorm study before Yuki finds her. It's not hard—Kaia's workstation is always the same: back row, three from the end, chair jammed against the condensation-crusted window. She prefers the cold. It sharpens her. And today, she needs every edge she can get.

Yuki feigns needing a stylus, but the pantomime is unnecessary; they both know exactly what the other means. Yuki's hair is shorn close, her face raw with sleep deprivation and fluorescent abuse. She plops into the adjacent chair, makes a show of rummaging through Kaia's pens, then angles her body so the two of them present nothing but the blandest silhouettes to the overhead lens.

"Find anything interesting?" Yuki whispers, eyes on the blank page of her own pad.

Kaia risks a half-smile, the kind that looks neutral to anyone outside the blast radius. "Depends. Is 'history' still defined as what survives the redaction, or is it now just whatever fits on a slide?"

Yuki's eyes crinkle at the corners. She leans in, her voice a vibration that barely reaches Kaia's ear: "Show me."

Kaia pulls the battered history book from her backpack, opens to the marked page, and tilts it just enough for Yuki to catch the margin. There, next to the official diagram of "Media Regulation Bureau, 31.7A Construction," someone has drawn a symbol: a three-pronged swirl, the kind of thing you see on forbidden street tags, but smaller, tighter, etched in a hand desperate not to be noticed. It matches the graffiti pattern they'd seen outside the old Codex Vault.

Yuki traces the symbol with her pinky. "You know what that means," she says, not really a question.

Kaia nods, keeping her own hand braced across the lower corner of the book, thumb covering the first letter of her mother's name in the copyright line. "Means it's not just us. Someone on the inside—maybe years ago—knew to leave a trail."

Yuki snorts softly. "Or it's bait. Or a plant for sentimental types like us."

"Or both."

Yuki grins, all teeth, then sobers. "Page?"

"One-nineteen. But it's everywhere, if you know how to look." Kaia turns to the earlier section: "Formation of the League." The text is thick with the language of necessity, every paragraph justifying the crackdown as civic hygiene. Kaia points to a footnote: "For further context, see: 'Suppression of Proto-Collectives, Isleblock 2, 18.5.4.'" But next to it, in a hand even smaller, a marginal note: "Lies. See early 17.6.2, unredacted version."

Yuki's mouth tightens. "They never stop, do they? Even when they think they've burned every copy, someone finds a way to make the ashes speak."

Kaia flips forward to the section on the "Information Crisis." The text claims the MRB—Media Regulation Bureau—was formed to "protect public safety and ensure uninterrupted access to the correct narrative." But in the margin, the last word is overwritten: "true" replaced by "approved."

Yuki catches the edit and laughs, the sound dry and exhausted. "Truth is always a moving target."

Kaia lowers her voice further. "They called it the Blackout. Said it was 'engineered by dissident forces.' But here—" she runs her finger under another hand-inked note "—'Systemic failure after League hack. Citizen-led. See Sato file.'"

Yuki goes very still at the mention of "Sato." It's an unspoken rule between them never to bring up Yuki's brother—missing, presumed dead, after the last round of purges. The silence hangs. Kaia doesn't fill it.

Instead, she slides her thumb down the outer margin, where the pages are thickest. It's a trick she learned as a child, searching for the spots where library books had been hollowed to hide forbidden chips. Here, on page 168, she finds it: a slim, torn slip, so thin it almost escapes notice.

She palms it, shielding the motion with the edge of the textbook. The slip is a fragment, the top edge rough, the ink a faded green:

"...remembered differently, in the streets and skyways, than it is here. Resistance never ended. They only made it smaller, made it go underground. Story is the last territory."

Kaia can't help it—her hands shake. Yuki sees the tremor, and for a split second, their eyes meet: panic, elation, and something else. Yuki's hand closes over Kaia's fist, anchoring it, then pulls back with the practiced flick of one used to secreting answers.

"Careful," Yuki says. "Keep that in your pocket, and you'll be next on the interview list."

"I'll take my chances."

They sit like that for a while, pretending to scroll on their screens, both reading the same slip of paper behind cupped palms. Kaia memorizes every word, every break—every sense that the truth is still alive somewhere, waiting for air to escape.

From the outer corridor, a bell rings—lunch rotation, or maybe a power cycle. The room shifts as some bodies stand and others shuffle for position near the exits. The drone above pivots, the lens centering on the two of them for a heartbeat too long.

Yuki tucks the stylus behind her ear, stands, and murmurs, "Later. Be careful where you carry that." Her face is bland, perfectly unmemorable; only the angle of her jaw, set in private anger, gives her away.

Kaia nods. As Yuki leaves, she sees the slip pass from her hand to Yuki's—motion invisible to anyone already in on the scheme. They are good at this. They've had years to practice.

Kaia tucks the history book away, heart still sprinting. She runs her finger along the inside of her sleeve, where her mother's ribboned token waits, warm against her skin. She remembers the mantra from the slip, and from her mother: Story is the last territory.

She glances at the dorm window. The view outside is nothing but city grid and the scorched haze of the lower sky; but if she blurs her eyes, she can almost see it—the real Aetherra, where isles floated and history belonged to the people who lived it, not to the machines programmed to erase it.

She closes her eyes, just for a second, and lets herself remember.

Aetherra was never just a city. It was hundreds—maybe thousands—of floating isles, each unique in culture, each a splinter of the world before. The Cataclysm had shattered the planet's surface, but the fragments rose, orbiting in slow parabolas above the broken crust. For a century, the isles feuded, fused, and sometimes forgot themselves, but what survived was always the memory—the story—of what had been. It was the only thing the League couldn't regulate.

Then came the Information Crisis. League agents seeded distrust, cut off networks, burned old libraries until only ghosts and orphans could tell you what a "story" even was. The Blackout Protests tried to stop the erasure, but the violence was quick, surgical. No one even knew how many died. That's why the history books were always so thin, why every "official" record was more glue than truth.

Kaia opens her eyes, sees the world as it is: a discipline grid, a thousand pairs of eyes waiting for you to slip. But she's not alone. She has the slip. She has the ribbon. She has the memory.

She slips the textbook into her bag, feeling the weight of all the missing pages. When the next bell sounds, she files out with the rest, head down, but spine locked. She knows Yuki will read the slip, memorize it, and pass it on. That's how you make a story survive. Not by keeping it—by giving it away, a piece at a time, until it's everywhere again.

Kaia walks the corridor, the world suddenly less empty, the chill in her veins replaced with a bright and terrible hope.

It's after lights-out, the corridors a procession of shadows, when the last scene replays itself: Kaia seated at her habitual corner desk, thumb running raw circles over her mother's ribbon, the battered textbook still open to its evidence.

The transition from study period to night is never subtle. Doors lock down, the buzz of student energy replaced by the white noise of ventilation and the insistent tick of ceiling clocks. The only real light is a feverish orange, designed to induce sleep. Kaia lingers, copying notes, waiting for the right moment to duck out. Yuki has vanished—left before the end of period, a calculated risk.

She feels him before she hears him: Lt. Dojo, standing at the end of the row, not moving, not even pretending to check the time. He's dressed in full regulation, but his hair's still wet from shower and the crispness of his collar does nothing to hide the impression that he's been watching, and waiting, for this exact moment.

"Productive research, Recruit Mori?" His tone is conversational, but the sentence lands with surgical precision, drawing the gaze of every straggler in the room.

Kaia closes the book with a slow deliberateness, refusing to fumble, refusing to glance at the altered pages. "Just reviewing the standard curriculum, sir." Her voice is even, but inside every cell is pitching forward, ready for flight or incineration.

Dojo walks the row. He stops at her elbow, the silence a challenge. "I notice you've spent more time with that particular volume than any other recruit this quarter." He lets the words hang, then softens them with a half-smile, the kind that looks almost sincere until you spot the calculation in his eyes. "You have an affinity for lost causes?"

Kaia shrugs, keeping her expression somewhere between bored and tired. "Only if they're worth the effort."

For a few seconds, the two of them exist outside of protocol, neither yielding, neither pushing. It's not a contest of strength. It's a contest of who will risk being seen.

At last, Dojo gestures. "May I?" He extends his palm for the book.

Kaia's grip tightens before she relents, letting the cover slip from her to him. His hands are steady, nails perfectly clean, but when he takes the book, he doesn't open to the title page or the section labeled "Crisis and Correction." He flips straight to page 119—the one with the blue ink bleeding in the margin.

He doesn't react, doesn't so much as blink, but Kaia can feel the tension radiate off him like static. His thumb brushes the margin graffiti, then rests there, as if weighing the reality of it.

"Thank you, Recruit," he says. "I'll make sure this returns to its proper place." He turns away, leaving the rest of the sentence unfinished. Kaia doesn't miss the message: that's enough for today.

She packs her things deliberately, slow, eyes following the line of his back as he exits. She's not sure if he's won, or if she has, or if it even matters.

After midnight, a summons arrives: Hallway F, Level 2. The old admin corridor, barely used since the last round of budget cuts. The summons is unsigned, but the font is unmistakable: Dojo.

She goes.

The hallway is colder than the rest of the building, windows blued out by a film of dust and neglect. Dojo stands at the far end, his posture casual, one boot up against the wall. He's reading from the same battered textbook, head bowed, a strand of hair fallen loose over his temple.

"You know, they burned half the original editions after the Second Blackout," he says without looking up. "The rest, they just rewrote."

Kaia doesn't answer but stops three meters away—close enough for confrontation, far enough for plausible deniability.

He closes the book, holds it out to her. A new crease runs along the spine, and the margin ink looks somehow darker now, as if the words have seeped in deeper.

He says, "Be careful what questions you ask, Mori; some answers aren't worth the cost."

Her throat aches, but she forces the words out: "I'd rather know than live in the dark."

He holds her gaze for a long time, and in that moment, the mask of authority drops just enough to reveal the person underneath: tired, brittle, but not unsympathetic.

He hands her the book, but when she takes it, she feels that something is missing.

She checks the inside cover. The slip of green paper—the resistance narrative—is gone.

Dojo's voice is so low it's almost lost in the hum of the air system. "Loose pages have a way of blowing away, don't they?"

She meets his eyes, and in the shadow between them is the promise of reprisal, and also the smallest glimmer of alliance.

He steps back, the interview over, and with a crisp pivot he's gone down the hall, leaving her alone with the returned book and the hollow where the slip used to be.

Kaia presses the book to her chest. The cover is still warm from his hands. She catches a whiff of ozone, maybe sweat, maybe just the lingering aftermath of electricity and fear.

When she cracks the spine, she sees it: a thin black line along the lower edge, as if the book had been caught in fire—and barely survived. A scorch, subtle but permanent.

As Kaia settled into her room, the flickering light of a single candle danced across the walls, casting shadows that whispered the secrets of the world outside. She placed the book on her desk, its weight a reminder of the knowledge it held within its pages. The ribbon, once a symbol of her mother's love and guidance, now felt like a beacon of strength in the midst of uncertainty.

She sat on the edge of her bed, thoughts a whirlwind of determination and defiance. The world may burn, but she refused to be consumed by its flames. With a deep breath, she untied the ribbon from her heart and tied it around her wrist—a silent promise to carry on.

As the night deepened, Kaia leaned her head against the window, gazing out at the stars that shimmered in the dark sky. Tomorrow promised a new day—a chance to rise from ash and stand tall against the chaos threatened to engulf them all.

With a sense of quiet resolve, Kaia closed her eyes, her mother's ribbon a comforting presence against her skin. Tomorrow, they would try again, and no matter how fierce the flames burned, she would carry the heat with grace and strength. For in the midst of destruction, there was also the promise of renewal, of a future where hope could blossom once more. With that thought in her heart, Kaia drifted off to sleep, ready to face whatever challenges tomorrow may bring.

Chapter 6: The Codex Vault

D awn has no purchase here. The corridor outside the Codex Vault is buried three levels below the LDC Academy, sealed off from the rest of the world by reinforced steel, electromagnetic dead zones, and the weight of institutional secrecy. The only light is the soft, sour pulse of the floor LEDs and the liquid shimmer of the vault's insignia—twisted torch, open book—projected three meters tall on the door itself. The effect is not subtle. You could mistake this for a tomb or a fortress, and you'd be right both ways.

Kaia stands sixth in a line of ten. They have been told to stand at parade rest, but tension leaks out regardless: hands wringing, boots shuffling, nervous coughs half-swallowed and buried beneath a practiced mask. No one jokes. No one speaks. Every recruit here has been handpicked, told only that today would be their "orientation in special access protocols." In Kaia's head, the phrase loops: special access, special access, as if by repeating it she might strip it of danger. It never works.

The door is absurd—three meters high, ribbed with blast-dampeners, its surface glossier than a fresh bruise. At eye level, a single iris scanner sits above a fingerprint reader, the whole guarded by a thin beam of red light. Above, motion-capture domes stutter quietly, tracking every breath. Rumor held that nobody could force this door, not even from the inside.

At 0702, the footsteps echo. From the right—a side passage so narrow it looks drawn in by a ruler—an officer emerges, flanked by two junior aides. She is older than the average cadre, her silver-streaked hair coiled tight against her head, every movement deliberate, controlled. Her face is sharp enough to slice bread; her eyes shaded by plastic-rimmed readers that seem surgically bonded to her skull. Her uniform is immaculate, not a thread loose. She wears the rank of Commander, and her nameplate—VOSS—looks freshly etched.

She surveys the line with a glance so swift it feels like a scan. "You will address me as Commander or Ma'am. We will not waste time on pleasantries."

There's a shift along the line, as if every vertebra recalibrates at once.

"This is the Codex Vault," Voss continues, gesturing at the behemoth door as if it were a mere inconvenience. "It is the digital heart of the Literary Defense Corps. Everything we have ever preserved—every text, every image, every byte—lives here. You are about to enter the most secure library in the hemisphere. If you are here, it is because you are trusted." She lets the word hang, lets its weight be known.

Kaia fights the urge to look down, instead fixing on a scratch in the floor three meters ahead. She counts breaths, bites the inside of her cheek, and unconsciously brushes her left wrist. Beneath the sleeve, stitched into the seam, the blue ribbon bookmark presses cool and steady against her skin. It's just enough to keep her upright.

"Prepare for access," Voss orders.

As the line inches forward, a sense of anticipation hangs thick in the air, each heartbeat synchronized with the rhythmic progression. The technology hums with precision, designed to swiftly process each individual in a mere heartbeat: the piercing gaze of the iris lock, the imprint of a thumb, and the whispered mantra ingrained deep within their being ("To preserve is to remember"). With every flicker of green from the scanner, hope surges through the recruit as they step closer to their fate. But when the dreaded red light casts a shadow, a collective tension grips the line, holding them in suspense.

Amid this sea of nerves and trepidation, Kaia stands sixth in line, her very essence trembling with intensity. An orchestra of emotions swells within her, threatening to overwhelm even the faultless protocols of the scanner. Yet, with sheer determination, she places her thumb on the sensor, locks eyes unwaveringly with the azure diode, and breathes out the sacred words: "To preserve is to remember".

The light blinks green. She steps into the vestibule.

Inside: a decontamination chamber. Air jets from the walls in a violent, skin-needling blast, followed by a haze of ozone that tastes like burnt plastic and old rain. The chamber is glass on three sides, perfectly clear; from the inside, you can see the next recruit enter and the previous one exit, but there's no way to make eye contact. Kaia stands still, letting the cold air do its work, arms out as instructed. She flexes her hands, fighting the urge to shield her face. The ribbon at her wrist trembles with the rest of her.

When the chamber clicks open, she steps through and finds herself at the edge of a wide, half-lit anteroom. The other recruits have clustered by the rail, all of them studiously avoiding the gaze of the man standing just off to the left—Lieutenant Dojo.

He's in full LDC parade uniform, blue so deep it looks black at a distance. His boots are, as always, polished to mirror. He stands with his hands clasped behind his back, chin high, eyes scanning the group not as individuals but as a collective equation—inputs, outputs, variables to be managed. The only sign of warmth is a half-inch of open collar, as if even he can't stomach the Academy's new button policy.

"Eyes front," Dojo commands, his voice a shade gentler than it was in the yard. "The Vault opens in thirty seconds. Prepare yourselves."

Kaia's breath hitches. She feels the blue ribbon with her thumb, anchoring herself. She glances sideways, catches the edge of Dojo's expression—rigid, unreadable, but not hostile. He looks at her for half a second longer than necessary. She wonders what he's looking for.

A hiss, low and hydraulic. The vault door slides open—not fast, not slow, but with the implacable certainty of a natural disaster. Cold air spills out in a river, flooding the anteroom with a sudden, glacial chill. Kaia shivers, her body unsure if this is awe or fear.

Inside, the Codex Vault bears no resemblance to the public archive rooms above. The ceiling vanished into shadows, far above the polished floor. The walls are lined with server banks stacked four stories high, each bank caged in mesh and bristling with status lights. Along the central aisle, columns of glass—filled with holographic projections of books, newsreels, images of vanished cities—pulse in rhythmic sequence. The air hums with the low, omnipresent song of machines at work.

Kaia steps forward, feet numb from cold and nerves. The temperature here is engineered for the comfort of data, not people. She wrapped her arms tight around her ribs—half hug, half self-defense.

At the far end, a dais rises—half stage, half altar. On it, an old-world desk sits beneath a waterfall of blue-white light. Commander Voss moves to stand behind it, her presence magnified by the LED haze. She gestures for the recruits to approach.

They filed in, forming a rough arc around the dais. Kaia found herself standing between two boys who seemed desperate to be anywhere else; their faces pale, eyes darting from server banks to the silent glass columns and back.

"This is our responsibility," Voss declared. "It's not about the building or the machinery; it's about preserving memory itself. Every byte stored here is unique—irreplaceable. Hesitate or fail, and there is no duplicate, no backup, no rescue. We are the final defense."

In the humming room, Kaia stood by the whirl of holographic displays. Her gaze drifted toward a vibrant collage of images and words, each projection telling its own story. The weight of longing hangs heavy in her chest as thoughts of her mother's tales flood her mind, painting a picture of vast libraries lost in time.

Voss's declaration pierces through the murmurs, her words laden with expectation and intensity. The air crackled with anticipation as Dojo's strict instructions reverberated through the space, drawing a stark contrast to the ethereal glow surrounding them. A sense of foreboding lingered, each command etching deeper into the mission.

As Kaia absorbed the gravity of their charge, a symphony of emotions culminated within her, blending determination with uncertainty. The challenge ahead looms large, casting a shadow that stretches beyond the confines of the room. In that moment, every spoken word carried profound resonance, igniting a fire within each person present—a flame fueled by duty and destiny.

As the speech winds down, Voss gestures to the group. "If you are here, it is because you are believed to possess the discipline to access, and defend, the Codex. That is your charge." Her eyes landed on Kaia for a split second—measuring, challenging, or perhaps warning.

From the shadows, Dojo steps forward. "You will tour the main stacks in pairs. No deviation from the route. No unauthorized access. Infractions will be reported instantly. Is that understood?"

A lifeless unison: "Yes, sir."

Kaia is paired with the boy to her right, whose name she vaguely remembers as Taro. They are assigned Row 6: "Historical Memory—Pre-Unity." A robot glide-cart, shaped like a stunted ostrich, whirs ahead of them, emitting a thin blue guidance laser for them to follow.

As they walk, Kaia's fingers drift to the ribbon in her sleeve. She rolls it between thumb and forefinger, lets the feeling settle her. The cold is worse here, slicing through the uniform, but she doesn't mind. It means the memory is still real, still solid, still somewhere that cannot be touched or overwritten.

Kaia tried not to stare at the glass columns, but it was impossible to look away. At one point, a projection flickers to life—an ancient children's book, its illustrations lush and strange. Kaia recognizes it instantly. She nearly tripped over her own feet.

Taro sees her freeze and whispers, "You know that one?"

Kaia nods. "My mother used to read it. Before—" She stopped, clamped her jaw tight.

Taro says nothing, but for the first time, his face softens.

At the end of the row, the robot cart halts. A holopanel opens, requesting input: "Enter search query."

Kaia hesitates. She wants to type in her mother's name, or the title of the forbidden book, or even just "truth." She settles for "archive access protocol."

The screen blooms with a menu: not words, but a map—a web of connections linking one fragment of memory to the next, a constellation of knowledge. Kaia is lost instantly, and happily.

Commander Voss's voice echoes from the center: "Return to the main aisle. Group rotation in sixty seconds."

Kaia pulls herself away. While they return, she meets Dojo's gaze. He's observing her, and for the first time, she wonders if he's not searching for mistakes—perhaps he's looking for something else.

Back in the central space, Voss waits, hands folded. "Any questions?" she asks, the words clipped and expectant.

Kaia thinks of a hundred, but says none. She stands, hands at her side, the blue ribbon a secret pulse beneath her skin.

The Vault is cold, but the memory burned. Kaia lets it anchor her as the group is herded deeper into the labyrinth of preserved, forbidden things.

The main aisle of the Codex Vault was a corridor of worship—nothing but clean lines, mirrored floors, and twin rows of server towers blinking in unison. The noise here is constant but strangely lulling: the gentle churn of fans, the pulse of liquid-cooling arteries, the distant click of a relay cycling over and over. It's the sound of memory in suspension, of history defying entropy by sheer, relentless effort.

Voss marches the group to the center of the vault, a node where four broad aisles converge beneath a glass dome. Even the light is curated—blue-white and shadowless, draining every face to a spectral pallor. The dome overhead projects a slow-motion panorama of old-world libraries, their domes and arches flickering in and out as if the system can't decide which to miss more. Kaia catches her reflection in the floor—pale, eyes too large, mouth tight set. The sight offers no comfort.

"All eyes here," Voss calls, and the recruits assemble around a waist-high dais topped with an interface slab. It's nothing like the clunky access panels in the public library; this console floats the holo a full half-meter above the glass, the data rendered as a luminous, shifting lattice. Voss touches the surface, her movements precise, and the lattice unravels to reveal a spinning globe of virtual bookshelves.

"This is the Codex proper," she says. "It contains every volume we have ever intercepted, scanned, or restored, including partials and unapproved. The core is updated nightly. There are no blank spots, no deliberate gaps. If you can't find something, it was never there to begin with."

A ripple of awe moves through the group. The boy next to Kaia—Taro—leans in, eyes bright. "Is it true some texts are encoded in three layers? That if you know the right phrase, you can unlock a whole shadow archive beneath the main one?"

Voss's mouth twitches, not quite a smile. "That's classified. But you're not wrong."

She demonstrates, dragging her finger across the holo to select a title: "The Complete Works of Shakespeare." The system flickers, conjuring a perfect simulacrum of the First Folio, pages fanning out as if caught in a phantom breeze. Every word, every marginalia, perfectly replicated. You can even see the stains and the pressed flowers from some long-dead owner. Kaia feels the group sway forward, hunger and disbelief mingling on their faces.

"This is how we preserve knowledge," Voss says. "No physical contamination, no risk of loss to fire, flood, or theft. It's not about the paper. It's about the pattern of meaning—the code of the past."

Kaia wants to believe it, but something inside her resists. She remembers the old library from her childhood—the real, forbidden one, with sagging shelves and the thick, mineral smell of old glue. Her mother's hands, ink-stained, tracing lines down a page; the way stories seemed to breathe when you pressed your cheek to a stack of them. This? It's dazzling, but it's not alive.

She looks down, fingers unconsciously stroking the ribbon at her wrist—a gesture so practiced she barely notices. Across the console, Dojo is watching her. He doesn't blink, doesn't shift, just fixes her with that low, clinical stare. It makes her feel seen and invisible at the same time.

Voss beckons for a volunteer. "Who here wants to try the interface?"

A dozen hands go up. Voss picks the tall girl from the left end—Hana, if Kaia remembers right. Hana steps forward, nervous but excited, and Voss walks her through the gestures: how to search, how to bookmark, how to run comparisons between editions.

Kaia drifts back a half step, letting the others crowd the demo. She watches Hana's hands as they swipe and pinch at the air, leaving trails of phosphor light. The system is beautiful, yes—but it's cold. The pages have no weight, the ink no bite. You could erase or alter anything here and no one would know.

Behind her, Taro murmurs, "Wish my old man could see this. He always said the League would burn itself out, but this...this is better than anything they ever made."

Kaia nods, not trusting herself to answer. In her head, a loop of old argument: Is it better to lose the page but keep the words, or lose the words and have nothing at all? She suspects there's no answer, but she aches for one anyway.

At the console, Voss shifts the display. "Many of you have been taught that books are dangerous because they are hard to control. That's true. One contaminated text can undo decades of order. But in here, we control the content. If something is wrong or harmful, we correct it instantly. There is no threat of dissidence escaping into the wild anymore."

The recruits take this in. A few glance at each other, the tension barely masked. Kaia looks at Dojo again, and this time he holds her gaze for a full two seconds. There's a question in his face—maybe even a challenge.

Voss flicks her finger, and the Shakespeare folio dissolves into a cascade of metadata: every edit, every change, every curation decision annotated and time-stamped. "Transparency," she says. "That's the advantage. We can see everything, track every version, every voice."

Kaia wonders if her mother's annotations survived the purge. She wants to ask, but the voice won't come.

A new recruit, braver than most, pipes up: "But if it's all digital, what happens if the Codex fails? What if there's a glitch, or sabotage?"

Voss answers without hesitation. "There are redundancies. But more important—everyone here is the backup. You will memorize, you will internalize, you will become living copies. The LDC is not just a storage unit. It is a society of walking archives. If we lose the machines, we have each other."

A hush falls. For the first time, Kaia feels the gravity of the job—the weight of being not just a protector, but a vessel.

But still, her hands itch for a real book, a real page.

As the session ends, Voss waves them away. "Explore. Pair off. Review your assigned sections. This is your home now."

The group fragments. Kaia hangs back, her heart heavy. She's not sure what she expected, but the sense of loss is sharp and fresh.

She drifts to the edge of the dome, sits on a low bench beneath a projection of the Library of Alexandria burning, its columns dissolving in digital flame. The holo is so realistic she can almost feel the heat, almost smell the smoke. She clutches her sleeve, the blue ribbon crumpled in her palm.

A shadow crosses her vision. Dojo stands above her, hands still clasped behind his back. "Having second thoughts?"

Kaia shakes her head, not trusting herself to speak.

He sits beside her, not close, but not distant. "It's not what you expected, is it?"

She shrugs. "I thought there'd be more...books."

He allowed himself the smallest smile. "So did I. But things change. Adapt or disappear."

They sit in silence, the server song and the faint screams of digital Alexandria mingling in the air.

Dojo says, "You know, most of what matters is still in people's heads. The Codex just helps us remember the rest."

Kaia nods, her jaw tight.

He stands, then turns to her. "The ribbon in your sleeve," he says, voice so quiet it barely carries. "Don't let anyone take it, all right?"

She meets his eyes, surprised. There's nothing mocking in his face, only a hard-earned empathy.

She says, "I won't."

Kaia's fingers clung tightly to the crumpled blue ribbon in her palm, the fabric rough against her skin.

He nods, then disappears into the blue-lit maze.

In that moment, Kaia realized the future was uncertain, filled with twists and turns she could not foresee. But as long as she held onto the memories that shaped her, she knew she could weather any storm that came her way. With a renewed sense of determination, she tucks the ribbon safely into her pocket, ready to face whatever challenges lie ahead.

The blue light of the maze flickered and faded, casting shadows that danced around her. Kaia took one last look around, imprinting the scene in her mind before stepping forward, ready to embrace whatever came next.

The end of the tour was a cul-de-sac, set in the shadow of the tallest server racks. The air here was colder, tinged with the antiseptic tang of ozone. At the far side, a glass case sat on a plinth—unadorned, deliberate. Inside was a single book, nothing digital about it: cracked leather binding, cover faded to the shade of old bone, the title stamped in black but nearly gone. If you looked close, you could still read the last fragment of the original type: Fahrenheit 451.

Kaia heard her mother's voice, vivid and defiant: "Don't let them tell you what to think. It's the writers who will be burned next, when the firemen are done." She touched the glass and imagined the paper inside, the way it could catch and curl. The flames outside danced in perfect pixels, but this fire was real.

The group clusters around the case. Even the bravest of the recruits are quiet, the presence of the artifact drawing a hush more profound than anything in the server vault. Kaia finds herself at the front, separated from the others by accident or gravity. She can see the book perfectly: the way the pages have swollen with age, the little scars at the corners where it was probably pried from some secret hiding place.

Commander Voss speaks in a calm, steady tone, not needing to amplify her voice. "This is a major contraband item," she informs the group, her gaze moving across them. "It was confiscated six years ago during a raid on an illegal archive in the Lower Archipelago. The archive was eliminated, and the perpetrators received the standard punishment: a complete memory audit followed by reconditioning." There's a beat where no one breathes. Kaia imagines the archive's destruction, knowledge snuffed out in the name of protection.

Voss continues: "You've been taught to fear what's inside a book. That's only partially true. The real threat is the medium itself." She taps the glass with a sharp sound. "Paper can't be traced. It can be transported, duplicated, concealed. No code can neutralize it, and no firewall can erase it. If a text survives long enough out in the world, it turns into a virus—infecting minds and creating unauthorized memories." Yuki shifts uneasily beside Kaia, eyes flicking to the book then away. Kaia wonders how much of this is preservation, how much is control. Voss's voice pushes on: "Digital content, however, is always in our control. We can redact, update, delete it. There's no transmission we can't monitor. That's why we do what we do."

Kaia can't look away from the book. She's never seen a real one up close—never smelled the dry, earthy exhale of old pages or touched the warped edge of a cover softened by a hundred hands. She tries to imagine her mother with something like this, reading it by forbidden lamplight, hiding it in the walls when the Censors came. A sudden wash of memory: the door ripped open, her mother's voice caught mid-sentence, the book torn from her hands and the hands cuffed behind her back. Kaia's stomach knots so fast she has to clench her teeth to keep from retching.

On the plinth, a holographic display flickers to life, casting an orange wash across the group. The display plays a looped sequence—first, the raid itself: men in matte armor, faces erased by visors, flooding a tenement and smashing shelves of real books. Then the aftermath: a fire in the courtyard, civilians kneeling, hands on heads, as the pages go up in gray-black sheets. Voss's voice is stripped of sympathy. "The penalty for possession of primary contraband is, and always will be, absolute. The penalty for distribution is worse. We are not here to judge. We are here to prevent a repetition of history."

Kaia's pulse thrums in her ears as the core paradox twists in her mind: preserving knowledge not for learning, but for surveillance. The book seems to glow in its case, a dangerous flare against this world of sanctioned memory.

Kaia's hand finds the blue ribbon at her wrist, squeezes until the blood drains from her fingers. The sensation is sharp, grounding, and for a moment she's not in the Vault but in her childhood bedroom, listening to her mother read forbidden stories in the dark.

She tries to let go, but can't. The urge to protect the ribbon, to keep it hidden, is overwhelming.

From the corner of her eye, she sees Dojo watching her. His face is unreadable, but there's something in his gaze—not accusation, not yet, but a taut thread of warning.

A recruit behind Kaia clears his throat. "If the books are so dangerous, why keep even one in the Vault? Why not just burn them all?"

Voss regards him for a long moment. "Because you cannot understand the past unless you see what it looks like. To fight an enemy, you must know them. If we destroyed every artifact, we'd be no better than the revisionists."

The recruit seems satisfied, but Kaia is not. Her thoughts race: How many other books lie locked in glass cases, preserved as warnings rather than for learning? How many stories have been lost forever—their only evidence a specter in a database or a fragment fading in someone's memory?

Voss steps back, gesturing at the display. "You are the future of the LDC. Your duty is not to hate books, but to outsmart them. To understand the flaws that allowed our ancestors to become addicted to unregulated narrative. You must remember what happened, so you can prevent it from happening again."

Kaia's palm aches. She glances down, sees a thin red line where the ribbon has pressed into her skin.

The hologram resets, looping the footage: the raid, the burning, the kneeling civilians. This time, Kaia looks for the faces—searching for anything familiar, even though she knows her mother's arrest was never televised, never given the dignity of being archived. The rage that rises is white-hot and clean— the kind that roots her to the spot.

There's a question burning in her throat, but she doesn't dare ask it. She wonders if the LDC would ever preserve memories of people like her mother—or if that is the next frontier in "authorized curation": a world where even sorrow is managed and redacted.

Voss dismisses the group with a nod. "Tour is over. You may review the Vault at your leisure. Any questions must be cleared through your unit commander. Remember your protocols."

The recruits scatter, some in pairs, others dazed and wandering. Kaia stays by the case, eyes locked on the book. She wonders what story is hidden inside, if any of the pages are annotated, if a single word remains uncensored. She leans in until her breath fogs the glass.

Behind her, Dojo waits. When she turns, he doesn't move. He just looks at her—long enough that his gaze becomes something other than authority: perhaps kinship, perhaps scrutiny.

She doesn't know if he saw her clutch the ribbon, or if he cares.

But then he does something unexpected: he tilts his head, the barest nod, as if to say he saw everything and will keep it between them. Maybe it's a test. Maybe it's a gift with strings attached.

Kaia straightens her spine, lets her hand relax. The ache in her palm lingers, but now it feels like a promise.

She gives the nod back, almost imperceptible. She wonders what it costs her.

Then she turns away from the glass, walks into the blue-lit maze, and lets herself hope—for the first time in a long time—that not everything precious must be destroyed to be saved.

As Kaia navigates the twists and turns of the blue-lit maze, her footsteps echo softly against the cold walls; a newfound determination blooms within her. The encounter with Dojo, though brief, kindled a spark of hope in her heart—a belief that, in the midst of chaos and uncertainty, a chance for redemption still lingers.

Every fiber of her being tells her to keep moving forward, to push through the doubts and fears that threaten to engulf her. The ribbon in her hand serves as a silent reminder of the past, of the sacrifices made and the secrets buried deep within her soul.

As she reaches a junction in the maze, Kaia comes to a sudden halt, her breath catching in her throat. Before her lies a path bathed in a soft golden light, beckoning her towards an unknown destination. Instinct guides her as she takes the first step onto the illuminated path, her heart pounding with a mixture of trepidation and anticipation.

In the distance, a faint glimmer catches her eye—a flicker of something ancient and powerful, calling out to her from the shadows. With each passing moment, the weight of the past begins to lift from her shoulders, replaced by a sense of clarity and purpose she thought she had lost long ago.

As Kaia moves deeper into the maze, the walls around her seem to shimmer and shift, revealing a pathway that leads to a place she never imagined she would find. And in that moment, bathed in the gentle glow of the golden light, she knows that the journey ahead will be fraught with challenges and sacrifices, but also with moments of profound beauty and grace.

With a steadying breath, Kaia sets her sights on the horizon, her gaze unwavering and her spirit unbroken. For in the heart of the maze, surrounded by shadows and light, she discovers a truth that resonates deep within her soul: that sometimes, in the darkest of nights, the faintest glimmer of hope is all it takes to illuminate the path towards a brighter tomorrow.

Chapter 7: Breach Simulation

The Academy's urban training wing is three stories of staged squalor, each corridor made to look like a slice of the real Aetherra: crumbling ferrocrete, acid-stained windows, a fake wind that brings the faint smell of old oil and ionized blood. It's 0500, and in the prep bay, Kaia sits on a wire bench next to nine other recruits, all of them cinched into tactical gear and stripped of any hope of sleep.

"Thirty seconds to breach," the intercom intones, and every head lifts in unison. No one is truly awake, but no one dares to slack. The air smells of recycled sweat, ozone, and the metallic tang that means the cleaning bots have finished their rounds but the blood from the last sim still lingers somewhere below.

Kaia runs her fingers along the Velcro strip of her vest, thumb hitching on the plastic tab. Her hands shake—not from fear, exactly, but from the anticipation that always grips her before a drill. Beneath her left sleeve, tight against the wrist, is the token: blue ribbon, pressed feather, mother's memory. She touches it once, brief and private, before pulling her glove on.

The squad leader, a wall of a girl whose arms look sculpted for battering down doors, checks the clock again. "Final check," she says, voice low and mean. "Vests. Ammo. Comms."

Kaia taps her chest, then her belt, then the mic at her throat. The checklist follows a script, but it steadies her. Around her, the others do the same. She sees Yuki, hair hidden under a skullcap, fussing with the latch on her sidearm; sees the boy with the broken nose (Recruit #7, she thinks, though no one uses names in drills) staring ahead, eyes flat and unblinking.

The mission parameters scroll on the wall screen: Simulated Hostage Recovery. Two targets, neutralize all enemy dummies, fifteen-minute time limit, full failure if any recruit is "lost" before breach point.

"Clear on tactics?" the squad leader asks.

A chorus of yeses, Kaia's half a second ahead.

"Entry pattern?"

"Four in wedge, six in cover. Sweep stairs, secure east block, push to objective."

"Who takes point?"

No one hesitates. They all know—it's Kaia, it's always Kaia. Even when she's not assigned, she finds the gap and wedges herself in.

The squad leader nods, a grudging respect. "You hear that, Mori? This time, no fancy moves. No detours. No heroics. We do this by the book or not at all."

Kaia bites the inside of her cheek, words sticking, but she says, "Understood."

The lights in the prep bay shift from blue to orange, and they're out: the corridor's dim and cramped, a tunnel of cracked panels and fluid stains. Kaia moves fast, not waiting for cover. She knows the map, knows the real thing even better. Her breath thins as she pushes to the stairs, a rattle of boots behind her. Grinding servos, simulated gunfire—she's halfway up when Recruit #7 collapses. The enemy AI is relentless. Two more go down. The wall screen showed three rooms, but now it's dropped all the black markers, every drone live and lethal. Kaia knows the drill. "Push forward!" she shouts. Her voice barely slices through the chaos. They hit the second floor, a maze of false walls and low ceilings. The bodies pile up: Yuki yells but Kaia can't slow. She takes a corner, takes the lead, fakes left, fakes right. She hits the door to the east block with two recruits left. The hostages are close. She can feel it. She can feel the pattern change. She kicks in the final room; orange to red, too quick. Her chest's a fist of failure. The sim's a kill box, just like last time.

Ten seconds to breach.

Kaia glances down the line. Yuki gives her a quick, savage grin. The boy with the broken nose won't meet her eyes, but Kaia catches the twitch of his jaw—nerves or anger, impossible to say.

"Comms check," the squad leader says.

Each recruit taps their mic in sequence. Kaia's buzzes twice—she's always had a glitch with the cheap equipment they issue to her section.

"That's your last warning, Mori," the squad leader says. "Get your act together or go home."

Kaia's reply is a clipped "Copy," but in her head, she hears her mother's voice, old and warm: If the world closes, you wedge a story in the crack and lever it back open.

The breach alarm sounds, shrill and close, and the wall panel rolls aside.

They're in.

The first corridor is a nightmare of strobing lights, the floor slick with synthetic grime. Kaia moves low, knee almost skimming concrete, the shotgun weight in her arms perfectly familiar. Her boots slap once before she finds the cadence, the rhythm of their old marches. A simulated gunshot cracks the air. She hears Recruit #7 go down, a thud of servo and bone. She pushes forward, urgency in her breath. The east block's a floor up. The stairwell narrows, its steps caked in rubber dust and old oil. Two more fall behind her. Kaia sees the black markers drop on every room. The AI's shifted the pattern, turning dummies to drones. "Push forward!" Her voice scrapes the chaos. She hits the second floor, a maze of false walls and low ceilings. Yuki yells but Kaia can't slow. She takes a corner, fakes left, fakes right. The hostages are close; she can feel it. She kicks the door, orange to red, too quick. Her chest's a fist of failure. The sim's a kill box, just like last time.

"Left, left," Yuki hisses, and Kaia mirrors the call, the whole wedge pivoting around her.

Up ahead, the sim has staged a barricade—broken furniture, an overturned server rack, the legs of a dummy in League armor poking out from behind a crate. Kaia signals halt, raises a fist, but instead of regrouping, she does the thing she shouldn't: she slips out two steps ahead, sighting over the barrel.

It's a risk, but it's what she does. She sees the motion before the rest—the dummy's head, servo-jerking to target them. Kaia fires once, a thunderclap in the echo chamber, and the dummy folds with a spray of red paint.

"Clear!" she calls, but the squad leader is already at her elbow—grabbing her shoulder, spinning her back into line.

"What did I say?" the squad leader snaps, teeth bared.

"Dummy had first shot," Kaia replies. "If I waited, we'd lose two at the breach."

Squad leader glares, but they both know she's not wrong.

"Stick to the plan," the leader growls.

They move. Second corridor, second sweep: tight, stacked with mock debris, the smell of tear-gas simulant burning the nostrils. The squad is good, disciplined. Kaia and Yuki in the middle, two go high, two go low. The black markers shift, turning dummies to drones. AI's changed the pattern. The enemy is smarter—one fires from cover, the other tries to circle. Kaia predicts the move, signals with a chop of her hand. They split the group, cut the AI off. A quick twist of focus. They clear the hall in under thirty seconds.

"Downstairs," Yuki says, voice thin over comms. "Hostages are flagged in lower east."

Kaia is first down the stairs. She feels the old rush, the same sick joy as when she'd sneak forbidden books from the roof vents in her childhood, every step a wager that she'd make it and no one would notice. Here, the risk is calibrated, safe, but her pulse is the same.

At the bottom, a fork. The plan says left, clear the storage first, then sweep the cells. But Kaia sees a shadow at the far end, a flicker in the strobing red lights. Maybe it's nothing, but it sets her teeth on edge.

She hesitates.

The squad moves tight down the hall, banking left at the ground floor fork. Kaia stays, just half a step, just long enough for the gap to widen and shadows to bleed into the breach. They ignore the plan, ignore the map—she knows the sim will try to flank if she ignores it.

"Movement right," she whispers, "possible flanker."

The squad leader hisses, "Stick to the plan, Mori. Left block first, then right. That's the protocol."

But Kaia can't. She edges toward the right fork, gun up, nerves screaming. The hallway is deserted, silent except for her own breath. Yuki curses from down the hall.

At the end, a door. She kicks it open, hard; the hinges groan. Inside, nothing—a closet, a decoy. Kaia swears, but then, behind her, a blare: breach alarm, loud and sudden, drowning out all other noise. She's triggered the sim's trap. Instantly, the lights snap from red to white, and the enemy dummies in the left block activate early, pinning the squad with a hail of paint rounds.

"Damn it!" the squad leader yells, "They're behind us—Mori, you set off the breach!"

Kaia wheels back—caught in the crossfire. Paint slaps her vest, stings her neck, dribbles down inside her collar. The others are forced back, stumbling over each other. The left block is chaos—every plan shredded.

Kaia's heart hammers, her mouth thick with the taste of old batteries and fake blood. She dives for cover, rolling behind a tipped filing cabinet. The comms are a storm of static and shouted curses.

Yuki's voice cuts through: "Regroup! Kaia, can you move?"

"Yeah," Kaia spits, wiping paint from her cheek. "On your six."

They form up behind the cabinet, just three of them—Yuki, Kaia, and the broken-nose boy, who is bleeding real blood now from a cut on his cheek. The rest of the squad is down, marked by the sim as "eliminated," their armor pulsing with angry red LEDs.

"Time?" Kaia asks.

"Five minutes to deadline," Yuki says. "Two hostages, both still live. We go now, or it's a fail."

Kaia nods, and together, they break from cover, charging into the fire. The dummies are accurate, but not creative. Kaia uses her body as a shield, draws fire, while Yuki and the boy flank the enemy.

It almost works. They take out two, but then a spray of paint rounds catches Yuki in the thigh, dropping her hard. Kaia keeps moving, the mission shrinking to a single, burning goal: reach the hostages. She barrels through a side door, into the cell block.

Inside, the hostages—two dummies, tied to chairs—wait in the center. Kaia rushes to them, ignoring the pain in her side from a fresh welt.

She yanks the bindings off, checks the timer. Thirty seconds left.

"Go, go," she urges the hostages, but they don't move—the sim requires both to be escorted. Kaia grabs one under the arm, hauls it upright.

Behind her, the broken-nose boy limps in, paint streaked down his vest. He grabs the second hostage.

They make it three meters before the final wave hits: enemy dummies, six of them, all firing at once.

Kaia shoves the hostage forward, throws herself over it as a shield. She takes three, four more rounds, paint everywhere, stinging and cold.

The timer runs out.

The sim freezes. The lights come up. The world goes silent, but for the sound of Kaia's breath and the ragged gasp of the boy next to her.

She sits up, blinking against the harsh white. Yuki limps into the room, clutching her thigh, eyes wet but not from pain.

"Mission failed," the intercom says, cold and flat.

The squad leader, alive again in the restart, appears in the doorway, arms folded. She looks at Kaia, at the mess on her vest, at the hostages on the floor.

"Good job, Mori," she says, voice thick with sarcasm. "You just got us all killed. Again."

Kaia opens her mouth, then closes it—the heat in her face brighter than any sim paint.

She waits for the next words, the ones she always expects—the threat, the warning, the lecture.

But the squad leader just shakes her head, a mix of anger and something like confusion.

"Debrief in five," she says, then leaves.

Yuki helps Kaia up, her touch rough but not unkind. "You saw the movement, right?"

Kaia nods, unable to meet her eyes.

"Sim's getting better," Yuki says, voice softer now. "Or maybe you are."

Kaia manages a smile, crooked and bloodied. She glances at her sleeve, at the blue ribbon dark with paint but still intact.

She thinks: If the world closes, wedge a story in the crack.

But what if you're the crack?

She doesn't have the answer. All she has is the aftermath, the memory, and the hope that next time, maybe, she can hold the world open long enough for the story to matter.

The paint dries cold on her skin, but the fire inside her is anything but.

The debrief offers no relief. The simulation restarts in under a minute—this time, just six participants remain, as the other four are sidelined for "injury recovery" in the medical wing. Kaia wipes paint from her lips, the mix of blue and red now a symbol of her shame and fatigue. Her ears echo with the squad leader's reprimand: Next time, maintain formation. Next time, don't be the reason for our failure. She doesn't get a next time, not really.

The alarm blares, throwing them back into the corridor mid-mission, all previous errors compounded. The enemy has adapted—now, instead of dummies, half a dozen automated drones hover down the hall, their gun-arms clicking with anticipation. Kaia catches the shimmer of their shields as the lights flicker; the bots map trajectories, update threat matrices. She remembers a line from the manual: "Each simulation is unique, but every mistake is remembered."

Pressed against the wall, Kaia feels her breath sear her nostrils as she waits for the first drone to commit. The whine of capacitors fills the air—a shivering, high-pitched scream. Yuki gestures from ahead, a silent three-count. They break cover sprinting low and hard for the next barricade.

The drones react instantly, rounds of paint and rubber ricocheting off the concrete. Kaia's world shrinks to the pounding rhythm of her heart and the thudding of her boots against the ground. She acts on instinct now—muscle memory guiding her through the maze of chaos. Left, then up—vault over debris. A round cracks off her helmet—the world dances with stars, but she keeps moving.

"Keep moving!" bellows the squad leader over comms, panic tinging her voice as realization dawns that any mistake now is fatal.

They're almost to the east block when Kaia hears it: a wet, desperate shout from behind.

Spinning around reveals Recruit #7 pinned beneath a tangle of collapsed scaffolding. One arm flails, his face twisted with pain. The sim has shredded his armor at the shoulder—paint streaks down to his joint. However, what matters most is the drone overhead with its laser dot tracking slow across his chest.

"He's down," someone hisses. Ignoring commands to keep moving, Kaia sprints back—low and desperate—to aid him. Every breath tears at her lungs; every step feels like wading through glue in the smoky corridor that reeks of propellant and old sweat.

Yuki shouts after her: "Kaia! Ignore it! Keep moving—that's an order!"

But Kaia disregards commands in favor of saving a comrade in need.

The drone targets her; she senses the prick of its laser and hears the click as its gun arms adjust. She dives hard—slides under its line of fire, rolls to the base of the scaffolding, dodging paint rounds exploding near her face. Gripping under the steel beam pinning Recruit #7's chest takes monumental effort; She grits her teeth against pain, letting it guide her anger.

"Go," pleads Recruit #7. "Just go—it's a sim."

"Shut up," she whispers during trembling effort. "It's still us."

With a pure, animalistic howl, Kaia shifts the beam enough for him to free himself from entrapment.

Another drone rounds a corner—Kaia sees it but knows escape is impossible at this point. Shielding Recruit #7 with her body while bracing for impact seems to be their only recourse now.

The sim freezes abruptly.

Silence descends upon them following chaos that reigned moments ago. Kaia remains on her knees; Her hands still locked on the steel beam show signs of strain: cracked nails and raw palms. Recruit #7 breathes fast yet shallow—a sign he's alive despite everything they faced together.

"Why?" he asks, not angry, just tired.

Kaia's answer is a rasp: "Because they never mean it, you know? When they say it's 'just' a sim. It's always real. Always practice for what comes next. If we don't save each other now, we'll never do it for real."

The boy nods, and for the first time, his eyes meet hers with something like respect.

A voice on the overhead: "Simulation complete. Debrief in ten."

Yuki is there, crouching beside Kaia, hands on her knees. "You're insane," she says, but it's half a laugh, half a sob.

Kaia shrugs, winces at the pain. "Maybe."

They stand, together, supporting each other. The squad leader approaches, helmet off, face flushed with embarrassment or anger or both.

"You fucked the mission," she says, tone flat.

Kaia nods. "Yeah. But I didn't fuck the squad."

A long silence, broken only by the hum of the deactivated drones. Finally, the squad leader says, "Next time, you better be sure it's worth it."

Kaia looks around at the faces—bruised, battered, and alive. "It was," she says.

She rubs her wrist, feeling the faint bulge of the ribboned token beneath her sleeve. Even here, under fake lights and fake pain, it still means something.

In the end, that's enough.

The six of them limp back to the prep bay, not winners, not really even survivors, but together. Kaia doesn't know if she passed or failed. All she knows is that when the world comes for her, for all of them, this is what she'll remember: not the victory, but the refusal to leave anyone behind.

She sits, sweat drying cold on her skin, and waits for the next fight.

The debriefing room is colder than the sim chamber—on purpose, probably, to keep the sweat from turning into stink. The six remaining recruits stand at attention in a ragged line, gear stowed but bruises, welts, and paint still visible on skin and hair and undershirts. Kaia holds her ground in the center. She can feel the heat of Recruit #7 on her right, not anger, not now, but a residual pulse of adrenaline and something harder to name.

Nobody speaks. Yuki keeps her hands jammed in her pockets, eyes half-lidded, mouth drawn in a line that means she's replaying every second. The squad leader—wary now, not triumphant—stands at the far end, studying her boots with a tension that threatens to break bones.

Lt. Dojo enters like a force of gravity, posture perfect, uniform fresh, expression as unreadable as the ocean in winter. He doesn't bother with a clipboard or notes. He surveys them, his face blank and expectant, letting the silence dig trenches in the room.

"You're all still alive," he says at last, voice softer than a reprimand but sharper than any praise. "That's something."

Nobody relaxes. Kaia feels her jaw tighten, then deliberately unclenches it.

Dojo stops in front of her, hands behind his back. For a moment, Kaia thinks she can smell ink and ozone on his skin, the chemical burn of a print shop before the League shut them all down.

"You failed the primary objective, Recruit Mori." Flat, declarative. "You lost the hostages, compromised the team, and allowed yourself to be flanked."

Kaia straightens her spine. "Understood, sir."

"But," Dojo says, the word a razor, "you also disobeyed a direct order to leave a fallen comrade. You demonstrated initiative, personal courage, and a certain contempt for easy decisions — all qualities we prize when properly aimed."

A hitch hangs in the room. Even the squad leader blinks.

Dojo pivots, addresses the group. "Sometimes the mission isn't what you think it is. Sometimes the job is just to come home alive."

He walks the line, pausing at each recruit, eyeing their injuries, their posture, the way they hold disappointment or relief.

"Make no mistake," he says. "You will be penalized for the loss. But you won't be penalized for acting like humans. That is, after all, what we're defending."

He looks back at Kaia, and for the first time, there's a glint—approval, maybe, or the memory of something he once believed. It's gone as fast as it comes.

"Dismissed. Clean yourselves up. Report to the mess for full debrief at 1900."

They file out, slow and battered. Yuki hangs back, giving Kaia a look equal parts admiration and warning. The squad leader walks ahead, her pace slower than usual. Kaia tucks her hand into her sleeve, feels for the blue ribbon, the feather pressed flat, the old blood crusted at the edge.

She breathes in, lets it anchor her.

In the hall, the other recruits cluster closer than before. Nobody jokes, but nobody glares, either. The paint on their faces is a badge now, not a shame.

Recruit #7 falls into step beside her. His limp is slight, more pride than injury.

He says, low, "Thanks for coming back for me. Not everyone would have."

Kaia shrugs. "We only get one shot at this. Might as well make it count for something."

He grins, teeth pink with paint. "Guess so."

At the exit, Yuki nudges her in the ribs. "You realize you just made life a lot harder for the rest of us? Now we have to actually give a damn."

Kaia grins back. "Figure it's time somebody did."

They walk on, the cold of the corridor fading as they near the mess. Kaia feels the bruises, the ache in her bones, but they're good aches, the kind that prove you were there, that you mattered.

She touches the token, just once, then squares her shoulders.

She failed the mission, sure. But she didn't fail herself.

And in a place built on the bones of stories, that felt like the only win that mattered.

Chapter 8: Unspoken Words

There are three ways to slip unseen into the archive wing during free period: the long crawl through the ductwork (risky if you're tall or unlucky), the back stairs by the mail chute (better, but the keypad is logged), and Kaia's favorite—the water closet behind the maintenance office, with a loose panel leading straight to the auxiliary stacks. No one uses it; no one expects a recruit in the LDC's least glamorous hall—not unless you're hiding something or looking to steal it.

Kaia, of course, is both.

She slides the panel aside with practiced, silent care. Beyond it: a four-meter stretch of corridor, unlit except for the jaundiced spill of a single bulb and the neon flicker from the exit sign at the far end. It's a reliquary of neglect, lined with boxes the color of dishwater and crates stenciled "REDUNDANT" in five languages. The dust here is old—less like powder, more like the skin of something dead and unclaimed.

Kaia advanced, careful and feline, each step surgically considered. She'd trained her footsteps to the rhythm of the hum in the walls—two beats on the pipes, one on the tiles, one on her pulse. She could map this corridor by memory, even in blackout. At the midpoint, where the geometry kinked sharply and the walls seemed to close like a windpipe, she stopped at a door with a battered plate: "MEMORY SUPPLEMENTAL: LEVEL 2." The mechanism was ancient, sticky from years of oil and skin cells, but she jimmied it open with a swipe of her badge and a gentle backward shove. Inside, the vault of castoff memory.

This was where the discarded went—the indexes nobody ever referenced, the old legal digests, the public records out of fashion and favor, their contents neither dangerous nor sufficiently mythic to warrant erasure. A mausoleum of the unremarkable. The burnout recruits sometimes used the room for illicit naps, the supervisors for hiding contraband or dalliances. Kaia alone came here for the ghosts.

The stacks here were not the ordered, threatened beauty of the main archive, but a crumbling, half-lit labyrinth. Shelves sagged under the weight of their own obsolescence, like backs permanently bent under the memory of labor. The air held the musk of decomp, the sour tang of glue and ink leaching upward from pulp. A faint current from the air vent set the dust motes to jittering, as if the whole room vibrated with the slow panic of being forgotten.

Kaia paused to listen, motionless in her shadow. There were no voices, no footsteps in the corridor outside—only the slow tick of the wall clock and the groan of the building's ancient ventilation. She exhaled, then navigated to her refuge: two aisles down, left, a nook hidden behind a collapsed column of city ledgers. She ducked beneath the belly of "Municipal Tax Code, 2144-2165," squeezed past a lasagna of "Official Notices—Obsolete," and found her cubby, the hollow at the bottom just wide enough for a person desperate to vanish.

She crouched, knees to chest, and retrieved the battered logbook she'd stashed in the crawlspace weeks prior—"Community Proceedings, Volume CXL." Its spine was scarred by the graffiti of generations: insults, love notes, a crude rendering of a bird in flight. The pages were fragile, the paper gone to the consistency of onion skin, but Kaia handled it with respect, almost reverence. There was power here, she believed, in the way memory clung to the edge of decay.

She opened to her marker—a purple thread from her own uniform, wound around page 67. She picked up her search where she'd left off, this time reading slower, letting each page settle before she turned to the next. She wasn't searching for secrets or heresy; she wanted the residue, the proof of hands and minds that had once touched these leaves. The world outside, the world she was training for, didn't care about who made the marks or why. But here, in this tomb, those tiny thumbprints—smudges of ink, the oily shadow of a palm—were evidence that someone had survived the forgetting, at least for a while.

On page 67, a hitch. Two pages stuck together, edges yellowed and delicate, but at the margin a shadow, a seam where the light refused to penetrate. Kaia's breath went paper thin. She worked a fingernail into the gap and, with surgical patience, teased the leaves apart. Hidden, compressed by decades, was a slip of paper: two centimeters by four, the color of old teeth, folded first in half and then again. The edges were frilled, almost lacy, where the fibers had surrendered to pressure and time.

She freed it, cradled it in her palm. The ink had faded from black to rust, but the handwriting—tight and slanting up, almost frantic—remained. She opened the fold with reverence, terrified some essential part would crumble away. The message was short, just a line and a half, severed at both ends: "...when they take everything else, they cannot take what we felt in that moment—"

No signature, no context. The violence was not in the content, but in the ragged way it ended, as if the rest had been torn away for security, or left unwritten in the panic of discovery. Kaia's throat tightened; her thumb drifted, as if by reflex, to the inside of her sleeve, to the old token she always carried—a strip of blue ribbon, a feather, the memory of her mother's hand. She squeezed it, grounding herself in the present, then returned to the message, reading it again and again.

Who wrote it? A lover? A prisoner? Someone about to be erased? Maybe all of these, maybe neither; the personalness of it was the danger, more than any call to arms or forbidden doctrine. The system could survive a thousand rumors, but not one person who remembered how it felt.

Kaia pressed the slip to her knee and inhaled. The ink had a faint, metallic tang, and if she closed her eyes she could almost conjure the smell of skin, the cramped heat of a hand squeezing the words onto the page before someone came through the door. She flipped the scrap, found the watermark: an official grid, standard issue, a faint imprint of the old regime. Even rebellion preserved the forms; even love learned to write itself in code.

She wondered if anyone else had read this, or if it was her alone. Did it matter? She remembered a story her mother used to tell, back in the safer years, before the raids—how sometimes the only real memory that survived was the feeling, not the words themselves.

Kaia closed her eyes. The memory was sharp, a scalpel: her mother's fingers braiding her hair, the whisper of a forbidden ending, the way she would tuck a thumb under Kaia's chin and say, never forget the feeling, Kaichan. That's what they can't rewrite. Not if you keep it alive. Kaia let it wash over her, the ache of loss blended with the stubborn, volcanic warmth of something preserved. She held the slip of paper to her heart, then refolded it precisely, aligning the old creases, and tucked it back into the logbook. She marked the page with a new thread, one plucked from the cuff of her own uniform—a small, deliberate wound.

It would be safer to keep it, to pocket the message for herself. But she didn't. Kaia understood, with the slow certainty of grief, that real memory was never private. It had to be left for the next one, the stranger who would need it most.

She rose, shaking the pins and needles from her legs. The room had grown colder, the shadows longer; outside, the building's hum was joined by the distant stutter of the intercom. She closed the book, repositioned the ledgers to hide her trail, and stepped into the aisle, pulse steady. No one waited in the corridor. She retraced her steps, ears tuned for the scrape of a boot or the static of surveillance. Nothing, only her own breath and the echo of what she'd just read, pulsing in the space behind her eyes. At the panel, Kaia steadied herself, pressed her ear to the metal, and counted to five: a trick her mother taught to flush out the watchers. Silence. She slipped into the gap and eased the wall closed behind her. By the time she reached the long corridor to the main hall, her passage was perfectly erased, except for a single, knee-shaped print in the dust behind "Community Proceedings, Volume CXL."

She walked, eyes fixed ahead, the stolen sentence burning quietly in her hand. Each step felt deliberate, less an escape than a pilgrimage. She wondered if the message would last, if anyone would ever find it again. She realized, with a pulse of certainty, that it didn't matter. What mattered was that it had survived long enough to be felt.

And maybe, she thought, they really couldn't take that, not even when they took everything else.

The sound that gave Dojo away was never his boots—he could walk silent on broken glass—but the faint metallic click as he reset the outer corridor's access latch. If you weren't listening for anomalies, you'd miss it; the building was a constant churn of electric fidgets: pressure sensors, coolant pumps, the subtle exhalations of cycle fans. But Kaia had made a study of those sounds, catalogued and cross-referenced every tone, and the click struck her like an errant pulse. By the time he rounded the corner—just a shadow in the jaundiced corridor—she was already upright, her posture set to parade-ready, hands folded at her lower back, face scrubbed clean of all affect except the bland alertness of a model recruit.

It was a performance, and she knew it. But the truth was, it had never worked on Dojo.

He lingered just at the boundary of her territory, his presence outlined in the dim spill of the hall. Sharp-collared blues, LDC insignia crisp at his throat, the battered sash of a service medal hanging beneath the fresh lacquer of a new reprimand ribbon. The contrast wasn't lost on her: the tension between what he was and what he was supposed to be. He studied the stacks ahead of him—not entering, not even leaning in—just letting his energy fill the space, as if he could nudge her back into line by sheer force of discipline.

"You're off schedule, Recruit Mori," he said, voice pitched low.

Kaia's mind spun for a cover story. "Maintenance detail, sir. Leak by the stairwell—Hydro sent me to check for water damage in the analog archives." She tried to land the delivery in that sweet spot between bored and dutiful, but even to her own ears it rang forced.

Dojo's gaze drifted over the scene: the toppled ledgers, the open logbook, the dust unsettled by her passage. He noticed everything, catalogued it, but said nothing about the evidence. His attention arrested on her left hand, where the ragged slip of paper had migrated from knuckle to palm, pinched in a way that made hiding it impossible. Still, he gave her the grace of pretending not to see it immediately, as though he was offering her the chance to make it right.

He stepped forward, closing the gap so that she could smell the ozone tang of his pressed uniform, the memory of old disinfectant in his hair. Then, quietly, "Show me."

Kaia hesitated. A flicker, maybe a single frame's worth of time, but it was enough for the air to tighten between them. Her fingers flexed; she could have crumpled the fragment, swallowed it, or tried sleight of hand, but her body chose honesty. She unfolded her fist, presenting the slip by its corner like a rare, forbidden stamp.

Dojo pinched it from her, but didn't look at it right away. Instead, he examined her face—eyes, then jaw, mapping the muscle tension, the blush racing up her collar. For a moment, she saw something almost human in him, a glint of what he'd been before the wars and the tribunals. Then the bureaucratic mask slid back into place, and he read the fragment aloud, voice barely more than a vibration:

"...when they take everything else, they cannot take what we felt in that moment—"

He stopped, jawline setting hard as if the words had been a dare.

He flipped the scrap over, seeking a code or an embedded threat, but the reverse was blank. "Not Corps-approved," he said, returning it to her with an odd delicacy, as if passing a hot wire or a living insect.

Kaia accepted it, gentle, all reverence. "It isn't instruction, sir. Just memory." The distinction mattered—she wanted him to know she wasn't reckless, at least not in the ways that counted.

Dojo held her gaze, unblinking. "That's exactly the problem, Recruit. Memory is never just memory. It's how we end up with martyrs. Radicalized cells. The last ten years of our lives." His voice dropped, and for a second Kaia was certain he was remembering something of his own, some line of poetry or plea for clemency read out at a sentencing. "Unvetted emotion gets people dead. On the page or in the street, it makes no difference."

There was a silence—physical, charged. Kaia stood her ground, knowing a single twitch or tremor would give everything away. Dojo's gaze flicked to the blue thread at her wrist, then out again into neutral. "I'll log the infraction," he said. "But I won't escalate. Not today."

His words stung with implication. She wanted to argue, to ask what difference it made if a scrap of someone else's longing survived in these dead stacks. Instead, she dropped her chin—refusal, not compliance—and said, "Understood."

Dojo leaned in, just enough that only she could hear him above the static hum.

"Don't get sentimental, Mori. Personal attachments are liabilities in the field." There was no threat in it, only a strange tenderness, as if he'd spoken from the bottom of a wound.

She wanted to laugh, or shout, or press the fragment to his chest the way you might stop someone bleeding. Instead, she watched his eyes: how they flickered, how the mask frayed at the edge.

He stepped back, the mask snapping shut for good. "Clean up and report to squad prep. Field exercise in forty minutes. I don't want to see you on remedial again." Then, lower, "Or on a casualty list."

He retreated down the corridor, the air behind him collapsing as if he'd never been there. For a long moment, Kaia stayed where she was, counting the slow contractions of her heart, the paper fragment pulsing in her hand. She pressed it to her lips—a silent benediction—then folded it sharp and small, quartered and then halved again, and slipped it into her side pocket, the one where she kept the bandages and the sugar tabs and all the other things you weren't supposed to need.

She cleaned her work, brushing the dust back into even strata, stacking the logbooks and replacing the ledgers so precisely they looked untouched. By the time she left, the only trace she'd been there was a faint oval in the carpet, a knee-shaped impression that would fade by lights-out.

The main hall was louder now, filled with the clatter and echo of other recruits. Kaia slipped into the flow, head down, the blue thread at her wrist hidden by her sleeve, the secret in her pocket thrumming with its own heat. She felt the gaze of cameras, the disinterested stares of senior staff, and the ever-present awareness that her presence was always a kind of trespass.

But the scrap of memory—what we felt—reminded her that not everything could be filed away, not forever. Some things survived. She reached into her pocket, touched the folded edge, and thought, Maybe this is enough. Maybe it's everything.

They can't take that from her, either.

Chapter 9: Family Secrets

Two hours past lights-out, the LDC Academy felt like a mausoleum with opinions about trespassers. Corridors stretched wide and mostly empty, floors so clean they mirrored the ceiling's surveillance domes, doubling the weight of paranoia. Each footfall is a crime, amplified and catalogued. Kaia moved with the rehearsed tension of a cat in someone else's kitchen—never a straight line, never a stride longer than necessary. When the security drone glides past at corridor delta, she melts into the shadow of a janitorial bot, heartbeat loud as a drumline, eyes squeezed shut against the urge to run.

The route to the restricted archives is a map of near-misses. Past the admin wing—where even the air tastes of bleach and disappointment—then through a supply closet whose mop stink is sharp enough to burn memory into the nose. Kaia's left hand finds her wrist by reflex, thumb kneading the blue ribbon beneath her sleeve, an old comfort and a reminder of purpose. Every time she freezes, she counts to four. Never five. Four means courage, five means indecision, and her mother had always said courage doesn't linger.

The access panel guarding the MRB subbasement is a square of black glass, indifferent to all but the proper sequence. Kaia takes the code from memory, not daring to check the note she'd scrawled under her pillow: 44-DIA-67. The string enters easy; the red light cycles, then blinks green. The door sighs open, heavy and faintly resentful.

Inside, the air is colder, with a chemical flatness that makes Kaia's teeth ache. Rows and rows of steel filing cabinets stand at attention, their surfaces matte and label-free, broken only by thin bands of barcode and the ghost prints of nervous fingers. At the far end, a fan of blue light from the main data terminal sifts dust motes like glitter through a waterfall. She scanned the ceiling—two cameras, one real, one dummy—and sidled between the cabinets, pressing close enough to leave a heat trace.

She wants to run, but makes herself walk. Every third cabinet holds a slim touchpad and a digital reader; the rest are unlocked, useless to her purpose. She finds the terminal, palms it awake, and whispers her mother's name as if she might conjure her from the machine: "Hana Mori."

A stutter. The cursor blinks, then leaps to a hit: Case ID 0094287, "VERBAL CONTAMINATION—SUSPECT: MORI, HANA." The language is bureaucratic, hollowed-out, but each word is a nail.

Kaia's hands sweat so badly the scanner slips twice before she steadies. The terminal demands a secondary credential; she gives it the bootleg code, fingers trembling, and prays the botnet hasn't been scrubbed from the system yet. The light bars flash through the warning colors—amber, then a sickly green—and the drawer in front of her pops with a muted click.

She pulls it open, breath shallow as if lifting the lid on a crypt. Inside: a thick manila folder, edges crisp, the weight of it heavier than she expects. There is something about physical records that still feels dangerous, like a weapon with the safety off. Kaia closes the drawer with her hip and backs up two paces, folder held in both hands.

She doesn't dare open it here. Instead, she drops to one knee behind the cabinet, presses her body into the space where two units meet, and lays the folder flat on the cold linoleum. The stillness is absolute, but for the hum of the main server rack, a low and constant warning that this place is always listening.

She peeled the clasp, every movement slow and deliberate. The first page is a booking warrant, the League seal stamped in blue at the top, the rest filled with lines of all-caps certainty:

OFFENSE: VERBAL CONTAMINATION, CLASS B

SUBJECT: MORI, HANA

ACTION: DETAIN AND AUDIT

Kaia's chest tightens. She skips the procedural language and finds the interrogation log, but nearly half the lines are redacted, black bars fat as worms crawling across the text. Still, she recognizes the cadence of her mother's speech in the surviving fragments. There is a question, a long pause, and then: "The only memory that matters is the one you refuse to surrender." The line was underlined three times in red pen, someone's comment scrawled beside it: "Repeat noncompliance. Elevate protocol."

Kaia presses the page to her nose, not sure what she expects—cologne, tears, the old library's dust? There's only the sharp, bitter note of toner and solvent, a disappointment as complete as the page itself.

She turns to the next sheet. It's a photo: the intake booking shot, dated three years prior. Her mother's face is half-shadow, the bruise along her cheekbone dark as a fingerprint. The defiance in her eyes is alive, but so is the exhaustion—the kind that can't be hidden by posture or even bravado. Kaia's breath comes in sharp, uneven pulls. She runs her thumb along the edge of the paper, careful not to smudge it.

Next is an inventory list, "Seized Materials—Subject Mori." Most of it is unremarkable: keys, ID, an old pen, a plastic card. But there, at the bottom, Kaia sees it: "1x—Handwritten Poem, yellow scrap, RECOVERED POCKET L." The last column reads "DISPOSED: scheduled for incineration."

Her vision tunnels. She flips the folder, digs through the annexed slips, and finds the evidence bag, clear and crinkled, heat-sealed at the top. Inside, the yellow scrap. Kaia rips the bag open with teeth she didn't know were bared. The paper is so thin it nearly disintegrates. On it, in her mother's looping script:

When the wind howls, shout the truth through cupped hands.

If the world closes, wedge a story in the crack.

If the world burns, let the ash spell your name.

There is no signature, just the word "Kaia" at the bottom, the ink smudged by water or sweat or both.

She can't breathe for a minute. Her pulse is a siren in her ears, every cell boiling with the knowledge that none of this was an accident. She understands, now, what Dojo never said outright, what the League always left in the spaces between words: It was always going to be personal. The hunt, the audit, the erasure. They didn't just want her mother's silence—they wanted to make sure that nothing survived of her but the official story.

Kaia kneels there, poem in hand, letting the grief run through her, hot and raw. Her hands shake so badly she nearly tears the paper. She folds it once, again, then slides it into her boot, next to the ribbon, the feather, and the small bloodstained thread—the last remnants of her true history.

Footsteps. Distant, but moving closer—measured, not rushed. Someone making rounds, maybe just another insomniac staffer, maybe not.

Kaia snaps the folder shut, replaces it in the drawer, then wipes down every surface she touched. She paces her breath: in, out, three seconds each. On the way out, she casts a last look at the terminal. The cursor blinks, expectant, as if waiting for a better answer.

She leaves through the janitorial route, heart in her mouth, not stopping until she's back in the safety of the stairwell, hands pressed to cold concrete, the poem burning a hole in her boot.

At her bunk, she doesn't sleep. She just lies there, the ribbon in her left hand, the poem in her right, and lets the pain and the memory braid together until she is certain—absolutely certain—that she will never let them win.

Above her, the ceiling fan circles, lazy and silent, oblivious to the war that just started.

Kaia spends the next day a storm system on a slow, grinding course: nothing breaks, but nothing heals. Her anger stalks her through every drill, every choreographed recitation, every tasteless meal. When Yuki tries to corner her at lunch, she shakes her off with a silent glare that says: not now, maybe not ever. By dusk, the weight of the folder in her pack is physical, like an extra organ pressing against her spine. She can't bear the thought of sleep—not tonight, not until she's gotten answers.

She catches Dojo between shifts, in the margin between yard detail and admin rounds. He's at the end of a secondary corridor, sipping from a battered mug and watching the evening rotation of drones flicker by on the security monitor. His posture is looser than she's ever seen it, almost relaxed. It makes her hate him a little more. She closes the distance in five purposeful steps. When Dojo finally registers her, he straightens, but not enough to erase the fatigue in his eyes.

"Problem, Recruit?" he asks, his voice colored by something suspiciously close to boredom.

Kaia's hands are fists at her sides, but she doesn't bother to salute. "You lied to me."

Dojo sets down the mug, the clack loud in the hush. "Careful," he says. "You're two sentences away from disciplinary."

She doesn't flinch. She pulls the manila folder from her bag, thrusts it at him. The pressure from her grip warps the edges.

"Did you know about this?" Her words hiss, sharp as any alarm.

He eyes the folder, glances at her, then back to the folder again. He takes it slow, deliberate, as if giving her time to reconsider. He opens the cover, skims the first page. When he hits the photo—the one with her mother's bruised cheek and defiant eyes—his fingers freeze for just a fraction of a second.

Kaia sees it, cataloguing every millimeter of his reaction, refusing to blink.

He closes the file, thumb still marking the page. "I know what's in there," he says, voice low and dry.

"Then why did you pretend otherwise?" She steps closer, not quite in his space but enough to make the threat real. "Why act like my mother just...disappeared?"

Dojo's jaw sets. "She didn't just disappear, Mori. She was processed by the same system that processes everyone here. That includes me. That includes you."

"You sound like a manual," she spits, the words almost cracking. "Is that all you are? Just another echo?"

His lips quirk, humorless. "You're not the first to ask."

She presses on, her voice trembling at the edges: "The MRB has been targeting literary dissenters for decades. You knew that. You know exactly what happens to people like her. Like me." The last two words land with a weight she can't modulate.

Dojo doesn't answer right away. Instead, he runs a hand over his scalp, the gesture more nervous than she's ever seen him. "There are things you learn when you make it past year two here," he says, gaze fixed on the blank wall over her shoulder. "I once thought like you—" he cuts off, voice suddenly raw. "Some things you have to pretend you never knew—or you don't last."

"That's bullshit," Kaia snaps. "You're supposed to be protecting knowledge, not helping them destroy it."

His voice comes back measured, but now there are cracks: "It's not that simple. The LDC isn't just preservation. It's also containment. If I didn't follow protocol, if I even asked the wrong questions—" He breaks off, then laughs, a sound as empty as a popped blister. "You think the League would let me lead a squad if I carried a memory like that?"

Kaia's jaw clenches so hard it aches. "So you toe the line, and people like my mother vanish? You get to survive, and everyone else gets—what? A number and a black bar?"

Dojo lifts the file, shakes it slightly. "She wasn't the first. She won't be the last. That's the truth you're looking for, isn't it?"

The two stand locked, the corridor as tight as a confession booth. The blue-white flicker from the monitor gives Dojo's face a death-mask hue; Kaia's own shadow blurs across the floor, sharp with the energy of things unsaid.

He lowers his voice, and for once it isn't a threat. "They watch for anomalies. For memory that doesn't fade. I've seen what they do to people who can't let go. If you keep poking at this, you'll be flagged. I can't help you if that happens."

Kaia's next words are nearly a whisper: "I'd rather be erased than live like this."

Dojo's mask slips for just a second, and behind it is an old wound. "You say that now. But you don't know what they do to people who refuse to forget."

Kaia leans in, almost nose to nose. "I know exactly what they do."

Footsteps, quick and regular, echo from the far end of the corridor. Kaia jerks back, almost shoving the file into her bag before she remembers it's not contraband—at least not until someone says it is.

Dojo straightens, his face once again regulation-perfect. The approaching figure—a senior aide, eyes on her clipboard—nods at both of them, oblivious to the static in the air.

"Report to the quad, Recruit Mori. Now," Dojo says, voice sharp enough to carry.

Kaia meets his eyes one last time, expecting contempt or disappointment—but instead she catches something else: envy, or perhaps just the memory of it.

Kaia pivots and walks away, pulse hammering at the base of her skull, every cell screaming for violence or a scream—yet she offers neither. She saves it, banks it, lets it simmer.

Behind her, Dojo says nothing. But she knows he's watching, and that's almost enough. Almost.

In the lowest hour of night, the dormitory is a quarantine for unsanctioned emotion. Even the light is rationed: a stingy oval from the desk
lamp, not enough to fill the corners. The walls are an institutional gray,
the kind that swallows color, absorbs breath. Kaia sits cross-legged on
her bunk, the blue ribbon cinched so tight around her left wrist it has
left the flesh ridged and white. The folder rests in her lap, the poem
extracted and laid flat beside her like a relic.

She reads every page in sequence, careful to align the dates, to see
the story as a whole and not just a chain of losses. There is something
devotional in the way she touches each sheet, fingertips tracing the
lines of redaction, the marginalia, the stains of official ink. Her body
is still except for the minor tremor in her left leg, the only movement
she allows.

Outside, the world is silent but for the hum of the ventilation and
the odd tick of pipes. Inside, her own breathing is loud. She catches
herself holding her breath after each discovery, as if oxygen might erase
the meaning if she's careless. She forces herself to breathe: in, out, like
her mother's old lesson—never let the world see you starved for air.

She lingers on the booking photo, tracing her mother's face with
a blunt fingernail, daring herself to find the resemblance. It's there,
in the chin and the set of the eyes, but Kaia thinks maybe the real
inheritance is the refusal to yield, to let a system decide how the story
ends.

The poem, once she reads it again, hurts more than the rest. The last
line—let the ash spell your name—burns its way into her, a warning

and a demand. She tucks it under the ribbon, over the pulse in her wrist, as if that might keep it close enough to change her.

She sorts the papers, arranges them by time, looking for the pattern. There is one: the gradual tightening of language, the shift from inquiry to accusation, the way every gap in the record lines up with a policy change or a sudden spike in disciplinary actions. It's all there, hidden in the margins, in the places nobody is supposed to look.

She wonders if anyone else in the dorm is awake, if the silence is communal or just her own. She looks at the door, twice, three times, each time expecting a shadow or the scratch of boots on resin tile. Nothing. Even Yuki, the best at sniffing out trouble, is absent—maybe by design, maybe because some nights you have to fight alone.

At last, when her hands stop shaking and her heart is only a dull thump in her ears, Kaia folds the records. She tucks the poem inside, then strips the blue ribbon from her wrist and knots it around the packet, a chokehold rather than a bow. It looks almost silly, the childish color against the brown and gray, but she decides it's perfect. It's her line in the sand, her promise to keep the story alive.

She slides the bundle under her bunk, into the shallow crawlspace left by a warped floorboard. The panel yields with a hollow pop; she presses the file flat, hearing it sigh against the concrete. When she replaces the board, the surface is flawless, no trace left.

She sits back on her bed, hands empty now but not idle. She rubs the wrist where the ribbon was, feeling the imprint.

In the stillness, a plan starts to take shape, not yet words but momentum, a hunger that will not be denied. She will learn what happened to her mother—not the League version, not the sanitized story, but the truth, raw and ugly as it needs to be. She will not be another black bar, another lost name.

Kaia switches off the lamp. The darkness is immediate, complete, but she finds she's not afraid. She listens to the sound of the world's machines, the pulse in her own body, the whisper of her mother's words still alive inside her.

She lets her head fall back onto the thin pillow and closes her eyes. Her hands, for the first time in weeks, are steady.

Somewhere beyond the gray walls, the wind howls. Kaia smiles, teeth bared, and waits for morning.

Chapter 10: Pages in the Wall

There is a trick to slipping the leash at LDC Academy. You have to act like you're where you belong, even when every cell in your body wants to bolt. Kaia Mori is a master of this, but tonight—the corridor outside Dorm South D, at the edge of curfew—her hands are slick, and her nerves spark off the rails.

The maintenance rotation is easy to duck, if you know the schedule: janitorial bots at 21:00, drone pass at 21:05, human patrol on the quarter hour. Kaia times her exit for the moment after the last bot clears the lower hall, the air behind it stinking faintly of disinfectant and scorched ozone. The corridor she targets lies two stories below, officially condemned and marked by a sun-bleached "UNDER RE-PAIR" banner that flaps against the cinderblock like a dying flag. Nobody is supposed to use this wing—too much risk of falling masonry, or so the risk assessment says. Kaia read it, three times, until she could see the floor plan in negative behind her eyelids.

She goes silent past the landing, boots rolling on the balls of her feet. The walls are a wash of institutional green and off-white, but here, beneath neglected fluorescents, the paint cracks and flakes in long, curling strips, afflicting the place like a skin condition. The further she walks, the more the Academy feels like a body after the nerves have died—lights flicker in and out, the hum of the old vent system phasing in and out like shallow breath.

She's supposed to be in her bunk, reviewing codex audit protocols. Instead, she moves through the dead wing, counting the time between each buzz of the distant drone, hyperaware of the dust that settles in the gaps between her steps. Every sound she makes is instantly swallowed; every motion a trespass against the stillness.

At the third door, she halts. The room is listed as "STORAGE—NONACTIVE," but the latch is missing, replaced by a wedge of folded cardboard and a strip of painter's tape that's gone the color of old teeth. Kaia thumbs the cardboard aside and slips inside. The room stinks of mildew and damp, the air stale enough that her first breath tickles the back of her throat. Inside, it's nothing but stacked boxes, mostly empty, and a series of steel shelving units so bent they look like they're leaning in to gossip about her.

She closes the door behind her, then moves to the far wall, the one that runs parallel to the city-facing side. Here, the paint is layered on thicker than the rest; at the corner, someone's half-hearted repair job has left a trowel-sized bulge and a lumpy seam. Kaia reaches out, runs her fingers along the line—up, across, down—feeling for the pulse that tells her she's found the vein.

There: a rough rectangle, five by ten centimeters, set lower than the rest. If you squint, it looks just like every other brick, but the color is a shade off—less jaundiced, more pink, as if the Academy's blood has surfaced here, in this one forgotten spot.

She risks a look over her shoulder. Nothing. No footsteps. No warning.

Kaia crouches, slips her knife from her boot, and works it under the edge of the brick. The mortar crumbles with barely a whisper. A careful twist, a slow pull—and the brick slides free, revealing a shallow cavity lined with soft, rotting cloth.

Her pulse roars, drowning out the world. She slides her hand in, breath caught halfway to her lungs.

Inside: stacks of paper, folded tight and wrapped in clear film. Not standard-issue, not printed—these are handmade, the edges deckled, the ink bled into the fibers. Beneath them, a smaller packet: a rectangle of old-fashioned parchment, the kind they say was banned after the Second Blackout, tied with a faded shoelace and sealed with a thumbprint of blue wax.

Kaia pulls out the first stack. The film is brittle—cracking as she bends it—and the top page slips free. Her hands are shaking, but she forces herself to steady, to read.

It's poetry. Handwritten, the lines cramped and urgent. She recognizes the shape of the letters: a left-handed writer, probably a woman, the same pressure on the descenders as the notes her mother used to scribble on ration chits. The title at the top reads, "AFTER THE FIRE." She reads the first stanza, lips barely moving:

Ink bleeds truth through broken bars.

We burn for what they cannot kill.

When morning comes, we haunt the scars;

The world rewrites, but we are still.

Her vision blurs. Not tears, not yet, but the ache is there, a slow acid at the base of her throat. Kaia flips to the next page, then the next. Each is a different voice, a different hand—some neat and academic, others scrawled in lines so dense the words are a dare to decipher. But every page is a story of survival, of memory, of fighting to outlast the erasure.

She glances at the old parchment. It's heavier, the color uneven, the tie holding it together so tight she has to pick at the knot for nearly a minute before it loosens. She breathes in, sharp and deliberate, and the scent—musty, mineral, like wet earth after a bomb—hits her with a memory so sudden she nearly drops the packet.

Years ago, her mother's voice, reading by flashlight, had the same timbre. The same breathless urgency.

Kaia untwists the parchment, careful as surgery. Inside: a lullaby, written in code. The words are nonsense, at first, but Kaia's mother taught her how to strip the ciphers bare, how to find the rhythm beneath the noise. She parses the first line, then the next, and the meaning unfolds in her head like a map. A promise of meeting places, of times to watch the sky for signals, of who to trust when everything else falls away.

She clutches the blue ribbon at her wrist, the one she's never let anyone see. She thinks of her mother, of the stories that survived in the cracks and never made it past the censors. The ache in her chest swells. She wants to scream, but instead she sits cross-legged in the dust, knees tucked to her chin, and lets herself feel the words, every one of them, until her whole body vibrates with the echo.

She reads for minutes or hours, it doesn't matter. Every poem, every scrap, every encoded lullaby—she memorizes them the way her mother taught her, imprinting the lines behind her eyes, making herself a living book.

At last, when her legs go numb and her head swims, she wraps the cache in the cloth, packs it back into the wall, and slides the brick into place. She wipes the dust from her hands, stands, and breathes the stale air, waiting for her heart to slow.

She is not alone, she thinks, not ever. The stories outlive the stone, just like her mother said.

Kaia checks the corridor once more. The night is silent, save for the far-off whir of the last drone shift. She returns to her bunk, slips the blue ribbon under her pillow, and dreams of fire that writes new stories in the air.

The next day, she will go back. There are more secrets to find, and now she knows: she is the only one left to remember.

The next night, Kaia doesn't sleep at all. She's up at the first drone sweep, uses the cover of morning drills to pocket her comm pad, and spends the day rehearsing excuses for wherever she's supposed to be at 22:00. When the time comes, she slides out of her bunk with the slowness of a diver approaching the surface: one careful movement at a time, no ripples, no noise.

She moves through the halls as if gravity itself has halved. Down the back stairs, past the blackout curtains of the AV room, until she's once again at the dead-end corridor. The air is thicker tonight, charged with something that stings her skin. Kaia hesitates at the door—half-expecting to find a ghost, or worse, an audience—but it's only the hush, as loyal as ever.

Inside, the boxes haven't shifted, but the scent is different: old metal, wet cement, a thread of ash like the ghost of burned paper. She kneels at the wall, peels away the brick with hands that tremble despite her best efforts. This time, she doesn't try to fight the feeling—she just lets the quake run through her, unfiltered.

The cache is right where she left it, but tonight she pulls the entire bundle into her lap. The cloth is damp, maybe from condensation, maybe from sweat. She shivers, unpacks the first packet, and fans out the sheets of paper on her thigh. They are warped, each page a little different in heft and color, but all of them are crowded with the same cramped, urgent script.

She begins with the top sheet: a poem in blue ink, its title underlined three times—"Cellblock Lullaby." She reads the first line out loud, so soft it's just the brush of her tongue on the air.

The walls are thin between our cells,
I hear your breath, your hungry heart.
When lights go out, the old world tells
The secret ways we never part.

She lets the words sit. Her breath is shallow; her chest feels too small for the heart beating in it. She reads the next line, then the next. The last stanza is a whisper:

I speak to ghosts who dared to dream,
Their voices folded in the seam.
If you remember how to sing,
Tomorrow, love, we'll break the ring.

Kaia runs her finger over the lines, tracing the ink as if it might smudge back to life. The handwriting is not her mother's, but the rhythm—the slide of syllables, the lullaby cadence—hits her like a slap. She almost laughs at the pain of it, then bites the inside of her cheek to stay quiet.

She reads another, this one in black—the script jagged and desperate:

They said we'd never see the dawn,
They lied, they lied, they lied.
I found the sun behind your eyes

And so I never died.

The words are cliché, even corny, but Kaia feels them in her veins, in the way her knees have started to shake. She thinks of the Silence Drill, of the hours spent locked in formation, sweating out the hope that anyone remembered why they were even there. These poems are nothing like the cold logic of the Codex—they're alive, wild, messy. The kind of thing you keep secret because to read them is to admit you want more than what you're allowed.

She flips to a different sheet, this one a list—maybe a code, maybe just a stream of words, but she knows how to read between lines. She memorizes the odd turns of phrase, the hints at places and times: "3rd shift, roofline, bring blue," "Jasper sees more than he lets on," "If you get to the blackout, wait four seconds—then run."

She reads the phrase "bring blue" and feels the ribbon at her wrist prickle against her skin. She tugs it out, lays it flat beside the page, and tries to imagine all the others who might have read this, who might have worn their own piece of blue as a promise to themselves.

Now she is crying, silently—tears hot, salty, uncontrollable. The blue light of the comm pad—dimmed to bare visibility—casts her face in the same shade as the ink, as if the lines are tattooed on her skin. She snaps photos of every page, the shutterless flash a mere flicker, then tucks the pad away and resumes reading.

One note catches her: a single line, written in the shaky hand of someone at the end of their rope:

"If you find this, you are the memory. Don't let them convince you otherwise."

Kaia breathes out, slow, and feels her anger coil tight. She doesn't know who wrote it, doesn't know if they survived, but the force of the plea is electric. She copies the line in her own notebook, the one hidden in the lining of her boot, then whispers the words like a prayer.

She keeps going, greedy for the feeling. The pages blur together: some jokes, some insults aimed at the instructors, some lists of what's been lost—"Luca, last seen night 29," "Yuli, transferred, no return." Some drawings: a map of the yard, a cartoon of a squad leader with teeth for eyes. All of it is raw and immediate and alive.

She reads one more poem, this one unsigned, the handwriting big and childish:

There's no end to the stories,
Only hands that won't hold them.
I keep mine in the dark,
Waiting for a time when they can fly.

Kaia tucks the ribbon back in her sleeve, swipes her eyes, and tries to laugh, but it comes out as a hiccup of something broken. She wants to tell someone, anyone, but knows that would be fatal—these words are dangerous because they're true, and in the Academy, truth is always a liability.

She repacks the cache, careful to align the pages as they were, but she hesitates at the last. The blue-inked "Cellblock Lullaby" is not going back. She folds it, twice, then slides it between the lining of her jacket and the curve of her shoulder. If anyone finds it, she'll be dead—but she'd rather risk that than let it rot in the dark.

She replaces the brick, wipes down every trace, and sits for a minute with her eyes shut, letting the feeling fade. Her pulse is still too fast, her mouth dry, but she forces herself to steady.

On her way out, she rehearses the cadence of her mother's lullabies, humming them under her breath, slow and soft and full of anger. She thinks of all the ghosts who dared to dream, of all the hands that wrote these words and then vanished.

She will not be the last. That's a promise.

In her bunk that night, she presses the folded poem to her heart, and for the first time since the arrest, she sleeps without fear.

The world comes back in a snap: the whir of a drone somewhere down the corridor, then the click of reinforced boots on tile. Kaia flinches, hands frozen in the act of folding the last page. She's been here too long. The night is thinning; patrols are early or late on purpose, just to catch people like her.

She sweeps the cache together, adrenaline spiking so hard her fingers go numb. She grabs the poem with the lullaby cadence—the one she can't let go—and stuffs it into her sleeve, flattening it against her forearm with the blue ribbon. The rest, she jams into the cloth, rolls it tight, and crams the whole packet back into the hollow behind the brick. She wipes the sweat from her forehead, checks the hall through the crack of the storage door.

The drone is closer now, its camera-eye flickering as it scans the walls for movement. Kaia knows the algorithm: it searches heat first, then motion, then—if it's been recently updated—reflected light. She presses her back to the wall and counts her breaths—four in, four out. Like the Drill. Like the silence.

She hears the boots again, two pairs, then three, one heavy with a limp, one lighter and fast. They're talking, but not in words—just the code-phrases of the graveyard shift, bored and mean. Kaia edges along the back of the shelves, finds the notch where the racks part just enough for her to squeeze into the space between wall and metal. She presses herself flat, cheek mashed against freezing stone.

The drone pauses outside the door. There's a hiss, then the red diode blinks green. Kaia's eyes water from the cold, but she doesn't blink. She remembers the penalty for being found outside her bed at this hour: a week of kitchen rot, or worse, a full wipe of non-curricular memory. If she's caught with contraband, with banned material—even a fragment—she'll be erased. No warning, no appeal.

She listens as the drone's rotor idles. The camera whines as it tracks the seam of the door, then it zips down the hall, off to terrorize some other shadow. The boots are next, and this time they stop right outside. Kaia can hear the scrape of one heel as it plants, the grind of cheap synth leather as the guard shifts weight. She thinks she hears a sniff, a cough. Then, from the opposite side of the wall, a voice:

"Clear. Next block."

The boots move on. She waits thirty seconds more, counting each heartbeat. The silence after the echo is almost as loud as the chase.

She slinks from the alcove, slides the brick flush, and rubs her hands down her thighs to get the circulation back. The backs of her calves are damp with cold sweat; her mouth tastes like tin. She checks the corridor once more—empty—and sprints for the stairwell.

She doesn't take the main route. Instead, she ducks into the janitorial access, the one that runs parallel to the heating pipes. The shaft is barely wide enough to crawl; it stinks of lye and something organic. She braces herself on elbows and knees, moves forward a meter at a time, counting grates and junction boxes. At the fifth, she stops, listens. Nothing. She drops to the next level, careful not to jar the pipes, then cuts right, toward Dorm D.

At the end, there's a hatch. She pops it with the edge of her comm pad, slides through, and lands hard on the resin floor. Her hands are raw, her jacket is torn, and the poem in her sleeve is wrinkled but still there.

She walks to her bunk, boots silent on the tile, and slips under the covers before the hour bell sounds. Nobody stirs. She lies on her back, head pounding, and pulls the poem free. She unfolds it, smooths the creases, and reads it again in the glow from her pad.

If you are the last, be the first to speak.
Ink your truth into the wall of night.
If memory is a cell, break it.
If history is a chain, melt it.
There's no one left to save you, so
Save yourself.

She smiles, and this time the tears are hot and happy and full of rage. She reads the poem three more times, then tucks it in the lining of her jacket. She knows, now, what she has to do.

It's not enough to remember. She has to make the memory real, has to give it away. She will take these poems, these secrets, and scatter them—one for every drone, every patrol, every recruit who ever wondered if there was more to the world than what they were told.

She will not be the last. She will not let them win.

Kaia closes her eyes, fists the blue ribbon in her hand, and dreams of a world where the story survives.

Chapter 11: The Whisperer

The Academy library after curfew is a crypt for the once-worshipped, its air sharp as antiseptic and heavy with memory. The sanctioned lighting—cold blue, UV-tinged—lays a pallor over every surface, flattening even the most ornate stacks to bureaucratic sameness. The place is empty except for the whir of air handlers and the faint, spectral rustle of dust settling over centuries of failed utopias. And Kaia, solitary as a minor heretic, entombed in the restricted section with nothing but her assignment and the smothering expectation that she'll finish it before morning.

Kaia hates this part of the job. The books are dead weight: "Pre-Regulation Literature: A Historical Analysis," "Crisis of Narratives, vol. II," "League Authorship: Methods and Motives." Each is a cross-section of a world that existed before the League, before the purges, and each is so thoroughly redacted it may as well be blank. She's meant to catalog these, to double-check for "unsanctioned supplements," but really it's a ritual of futility—busywork for the too curious, or the too suspicious.

Kaia flips another page, careful not to crack the already fragile spine. The binding's dry rot gave a tactile crunch, like old teeth, and the pages stuck at the margin where, long ago, someone had pressed too hard annotating in forbidden ink. She sniffed the edge out of habit—each volume carrying its own perfume, a commingling of preservation solvent and the particular tang of its era. This one smells like a hospital after a fire: medicinal and scorched, a threat barely scrubbed away.

Her eyes scan the lines, but her brain is numb, only half attending. She's thinking about her mother's face—how it looked in the old booking photo, before the bruises bloomed, before the hope finally broke. Kaia wonders if anyone ever really saw her mother, or if they just remembered the cautionary tale.

A page turns, and something snags at the edge of her vision: a dot, no, a glyph—something so small she almost misses it, tucked in the lower gutter of the text block. She stares. The Academy trains you to spot annotation: blue for edits, red for challenge, black for refute. This is none of those. It's a single vertical line, not ink but a score, as if someone pressed a pin into the page. The pressure mark is precise, surgical. Intentional.

Kaia squints, lifts the book to catch the angle of the light. The mark is repeated at intervals—here, then forty pages ahead, and again. Each in the same position, the exact same depth. She frowns, tilts the page to the preservation lamp, and lets the UV light rip the color out of everything else. The line glows, faint and white, a scar running through the tissue of the page.

She traces it with her nail. This isn't an accident. And it's not Academy code. She's sure of it.

She flips forward, finds the next mark, and then the next. Each time, the page contains a phrase the League left unredacted—a survivor of the cull. She reads them aloud, barely a whisper:

"...prevalence of oral transmission among subversive cultures..."

"...counter-narrative as a vector for memory resistance..."

"...the final authority is not the text, but the witness..."

Kaia's skin prickles. She glances over her shoulder, reflexive, though she knows the security grid is programmed to ignore anyone with her badge after hours. Still, a chill crawls up her neck. She closed the volume, laid it flat, and logged its accession code on the digital sheet. But she can't let it go.

She stands, stretches, the motion cracking every vertebra down her spine. The room was so empty it echoed, and the hum of the lights made her teeth ache. She drifts along the shelves, scanning for other books from the same shelf code—maybe, if she's lucky, the same annotator left more of their story.

She pulls five more volumes at random, each a clone of institutional memory. Three are clean, their pages untouched. The fourth, "Revision and Recollection: League Protocols for Memory Management," has two of the same marks—one at the start, one at the end. She flips to the last one, "Oral Cultures: Survivals in the Regime Era," and her breath catches: the back cover has a dense array of pin-scores, maybe fifty in a block, like Braille for the blind.

She glances at the clock. It's 0220, a time so late it's not even night anymore, just prelude to the next day's punishments. She hesitates, then tucks the two marked volumes under her arm, logs them as "flagged for restoration," and heads for the auxiliary desk in the back. The seat is half-busted, the screen flickers with every touch, but it's far from the main desk—no chance of a surprise inspection.

Kaia arranges the books in front of her, flips to the marked pages, and lays them side by side. She ran her thumb along the scars, then pressed them lightly against her lips, as if some flavor might transfer. She traces the lines on the cover of the last book—too small to see, too purposeful to be random.

The marks are a pattern, she realizes. Not just random notes, but an alphabet. A code.

She lets herself smile, just a little, the old thrill back in her chest.

"Who are you?" she whispers, running her thumb along the page. "What were you trying to say?"

She pulls a sheet of scrap from the printer, grabs the red marker from the cup, and begins to chart the pattern: vertical, diagonal, triple dot. With every mark, her heartbeat picks up. This is what her mother used to call "the archive's true voice"—the story beneath the story, the one they could never erase.

A sound—soft, nothing, probably just a vent kicking in—makes her jump. She gathers the books, stacks them neatly, but leaves her code sheet out, weighted under her elbow. She listens, but the space is still dead, no footsteps, no whisper of comms. She exhales, long and slow.

She wanted to laugh at herself, at the paranoia, but the world had taught her well: always check, always be sure. She leaned back, as if bored, and scanned the corners for the security eyes. There were three in this section, all with their blue blinkers on standby. No one is watching live. She let her shoulders drop, feigning a yawn for the benefit of anyone reviewing the feed later.

She'll come back tomorrow, she decides. Finish her shift, then see if the code is repeated in any of the off-limits stacks. Maybe, if she's clever, she can find the whole message, piece it together like a scavenger hunt for traitors.

She logs off the terminal, tucks the code sheet into her waistband, and returns the books to their exact shelf order, except for the two with the densest markings. Those she logs for "urgent stabilization," and places in the lockup cabinet under the desk—a trick her mother taught her, a way to keep a book close without tripping the inventory.

On her way out, Kaia brushes the spines with her fingertips, one by one. It's a ritual, a promise. She feels the tiny dents left by the old annotator's code, and for a moment, she thinks she can feel their intent, warm and alive in the marrow of the paper.

She glances at the main desk—empty, as always. She leaves her code sheet out for just a second longer, then folds it tight and slips it inside her boot, with the ribbon, with the rest of her hope.

In the hall, the lights are lower, the air almost warm by contrast. She moved fast, head down, already plotting the next night's return. She has the taste of code in her mouth, and it is sweet, and she is hungry for more.

By morning, her mother's voice is with her again: Stories outlive the stone.

And Kaia, for the first time in months, believes it.

The next night, Kaia returns to the library in the deadest slice of time, when even the drones seem to be running half-speed and the only other humans are the ones who've long ago traded sleep for quiet. She walks past the main reading room, which is deserted except for a pair of upper-year Vanguards locked in a silent speed-reading contest, their faces set with the grim determination of doomed competitors.

She ignores them. Her world has narrowed to the books under her arm and the code sheet, now smoothed flat and annotated in three colors of stolen marker.

She settles at a secluded table in the study pit, one level below the security desk's line of sight. The lights here are dimmer, the blue more saturated, and the heat from the main stacks never quite reaches these corners. She prefers it; the cold keeps her sharp.

She unpacks the books and lays them out, left to right, in order of publication. She doesn't know why, exactly—just that sequence feels right, like it might unlock the next layer of sense. She fingers the spines, counting the ridges in the cloth, running her thumb along the margins until the familiar pressure marks jump out at her.

She flips to the first scored page in each volume and lines them up. The vertical lines, at first glance so uniform, now seem to pulse with a deeper rhythm: some double, some single, some clustered in triplets with a faint diagonal scratch connecting them. She realizes, with a thrill like falling, that it's not just a code. It's a cipher, one she's seen in the old LDC field manual—dot, line, slash, the archaic notation used for transmission of "contraband intelligence" in the pre-regulation era.

She digs in her pack for the battered field manual, the only physical book she owns that isn't officially assigned. She props it open with a pencil stub and skims to the relevant page: "Cipher Types, Outlawed or Obsolete." The translation grid is faded, but Kaia commits it in three reads.

She starts mapping the marks, first by column, then by row, each combination of lines yielding a crude letter. At first, it's gibberish, but when she shifts the starting point—old code often loops, her mother used to say—the message resolves, hesitant, like a stutter finding its voice.

N O T A L L G U A R D I A N S W E A R U N I F O R M S

She mouths it, hardly breathing. Not all guardians wear uniforms. The words spark in her brain, feeding on the loneliness of the hour and the cold certainty that she is being spoken to, directly, from the past.

She traces the next line, working faster now, heart drumming in her ears. The message continues:

L O O K F O R T H E B O O K M A R K

Kaia's hands trembled, just a little. She glances up, as if the message might have triggered a silent alarm. The Vanguards are still buried in their own reading, oblivious, and the security grid shows no change—no red dots, no sudden heat signature drifting her way.

She flips the books, one by one, searching the inner spines. Nothing in the first. Nothing in the second. In the third, a sliver of red peeks out from the top margin—at first glance, just a stray thread, but when she tugs it, a thin, ancient ribbon pulls free, so faded it's nearly pink.

She holds it up to the desk light, squinting. There's writing on it, but so faint she has to twist the ribbon and hold it just so. At the midpoint, in microscopic script, a sequence of numbers, dots, and dashes. Not a message, this time, but coordinates.

She scans the ribbon under the blue lamp, and the numbers flare: 4.44-N 2.21-W, followed by the sigil of a torch and book—an old symbol for the pre-league "Keepers of Memory." Kaia's mouth goes dry.

The Library's own preservation lights make the ink visible; under any other color, the ribbon would be blank.

She wants to stand, to run, to shout at the old men on the wall screens that their secrets aren't safe, not really, not if you know how to look. But she forces herself calm, winds the ribbon tight around her finger, and pretends to study a random page of "League Authorship."

Her thoughts buzzed so loud it was hard to keep still. If she reported the find, it'll be confiscated, and she'll get maybe a commendation and then a year of surveillance. But if she keeps it—if she follows the coordinates—she might finally learn what her mother tried to teach her, the part of the story that survived the fire.

She tucked the ribbon deep in her pocket, replaced the books in perfect order, and logged out with a time stamp. On the way out, she glanced again at the upper-year Vanguards. The boy with the scarred knuckles glances up, meets her gaze for half a second, then looks away. For a moment, Kaia wonders if he's part of the message too, or just another ghost in the archive.

In the corridor, she presses the ribbon to her cheek, the cool fabric tingling with the ghost of invisible ink. She recites the coordinates, memorizing them, then buries the slip in the secret pocket of her sleeve, next to the blue ribbon she's never let go.

"Not all guardians wear uniforms," the message echoed. Kaia grinned, wide and wild, daring the library's walls to forget her.

They won't. She'll see to that.

The next morning, Kaia studies the coordinates over and over until she's sure they're not only a place but a test—a way of seeing if she'll risk the penalty for being curious. The numbers point to a far end of the library, a place where the stacks thin out and the lights flicker on motion sensors, the temperature always a few degrees below the rest. She waits until midday, when the upperclassmen are in tactical theory and the lower ranks are too scared to break routine. Then she goes, moving quick but measured, not so fast as to draw attention but not so slow as to look like she's stalling.

The section is linguistics: dusty, unexplored, mostly reference and a few case studies from before the League's language reforms. The book the coordinates map to is "Structural Morphology: A Comparative Atlas," its spine undamaged, the dust on it undisturbed except for a single finger-track from someone who thought better of pulling it down.

Kaia slides the volume free. It's heavy, dense, the kind of book you could weaponize in a riot. She flips to the designated page—4.44, as marked on the ribbon—and there, between the leaves, a slip of paper folded so tight it leaves a crease sharp enough to cut skin. She unfolds it, hands shaking.

The handwriting is fine, precise, almost mechanical. The message reads:

The stories they erase still exist in memory.

Meet me where water meets stone.

Tomorrow. Dusk.

Kaia reads it three times, the pulse of adrenaline so loud she couldn't hear anything else. The phrasing—it's not just a summons, it's a dare. She looks up, scans the stacks for movement, for eyes, for the red dot of a camera laser. Nothing. But she knows better than to trust nothing.

She folded the note and stowed it in her boot, fingers lingering on the edge, half hoping it was a hallucination. She slides the book back in place, aligns it exactly, then stands, letting her eyes adjust to the gloom. The message echoes in her head, a drumbeat she can't drown out.

If she turns in the note, she's a hero: fast-track to merit points, maybe even a mention in the newsletter, a guarantee of surveillance but also protection. But the message—it sounds like her mother, or at least the story her mother always wanted to tell. If she pursues it, she risks everything. But it's also the only thing that feels like hers, not just another borrowed piece of history.

She starts to leave, but the motion sensors trip, and the far light pops on. In the new glow, she sees movement—a shadow, then the unmistakable shape of Lt. Dojo, standing at the end of the row with arms folded and gaze locked to her position.

Kaia's stomach plummeted. She put on her best bored-cadet face, grabbed the nearest volume, and flipped it open to a random page, pretending to be engrossed.

Dojo approaches, his pace deliberate, boots so silent they seem to suck sound from the aisle. He halts a meter away, eyes scanning the shelves, then her, then the shelf again.

"Linguistics, Mori?" His tone was low, amused but edged. "Didn't peg you for a language chaser."

Kaia shrugged, keeping her voice level. "Just following research protocols, sir. Some of the Codex references in the upper stacks crosslist to language studies. I wanted to see how the field manuals lined up with the historical perspective."

He narrows his eyes, not buying it but also not calling her out. "You're off schedule. Training block starts in fifteen. If you're late, you'll lose the privilege." He looked her over, scanning for tells. "And don't abuse open access. I'll know."

She nods, "Understood, sir." She waits for him to walk off, but he doesn't.

He leans in, voice so quiet it's barely audible. "Curiosity is good, Mori. But curiosity without discipline?" He let the silence stretch, a threat and a warning. "That's how people end up as footnotes."

She meets his gaze, searching for malice or sympathy. It's neither. Just calculation.

He turns, disappears into the dark, leaving her alone and shaking.

Kaia waits until his footsteps are gone, then tucks the book under her arm and returns to the main corridor, where the world is brighter but also much less real.

She carried the note in her boot all day, pressing her heel against it with every step. The message ate at her, splits her attention. At lunch, Yuki tries to corner her with a question, but Kaia blows her off with a look so cold even Yuki flinches. She spends the afternoon drills half-present, the other half running permutations of "where water meets stone." It could mean the irrigation canal by the old field, or the east end of the courtyard where the maintenance fountain is always half-frozen. It could be a joke. Or a trap.

At night, she re-reads the note by the blue light of her pad, letting the words sink into her as if they might fuse with the bone.

Tomorrow. Dusk.

She stared at the ceiling until her eyes blurred. She had made her decision, but the consequences remained a mystery.

If it's a trap, she'll know soon enough.

But if it's not—if the message is real—maybe, just maybe, she can claw one more story from the fire.

She grips the blue ribbon on her wrist, feeling it pulse like a vein. For once, she doesn't dream.

She waited for tomorrow, and the next test.

At dusk, the world pulls itself taut, every edge sharpened by the cold and the risk of being seen. Kaia faked a stomach virus, presented her case to the med drone with a mix of sweaty palms and half-truths, and was excused from the evening's practicals. She waits a full hour after lights dim before slipping out the service corridor, moving under the cover of orange sodium haze and the dead space in the security camera cycle.

The route to the boundary fountain is a corridor of exposure: past the compost heaps, over the old athletic field, through a gap in the perimeter hedge that only the most desperate or the most foolish would bother to find. Kaia is both. The air bites at her ears, and the strip of blue ribbon on her wrist is a pulse of old defiance, hidden under her cuff but present, always.

She finds the fountain where memory and rumor said it would be, a squat cylinder of concrete and basalt half-sunken into the ground, more pit than sculpture. A thin spill of water dribbled into a grate at its base, while moss crept over the lip like an unhealed wound. The campus boundary wall rises behind it, imposing and indifferent. In the dying light, the place feels abandoned—one more relic nobody has had the time or the cruelty to fully erase.

Kaia glances at her watch: four minutes early. She crouches on the low rim, back to the wall, keeping her hands out of sight. Every sound is an alarm—her own breathing, the crunch of gravel, the click of a distant gate. She rehearses her story: she got lost, she tripped and hit her head, she's here for the silence. But none of them will matter if this is a setup. Or if she's truly alone.

At first she doesn't see him: the old man sitting in the shadow of the wall, hunched in on himself, the gray of his coveralls almost the same shade as the stone. He blends, not just visually, but in the sense that he's not meant to register to anyone in power—a ghost in the system.

She startles when he moves, a small and deliberate shift. He pats the rim beside him, not looking at her. "Sit if you want," he says, voice thick with the phlegm of years spent breathing in bleach and floor wax. "Or stand. Doesn't matter."

Kaia's heart hammers. She slide onto the edge of the fountain, keeping her weight light, ready to run. The man coughs, then spits neatly into the grate.

"You found the note," he said. "Didn't expect a first-year to do it." He rubbed his palms together, then wiped them on his knees. "Or maybe I did."

Kaia studies his profile: pockmarked, nose wide and flattened by age or accident, eyes hooded and yellowed. She recognizes him—a janitor, always with a cart and a humming drone, never speaking, never making eye contact. She's passed him in the halls a dozen times and never thought twice.

She says nothing, uncertain of the rules here.

He waits, then shrugs, "No need to talk. They bug the drains, sometimes, but nobody listens to the old pipes."

Kaia swallows. "What is this?" she asks, voice thin in the chill. "A test?"

He barks a laugh. "Everything's a test, Mori. The real ones don't have right answers." He glances at her, quick, then back to the wall. "You know the codes. You care enough to chase them. And you don't rat. That's three more things than the last one had."

He reaches into his pocket, pulls out a foil-wrapped lozenge, and pops it into his mouth. The act is so ordinary it almost breaks the spell.

"My name's Hideo," he says, as if reciting the least interesting fact about himself. "I used to be a librarian, before the purge. Now I mop floors, scrub the blood from the training mats, and keep my head down. But I remember."

The word lands with a weight. Kaia grips the fountain, letting the wet seep into her palm. "Why me?"

He gives her a sidelong look. "Why anyone? You're the one who answered."

Silence. Then, "You wrote the message?"

Hideo nods, slow. "Took years to find the right way. Used to carve into the wood, but they scan for that now. Ink's easier, but you have to hide the color. I tried glue, I tried heat, I tried the bleach trick. In the end, memory is best—if you get them to remember, they do the rest for you." He smiles, showing a row of teeth too perfect to be real.

Kaia's eyes narrow. "What do you want?"

He leans forward, arms on knees. "Nothing. Everything. To see if there's still someone in this building who remembers what a story is. To see if the line survived." He looks at her ribbon, the blue peeking from her sleeve. "You were taught, weren't you? Not just the rules. The real stories."

She nods, barely.

He snorts. "They tried to erase us. That's the joke—it never works. The more they cut, the more grows back." He pulls a slip of paper from his sleeve, passes it to her with the care of someone who's used to losing fingers for less.

Kaia unfolds it. The handwriting is blocky, but neat.

If you want the truth, bring a story of your own.

Same place. Next week.

She looks up, unsure if she's angry or grateful. "What if I don't?"

He shrugs, as if the idea of her failing is unworthy of consideration. "You will."

They sit in silence, the sky gone purple overhead, the last of the water trickling in the grate below.

Finally, Kaia asks, "What happened to my mother?"

Hideo is quiet a long time. "She left," he says. "Not by choice. But she left something behind."

He stands, bones popping. "Don't wait for permission. If you do, you'll die old and empty like the rest of us."

He walks off, no hurry, no fear. Kaia listens to his footsteps fade, then watches the spot where he vanished, half-expecting him to come back and say it was all a mistake.

She reads the note again, commits the words to memory. Her hands are shaking.

She sits on the rim of the fountain until her legs go numb and the cold creeps through her jacket. Only then does she stand, stretching until the ache subsides.

On the way back to the dorm, she feels the eyes of the surveillance drones, the cold stare of the night shift, the thousand invisible lines of code waiting to catch her. But none of it matters now.

She has a story to write.

And this time, she won't be alone.

Chapter 12: Underground Memory

The world above is asleep, or pretending to be, but the guts of the LDC Academy never stop grinding. In the corridor shadow behind Barracks South, Kaia waits, counting out the seconds until the patrol drones sync their searchlights to opposite ends of the service quad. Kaia keeps her back to the wall, fingers the edge of her sleeve, pressing the blue ribbon flat against her skin. The nerves in her arms buzz so hard she wonders if the cameras will pick up the heat.

Yuki signals from the next alcove with two quick hand chops. Kaia flattens herself and slides after her, moving quick but with the memory of silence drilled into every muscle. Mikihisa is last, as always, a foot taller than either of them and twice as likely to catch his elbow on a pipe. He's sweating already, hair stuck to his temple, but his mouth curls in the crooked smile he uses to mask terror or delight—it's the same, with him.

The tunnel mouth is just past the perimeter trash chute, a hole carved out of the concrete decades ago for access panels and then promptly forgotten. They slip through in single file, breath close, the air thick with mold and burnt plastic from old wiring. Kaia's eyes adjust slow; she keeps one hand on the wall, knuckles scraping paint, and lets Yuki take point. Yuki always knows the route. She claims to have mapped every tunnel in the first month at Academy, out of boredom and a gnawing need to control the only thing that could kill her without warning.

Mikihisa can't help himself: "If we die in here, does the League even bother logging it, or do they just mark us 'lost to entropy' and move on?"

Yuki doesn't turn, but her voice floats back: "Entropy would've gotten you years ago, if you weren't so damn dense."

Kaia nearly laughs, but clamps her jaw. She's too excited for humor, her heart jacked by the risk. Every time she does this—every time she lets Yuki talk her into a blackout errand—she promises herself it's the last, that next time she'll toe the line, that next time she'll stop being a character in someone else's narrative. But now, with the dark pressing in and the scent of old oil in her nose, she remembers what Hideo said last week: If you wait for permission, you'll die old and empty. She's not ready for that.

Down two meters, they reach the main trunk. Here the ceiling lowers, forcing them into a crouch. Water drips somewhere ahead; Kaia wipes her palm on her uniform, then grips the ribbon again, rolling it between thumb and forefinger until the sting in her wrist becomes a grounding pulse.

Yuki stops at a junction and puts her finger to her lips—like Kaia needs the reminder. She risks a glance at Mikihisa. He looks back, eyes huge in the dark, and whispers, "Odds of getting caught just went from one in ten to one in three. Anyone wanna update their will?"

Kaia smiles genuinely this time. "You're first in line for my socks. Good luck to you."

Yuki gives them a look. "Focus. Drone pattern's changed. Listen."

They hush, straining for it. The drone's whir starts faint, then swells—closer than last time, and not on the published rotation. Kaia's scalp prickles. She flattens herself into the crook of the junction, Yuki curling in beside her. Mikihisa barely fits, but he folds up, somehow, and for a moment the three of them are compressed to a single shivering mass. Kaia can feel the heat off Yuki's body, the faint shudder in her chest as she holds her breath.

The drone passes overhead, a judder in the pipes, the whine of its camera lens tracking left and right. For three seconds, nothing else exists. Kaia shuts her eyes and counts—one, two, three—then the sound recedes, replaced by the slow drip of the leak and the frantic pace of her own heart.

Mikihisa exhales, shaky. "Thought they'd upgraded to thermal sensors."

Yuki: "Maybe they have, but we're not interesting enough for the good hardware. Move."

The next segment is narrower, painted the color of old phlegm and lined with insulation that flakes on contact. Kaia breathes through her nose, matching their pace. She thinks about the rumors—about kids who got caught sneaking the tunnels, never seen again, or recycled into mindless admin labor. She wonders if her mother ever had to crawl like this, before the League took her, or if she'd just walked out the front door, head high, the story of her life already written and waiting for the next reader.

The tunnel opens up at a sub-level junction, just beneath the mess hall. Here, Kaia recognizes the faint reek of cooked protein and the ozone tang of sterilizer. They pause at a grated vent, listening for voices, but there's only the hum of refrigeration and the click of a loose light fixture, swinging somewhere far above. Kaia lets herself breathe, but only for a second.

Yuki checks her pad, screen dimmed to red, and traces a route on the cracked display. "Left here, then down. There's a hatch at the old service stair. That's the handoff point."

Kaia: "How sure?"

Yuki's smile is all teeth. "I trust Hideo more than I trust the League to keep their own secrets. That's enough."

They move again, the last stretch a tight crawl, hands and knees on cold cement. Mikihisa grumbles, "If I blow out my ACL on this, someone better at least memorialize me in the quad." Yuki huffs, but her voice is softer now: "You'll be lucky if they even spell your name right."

At the bottom of the crawl, the tunnel ends in a rusted steel door. There's no handle, just a pattern of pits and gouges, old paint flaked away by years of neglect. Kaia's eyes pick out the mark instantly: three wavering lines, barely visible, carved at chest height. If you squint, they look like an open book, the oldest symbol for the Keepers of Memory.

Yuki wipes sweat from her brow, then presses her knuckles over the mark. She raps out a series of knocks: two, then three, then two again, with a pause in the middle. Kaia feels each strike in her rib cage.

On the far side, nothing happens. Then, a click, followed by the hiss of a pressure seal releasing. The door swings inward, slow and silent, revealing a slice of yellow light and the blurred shape of a figure hunched in the gloom.

Yuki steps through first. Kaia and Mikihisa follow, blinking at the sudden brightness. The person on the other side wears a mask, just gauze and plastic, but Kaia recognizes the eyes: sharp, old, seeing everything. Hideo.

He nods, waves them inside, and pulls the door shut. The tunnel beyond is wider, lined with battered benches and the warped shadows of dozens of old crates. Kaia lets her eyes adjust, heart slowing from panic to anticipation. This is the underground reading salon, the one her mother always hinted at, the one the League swore didn't exist.

She tucks the blue ribbon tighter beneath her sleeve and follows the others, her own breath finally quiet enough to let her hear the story waiting on the other side.

The reading salon isn't what Kaia expected. The maintenance chamber has been softened into something almost sacred: benches scrounged from a dozen decommissioned classrooms, ends chewed raw by teeth or time, arranged in a crescent that faces the makeshift stage—just a stretch of clean cement, backlit by a run of ancient pipework. Someone's strung patched curtains from the overheads, fabric the color of marrow and rust, patched with squares of old uniform and riot tape. Every seam in the fabric throws shadows on the faces turned toward the center, where a ring of storm lanterns burns yellow and alive.

Tonight, there are maybe twenty people present, most of them young, a few older than Academy would ever admit. Their eyes follow every movement; their bodies are rigid, postures drilled but eyes soft, almost desperate. Kaia, Yuki, and Mikihisa slip to the last bench. Mikihisa folds his long frame in on itself, making himself as small as possible. Yuki stays alert, gaze flicking to entrances and exits, cataloguing every threat. Kaia watches the crowd, fascinated by how no one speaks, not even a whisper—how the anticipation in the room has condensed into a single, quivering hush.

At the center of the space, Hideo sets up a battered folding stool. He wipes it clean, then steps back. A woman takes his place—a legend of a woman, if the rumors are true, but Kaia can't assign her an age. Her hair is a tangle of black and silver, her face lined with scars and the trace work of old burns. She moves slow, but not with age—with ceremony. Every step is measured. Every gesture lands.

The woman sits, then produces a book from the inside of her coat. The crowd ripples at the sight of it—not fear, but awe. Kaia's lungs seize up. It's not just any book; it's a relic, battered and waterlogged, its jacket patched together with layers of black tape and something that looks like skin. The edges are foxed with time, but the spine is intact. Kaia recognizes the title—almost—but the letters have been scrubbed down to ghosts.

The performer opens to a marked page and waits until the silence is complete. When she speaks, her voice is low and even, carrying through the room without need for force.

"I'm going to read to you from a story that's not supposed to exist. If you know the ending, don't say a word." Her eyes scan the room, searching for the heretics who might spoil the only joy left. "If you don't—listen, and let yourself believe."

She begins.

The language is simple, direct, but alive with a rhythm that cuts through the years of curation and official protocol. Kaia loses herself in the sound of it, in the way the woman's voice rides the edges of each word. The story is about two lovers, separated by a war no one wins. Each is conscripted to a different side. The only thing that survives the divide is their memory of a single book—one they read together, then tore apart, each taking half.

"On the first night of the siege," the woman reads, "he found her handwriting scrawled in the margin, just above the place where the hero loses his name. The words were code. She told him: I am not gone. I am only rewritten."

A sniffle in the room. Kaia looks down the line—two seats over, a boy holds a fist to his mouth, fighting tears. Yuki is rigid, her jaw set so hard it must hurt. Kaia flexes her hands in her lap, realizing she's been clutching the blue ribbon the entire time, knuckles pale as pressed paper.

The story winds on, each chapter a new hardship, a new method for smuggling words across the front. Once, the lovers meet by accident at a checkpoint, and neither can acknowledge the other. Instead, they exchange contraband: a book, hollowed out and filled with pages of memory. The woman onstage reads it with a lilt that makes it sound like a lullaby, then like a knife.

"War is not the absence of love," the woman recites, "but its multiplication. Every pain is a proof of the heart's persistence."

Kaia's throat is raw. The memory of her mother reading by flashlight, voice thinned to a whisper, is so vivid she nearly stands up to stop the story, to save the ending before it can break her. But she sits, lets it happen.

Yuki leans in, just slightly, and her arm presses against Kaia's. The contact is electric. Neither says a word.

Mikihisa is silent, for once. He stares at his shoes, but his shoulders shake. Kaia is certain he's not laughing.

The story's end is simple and brutal. The lovers reunite, only to find that neither remembers the exact words of their shared book. But it doesn't matter, because every effort to remember is an act of love itself—a refusal to let the world finish the work of erasure.

When the performer closes the book, the room holds its breath for a full minute. The only sound is the hiss of a lantern, the slow tick of pipes cooling overhead. Kaia sits back, chest aching, tears running down her cheeks before she's aware of them. She wipes them away, angry and grateful at once.

The woman stands, tucks the book away, and lets her eyes sweep the room one last time. "Carry it with you," she says, softer now. "Every story is a weapon. Use it wisely."

Hideo returns, offers her an arm, but she declines with a crooked grin. She limps to the back, her departure as silent as her arrival.

The room remains suspended in a moment of perfect, collective memory, the last word still echoing in the stone.

Kaia thinks: If she never hears another story, this one will last a lifetime.

But she knows she'll be back, as long as the books survive.

There is no warning before the world shifts. One moment, the room still hums with the residue of story; the next, a dull red light pulses from the emergency sconces, strobing the crowd in bursts of panic. Someone at the front hisses, "Patrols—now," and the group dissolves, not in chaos but in the practiced discipline of people who have rehearsed escape more than they have the art of reading.

Hideo shepherds people to the nearest exit, hands urgent but quiet. Yuki springs into action, grabbing Mikihisa by the wrist and jerking her chin at Kaia: Go. But Kaia hesitates, her feet heavy as the story's ending churns in her chest. The performer is already halfway to the shadow of the back curtains, book pressed flat to her side, coat buttoned to the throat. Kaia darts forward, propelled by a question she doesn't understand until it's out of her mouth.

"Was that the real ending?" Her voice comes out thin, childlike, but it's all she has.

The woman stops, turns, and studies Kaia with an intensity that's almost clinical. Her eyes flick to the sleeve, to the faint outline of regulation stitching, then to the blue ribbon peeking from beneath the cuff. There's a pause—an assessment, a weighing of trust and risk. Then the woman smiles, an old and brittle thing.

"Stories don't end, child. They live in the ones who carry them." She steps closer, her movements fast for someone with such visible pain. She brings her hand up, slow, and pushes a folded page into Kaia's palm. "Choose carefully who you share it with," she whispers, voice gone dry. "Some stories are more dangerous than others."

Kaia folds the page into her fist, tucks it into the lining of her boot; the paper an electric presence against her skin. She can't speak—there's no time, and nothing she could say would match the gravity of the gift. Instead, she bows her head, a reflex from a thousand hours of obedience drills.

Yuki's fingers hook her collar and yank her back. "Move, Mori. They're sweeping the east block in two."

Mikihisa leads the way out, not with courage but with the terror of someone who's survived too many close calls. The tunnels are a centrifuge of bodies: students, staff, and faces Kaia's never seen. The escape routes branch and diverge. They take the leftmost, Yuki's call, her logic always a step ahead.

But the drones are faster this time. At the first junction, a whirring eye sweeps the corridor, lens catching on Mikihisa's pale face. He slaps a hand to the sensor, buys a second, and they duck into an alcove no wider than a coffin. They huddle in the dark, Kaia's shoulder blade digging into raw stone, Mikihisa's breath sour with adrenaline.

Outside, the drone pauses. A voice—bored, mechanical—announces "Clear. Proceed." They don't move, not until Yuki counts down from ten, lips moving silently, then signals the all-clear.

They double-time it through the last stretch, crawling and gasping, dirt smearing every inch of uniform. The blue ribbon is sticky on Kaia's wrist, sweat or blood, she can't tell. The page in her boot is a burning coin. She can't feel her toes.

At the tunnel mouth, the night above is beginning to pale. They tumble out, backs pressed to the shadow of the barracks, lungs heaving. From inside, the sound of alarms and shouted code ripples through the steel and concrete. Kaia thinks of all the people still running, still hiding, and wonders how many will be missing at roll call.

Mikihisa is first to speak, voice raw: "Worth it?"

Yuki just laughs, a single, brittle note. "We're still breathing, aren't we?"

Kaia nods, but the weight of the paper in her boot is more real than any answer. She wants to tell them what happened, about the woman and the warning, but something inside tells her not yet. Instead, she just holds the memory, presses it to her heart.

They sneak back to their barracks, timing their dash to the last gap in the patrols. Inside, the other beds are cold, but no one notices their absence. They peel off their dirty clothes, roll them tight, and hide them in the laundry chute for the maintenance bots to devour. Kaia changes in the dark, careful to keep the page hidden, careful to show no trace of what she's become.

The morning alarm rings before she can close her eyes. She lies on her back, stares at the ceiling, lets the weight of exhaustion pin her flat. The page in her boot is a promise—a story with no ending, a seed she'll have to choose how and when to plant. The fear is real, but so is the thrill. For the first time since the League took her mother, Kaia feels the line of memory running unbroken through her, fierce and alive.

She swears she'll never let go.

She drifts off, the blue ribbon wrapped twice around her fist, the taste of forbidden words still sweet on her tongue.

Chapter 13: The Cipher Exam

The exam chamber was a cube of absence: no windows, no clocks, nothing to mark time except the low hum of recirculated air and the blue-white haze of holographic projectors lining every wall. Rows of identical desks marched from the door to the far bulkhead, each a perfect square of resin and alloy, outfitted with a blank display and the unforgiving logic of a digital input pad. Overhead, a single countdown clock hovered in the center of the air, digits frozen at 15:00—an hourglass filled with ice instead of sand.

The recruits filed in as if called by algorithm, not voice. Every step was catalogued, every face already indexed: Yuki at the front, eyes narrowed and mouth set in a line that meant she'd already mapped the room for exits, sight lines, blind spots. Mikihisa lags just behind, a nervous tic jerking his left shoulder every third step, his eyes flickering between the clock and the uniformed figure at the head of the chamber. Lt. Dojo stood with his hands behind his back, face expressionless, the burnished blue of his Literary Defense Corps badge absorbing all the light that found it.

Kaia entered with the third wave, neither first nor last, and seated herself two rows from the front, left side—prime position for both visual sweep and tactical withdrawal. Her palms sweated, but her breath remained steady. She noted, with satisfaction, that the desk surface was still cool—untouched by previous bodies, untainted by fear.

Yuki catches Kaia's eye and gives the barest twitch of a smile—solidarity, or maybe just the old dare to try. Mikihisa attempts a wink, but his eyelid quivers, unsure of itself, and he settles for rolling his cuffs with exaggerated focus, as if any sliver of exposed skin might mean instant failure.

The rest of the room fills with a scatter of half-familiar faces, each rendered anonymous by the Academy's taste for conformity: hair cropped to regulation, uniforms scrubbed of all color but navy, boots identical down to the mud on the soles. At 14:59:59, the last recruit slides into place, and the door hisses shut with a finality that silences even the rustle of cloth on plastic.

The lights dim. The only illumination now is the spectral blue of the projectors, painting every feature in sharp relief.

Lt. Dojo surveys the room, eyes like searchlights, and then speaks. His voice is quiet, measured, not needing volume to carry. "This is the Narrative Cipher Test. You have fifteen minutes to decode the embedded message. Three errors will lock your terminal. There are no makeups, no appeals. Begin."

As if triggered by his words, every screen blazes to life at once. Kaia's retinas flinch, but she recovers fast, focusing on the stream of symbols that race across the display—letters and numbers, yes, but also sigils, fragments of punctuation, even mathematical operators rendered in a script designed to resist pattern recognition. The text slides, flickers, then resets, always different but always the same.

Kaia's fingers hovered, then landed on the keys with a certainty she did not feel. The first instinct is to brute-force it, to search for familiar ciphers, substitution patterns, anything the League might have recycled from old exams. But this—this is different. The rhythm of the characters is wrong: too variable, too alive. Kaia squints, ignores the margins, and lets her vision blur, softening the edges until the code ceases to be code and becomes shape, negative space.

Next to her, Mikihisa's breathing grows audible, a faint hitch every time the symbols slide too fast. Two rows ahead, Yuki is already typing, her strokes precise, surgical, as if she's reading a language only she remembers.

Dojo watches from the front, face unreadable, one hand now resting on the base of the countdown clock. He is still as a statue, but Kaia can sense the tension in the set of his jaw, the way his gaze lingers a beat longer on each recruit as if searching for the first signs of collapse.

The test has only been running a minute, but already a kind of vertigo has set in. The lights, the shifting text, the relentless pressure of the clock—every element designed to erode focus, to reduce a mind to raw nerve.

Kaia centers herself. She remembers her mother's voice, low and steady, teaching her to find the story beneath the noise: "Every code is a confession," Hana used to say. "Even if you can't see it, the shape of the lie will tell you what's missing."

She scans the screen again. On the fourth repetition, something jumps out: every fifth line starts with a double space, an anomaly so subtle it would have gone unnoticed by anyone less obsessed with margin. Kaia highlights the lines, strings the leading characters into a new sequence. It's nonsense, at first, but then she sees it—a pattern in the seeming randomness, like a faint melody beneath a wall of static.

She types, careful, methodical. The input pad is merciless, each error followed by an angry red flash and a microsecond of added lag—punishment for hesitation. Kaia doesn't make the same mistake twice. Every letter is an act of memory, a wager that what she sees is real.

At 10:43, the first recruit slammed a fist on the desk, mouth tight, eyes wet with the threat of failure. The room doesn't react. The test is a predator, and weakness only feeds it.

Yuki was two rows ahead, her posture unchanging, eyes flicking between screen and pad, every move so minimal it might have been pre-programmed. She finishes the first block, leans back, and closes her eyes—resting, or maybe just letting the solution marinate. Kaia envies the confidence, but she knows Yuki: it's not arrogance, it's the habit of winning.

At 7:22, Mikihisa dropped his stylus, swore under his breath, and wiped his forehead with the back of his hand. The sweat leaves a dark stripe on the fabric. He starts over, slower now, the panic in his hands, not his voice.

Kaia keeps going, consumed by the rhythm. She sees the pattern resolve into language—fractured, broken, but language all the same. It's a story, she realizes, or the skeleton of one: characters in conflict, hints of place and time, a through-line masked by the smoke of deliberate error.

She almost laughs. Of course the Academy would hide its secrets in narrative. Even the League, for all its hatred of unauthorized story, cannot help but betray itself.

She types the reconstructed message line by line, watching the red error count refuse to tick up. Each input that survives is a victory, a step closer to the end.

Behind her, someone is sobbing—quiet, but present. Kaia does not look back. The clock is now her only enemy.

Dojo paces, slow and deliberate, his eyes never leaving the rows. His mouth is set, but Kaia catches a flicker of something in the corners—approval? Or just the pleasure of watching pressure do its work?

At 2:11, Yuki's screen flashes green—done. She sits motionless for a moment, then turns to scan the room, her gaze skipping over Kaia and lingering, just a fraction of a second, on Mikihisa's trembling form.

Kaia is nearly finished. The last segment of the code is dense, overwritten with false trails and double negatives. She has to slow, to parse each line, to force the pattern to reveal itself. She feels the sweat pooling under her collar, the pulse in her throat now louder than the ambient hum.

The final phrase is a punch in the chest: MEMORY OUTLASTS INK.

Kaia types it, careful, not daring to trust her fingers. The screen hesitates, then flashes green. The input pad unlocks, soft blue light replacing the angry red.

Kaia leans back, lets the breath out, and only then realizes how tightly her body has been wound.

The clock shows 00:41. She beat the test by less than a minute.

Dojo's voice fills the chamber, low and unhurried: "All terminals locked. Recruits, stand and face the display."

Kaia stands, legs shaky, and turns to the projector wall.

On the screen, the decoded message assembles, line by line, a testimonial in plain language:

"STORIES ARE MORE THAN DATA. THEY ARE MEMORY MADE REAL. MEMORY OUTLASTS INK."

Kaia's throat tightens. She looks to Yuki, who is grinning wide, teeth bared like a challenge. Mikihisa wipes his face again, this time with a kind of pride, as if surviving is victory enough.

Dojo watches them all, then nods. "You've done better than most. But remember: the world outside does not care how clever you are. Only if you survive."

He dismisses them with a gesture, the door opening as if in apology for its earlier cruelty.

Kaia files out with the rest, the message echoing behind her: Memory outlasts ink.

She does not look back. There is no need.

She settles into the test like an old fever, letting herself slide under the surface of the code until the outside world is an abstraction and every breath is a matter of parsing, prediction, response.

The first hundred lines are ceremonial—League code always opens with a burst of digital camouflage, a blitz of randomized characters whose only job is to batter the reader's confidence. Kaia knows the trick: ignore the white noise, hunt for rhythm, for the pulse that reveals intent. Her fingers skim the keys, backspacing only when the data pattern refuses to yield. She sketches the first column of output on her scratchpad, just to let her hands remember the drag of pen on paper, the left-to-right motion so old it feels ancestral.

The lullaby pattern emerges almost immediately. Every fourth block of text recycles the same motif—a cluster of consonants, a pair of slant rhymes, then a numeric glyph that lands like a rhyme at the end of a stanza. Kaia's mouth curls, involuntary. It's the same trick her mother used to use, burying forbidden stories inside bedtime rituals, the narrative couched in such dense repetition that a listening bot would flag it as noise, not message.

She hums the pattern under her breath, low and private, audible only to herself. The tune helps her fix the cipher's pivot points, the places where the code doubles back on itself or slips in a deliberate error. Every so often she glances up, not at the clock but at the spaces between the digits, watching for the microsecond when the test re-seeds itself. Her brain is part engine, part wound—a place where memory fuses to analysis and nothing, not even League math, can break it.

To her left, a recruit slams his stylus against the desk, muttering a curse so obscene it would be an instant demerit if the proctor cared to notice. The recruit's face is already splotched with the red flush of defeat. He tears the scratchpad in half, then just sits, paralyzed by the reality that the only way out is through.

Ahead, Yuki's posture is tranquil. Not a wasted movement. She types with a deliberate slowness, savoring each key press as if it's a blow to the test's ego. She's not in a hurry. She never is. Yuki's only mission is perfection, and she's content to let the clock come to her.

Mikihisa is a disaster. The tip of his tongue pokes from the corner of his mouth; every five seconds he swipes a sleeve across his brow, leaving a sequence of damp streaks like a barcode of panic. His screen is a gridlocked snarl of error messages, red overlays obscuring half his output. He grimaces, shakes out his hands, then tries again, slower. Kaia can hear the grind of his molars from two desks away.

But it's the middle of the room—the hinterland between the practiced and the lost—that holds Kaia's attention. A girl two rows back is chewing her lower lip bloody, eyes locked to her display, hands trembling over the keys. Another, a boy Kaia barely recognizes from conditioning drills, is already staring at the screen saver, resigned to failure, his pad untouched.

Kaia returns to her task, methodical as a forensic pathologist. She replays the last stanza, traces the lullaby pattern, and starts to sketch the logic. Each "chorus" of the code is a direct lift from a field manual—a double meaning, then a misdirect, then the truth hidden in plain sight. She grinned. This was old work. This was her mother's work.

But then, halfway through, the world flips.

Her screen seizes up—every line turns the color of raw steak, overlaid with a stuttering glyph she's never seen. For a second, the cursor freezes. When it comes back, the output is corrupted. Every word she typed is replaced with asterisks, each asterisk flickering like a dying star.

Kaia's heart spiked, her hands suddenly cold and rigid. She checks the pad, the stylus, the interface. All normal. The error is intentional—League sabotage, a curveball designed to break the cocky ones who think they can skate through on pattern alone.

The panic is instant and cellular. She stares at the glyph, willing it to resolve, but the more she focuses, the less sense it makes. It's a fracture in logic, a cut in the song.

For a long second, Kaia just breathes. Her chest aches. The room feels colder, as if the ventilation has kicked up a notch just to see who will shiver first. She looks at the desk, at the ghost of her own fingerprints on the resin, then at the scratchpad, where her penmanship has gone ragged and uneven.

She wants to slam her fist down, to cuss out the program, but all she does is slide her hand to her pocket and find the hard edge of her mother's bookmark, pressed flat against the fabric. It's nothing—just a sliver of blue acetate, too thin to even serve as a proper blade—but she curls her fingers around it, lets the chill seep into her skin.

She closes her eyes. She thinks about the night her mother taught her the last lullaby, the one that didn't bother to rhyme because it was too busy hiding. She can almost feel the weight of the blanket, the scratch of her mother's voice:

"If the code turns on you, rewrite the question. The answer will find you if you make room for it."

She reopens her eyes, and looks again. The error is no longer a corruption, but an overlay—a second channel running beneath the first. The asterisks aren't blank, they're placeholders, waiting to be filled. The strange glyph is a pivot, a cipher that unlocks the next tier of pattern.

Kaia sketches it, top to bottom, then flips the symbol as if she's rotating it in space. Now, as if conjured, it forms a sequence—three characters, then a space, then three more. It's a seed code. A recursive prompt.

She grins, all teeth, and starts to rewrite. This time, she ignores the color, the error overlays, the entire performative stress layer the League has engineered to break her. She focuses on the undertext, the story hiding inside the sabotage. Every input is a call-and-response, a test of faith. She enters the new logic, and the screen starts to behave—slowly, grudgingly, as if offended by her refusal to fold.

To her left, the panic has spread. Two recruits are crying, one quietly, the other in a muffled snarl. At the front, Dojo is as still as ever, but his eyes are alive, tracking every loss of nerve, every collapse. He wants to see who breaks, Kaia thinks, and for a moment she pities him.

Mikihisa is pale, hair pasted to his scalp. He mutters, "Come on, come on, come on," and when his screen flashes red, he drops his head to his arms and does not move.

Kaia tuned it all out. She was running hot again, the cadence of the lullaby merged with the new logic, her mind a metronome set to maximum. She types, and the output aligns. She types, and the test stops fighting her. She types, and the narrative emerges, the message folding out of the data like an origami truth.

There's a minute left. Kaia's hands are shaking, but her vision is laser sharp, all distractions flensed away. The last error resolves, the screen flashes green, and the final stanza assembles in plain text:

When all other stories fail,

Let the world be remade in the memory of a child who never learned to stop.

She stares at it, the words echoing in her head. For a moment, she wants to cry, but there is no time, and so she simply leans back, lets the screen go dark, and feels the chill in her bones recede.

The room is silent. Even the weepers have stopped, lost in the postmortem. Kaia wipes the sweat from her upper lip, then taps the bookmark in her pocket once, like a secret code, like a thank you.

She glances up at the clock: 00:13 remaining. She has time, for once.

She looks at Yuki, who is already watching her, eyebrow raised in solidarity and a touch of awe. Kaia winks, just a flicker, and Yuki winks back.

She scans the room, making note of every survivor, every shell-shocked recruit, every pair of eyes that looks anywhere but at the front. There are fewer than when the test began, and that, Kaia knows, is the point.

She pressed her hand to her chest, felt her heart hammering, and was glad for it.

They will have more tests, more traps, more moments designed to break them. But for now, the world is quiet, and she is undefeated.

With three minutes left on the clock, the room had gone predator-silent. There were no more outbursts, no more cursing—only the staccato tap of desperate fingers and the low, collective exhale of a class on the edge of erasure.

Kaia can feel the tension rising behind her, the psychic heat of a dozen minds caught between panic and resignation. She ignores it. The code has cracked wide open, the error state now a pathway instead of a wall. She hammers the input pad, translating each glyph sequence into language that feels—impossibly—like hers.

The fragments assemble themselves:

"...fight in the dark,

words left behind for the children of memory..."

"...our only hope is to bury the truth in plain sight..."

"...they will burn the stories, but the stories will survive in us..."

Kaia recognizes the cadence—field reports, the desperate confessions of old rebels, their messages encoded in book margins and ciphers and snatches of lullaby. She types faster, letting her hands run wild, trusting the muscle memory built from years of hiding, years of reading between the lines.

The last block of code resists—repeats itself, loops in a broken circuit. The countdown flashes from 00:49 to 00:30. Kaia stares at the screen, her reflection pale and sharp in the blue light. She tries the phrase as it appears, but the system rejects it. Two errors. One more and the desk locks.

She exhales, thumb flicking the bookmark's edge in her pocket, then looks again. The loop isn't a loop—it's a refrain, a chorus meant to be sung, not spoken. She closes her eyes, hums the fragment under her breath, and the melody unlocks the logic:

"Memory outlasts ink."

She keys it in, precise to match case, punctuation, the code's exact rhythm. The terminal hesitates, then floods green. The countdown freezes at 0:17, a moment of mercy.

Kaia leans back, hands limp in her lap; the rush of completion is vertigo, not victory.

Around her, the room is breaking apart. Two more screens flash red, terminals locking with a punitive hiss. Mikihisa slaps his palm against the desk, once, twice, then lets his head fall to the surface in abject surrender. Yuki, finished a minute before, is watching Kaia with open pride, arms folded, chin up, eyes gleaming with the thrill of shared success.

At the front of the chamber, Lt. Dojo is already moving. He stalks the aisle with predatory intent, pausing behind each finished desk, scanning the output with a practiced eye. Most recruits shrink under his gaze, but Kaia meets it when he arrives, refusing to blink.

He studies her solution, the lines of decoded narrative scrolling across the screen. His lips twitch—not quite a smile, not quite contempt. He leans in, voice pitched just for her:

"Mori. How did you recognize the structure?"

She considers the lie—something about intuition, about talent, about the old adage of "natural gift." But the room is too full of ghosts for that.

"My mother," she says, keeping her voice low but steady. "She hid stories in lullabies. I learned to hear the patterns, even when I was supposed to be sleeping."

Dojo's eyes narrow, as if the answer offends and impresses him at the same time. "You understand what that means, don't you?"

She does. She doesn't say so, but she nods, just enough for him to see.

He steps back, lets the silence do its work, and moves down the row. Kaia watches him interrogate the rest, but nobody else earns more than a grunt or a cursory glance. For a moment she wonders if that's good, or very, very bad.

As the test officially ends, the system releases the locks, and the room exhales as one. Some recruits slouch, some immediately start packing up, eager to get away from the memory of failure. Others linger, shell-shocked, staring at their screens as if they could will a different result from the data.

Yuki makes her way to Kaia, slides into the desk beside her, and leans in close. "You did it," she whispers, more reverence than envy. "That last sequence—how?"

Kaia shrugs, modest yet genuine. "You said it yourself. The League always gives itself away."

Yuki grins. "You're going to get us both killed, you know."

"Not if we're smart," Kaia says, letting the words hang in the charged air.

Across the aisle, Mikihisa has recovered enough to glare at Kaia, envy and admiration warring in his expression. He mouths the word "wizard" and then laughs, a brittle, exhausted sound.

The class files out, slower than before. Dojo waits at the exit, eyes on Kaia as she approaches, but he says nothing. Instead, he marks her name on his pad, then turns away to speak with a recruit whose hands are still trembling.

In the corridor, the world seems brighter, less hostile. The blue ribbon at Kaia's wrist is a live wire, the bookmark in her pocket a tiny shield against the day. She and Yuki walk together, silent at first, then in a low murmur of shared survival.

As they cross into the open hall, Kaia feels the eyes of the other recruits on her. Some watch with open respect, others with a wary, sidelong glance. She is marked now, not just as a top performer but as something else—an anomaly, a threat, maybe even a future ghost.

Yuki bumps her shoulder. "We celebrate tonight?" she asks, voice light, but Kaia can hear the tension beneath.

"Let's see if we survive to curfew," Kaia says, grinning despite herself.

They walk on, the taste of victory sharp and fleeting. Kaia knows it won't last, that the world is already recalibrating to make her pay for every answer she's stolen. But for now, she lets herself enjoy the sensation of being alive, of having a story no one can take.

At the far end of the corridor, the archive door looms, another test waiting, another code to break.

Kaia squares her shoulders, breathes in the cold, clean air, and keeps walking.

She doesn't look back.

Chapter 14: Paper and Blood

There's a rule, unspoken but known, that you never breathe easy in the tunnels beneath the city—not even when you're winning. Especially not then. If memory serves Kaia right, every close call gets banked by the universe, and the universe is a ledger that never misses a debt.

Tonight, the squad assembles at a dead-end junction three levels below the municipal library, where the air is so thick with iron dust it leaves a taste on the back of your tongue. Kaia checks her own pulse against the hum of the pipe overhead, then checks the faces of the squad: Yuki, Mikihisa, and the two new kids—one named "Recruit Seven" for lack of a better handle, and the other a skinny shadow who always wears her hood up, even underground.

Kaia gives the signal to kill headlamps, and a hush rolls in, the kind that feels alive and hungry. She presses her thumb to the blue ribbon beneath her wristband—a pulse of memory, a call to courage. It steadies her. Or maybe it just holds back the scream.

"Status," she whispers, voice pitched to land no further than a meter.

Yuki answers without turning: "Junction One clear. Motion sensors spoofed. Got five minutes to final point or we risk double cycle."

"Seven," Kaia prompts, voice low.

The tall kid checks the scanner, shaking only slightly. "No noise east. Thermal's dead except for a rat, or maybe a very smart pigeon."

Mikihisa manages a grimace. "Here's hoping it's the rat. Pigeons are snitches."

The joke barely lands—everyone too tight for it. Kaia shrugs on her pack, feeling the uneven weight of books and flash storage pulling her shoulders lopsided. She taps her comm: a metal button on her collar, styled like an old-school library pin. The current in it tingles her jaw—LDC standard-issue, no external light, all code and bone conduction.

"Let's move," she mouths, not even a whisper, and Yuki leads them in.

The tunnels themselves feel like memory: concrete poured before the regime, cracked now and veined with black mold pulsing faintly in the red glow of the emergency lights. Wiring droops from the ceiling like wet hair, and the floor is pitted by decades of runoff and boot prints. They walk single file, Mikihisa at rear, stepping exactly in Kaia's footprints—standard when you don't want to trip motion mines or wake the ultrasonic tripwires the MRB likes to hide in the seams.

Every ten meters, the pack stops for a full scan: Yuki with her custom pad, Seven with the bare-bones hardware. The hooded girl—nobody knows if she even has a name—carries a bandolier loaded with thumb drives and slips of actual paper, which she moves between pockets like a street illusionist.

Kaia feels her own heart keep time with their footsteps. Every so often, she'll risk a glance back; Mikihisa gives her a nod, teeth bared in a smile that looks like it hurts.

They pass a dead drone, its hull etched with graffiti: REMEMBER, in a child's block print. Yuki brushes a gloved hand over the word, then signals a halt. Up ahead, the passage doglegs into a room so black Kaia can't even see the outline.

She presses forward anyway, blue ribbon tight on her pulse. They enter the space and scatter to the walls, backs against cold stone. Yuki glides to the far side, scans the old access panel, then waves Kaia over.

"It's not locked," Yuki murmurs, barely moving her lips. "Someone's already inside."

Kaia bites the inside of her cheek, considers. "Protocol?"

"Could be nothing. Or it's a test."

Mikihisa, never one for patience, whispers: "If they're waiting for us, we're dead anyway. Let's get this over with."

Kaia runs a check on her own gear: all in place, safeties off, no alarms tripped. She signals the squad—count of three—and steps through.

The space is a former junction, once a power relay. Now it's been repurposed into a makeshift checkpoint, benches lined with empty cartons and the wrappers of nutrient blocks. At the far end, a man in civilian gray leans against the old battery cabinet, arms folded. He's older than Kaia, maybe by a decade, with a beard clipped down to stubble and a face so lined it looks carved.

He nods to them, eyes alert but not hostile. "You're early."

Kaia shrugs. "We prefer to disappoint. Easier to fix than being late."

He grins, showing gold at the side of his mouth. "Books?" he asks, looking not at Kaia but at the shadow-girl, who instantly tenses.

Kaia shifts, subtly shielding the girl from view. "We've got two bags. Some history, some lit. Four classics. Half a dozen flashloads." She speaks careful, the way Hideo taught her—never offer, only confirm.

"Nice," the man says. "Your payment's in the usual spot. You want a signature, or do you trust me?"

Kaia just stares, the kind of stare that leaves bruises. The man breaks first, coughs, and ducks his head. "Didn't think so."

He snaps his fingers; a second figure peels out from the dark, a woman built like a coiled wire, her hair in a white buzzcut. She carries a field bag and a pistol, but neither is pointed at the squad. She surveys the handoff, then slides a pouch across the floor—a toss, almost contemptuous.

Mikihisa retrieves it, pops the seal, inspects the contents. He raises an eyebrow: "Upgraded memory seeds. Old world type. Score."

The graybeard nods. "We keep our end. If you get in trouble at the next checkpoint, just say you're the courier for Section M."

Kaia files that away, then makes the handoff, careful to keep one eye on the shadows. Books and chips go in the bag, no words wasted. The other side inspects the goods, then shrugs. "See you next time," the woman says, already fading back.

As they withdraw, Yuki pulls Kaia aside. "We're not the only ones moving material. There's a third party on the tunnels tonight. Sigs are off, but the dust on the floor says at least three more. Armed."

Kaia considers this, fingers the blue ribbon. "Keep us off major junctions. No heroics."

Yuki's mouth twitches. "As if I'd let you."

They ghost out, keeping to the walls, senses dialed to maximum. The tunnel seems even tighter now, as if the very air was watching them.

As they near the next bend, Kaia halts the line, all at once. Something's off—she can feel it, the way a room feels before a quake. Seven tenses, primed for orders.

"Lights," Kaia says. Not loud, but commanding.

The squad goes dark, pitch-black but for the memory of the emergency bulbs.

In the darkness, a single voice—low, female, tired—comes from the passage ahead. "You're late," it says, mimicking the words from before, but this time with a bite.

Kaia doesn't flinch, but she can feel the ribbon on her wrist, hot as a warning. She draws breath, then lets it out.

"Correction," she calls back, "We're never late. You just ran out of patience."

For a second, nothing. Then a laugh, more bitter than amused. "Maybe so. Come forward, no sudden moves."

Kaia edges in, hands open, and finds the woman standing alone in the arch, uniform faded but clean, boots polished. Her weapon rests her hip, not drawn.

"What's the play?" Kaia asks.

The woman shrugs. "You're not the target. Someone's leaking. Higher-ups want an example, but you're too small for the headlines."

Yuki moves up beside Kaia, silent as breath. "So you're just here to scare us?"

"Not scare," the woman says, face neutral. "Remind. You get sloppy, you vanish. No one even remembers your name."

Kaia nods, the blue ribbon steady in her peripheral vision. "Thanks for the reminder. We'll be ghosts, then."

The woman steps aside, gestures them through. "Last warning," she says. "There are worse things than being a footnote."

They pass, single file, hearts thudding. Once out of earshot, Miki-hisa mutters: "Did we just get a pep talk from the secret police?"

Seven snorts, almost laughs. "If that's all it takes, we're lucky."

Kaia just grins, the old anger sweet in her tongue. "It's not luck," she whispers, "It's persistence."

They move, tunnel after tunnel, until the checkpoint is just a promise around the next bend. Kaia runs her thumb across the ribbon, the fabric worn but unbroken. She thinks of the world above, asleep in its ignorance, and the squad below, hearts stitched together by the stubbornness of memory.

If this is what it takes to keep the story alive, she thinks, it's worth every bruise.

And then, without another word, they press on—deeper into the dark, ready for whatever comes next.

The checkpoint is a maintenance vault five stories down, where the city's original arteries once pulsed with river water and now throb with the residue of black-market data. The ceiling is so low that Mikihisa's hair grazes a bundle of comm cables, and the sharp air makes everyone blink harder, as if the tunnel itself were trying to keep them honest.

Kaia scans the room: four doors, one vent, and a ghost-light over the breaker panel that could flicker out at any second. In the blue shadow of the far wall, three figures are already waiting. Not professionals—too jittery, too thin, wearing coats two sizes too large. Their eyes track every move Kaia makes, but their hands are open, palms displayed.

"Who's in charge?" asks the tallest, a woman with a stitched-up scar running from chin to collarbone.

"Whoever has the most to lose," Kaia says, barely above a whisper.

That's enough: the woman steps forward and offers a battered knapsack. Inside are a hundred chips, each encoded with a week's worth of banned pages. Kaia double-checks the seal, then slips it to Seven, who scans for malware or tracking. All clean.

Yuki makes the first handoff—a stack of battered print books, bundled in plastic and shielded with reflective tape. The civilians paw at them with trembling hunger, as if holding food for the first time in years. They flip pages, lips moving in silent proof, then tuck the books under their clothes.

"We thought it would be heavier," the scarred woman says. "The stories."

"They are," says Mikihisa, with a grin that's pure LDC. "You just don't notice until you try to run with them."

They are two seconds from done when the world detonates.

First comes the whine, a metallic scream as the motion sensor trips and the city's forgotten warning system jolts back to life. Second is the red pulse of the breach light, a strobe that bathes everything in slaughterhouse color. Last is the sound—a boom, not from explosives, but from boots on steel, too many and too close.

"Drop!" Kaia yells, but the civilians are already scattering, books clutched to their ribs.

The first round of fire is imprecise, just a warning across the mouth of the west tunnel. But the ricochet tears a strip of paint off the pipe beside Mikihisa's head and leaves a smoking dent in the wall. Kaia drags Mikihisa behind the old compressor, Yuki shoving the hooded girl ahead of her toward cover.

"East tunnel's the only exit," Yuki shouts, mapping the chaos in real time. "MRB's closing in on both sides."

Kaia grits her teeth, mind moving at a speed that feels both terrifying and slow. "Seven! Get the package to the vent. Yuki, you're with me—we cover the run."

Seven nods, face pinched and pale, and shoulders the bag of memory chips. The hooded girl is already crawling toward the vent, low and fast, but the bottleneck is obvious. It will take a miracle for them all to get through before the MRB closes the loop.

"Now!" Kaia hisses.

Seven hits the vent first, vanishes into blackness. The hooded girl is next, wriggling her thin frame through the oval. Kaia waits, counting the interval between shots. When it drops to less than a second, she risks a look.

Mikihisa is still at the compressor, body curled tight, but his face is off—jaw clenched, eyes darting. Kaia realizes he's prepping a throw. She shakes her head, but he's already in motion, flinging a smoke charge down the west corridor.

The response is instant—another hail of gunfire, this time closer, more focused.

Yuki appears beside Kaia, breathing hard. "He's buying time," she says, voice low and urgent. "But it'll cost him."

"Not if we move," Kaia snaps. She vaults over the compressor, grabs Mikihisa by the shoulder—except her hand comes away slick and red.

He's been hit already, she realizes. The blood is fresh, soaking into the seam of his uniform, warmth rising in a cloud she can almost taste.

"Mik," Kaia whispers, but he's grinning through the pain, eyes fever-bright.

"Just a scratch," he says, voice rough. "Get the others out."

She curses under her breath and signals Yuki to the vent. Then, bracing her foot against the compressor, Kaia half-lifts, half-drags Mikihisa back to the cover of the service wall. He stumbles, nearly falling, but recovers enough to slam his back to the stone.

"Pressure here," Yuki says, sliding a field wrap across the floor. Kaia wads it against Mikihisa's shoulder, feeling the thud of his pulse beneath her palm.

He tries for a joke, but it's just a hiss of pain.

"Shut up," Kaia says. "Let me work."

The gunfire pauses. In the echo, Kaia hears boots—too many, moving faster.

Yuki eyes the room, calculating. "You have thirty seconds, tops. I'll distract. You carry him."

Kaia shakes her head. "We both carry."

They get Mikihisa upright, each slinging an arm over their shoulders. The vent is too far for a sprint, but Yuki hauls him like dead weight. Kaia matches the pace, adrenaline turning her vision to a narrow, red-lit tunnel. Behind, the warning light flashes, strobing silhouettes against the far wall.

Ten meters to the vent. Eight.

A shot cracks, and Kaia feels a sting across her calf—just a graze, but enough to send her stumbling. Yuki doesn't slow, and Mikihisa, stubborn bastard, pushes off them both to fall the last three meters himself. He lands hard, face-first, but rolls and comes up grinning.

"You owe me," he pants, gritting through the pain.

"Add it to the tab," Kaia says, and together they drag him through the vent, scraping elbows and knees on rusted metal edges.

Inside, it's pitch black. Kaia can hear Seven ahead, breathing fast. The hooded girl is already gone, probably halfway up the crawl. Kaia pushes Mikihisa through, then follows, Yuki last, palming the vent cover closed behind them.

For a moment, there is nothing but the darkness and the sound of their own blood in their ears.

Then, from behind, the thud and clatter of MRB boots, the angry rattle of the vent cover as someone tests it from the other side.

Kaia presses her hand to Mikihisa's shoulder, applying pressure as he groans. "We need to move," she says, voice trembling but unbroken.

Yuki checks the tunnel ahead, then looks back. "They'll follow, but not for long. These shafts are too old for their gear."

"Lucky us," Mikihisa says, and this time the joke lands.

Kaia risks a breath. "Everyone alive?" She doesn't dare count until she hears the voices—Seven's tight and high, the hooded girl's low and flat.

"We're good," Seven says. "Package intact."

Kaia lets herself sag, just a moment, before the next task comes into focus. "We have to get to the fallback point. If Mik loses too much blood—"

"I won't," he interrupts, but Yuki is already tying off the wound, hands deft even in the dark.

"Pressure here," Yuki repeats, and Kaia presses down, hard.

Mikihisa winces, but grins through it. "You know, Mori, if you wanted to hold me this close, you could have just asked."

Kaia ignores him, focusing on the blood, the wound, the weight of the moment.

Ahead, the tunnel narrows, then opens up. Seven scouts it, finds a service door, and signals them through. Outside is a utility corridor—quiet, empty, the air blessedly cold.

They collapse in the shadow of an old conduit, Mikihisa slumping to the ground.

Yuki leans against the wall, eyes shut. "We did it," she whispers. "Or something like it."

Kaia cradles her hand, sticky now with blood. She looks at Mikihisa, then at the others.

"We did it," she echoes softly, as if convincing herself more than the others.

But already, she's thinking of the next tunnel, the next checkpoint, the next time they'll have to do it all over again.

She presses the blue ribbon to her wrist, feeling the beat of her own heart, and hopes it's enough.

The city is a labyrinth, its tunnels the veins of buried secrets. Kaia and her squad drag Mikihisa through them, the stink of blood and old mold thick enough to bite. Every dozen steps, they stop: Yuki signals for silence, and all five hold their breath, counting the seconds until the only sound is the drip of condensation and the thin, irregular moan of the wounded.

It takes them an hour to clear the outer ring. The path is never straight—Yuki knows all the old passages, every dead-end and culvert, and she leads them through a patternless web, always doubling back, never moving the way logic or fear says they should.

Twice, Kaia hears the distant clatter of boots, the blunt language of people who know they own the night. Each time, the squad huddles in a pocket of darkness, Kaia's hand pressed hard to Mikihisa's wound, his breath hot and ragged in her ear. He doesn't complain, but the effort of keeping quiet etches new lines in his face.

At last, they emerge in an old storage depot, a square of dry air behind a triple-locked hatch. The room is choked with dust and the ghosts of better times—shelves toppled, paper shredded into drifts, the graffiti of old resistance slogans barely visible under layers of whitewash.

Yuki checks all the seams, sets a tripwire across the door, then signals: safe, for now.

Kaia and Seven lower Mikihisa onto a crate. His face is gray, lips dry. The blood has stopped pumping, but only because it's pooling inside the uniform.

The hooded girl—Kaia still didn't know her name—broke open the med kit with fingers that barely shook. She cut away the ruined fabric, wiped at the wound with rough cloth, then glanced at Kaia for permission. Kaia nods, and the girl poured a stinging wash over the entry wound. Mikihisa hisses, but doesn't flinch.

"The bullet's still in," the girl says, voice flat. "It'll hurt to get out."

Yuki looks over, then at Kaia. "We don't have time for clean surgery."

Kaia pressed the blue ribbon to her lips—a reflex now. "Do it fast," she says.

The girl produced a pair of tweezers—LDC-issue, stamped with a number. She digs into the wound, slow and sure, fishing for the bullet. Mikihisa's jaw locks, eyes bulging with the effort not to scream.

Kaia held his free hand, her own nails biting deep into his skin.

There's a sharp metallic click, and the girl pulls the slug free. She tosses it onto the floor, then packs the wound with sealant, wraps it tight, and steps back.

Mikihisa's head drops. "How bad?" he asks, not opening his eyes.

"You'll live," the girl said. "But maybe not well."

He manages a weak laugh. "Guess we're all in the same boat."

The adrenaline is fading, leaving a cold, metallic taste in every mouth.

Yuki sets a hand on Kaia's shoulder. "You need to hear this," she says, holding up her comm.

The audio feed is static, then a voice—too loud, too eager, the way propaganda always is.

"...executed with precision by the Memory Regulation Bureau...arrest and purge of over two dozen resistance operatives...further enforcement actions currently underway in the Central South school district..."

Kaia's guts seize up. She closes her fist, feels the imprint of the blue ribbon against her palm.

The voice keeps going:

"...books confiscated...all students processed for re-education...teachers resisting arrest will be remanded to the sublevel for disciplinary action..."

Yuki flicked the comm off. Nobody speaks.

Mikihisa finally breaks the silence. "We led them right to it, didn't we?"

Kaia shakes her head. "No. They would've raided, whether we ran the op or not."

Mikihisa turns to her, face hollow. "You actually believe that?"

She wants to say yes, but it's a lie too heavy to lift. "I don't know," she whispered, her voice low and fragile.

Seven hugs their knees, staring at the floor. "It's all theater. They want people to see the punishment. To remember what happens if you try."

The hooded girl bandages her own hand, then looks up. "We're not dead yet," she says. "Maybe that's enough."

Kaia's pulse hammers in her neck. She closes her eyes, the afterimage of the blue ribbon burning against her eyelids.

More comm chatter filtered in: screams, running feet, the dull, official voice repeating phrases like "protective custody," "collateral containment," "compliance ensured."

Kaia's hands trembled. She dug her nails into her thigh, welcoming the pain. She pictures children lined up in the cold, faces numb with terror, books ripped from their hands and tossed in sacks. She pictures her own mother, face battered but stubborn, daring someone to erase her from the world.

"They're punishing innocents for our actions," Kaia said, her voice hollow as a shell.

Mikihisa, slumped against the crate, lifts his head. "Not for our actions," he corrected, wincing. "For their fear of what we protect."

The words rattle inside Kaia's ribcage, setting every nerve on edge.

Yuki cracks open a water pack, pours a thin stream into Mikihisa's mouth. She wipes his chin, then settles beside Kaia.

"We're going to make this worth it," Yuki says. "Or we're going to die trying."

Kaia nodded, the gesture a contract. She unties the blue ribbon from her wrist, ties it around Mikihisa's arm, just above the bandage.

"For luck," she said.

He laughs, and the sound is real, if only for a second.

The squad huddled together, battered and bleeding, the sound of the city's pain pressing in from every side.

Kaia stares at her empty wrist, then at the door, and then at the faces of her friends.

"I'm not done," she said, and nobody doubted her.

Outside, the world was still burning. But here, in the dark, memory survived.

Chapter 15: Dojo's Story

Night at LDC Academy isn't silent; it's predatory, poised for the first mistake. Every corridor Kaia takes is a wound in the building's body, lined with the kind of shadows that never fully go dormant. The hours after curfew bleed out any pretense of safety, and the regular patrols—man, machine, and rumor—hunt on muscle memory alone.

Kaia runs this gauntlet raw, ignoring the ache in her freshly patched leg, the crust of dried sweat at her neck. She tucked her chin and walked like she's supposed to be here, a little slumped, brisk but not rushed, just another ghost on overnight detail. The hard part isn't the cameras—they're easy to spoof if you keep your pulse slow and your face away from the lens. The hard part is not listening to the pulse behind your own ears. That, and not thinking of Mikihisa, arms slick with blood, or the way Yuki's voice went brittle after the last checkpoint. Or the possibility that the MRB broadcasts weren't exaggerating, that the entire school district above them is now a sheet of ash.

The air on this level is a sweatbox, moist and cold. The hum of the ventilation is so deep it vibrates through Kaia's bones. She counts the seconds between each drop of condensation from the overhead pipes, trying to pace herself against the rhythm of the building instead of her own nerves. Her boots, worn down by a hundred midnight errands, make less noise than the whine in her teeth. The strip lights overhead are set to minimum, cycling between deep blue and ultraviolet; every thirty meters, one flickers, casting the floor in strobe that makes her shadow lurch ahead, then fall behind.

She traced a route that doubles back on itself twice, then ducks into a service corridor behind the archives. The route is older than she is, and it still bears the smell of solvent and unvarnished concrete. The blue ribbon at her wrist is sticky with stress, the skin beneath ashy from where she'd rubbed it raw during the op. She tightened it now—pulse-check, superstition.

The cache is three walls down from the main archive entrance, set into a cavity behind a disused emergency panel. She stepped around the corner and hesitates, letting her eyes adjust to the dark. The walls here are slick, condensation thick enough to bead on her fingertips. She palms the edge of the seam, feeling for the microfracture where the concrete doesn't quite set flush. If she pushes just right—

—A voice, low but sharp, from around the next bend.

Kaia froze, hand halfway to the panel, holding her breath. The voices are muffled, but one is unmistakable: the clipped, metronome precision of Lt. Dojo, cutting through the artificial calm like a knife through old bread. The other voice she can't place—male, heavy, gravel-throated, probably another officer, maybe a new transfer. The angle of the hallway bounces their sound, makes it impossible to tell how far away they are.

Kaia retracted her hand, pressing her back flush against the wall. The concrete is icy, and she can feel the pulse of the ventilation system running through it, as if the Academy itself is trying to shake her off. She weighs the risks, not out of fear but calculation: if she aborts the mission, the hidden papers stay safe, but she loses a week of labor and maybe the only unredacted records of the last operation. If she goes forward, she risks discovery, or worse—an impromptu loyalty check.

She waited. Breath shallow, eyes half-closed, counting each drip from the pipe as if it's a countdown. She tried not to think about how close Dojo is, or how he would react to finding her here, out of bounds, with a backpack heavy enough to snap a regulation-issue shoulder strap.

The lamp at the far end of the hall flickered, the strobe catching the two officers in silhouette. Dojo is the taller, but only by posture; the other one slouches, hands deep in his jacket pockets. They stop at the turn, barely five meters from Kaia's hiding place.

She pressed herself into the cold, palm splayed, feeling the grit bite into her skin. The metal panel she's after is right at her hip, but to open it now would be suicide.

"Late rounds tonight," grumbles the other voice. "They've got us running circles for nothing. You see the new code they pushed out?"

Dojo's answer is crisp, automatic. "Saw it. It's bait. They're watching for anyone curious enough to look deeper."

The other man snorts, a wet, phlegmy sound. "Aren't we supposed to be training these kids to be curious? Isn't that the whole damn point?"

"Curious within protocol," said Dojo. "Curious with discipline. I'd rather cull one in a hundred than lose the entire block to stupidity."

Kaia's stomach tightened. She recognizes the argument—not just from Dojo's classes, but from the way he ran drills, from the way he once complimented her for "innovative insubordination," a praise so thin it left more wound than healing. She wondered if he's really as cold as he sounds, or if this is just another armor, a layer between him and the losses he never mentions.

The other officer laughs, then coughs—wet and phlegmy. "Sure. But you ever think, just once, that maybe a little more stupid would keep 'em alive? You read those reports from South District? They're butchering kids out there."

"South District got sloppy," Dojo said, quieter. "That's not my problem to fix."

The silence between them grows, a pressure drop that makes Kaia's ears ring.

"Still," said the other man, softer now. "Wouldn't mind a little less blood on my hands, next quarter."

Dojo doesn't answer. He stands perfectly still, the blue light from the lamp painting his profile in angles: jaw clenched, hands folded behind his back, boots aligned to the line of grout between tiles. For a moment, Kaia thought she saw him sway, just a hair, like he's absorbing the blow of the words before locking it away.

She realized her heart is thundering, that she's holding herself so rigidly her fingers have gone numb against the wall. She lets out a breath, slow and controlled, daring a glance around the edge. Dojo and his partner are now facing away, already drifting toward the next checkpoint. Their footsteps fall slow, measured, almost reluctant.

She waited until their voices fade, then counts to thirty, just to be sure.

When she moved, it is with an efficiency that surprises her—no wasted motion, no hesitation. She slid the panel, retrieved the bundle of papers, and tucked them tight to her chest. The wall cavity is barely large enough for the cache; she must flex her hand into the gap, scraping her wrist raw, to free it.

Her mind replays Dojo's voice all the while: the precision, the anger, the note of something else she can't name. Maybe regret. Maybe fear.

She replaces the panel, wipes away her prints with the edge of her sleeve, and slips back down the hall, boots soundless against damp tile. She takes the long route back, through the perimeter maintenance tunnel, even though it means more exposure to chill and the long, empty blue of unlit basement levels.

She doesn't let herself think until she's inside her cell, door locked, bundle hidden beneath the thin mattress. Only then does her body collapse, legs folded tight, forehead pressed to the cool resin floor.

She's shaking, but not with fear. It is the aftermath of knowing something new: that the man who taught her to outthink the system is as breakable as the rest. Even the best are haunted. And for all her anger, she does not want Dojo to lose another recruit—not to the League, not to the system, not to anything.

She closes her eyes, letting the rhythm of her own breath drown out echoes of old conversations. The blue ribbon at her wrist pulses with every heartbeat—a reminder that memory survives only if you fight for it.

Outside, the ventilation hums on, and the condensation drips in a tempo as relentless as time.

Kaia decided, right then, she'll risk everything to keep the story alive.

Even if it means becoming the next ghost in the corridor.

The vented passage behind the main comms hub echoes with things not meant to be heard. Kaia presses herself into the inch of shadow between bulkhead and air duct, knees tight to chest, every muscle stiff as dried cords. She'd slipped in during shift change—one errant sweep of a guard's torch and she'd be meat for the grinder, but here she's invisible. The low hum of the servers is a lullaby for the insomniac, yet Kaia is awake in every atom. She has a clear line of sound to the officers' rec room.

First, the low murmur of the other techs, laced with the clink of mugs and the crackle of a package torn open: protein snack bars, always the same flavor, always tasting of wet cement. Kaia lets it blur; she's here for the voices above that—Dojo's in particular, the one threading a reprimand sharper than wire through the air.

Footsteps: new. Slow, deliberate. The entry code panel chirps, and Kaia flattens against the vent, barely breathing. Through the grate she sees two silhouettes, backlit blue by the station monitors. The first is Dojo—rigid, every edge honed, even off shift. The second, thicker in the neck and with a limp that telegraphs ex-military: Sergeant Ishikura, whose sarcasm could etch glass.

They exchange the ritual of boredom. Ishikura pops the seal on a water bottle, takes a long swig, wipes his mouth on the sleeve.

"Didn't expect to see you tonight, Dojo," Ishikura said, voice a blunt instrument. "You on another audit, or just policing the living ghosts?"

Dojo doesn't rise to the bait. "Neither. Couldn't sleep. The wiring's a mess—someone keeps rerouting comms through auxiliary."

"Probably the new batch," Ishikura said. "Kids don't know a bus line from a backbone. Speaking of, had to pull a squad out of quarantine block this morning. Paper said it was a drill, but you know the look when a drill turns to a body count."

A silence, not comfortable. Kaia leans closer, feels the tickle of dust in her nose, clamps down on the urge to sneeze.

Dojo's reply is a cut below the usual discipline, rough at the edge. "Wasn't the first time, won't be the last."

Ishikura glanced over, reading the lines under the lines. "Something eat you, sir? Or just the usual?"

Dojo exhaled, rubs his palms together. The motion is restless, almost furtive. "It's nothing."

Ishikura snorts, fumbles in his pocket, produces a battered cigarette and a disposable lighter. The sound of the wheel sparking is loud in the vent, the first drag an exclamation point. "It's never nothing. Spill it, or I'll have to assume you've grown a soul."

Kaia's heart knocked in her chest. She's never seen Dojo so off-balance. Even in interrogation drills, he kept a lid on his insides like the world's best thermos. Now, the pause between his sentences is almost—almost—human.

"It was a clean operation," Dojo said, each word scrubbed of excess. "Everything by protocol. And still, people died."

Ishikura nods, ashes onto the floor. "That's the business."

A longer silence. Kaia counted six heartbeats, then Dojo's voice drops:

"Five years ago. Operation Blackwater Archive. You remember?"

Ishikura's cigarette stutters, a flinch. "Yeah. We lost good people. Wasn't your fault."

Dojo shook his head, barely perceptible, but Kaia sees it—a tremor in the rigid scaffold. "We were extracting pre-censorship medical texts.

I was team lead. They assigned us a civilian archivist—said she was the best. She believed in what we were doing." His hands clench and unclench, small motions against the cool table. "I told her we'd protect her."

The vent air is stale but suddenly electric. Kaia's fingers curl so tight around the lip of the vent she loses feeling in her pinky.

Dojo inhaled slowly and careful, as if rehearsing the words inside his lungs. "The MRB had mined the lower stacks. Remote detonation, set to trigger at ingress. I got the books out. I got the squad out. But not her."

Ishikura doesn't speak—just lets the smoke hang, then flicks the spent butt at the wall. It bounces, rolls, leaves a hot dot on the tile.

Dojo said, "Sometimes I see her face. Not in the dreams, just everywhere. Especially when we bring in a new cohort. There's always one who looks like her. Same age, same stare. Sometimes I think it's her, just rewritten."

Kaia's breath caught, a fish on a line. She knows the logic: loss is fuel for the machine. But hearing it here, in Dojo's own words, it lodges under her ribs like a needle. The idea that someone so strictly by the book could bleed regret is both a relief and a threat.

Ishikura shifts, the chair's legs scraping a jagged line across the tile. "You're not paid to remember, Dojo. That's what got us into this mess to start with. If you want to keep your head, forget the ghosts."

Dojo's voice is almost a whisper. "Can't. Never could."

The lights in the rec room dim; a silent warning for the end of shift. Ishikura stood, stretching until his vertebrae pop.

"Get some sleep," he said. "Or at least act like it. The ghosts aren't going anywhere."

Dojo stayed seated, hands flat on the table, eyes not on the screens but somewhere far away.

The rec room empties. Kaia waited, counting her own pulse, until even the servers sound bored. When she finally peeled herself off the wall, her arms shook.

She wanted to hate him—wanted the clarity of rage. Instead, there's only the slow creep of understanding, the ugly comfort of realizing everyone is a little bit broken, even the ones who run the drills.

She slipped from the vent, landed in the dust, and made her way back through the silent corridor. The world is unchanged, but she is not. She has seen the enemy, and he is all too familiar.

Back in her dorm, she lies on her bunk, replaying the words in her head until they lose their edge and become something else. Not forgiveness. Not yet.

But the memory of regret, passed from one lost soul to another, is its own kind of story.

And Kaia, despite herself, will remember.

The silence after the confession is a vacuum, a pressure drop that hums inside the ductwork. Ishikura tried to fill it, but even his voice—usually blunt enough to break stone—falters at the edge.

"You couldn't have known, Dojo," he said, tone less comfort than brute force. "None of us saw it coming."

Dojo's answer is sandpaper. "That was the job. To see. To anticipate. That's why they promoted me, why they made me take the needle and sign the oath." He flicks ash to the floor, the sound small but surgical. "I was supposed to out-think the enemy. Instead, I walked her right into it."

The smoke is thick enough to choke the sensors, but Kaia only feels it in the tightness across her chest. She shifts her weight, trying to ease the cramp knotting in her thigh. The metal at her back is cold, and the taste in her mouth is like old pennies.

Dojo's voice softens, just for a second. "She believed in the mission. Believed people could be saved by memory, by stories." He gives a low laugh, the kind that never makes it past the teeth. "I told her hope was a weapon. She told me it was a shield."

Ishikura grunts. "Maybe it's both."

Dojo grinds out the stub of his cigarette, thumb and forefinger stained yellow from years of the habit. "Sometimes I see her face in the new recruits. Especially that Mori girl—what's her first name? Kaia. Same damn stubborn idealism. She doesn't know how to stay down."

The words hit Kaia like a slap across the face. She tenses, and her elbow bumps the edge of the vent. It's a tiny noise—a metallic *ting*—but in the dead hush, it's a siren.

Both men freeze. Ishikura's eyes snap to the vent. Dojo's go narrow, calculating. Kaia's heart spikes, a wild animal in her chest.

Dojo stood, slow and silent, head cocked. Ishikura's hand drifted to the sidearm at his belt, but he doesn't draw. They step toward the wall, boots landing with the caution of predators.

Kaia doesn't breathe. She pulls herself tight, presses her spine flat against the duct, makes herself as small as a rumor. Her mind races: if they look inside, she's done. If they call for backup, there's no place to run. Every inch of her skin wants to scream.

But the men stop just short of the vent. Dojo stared into the mesh, his face unreadable.

He said, soft: "Next time you want to eavesdrop, Mori, clean the dust off your boots first."

Kaia is paralyzed, caught between the urge to bolt and the urge to vanish entirely. For a sick moment she thinks he's talking to her, directly, but then Dojo turns away, tension draining from his shoulders.

"Come on," he said to Ishikura. "Let's let the ghosts have their stories."

They walked off, the sound of their footsteps fading. Kaia waited, counts to a hundred, then to a thousand. When she's sure the corridor is empty, she uncurls, every joint screaming.

She drops from the vent, lands in a crouch. Her hands are shaking so hard she can barely untie the packet of papers hidden in her jacket. She clutches them to her chest, the last evidence of who she is, or was.

The way back to her quarters is a blur. The world felt too bright, every shadow a threat. She kept her eyes down, moved fast, and didn't stop until the door is locked behind her.

Inside, she sat on the edge of her bunk, the blue ribbon pressed tight to her wrist, pulse slamming underneath. She thought about the story she just heard—about the hope that's supposed to be a weapon, a shield, or maybe just a lie. She thought about Dojo, and the way his voice broke, and the way he looked right at the vent and let her go.

She laughs once—the sound brittle as snapped wire.

Then she untied the ribbon, smoothed it out, and pinned it to the wall above her bed—one small act of memory, stubborn and unbroken.

Kaia stared at it, and for the first time in a long time, she lets herself feel the weight of what she's carrying. The ache in her chest is real, and so is the heat rising behind her eyes.

She wipes it away, hands steady now.

The world outside is still broken, still waiting to grind her up and erase her name. But inside, the story survives.

And tonight, that is enough.

Chapter 16: Codex Rebellion

The LDC Academy archives at night felt less like a room than a state of being: negative light, a stench of ozone and old skin, each aisle a corridor between what was and what must never be again. Kaia worked in a hush calibrated for maximum plausible deniability—boots left by the door, comm pad slotted under a volume labeled "POLICY: RETENTION AND REGRET, 22nd Edition," an in-joke only the dead would enjoy.

Her fingers ache from the shift; she's been cross-indexing blacked-out yearbooks and lists of purge casualties, tracking the subtle drift of language from "storyteller" to "content technician" and then to "unauthorized vector." The more she compares, the more the lie seems to ripple beneath the surface, like a wound poorly stitched. She's about to log another dead-end when the new file—just dropped in the system an hour ago, "History: The Transition Years"—catches her eye.

The document loaded with the lag of a system that knew it was being watched. The first thirty pages are empty save for asterisks and blackout bars, as if the words themselves were radioactive and best left ignored. Kaia scrolls, frustrated, but then slows at page 44: there, in the center of a footnote, a phrase that should not exist outside family bedtime.

"See also: Codex Rebellion, Sub-Section E."

She sits back, lets her blood cool. The words are wrong, a spike through the graywash of League-speak. It's the name from her mother's forbidden stories—the bedtime tales told when Kaia was feverish, or when the hunger wouldn't let her sleep. The ones with heroes who bled for language, who hid books in floorboards and truth in the seams of their clothes.

Kaia's thumb hovered over the next link, suddenly unsure. The old anger is there, but so is a soft terror: what if the stories weren't lies? What if the Rebellion was real, and not just an oral virus her mother released for comfort?

She taps the reference. A new window opens, this time with almost no redaction. It's a personnel roster, a list of "operatives deemed essential for long-term memory containment." Three names are highlighted, the rest gone to static, but at the bottom of the page, a line of tiny text:

"The above remain under review due to unresolved protocol deviations."

Kaia skims the margin, and her heart does its best to escape her ribs. There, in the analyst notes, is an annotation in a hand she recognizes: her own mother's, careful, deliberate, a script unbroken by years of teaching or by the League's relentless enforcement of blandness.

She reads the note, mouthing the words to keep from shivering. "If this survives the cull, let it survive you. The stories need witnesses—even if all you witness is the loss."

She's not sure if she wants to laugh or cry. Her hands shake so badly she nearly drops the pad. Instead, she pulls up the camera, angles it so the blue light doesn't blow out the annotation, and snaps three shots—one from each side, just like Hideo taught her. She's putting the pad away when she hears the lock cycle at the far end of the stacks.

There's no time to run. Kaia slid the pad under the file cart and stepped into the shadows by the folio cases, her heart smashing itself stupid.

Boots on the tile. A figure in regulation LDC uniform, the navy and gray blurring in the dead light. It's Dojo, of course; nobody else walks with that contradiction of practiced boredom and predator's watchfulness. He scans the room, eyes not missing a trick, then calls out in a voice too soft to echo but too hard to ignore.

"Mori. Show yourself."

Kaia hesitates, then steps forward, keeping her face as blank as she can manage. "Sir."

He raises an eyebrow. "You're off shift by two hours. Explain."

She thinks fast. "I couldn't sleep. The Comparative Sects final is tomorrow. They said we could use the archives for night study."

Dojo scans her, searching for the seam in her story. Kaia stands straight, shoulders back, hands loose. The discipline is real, the lie only half so.

He drifts closer, the smell of burned coffee and something sharp—aftershave or maybe just institutional-grade antiseptic—preceding him. He glances at the table where her comm pad is hidden, then at the shelves behind her.

"You're working alone?"

Kaia nods, the picture of regulation compliance. "Yuki and Seven said they'd meet me here, but I guess they bailed."

He almost smiles, then doesn't. "You know what the penalty is for accessing restricted sub-sections without supervision?"

"I wasn't—" She starts, but he holds up a hand.

"You're not in trouble. But you should be more careful. Every log entry is permanent, and some ghosts don't like to be noticed."

He's closer now, standing so the light catches the scar on his left hand—the one everyone says came from a field op gone bad, but nobody knows for sure. He gestures to the terminal.

"Show me what you found."

Kaia feels the adrenaline burn in her arms. She scrolls back to the first page of "History: The Transition Years," careful to bypass the flagged notes. She lets Dojo read, keeping her eyes fixed on his, waiting for the moment he'll call her on the omission.

Instead, he just stands, silent, reading faster than seems human, lips moving in the tiniest of tics.

"You think there's more to the official story?" he said at last, voice so low it was almost a confession.

Kaia shrugs. "They say the best lies are the ones with a kernel of truth."

He studies her, then nods—once, curt.

"Be careful which ghosts you chase, Recruit Mori. Some are better left buried."

He turns and leaves, not looking back. The lock cycles, and Kaia sags against the shelving, the relief almost painful.

Only after she's sure he's gone does she retrieve the pad, open the roster again. Her hands still tremble, but less now; fear and curiosity in equal measure. She scrolls to the end, looking for a hidden signature, a date, anything.

At the very bottom, almost lost in the gutter of the page, is a symbol: a stylized flame wrapped around an open book. The logo of the old Keepers of Memory, but more importantly, the same shape as the pendant her mother always wore—until the day she vanished.

Kaia traces the outline, breath tightening in her chest. She wants to scream, to run, to smash the pad against the wall. But instead she just sits, cold tile seeping through her uniform, reading the annotation again and again until it burns behind her eyelids.

If this survives the cull, let it survive you.

She will. She'll make sure of it.

And she will chase every last ghost until the story is told.

Morning drills at the Academy are never just about muscle memory; they bleed yesterday's insubordination out through the pores and refill the body with acceptable error. The yard is slick with frost and sweat—coating her tongue with the bitter taste of others' fear. Kaia waits for Yuki at the perimeter, stretching in the prescribed "neutral" fashion, but her mind is still racing the archive circuit, piecing together what the night left unsaid.

Yuki arrives with her regulation-perfect stride, dark hair braided tight against her skull, eyes scanning the rest of the cohort for threats before giving Kaia a nod. Without a word, she steps onto the mat and sets her stance: left foot forward, right fist raised, the posture of someone who'd rather be hit than talk about it.

Kaia matches her, and for two cycles, they move as if on rails—strike, block, shift, reset. The routine should calm her, but it only makes the words build pressure behind her teeth.

"Ever hear of the Codex Rebellion?" Kaia asks, just loud enough for Yuki to hear over the yard sergeant's drone.

Yuki's punch stops midair, fractionally short of Kaia's jaw. Her eyes go blank, then sharp. She steps back, drops her hands. "Where did you hear that?"

Kaia shrugs, feigning the boredom that keeps people alive. "Found a reference in the archives last night. Wasn't in the mainline history, just a flagged note. Didn't think it was real."

Yuki glances left, then right, as if expecting the walls themselves to sprout ears. "You shouldn't say that name, even here. They listen for it."

Kaia can't help herself; she grins. "So it is real."

Yuki's face doesn't move. She steps close, voice so soft it's almost just breath. "My brother used to tell me stories about them. Said they went further than any of the sanctioned uprisings—past what's even legal to remember. They were the reason the MRB invented half the protocols we train with."

Kaia nods, the thrill of confirmation threading through her exhaustion. "Why'd they fail?"

Yuki's answer is flat. "Nobody knows. One day, they just stopped. Some say they were wiped out, others say they went underground and just waited."

Before Kaia can answer, a third body collides with them—Mikihisa, all elbows and misplaced confidence, tumbling onto the mat with a theatrical groan.

"Please tell me you two aren't conspiring without me," he says, sitting up and flashing a grin that's all teeth and no defense.

Yuki helps him up, but her expression is still pure ice. "Go back to your drama rehearsal, Mik. We're having a real conversation."

He dusts himself off, then leans in, lowering his voice. "That's exactly why I want in. My grandfather used to say the Codex Rebellion was a myth, but then he'd go and hide old books in the ceiling tiles. Used to think he was just crazy, but now—" he trails off, looking pointedly at Kaia.

She gives him the barest nod. "There's more. I found a document, but it's dangerous—could be a plant, could be a test."

Mikihisa's face goes from smirk to stone in a heartbeat. "Then let's be smart about this. Three heads, less chance of losing all of them at once." He tilts his head, signaling to the far end of the yard, where the instructors are too busy bullying the new batch to notice anything outside their immediate blast radius.

Yuki checks the perimeter again, then jerks her chin toward the old rec shed. "Five minutes. Bring whatever you found."

They break apart, shifting back into the normal churn of trainees. Kaia wipes her face with the heel of her hand, sweat and relief mingling over her skin.

In the shadow of the shed, away from the line of sight, Mikihisa is waiting, fidgeting with a strip of cloth that he's braided and unbraided so many times the edges are starting to fray.

"Show us," he says.

Kaia powers up her pad, flicks to the photo of the annotation. The blue light pulses against their faces as they all crowd in to read it.

"If this survives the cull, let it survive you. The stories need witnesses, even if all you witness is the loss."

Yuki reads it twice, then looks at Kaia, her voice soft for the first time all morning. "Your mother wrote that?"

Kaia nods, not trusting herself to speak.

Mikihisa blows out a breath. "My old man said the Rebellion wasn't just about books. Said they were working on something bigger: a way to preserve memory itself—not just words, but actual memory. He called it the Memory Codex."

Yuki's eyes narrow. "That's not possible."

He shrugs. "Maybe not then. But what if it was? Wouldn't the League want it erased more than anything else?"

They let the idea hang between them, the gravity undeniable.

"We meet tonight," Yuki says, decision already made. "After lights out. Tunnel access, like the old days."

Kaia and Mikihisa nod, the pact silent but binding.

They split up, blending back into the yard. Kaia can feel the weight of new purpose in her steps, but she doesn't let it show.

As she crosses the quad, she catches a glimpse of Dojo watching from the admin level, his face a mask, unreadable.

She pretends not to notice, but every hair on her neck stands up, waiting for the blow that's sure to come.

The crawlspace under the Academy is an inverted echo of the world above: same architecture, same logic, but in negative, stripped of ornament and hope. Every surface weeps with condensation; every footfall ghosts out in the mesh of pipes and power conduits. Yuki is first to arrive—gloves off, hands bare and blue with cold. She paces the length of the alcove, lips moving in silent calculation, then stops dead when Mikihisa slithers in from the east vent, clutching a battered polybag to his chest like it's the only thing keeping his insides from leaking out.

Kaia is last, cautious and watchful—her eyes adjusted to the dark and the dark's ways of lying. She checks the tunnel mouth twice, then ducks in, unslings her bag, and sets it between her feet.

Mikihisa wastes no time. He yanks the bag open, revealing a notebook so old the corners have delaminated to paper mush, the cover scrawled with a cipher Kaia doesn't recognize. He wipes his nose on the back of his hand, then starts flipping pages—careful not to let any one sheet linger in the light for too long.

"This is it," he says. "Everything my grandfather wrote down, after they pulled him from the old city." He passes the journal to Kaia, who takes it with a reverence she doesn't have for most artifacts.

Yuki leans in, trying to read over Kaia's shoulder, but the script is a hash of code, slang, and numbers. "Can you even decode that?" she whispers.

Kaia traces the writing, lets the pattern of numbers and misspellings settle. "Give me a minute."

While she works, Yuki perches on an upturned crate and says, "I started searching League records three months ago. The first thing that jumped out was how little overlap there is between resistance groups in the public archives. You can trace a group up until the moment they matter, and then the whole thing gets sanitized—names go generic, events get vague, no follow-up." But with the Codex Rebellion, it's not just vague. It's erased."

Mikihisa grunts. "My grandfather always said they were the only ones who scared the League. He talked about a blackout—like, literal darkness. Whole sectors lost power, communications dead, then boom, it's over. All the Rebellion people, gone."

Kaia runs her finger down a column of numbers, matching it to a series of short, sharp phrases. "This is a date," she murmurs, "and this—'BDAY'—I think it means the day of the blackout." She flips to the next page, where the handwriting shifts. "But here he's talking about someone named HANA. That's... that's my mother's name."

Yuki's breath catches, and for a moment, nobody speaks.

Kaia reads aloud, voice thin in the low light. "HANA delivered the child to safehouse. Final protocol engaged. All other vectors terminated. If this is the last entry, let memory be the message."

Mikihisa whistles. "That's not just a confession. That's a pass down."

Yuki looks Kaia dead in the eye. "Your mother was part of it—not just part—she was a leader. They trusted her with the last viable memory."

Kaia wants to deny it, wants to rewrite the words so they fit the story she grew up with, but it's there, raw and undeniable. The blue ribbon on her wrist burns with the pressure of the moment.

She slides the notebook to Yuki, who scans the remaining pages. "Most of these are lists—names, locations, codes. But here: 'LDC, recruited from archive staff. All compliance voluntary, no memory wipe.'" She flips again. "There's a cross-reference to 'Blackout Protocol' and then—shit."

She holds the page up to the failing bulb. "It's a list of League founders. The first three are crossed out, but the next two... one of them is Dojo's family. The other is High Archivist Saito."

Mikihisa's head snaps up. "That can't be. The founders were all career League."

Yuki shakes her head. "Not all. At least two came from Codex Rebellion stock. Means they weren't wiped—means they were either turned or embedded."

Kaia feels the world tilt. "You think they're still working for the Rebellion?"

Yuki's voice is dry, almost a laugh. "Or they killed it from the inside."

The three of them sit with the though; the grows heavy and slow.

Yuki is first to break the silence. "There's something else." She pulls a chip from her sleeve, smaller than a fingernail, transparent but for the glint of gold at its core. "I lifted this from the League comms two weeks ago. It's deadlocked, but I think it's coded with a key from the Rebellion. If we get it open..."

Kaia stares at the chip, then back at the journal. "You think it's the Memory Codex?"

Yuki shrugs. "Or just another piece of bait. But if we don't try, it stays erased forever."

Mikihisa flexes his hands, the old anxiety back. "We're not the first ones to try this. What makes us different?"

Kaia puts the pad and the notebook side by side. "We don't have to win. We just have to remember, and not let the story die."

They look at her—first skeptical, then with a spark of the same stubborn defiance that animated every ghost in the archives.

"We meet again tomorrow," Yuki says. "But offsite. I'll set the route, no repeats, no patterns."

Mikihisa nods. "And I'll see if I can find anyone else whose family got scrubbed in the blackout. Might be more of us."

They stand, the meeting over. Yuki moves to the tunnel exit, Mikihisa repacks his bag, but Kaia lingers, staring at the battered journal and the chip.

She almost doesn't hear the footsteps—soft, practiced, in sync with the electric hum beneath the old school's bones. By the time she reacts, the vent at the end of the alcove slides open, and a figure steps through, shadowed by a hood and the careful drape of worn fabric.

It's the Phantom Librarian, the ghost from every training cautionary, the bane of League digital security. Up close, the figure seems more smoke than substance, face masked by a strip of black mesh, eyes glinting with the cold humor of someone who knows all the punchlines before you even utter them.

"Congratulations," the Librarian says, voice equal parts purr and old gravel. "You've just set off every proximity alarm in the building."

The three of them freeze. Kaia clutches the journal, Yuki the chip. Mikihisa puts himself between the others and the Librarian, but it's a gesture more symbolic than tactical.

The Librarian moves closer, then pauses, surveying them with clinical detachment.

"I've been waiting for someone to follow the breadcrumbs. Took you longer than I'd hoped."

Yuki regains her voice first. "Why now? Why us?"

The Librarian shrugs. "Because you're the first cohort in five cycles to break protocol and collaborate. Every prior attempt ended in betrayal, or—" they snap their fingers, the sound sharp in the cold—"archive wipe."

Kaia lifts her chin. "We won't betray each other."

The Librarian tilts their head, as if amused. "You'd be surprised what people do under pressure. But that's not the test anymore. The real test is whether you can finish what your mothers and fathers started."

They produce a second chip—twin to Yuki's, but marked with a blue flame. They hand it to Kaia, the touch deliberate.

"This is the Codex Prime. It's a seed, a map, and a bomb, all in one. If you unlock it, you can rewrite what the League thinks it knows. But only if you're ready to risk everything."

Mikihisa's sweat beads again. "And if we fail?"

The Librarian's smile stays hidden, but Kaia hears it. "Then you'll be forgotten. But that's the baseline. Failure is always an option."

They turn to leave, but pause at the vent, hand on the frame.

"You've already made it further than most. Don't waste the head start."

And then they're gone, their footsteps' echo swallowed by the old pipes.

The alcove is silent, the three recruits standing in a triangle of cold light, two chips and a battered notebook between them.

Kaia studies the blue-flamed chip, the pulse of memory and purpose thrumming beneath her fingers.

"We do this together," she says, voice steady.

Yuki and Mikihisa nod, the pact now more real than ever.

As they leave the tunnel, Kaia feels the old fear, but also something new—a kind of hope, sharp and alive, the kind that cuts both ways.

Above them, the League's world spins on, oblivious for now.

But not for long.

Chapter 17:
Mission Redline

The LDC briefing room is a pressure cooker, cycling between near-frozen stillness and the frantic hum of pre-mission nerves. Cold fluorescent tubes overhead stutter, striping the concrete walls with staccato bands of white and blue. The lights reflected off the long table at the room's heart, painting every surface in shades of inter-rogation-room jaundice. Tactical maps smother the tabletop, corners curled and fraying, their surfaces pockmarked by years of caffeine rings and deliberate gouges. The focal point of every map is the same: a ragged sector of city grid, arteries converging on the skeletal outline of the communications hub at Sector 7.

Kaia couldn't stop worrying the blue ribbon in her palm—thumb rolling it, then flattening, then rolling again, over and over, as if she could squeeze the ghosts out by pressure alone. The habit is a tell; Yuki has clocked it already and meets her eyes with a look that says, sub-vocal, Enough. But Yuki's own hands aren't still, either. She's stripping her data-comm rifle with methodical care, laying each part out in surgical order before reassembling it. Mikihisa, on the other hand, has no patience for ceremony. He bounces his knee, shifting in his seat, mouthing old League anthems and tap-tap-tapping the barrel of a coil-pistol against his own teeth. If he's nervous, it doesn't show; he's made a career out of looking like he's not listening, even when he hears every syllable.

At the head of the table, Captain Reeves is more monument than man: all gray stubble and craggy jaw, eyes sunk so deep in their sockets they seem to be looking out from another room. He has the air of someone who would rather be on the front line than teaching it, and when he speaks, the squad listens without meaning to.

He slapped the tabletop with a palm like a shovel. "Listen up. This one's not a drill. Not a field exercise. The comms leak at 7-A has already torpedoed three of our ongoing operations. We are lucky—lucky—that last night's memory-siphon only scraped the surface. If they'd hit the deep archives, you'd be waking up to a city-wide lockdown, not this polite little after-school special."

Mikihisa winks at Kaia, low enough that Reeves can't see. "He means, we're getting the live ammo for once."

Yuki says nothing, but her cheek muscles tense, a microscopic shift.

Reeves continues. "Our window is sixty minutes, tops, before the MRB takes over. The leak is contained to the comms hub, as far as we know, but there's enough shadow traffic in that sector to hide a whole squadron of defectors. You three will be point on this; the rest of the team will cordon and delay. Priority one: trace the leak, root and stem. Priority two: bring in anyone who made contact. Priority three—" He raps the table twice, signaling this part is not negotiable. "No civilian casualties. None."

He waits, as if daring anyone to object.

Yuki is first to answer, voice a flawless monotone. "Rules of engagement, Captain?"

"Reeves's eyes flick to her, and for a second there's respect. "Non-lethal only. If you have to drop someone, you aim for reset, not deletion. The higher-ups want answers, not just a stack of new case files."

Mikihisa leans forward, finally dropping the coil-pistol into the mag well with a click. "What about potential friendlies? There's always a double-agent on the inside."

Reeves gives a smile so thin it might be negative space. "If you find a friendly, bring them in. Alive, conscious, and with their tongue intact. The last squad sent out on retrieval ended up with three bodies and zero intelligence. Let's try for a reversal."

He keys the wall display, and a crumbling schematic of the comms hub flickers into focus: four stories of decaying infrastructure, every floor a maze of old-world server racks and asbestos insulation, patched over with layers of LDC field tech. He taps a zone on the second sublevel—circled in red, the old cliché. "This is where we lost the signal last. If it's a ghost, root it out. If it's a plant, pull it up, roots and all. You have authorization for any digital intrusion short of a hard reboot."

He kills the map, and the room plunges back into its old black-and-white chiaroscuro. "Questions?"

Kaia opened her mouth, then closed it again, thumb white-knuckling the ribbon. She doesn't trust herself not to ask something that'll get her benched before the mission even starts.

Yuki, seeing this, stepped in. "Egress routes? Is the upper access still under repair?"

Reeves gives a grunt. "It's as clear as it's going to get. If you make too much noise, the roof stair is your only real escape. I'd recommend not making noise."

He checks the wall clock. "You roll in ten. Go."

The squad moves as one toward the armory, their steps out-of-sync: Kaia's stride quick and restless, Yuki gliding with mechanical grace, Mikihisa sauntering as if he has all the time in the world. Inside, the tech is racked by rank: pistols, charge packs, a whole buffet of non-lethal suppression tools. Kaia snags a baton and a clip of netting rounds, stows them in her vest, then checks and rechecks the tension on her belt until Yuki has to step in and physically steady her.

"Stop," Yuki says, voice so soft it's nearly thought. "If you over-tighten, you'll cut your own pulse," Yuki said softly.

Kaia nodded, let her hands drop, and breathed through her nose, just like her mother used to instruct. She wonders, briefly, if her mother's voice would sound like Yuki's, had she lived to see the inside of an armory.

Mikihisa pulled on a helmet, flicked the visor down, and stared at the pair of them through an orange mirror. "We look like kids playing at cops and robbers." He thumps his own chest with a knuckle. "I hope the bad guys don't mind getting embarrassed by the B squad."

Yuki ignores him, fingers running a rapid diagnostic on her comm pad. Mikihisa pulled on a helmet, flicked the visor down, and stared at the pair of them through an orange mirror.

Kaia runs a final mental inventory, but her mind drifts repeatedly to the ribbon in her pocket. The mission feels urgent, yes—but there's another edge to it, a shiver she can't trace to fear alone. She pushes it down, follows Yuki and Mikihisa to the bay where the transport waits.

On the way, the air changes: the white-noise hush of the briefing room replaced by the scent of metal polish and ozone, the floors here swept clean but still sticky in the joints. The squad moves with purpose, but every so often, Kaia glances up—some part of her expecting, or maybe hoping, to see a familiar face behind the observation glass.

She's almost disappointed to find only a blank row of mirrored panels, reflecting herself and the other two.

But as they pass the last door before the loading dock, a figure appears on the catwalk above: Lieutenant Dojo, arms folded, silhouette backlit by the ugly blue glow of the control room. He makes no movement, no gesture—just stands and watches. For a split second, Kaia meets his gaze—distant, and yet somehow a razor's edge beneath her skin.

Yuki sees it, too. "Don't let him rattle you," she murmurs. "He's just measuring for the postmortem."

"Cheery," Mikihisa says, his laugh hollow as a skull.

Kaia stares a moment longer, searching for a hint of approval, or even warning. But Dojo's face is unreadable—a wall of nothing, stone and air. She wonders if he's thinking of his own ghosts—or just counting down the minutes until he can add another line to her file.

The trio boards the transport; doors slam shut behind them with the finality of a book dropped from height.

Inside, the engine's hum drowns out everything but breaths and the occasional clatter of gear. Kaia sits by the window, tracing the city's fractured skyline as it flickers past, the blue ribbon coiled tight in her fist.

For the first time in a long while, she's not sure if she's the main character in her own story—or just a footnote waiting for the page to turn.

Either way, the mission is on, and the story's already writing itself.

Sector 7's comms hub looms over the intersection like a condemned cathedral—four stories of concrete rot, iron rebar poking through like fossilized nerve endings, every window panel either busted or replaced with plastic so old it's gone orange. The transport glides to a stop two blocks out, engine purring quietly, and the squad ghosts the last hundred meters on foot, boots tracing a rhythm only their hearts can match.

Inside, the hub is a labyrinth of dead light and stale air. Half the fixtures flicker, sputtering out more shadow than light; the rest exhale a low blue glow that sucks the color from skin and uniform alike. The walls are a palimpsest of faded propaganda posters and riot graffiti, slogans so layered and battered none are legible—just the sense of a perpetual argument, never resolved. Somewhere, water drips in a persistent code, pinging off the corroded stairwell and echoing through the skeleton of the building.

Mikihisa, first through the outer doors, signals clear with a two-finger flick, then moves to the side, weapon half raised. Yuki goes second, sweeping the entry with a gesture so smooth it barely exists; she's already mapping the room, every line of sight and every possible hazard catalogued in the staccato flick of her pupils. Kaia brings up the rear, breath caught in the cartilage of her throat, every sense dialed up until it hurts.

"Split and sweep," Yuki says, voice just above the tinnitus hum of the failing lights.

Mikihisa grins, but the set of his jaw betrays the joke. "I get the fun floor," he whispers, nodding to the sub-basement stairs.

"Try not to get lost," Kaia shoots back, but her own boots slide a half-inch on the floor, nearly losing purchase. The tile is covered in a slick layer of dust, mashed paper, and something that looks like it started as coffee and ended as a bacterial film. It's freezing in here, colder than outside, the HVAC a corpse but still leaking cold through the old city's marrow.

First floor is quiet, a kind of tension you feel before you see. Kaia takes the left-hand corridor, past a security desk that's been ripped up and tagged so many times the original color is a rumor. The floor tilts slightly downhill, toward the cluster of comms relay rooms in the building's belly. Every door she passes is either kicked open or jammed shut, hinges creaking or refusing to move at all.

She finds the first real sign of trouble at the end of a short hall: a heap of torn-up memory chips and a scatter of printouts, half burned. She kneels, tracing a finger through the char. The chips are the kind used in LDC field gear, but these are wiped—someone knew exactly what to erase, and what to leave behind for bait. She scans the papers: mostly blank, the few visible lines highlighted in angry red. "Transition event scheduled 15:00," one note reads, scrawled in a hand that looks too careful to be real.

A flash of movement up ahead. Kaia tenses, hand on her baton—but it is only a rat—no, two—fighting over a wedge of something unrecognizable. They scatter as she approaches, vanishing into a ventilation shaft that hisses a sour wind.

She checks her comm. "Main corridor, east. Evidence of data dump. No contact."

Yuki's reply is a whisper in the bone: "West side clear. Advancing to control center."

Mikihisa: "Basement access is a puddle. Smells like acid and death. Will update."

Kaia advances, tracing the breadcrumb trail of evidence—footprints in the dust, some fresh, some layered over each other in frantic back and forths. The footprints aren't League boots. Lighter, flatter.

Civilian? She counts the sizes—three, maybe four. Two heavier, one smaller, all moving with erratic urgency.

Halfway to the control room, she finds a blood smear on the wall, bright red against the graffiti. It's fresh—still tacky, the gloss untouched by air or dust. Her pulse doubles; her mother's old voice in her head: "Where there is fresh blood, there is either a friend in trouble or an enemy wounded. Never assume the difference."

Kaia signals a halt, crouches low, and listens. The comms hub groans, pipes ticking in the ceiling—nothing else. No voices, no footsteps, not even the whisper of electronics. She eases forward, every muscle coiled tight—baton drawn, thumb poised to pop the tip.

She rounds the last corner before the control center and stops dead: ahead, a makeshift barricade built out of wire racks and overturned desks blocks the corridor. Beyond it, in the sickly light, three figures huddle—two women, one man, all hunched over a tangle of what looks like scavenged LDC comms equipment and portable storage arrays. The man's arm is bandaged, the cloth already soaked through. The women work with desperate speed, pulling cables and slamming drives into place, all while stealing frantic glances at the barricade, as if expecting it to dissolve at any second.

Kaia's mouth goes dry. She edges closer, keeping to the wall, counting the heartbeats until she can see their faces. The man looks old, late forties, with a beard that's more stubble than hair and eyes bloodshot with exhaustion. One woman is maybe thirty, hair cropped close to the skull, hands stained with old ink and something blacker. The other is young—sixteen, seventeen, terrified and trying not to show it. There's a resemblance to the man, in the jaw and the way she hunches her shoulders: family.

Kaia takes one more step, the floor betraying her with a crunch of old glass. Instantly, the girl's head snaps up, eyes wide. The man moves to shield her, grabs a piece of bent conduit—barely a weapon, but held with the certainty of someone used to losing.

"They're here!" he shouts, voice raw and ragged with panic.

Kaia tries to shout back, to identify herself, to say something that will buy a second—but instinct overrides and she squeezes the baton's trigger. The round launches, striking the man square in the shoulder. He jerks backward, slams into the wire rack, and the whole barricade shudders. The older woman lunges for the floor, pulling the girl down with her.

But the barricade is unstable, a hastily engineered panic structure. The weight of the man knocks loose a top shelf, and it swings down, catching him across the brow and sending a hail of metal shards into the air. One jagged sliver flies—impossibly fast—and slices the younger woman's cheek open from chin to ear. Blood geysers, misting the wall and the stacks of papers she'd clutched.

She screams—a high, animal sound—and drops to her knees, hands clamped over her face. The man, arm dangling, tries to pull her upright, but only manages to spray more blood across the filthy tile.

Mikihisa arrives next, catching the last seconds of the chaos. He barrels through the corridor, ducks the low shelf, and slams the older woman to the ground with a practiced twist. "Easy," he says, voice soft and terrified at the same time. "We're not going to hurt you."

Yuki appears at the far end of the hall, her weapon trained but not firing. She takes in the scene—Kaia, frozen; Mikihisa, pinning a struggling civilian; the blood, the horror, the absolute failure of whatever plan they thought they had.

"Hold!" Yuki commands. The word bounces off the wall and sticks.

Kaia stands there, unable to move, baton still aimed at the cluster of bodies. She sees it, then: these aren't enemy operatives, not trained ones, anyway. They're just people. Civilians. Trying to... what? Steal data? Escape? Find someone, or something, they'd lost?

She lowers the weapon, the blue ribbon suddenly a garrote around her wrist.

Mikihisa has the woman in an arm lock but is speaking in a rush, the way you do when you're trying to calm a wild animal. "Stay still. Stay down. It's over. You're not in danger now."

The man groans, slumped against the debris. The young woman's hands are coated in blood, the gash in her face wide and weeping.

Kaia walks forward, legs numb. She wants to say sorry, or explain, or undo the last ten seconds, but all that comes out is a thin whisper: "We thought you were armed."

The older woman spits at her feet, a red-and-saliva glob that flecks her boot. "We're just trying to find our people," she hisses. "They said you'd have the names. That's all we want."

Yuki moves in, gun down, voice calm but brittle. "Who sent you?"

The man shakes his head. "Nobody sent us. We sent ourselves. There are people missing—friends, family. The LDC has the records. We thought—" He laughs, a short bark that breaks into a cough. "We thought if we could get them, we might get them back."

Kaia looks at the blood pooling on the floor, at torn-up faces and hands still trembling with adrenaline. She feels the story settle in her bones: not enemy combatants, not even dissidents. Just people, desperate enough to break into hell and drag their families out by memory alone.

She drops the baton—the plastic clatter as loud as a gunshot. She can't look at the young woman, can't look at anyone.

Yuki starts binding the man's arm, her motions clinical and quick. Mikihisa helps, still murmuring apologies that sound like confessions.

Kaia leans against the ruined barricade, staring at the spatter on her sleeve and the trembling in her fingers. The blue ribbon was stained now, blood soaking through, painting her mother's keepsake a dark, viscous red.

She tried to slow her breathing, to rewind, to remember a moment before all this. But there was no before anymore—only this, and whatever came after.

The comms center's flickering lights buzzed overhead, leaking ozone and futility into the world.

For a while, nobody spoke. Even the rats were silent, witnesses to the failure of good intentions in the face of raw fear.

Kaia stood, unmoving, as the echoes of the girl's scream bounced through the broken hub, and wondered if anyone would remember her as anything other than the one who pulled the trigger.

After is always quieter than before, but the silence in the comms hub after the chaos is funereal. The squad worked through the steps—stabilize the wounded, secure the site, log the evidence—on a kind of borrowed autopilot, hands moving faster than brains could process. Kaia's fingers shake as she binds the girl's split cheek with a med-patch from her kit. Blood beaded through the bandage, the gash too deep to seal, but protocol was a try. The girl won't look at her, and Kaia doesn't blame her.

Medical drones swept the corridors within minutes, trailing a stench of iodine and ozone. They descend on the man with the wounded shoulder and the girl with the torn face, their metal arms cold and precise. One drone floats close enough for Kaia to see herself reflected in its lens: skin pasty, lips bitten raw, her own eyes ringed with the kind of bruises you only get from not sleeping and seeing too much.

Yuki has set up a temporary field desk in the old break room, the only table left with more surface than graffiti. She sifts through the stolen data, scanning every memory stick, printout, and notebook page, cross-checking the names against League registry. "It's all personnel records," she says, not looking up. "Old district rosters. Family names. It's everyone who disappeared after the last round of contamination purges."

Mikihisa leans against the wall, one hand pressed to the older woman's shoulder to keep her still. "Why would you risk this for some names?" he asks, voice dull.

The man with the bandaged arm spits, a wet cough. "Because it's all we have left. They tell you people are gone, but nobody says where. Not even if they're alive. We thought maybe... just maybe..." He trails off, eyes rolling back in pain as the drone injects him with something clear and cold.

Kaia gathers the documents, the pages now soft and tacky with blood, and stashes them in a League evidence pouch. Every touch leaves a stain; the red climbs her wrists, paints her knuckles. She wants to wipe it off, but the blood is already drying, turning her hands into old brick.

In the hallway, the girl's scream lingers, stitched into the wallpaper and the old, peeling posters. Kaia tries not to listen, but it's in the echo of every footstep, in the whine of the lights, in the way her mother's blue ribbon—still wet, still knotted—sticks to her skin.

A memory: her mother once told her that every story starts with blood. "The trick," Hana Mori had said, "is to make it matter."

Kaia wonders if that's true, or if it's just another way to excuse the harm you cause.

Yuki emerges from the break room, eyes tired but intent. "Ready to exfil. HQ wants us back for debrief in thirty."

Kaia nods, helps Mikihisa half-carry, half-guide the wounded out through the same door they entered. The civilians go first, the drones hovering in silent escort. The older woman never turns around; she only looks down at her shoes, as if she's ashamed of the color.

Outside, the wind has picked up, blowing grit and frozen dust down the empty avenue. The city is lit in a perpetual blue twilight, the distant towers alive with thousands of windows, every one a potential watcher. The transport sits at the curb, doors open and engine idling. The squad piles the civilians in first, buckling them into the back row while the drones slot themselves in the cargo bay.

Kaia slides into the middle seat, evidence bag clutched to her chest. The blue ribbon, damp and sticky, slips from her pocket and lands on the floor. She watched it, not moving to retrieve it, as Mikihisa climbed in beside her. The transport doors hiss shut, sealing them into a private misery.

For a long time, nobody spoke. The engine's hum was the only sound, a low lull that numbed the mind. Every so often, the comms crackle with static or a fragment of League protocol chatter, but even that is muffled, like voices arguing in another apartment.

Kaia opens the evidence bag, sifts through the pages. Most are lists of names, highlighted or marked with desperate handwriting: "Where is M. Kondo?" "Last seen—disappeared 2/14." A photo slips out—two girls in a school uniform, smiling for a camera that must have been incinerated years ago. On the back, a scrawled note: "Will you remember me?"

She closes the bag, knuckles white.

Yuki stares out the window, face blank, but Kaia can tell she's doing the same inventory of guilt: running through the mission, parsing every second, looking for a decision that could have changed what happened. There isn't one.

Mikihisa tries for comfort, but his voice is a cracked reed. "You couldn't have known. None of us could."

Kaia wants to scream at him, to tell him he's wrong, but her mouth won't move. She looks at the blue ribbon on the floor, the stain blooming outward like a petal, and tries to remember the feeling of hope she had when the mission started.

The city blurs by, neon streaking the windows. It's beautiful, in the way decay is beautiful: slow, irreversible, indifferent.

Back at headquarters, the squad processes in reverse order—Kaia last, trailing a line of blood prints from her own hands. The med techs whisk the wounded away, the drones following in perfect formation. The civilians are sedated, faces slack, mouths open. None look back at her.

Inside the LDC's main entrance, the air is so clean it hurts. The walls are white, the lighting full-spectrum and sharp. For a moment, Kaia imagines she could just walk to her bunk and disappear, let the world keep spinning without her. But she has to make her statement, has to explain why things went wrong, has to catalog every error for the official record.

They're given ten minutes in the decontamination chamber, alone, before debrief. Kaia stands under the antiseptic mist, scrubbing her hands until the skin goes raw and the blood runs in diluted rivers down the drain. She wants it gone, but it stays—under the nails, in the creases, behind the eyes.

She looks up at the polished metal wall, at her reflection warped by the angle. Her face is pale, her eyes huge and black, the mouth a straight line that doesn't know how to smile anymore. She doesn't blink.

It's not the blood she sees. It's the memory of the girl, the wound, the scream, and the certainty that she is now part of someone else's story—the villain, the monster, the mistake.

The buzzer sounds, signaling the end of the cycle.

Kaia turns off the faucet, dries her hands, and picks the blue ribbon from the basin, twisting it once around her wrist.

She leaves the chamber, and her reflection lingers a second longer, unblinking, as if to say: this is only the beginning.

Chapter 18: The Ethics Debate

There's nothing soft about the LDC Academy seminar hall. If you licked the walls, they would taste of disinfectant and evaporated sweat. The ceiling hangs low, painted in a shade of off-white that seems designed to reflect the fluorescent strip-lights at maximum cruelty. Every surface is engineered to resist the organic—vinyl floors, alloy desks, a scent of ozone battling whatever lives on the skin of new recruits. The windows are a lie, just grayscale holoscreens rolling generic cityscape on endless loop, each cycle interrupted every fifteen minutes by an institutional PSA.

Kaia stands in the entry, blinking to reset her vision. The blue ribbon from her mother is twisted twice around her right thumb, a slow tourniquet she tightens when the hum of surveillance gets under her skin. Her classmates enter at regulation pace, passing one another without words, their faces already settling into debate masks. Today's topic is projected in five-foot-high red letters above the dais:

GOVERNMENT CENSORSHIP vs. FREE PRESERVATION: A Moral Dilemma

The phrase hangs there, pulsing with the building's synthetic heartbeat. Kaia's group—Opposition, in both name and spirit—has been assigned the "Free Preservation" angle. Which is a joke, because everyone knows the only thing less free than preservation at the Academy is the time between midnight and breakfast.

She slides into her assigned podium seat, the desk cold enough to numb her elbows. She palms the ribbon, running her thumbnail along the edge, then glances across the aisle to the Proponents' side. Tanner's already there, tie cinched to a perfect centimeter, posture so upright it hurts to look at. His hands are folded, the picture of earnest compliance.

Lt. Dojo occupies the moderator's chair at the front—upright, arms crossed, the face of someone who's memorized the outcome of this drill but still wants to see if any of the animals can escape their cages. He surveys the room like a chess engine waiting for a blunder.

Around the perimeter, a half-dozen security cameras pan and tilt in randomized cycles, the soft whir blending into the low buzz of the vent system. Kaia wonders if anyone has ever counted the cameras, or if there are more than even the staff realize. The walls are lined with posters—none of them motivational, all of them directives. Most are so heavy with blackout bars and redactions that the message is less about instruction and more about the threat that any knowledge not sanctioned is an act of sabotage.

Yuki slides into the audience row behind Kaia, spine straight but eyes soft. She gives a single nod: you got this. Mikihisa sits next to her, all restless limbs and overcompensation, mouth twitching in an approximation of a smile. He flashes Kaia a nervous thumbs-up, then immediately pivots his attention to the holoscreen, pretending to review last-minute notes.

The debate opens with a blare: a triple-tone that always pulls Kaia's mind toward hospital warnings or the onset of an air raid. Lt. Dojo stands without preamble, voice modulated just above the edge of human:

"Today, we challenge the ethics of knowledge control. As always, arguments will be judged on clarity, logic, and loyalty to Corps protocol. Personal narratives may be invoked, but only if grounded in substantiated evidence. Proponent: you have the floor."

Tanner stands, clears his throat—amplified slightly by the room's smart acoustics, a trick designed to give even the most fragile voice authority. He begins:

"Government censorship is not, as some believe, a violation of liberty. It is, fundamentally, a tool for maintaining societal order. In a world where information is weaponized, the careful regulation of knowledge prevents mass panic, disinformation, and—most importantly—cultural collapse. The Preservationists of the Codex Rebellion believed that all knowledge should be accessible. But what did that deliver? The Blackout, hundreds dead, and a generation traumatized. We argue not for the destruction of knowledge, but for its careful curation—"

He pauses, gaze locked on the audience, then on Lt. Dojo. The next sentence is calibrated to be memorable.

"—Because sometimes the truth is a greater threat than any enemy."

A handful of heads in the audience bob in silent assent. Kaia feels a cold pressure at her temples, the old anger and a new, sharper shame: she knows how much of this argument is historical fact, and how much is League-approved hallucination. But that's the whole point of the drill.

Dojo signals, "Opposition: respond."

Kaia stands. She's shorter than Tanner, but the room shrinks for her anyway. She tugs the ribbon, feeling the fabric cut into her finger until it almost hurts, then begins:

"Order built on silence is a type of death. A culture that erases its own memory—sanitizes it, scrubs it clean until only the version that flatters the powerful remains—is not stable. It's extinct, just waiting for the moment it forgets how to breathe."

She leans into the podium, the microphone catching the tremor in her voice and magnifying it. She lets the quaver stay—no point pretending she's not angry.

"The Codex Rebellion was a mistake. I agree. But it was a mistake born of the human need for story—for a place to put the pain and the hope. The League says it curates—but it's just a prettier word for burning the parts it can't control. My own mother taught at a public school before the cull. She was forced to recite only what was on the state syllabus, then watched as her students vanished, one by one, for 'content deviations' she had no power to prevent."

A silence grows. Not respectful, exactly. More like an uptick in tension before a power failure.

"If we allow the League to decide what is memory and what is myth, what remains isn't a culture—it's a vacuum. The same vacuum that killed my family—and many others here."

She sits, and the silence holds, stubborn and unyielding. The cameras whir; Kaia becomes sharply aware—more than before—of the audience beyond the room: admin staff in the booth upstairs, the AI sifting every word for signs of seditious patterns, the true purpose of the debate.

The cameras whir, and Kaia becomes aware—more than before—of the audience beyond the room: the admin staff in the booth upstairs, the AI combing through every word for signs of seditious pattern, the real function of the debate.

Yuki's eyes gleam; her mouth is set. Mikihisa wipes a sleeve across his brow, then gives Kaia a second, smaller thumbs-up—this time, it's real.

The Proponent bench regroups, whispering, but it's the kind of whisper meant to be overheard. Kaia catches the phrase "emotional manipulation" and "classic subversion tactic." She rolls her eyes, then twists the ribbon tighter. It's almost blue-black now, the old color faded from years of squeezing.

Lt. Dojo resumes, voice even:

"Thank you, both sides. The crossfire round begins. You have five minutes to challenge each other's logic and present evidence of systemic benefit or harm. Keep it civil. Begin."

Tanner's voice is slick, all the more so for the way it now addresses Kaia directly:

"Your narrative is compelling, but it ignores precedent. The pre-league era was a disaster of competing ideologies and rampant misinformation. The Blackout was not an anomaly—it was the result of too much access, not too little. Isn't it more ethical to restrict than to risk catastrophe?"

Kaia's mouth tastes of blood, where she's bitten the inside of her cheek. She leans back, voice flat:

"You call it a risk—I call it a cost. People are not safer just because you hide the evidence. They're just ignorant, and easier to control. If censorship worked, there'd be no Rebellion, no black market for memories, no one desperate enough to risk execution just for a taste of banned poetry. If your solution leads to more rebellion, maybe the problem is with the policy, not the people."

A murmur ripples through the audience; a few recruits stiffen, others drop their eyes to their notepads.

Dojo's face betrays nothing, but Kaia sees the way his left thumb presses rhythmically against his palm. He is, for all his rigidity, not immune.

Somewhere in the wall, a camera zooms in on Kaia. The soft tick is so faint, it would be easy to miss—but she doesn't.

She gives Tanner a slow, measured stare.

"Your answer," she says, "to every loss is more erasure. But erase enough, and eventually you delete what you're trying to protect."

The room goes still. Even the vent system seems to pause.

Yuki, in the back, nods once.

Mikihisa gives a soft whistle, then ducks his head, as if afraid the air itself might combust.

Dojo stands, finalizing the round.

"Final statements: thirty seconds, each."

Tanner's smile is back, but less certain. He reads from his pad, voice steady: "Preservation is noble. But preservation without order is chaos. The League exists to shield citizens from the dangers of unfiltered knowledge, and sometimes, protection requires hard choices. The alternative is not freedom, but the end of memory itself."

Kaia steps forward. She leaves the ribbon on the desk, just for a second.

"My mother told me, every story starts with someone making a choice. We pretend it's for the greater good, but really, it's just fear of what we might become. If the only way to survive is to forget what makes us human, maybe survival isn't the point."

She picks up the ribbon, lets it slide through her fingers—and then sits.

Dojo's voice slices the hush: "Debate adjourned."

The lights go harsh, flooding the room in cold blue.

Kaia feels the gaze of every recruit in the room, some curious, some hostile, a few—just a few—daring to look as if she's said something worth considering.

She wraps the ribbon around her thumb, tighter than before, and wonders how many stories are left to tell before the last page turns.

She waits, silent, for the next test to begin.

The closing statements have barely cooled before Tanner flips the switch from debate to demolition. He stands, eyes never leaving Kaia, and in a voice loud enough for the back row:

"Funny thing about the free flow of knowledge, Mori—it always seems to stream toward personal agenda. Maybe that's why your field record reads like a classified case study in collateral damage."

The words slap against the floor. Even the cameras hesitate, servos slowing as if savoring the moment.

Kaia feels the sting before the sense; her cheeks flush, breath goes shallow. She taps the ribbon against her thigh—steady, steady, don't rise to it—but the pulse of anger makes her leg bounce under the desk.

Tanner pushes on, smile cold. "Some of us," he says, "follow orders—instead of endangering civilians with personal crusades or risking team integrity because we believe the ends justify the means."

A buzz of conversation ripples through the audience—recruits exchanging glances, a few shaking their heads. In the front row, Yuki's mouth is a thin white line. Mikihisa looks like he wants to throw something but doesn't trust his aim.

Kaia keeps her voice low, controlled. "You mean the operation in Sector 7? The one where we saved three hostages and shut down the memory siphon?"

Tanner sneers. "At the expense of a dozen blackout victims and a city block's power grid. Or do you only count wins when they make you look like a hero?"

She feels the ribbon in her hand, the old acetate edge digging in until it's almost blood. Her voice sharpens.

"Better a hero than a ghost. Your type would have let the block be purged just to keep the paperwork clean. That's not protocol—it's cowardice."

The room stiffened, brittle as cracked glass. Several faces in the audience twist away, unwilling to be caught in the blast zone. The security cameras click into a higher sampling rate, lenses focusing so close Kaia can see her own reflection, eyes wide, jaw set.

She pushes up from her desk, ignoring the way her leg trembles. "We all took the same oath, Tanner. But some of us remember why we took it."

He laughs, but the sound is hollow. "Yeah? Remind us, Mori. Because some of us are tired of being judged by someone who still believes in fairy tales."

Kaia's knuckles go white on the edge of the podium. The scar on her elbow throbs, a metronome of rage and shame. She leans forward, voice vibrating with something she doesn't bother to mask:

"I believe in stories because they're all we have left. Every time the League wipes a page, erases a name, burns a book—another sliver of us dies. You want to talk about casualties? Let's talk about the six million stories incinerated by 'curation.' The art, the music, the memory—all of it gone, because people like you think silence is safer than truth."

There's a long, cold pause. The vent system kicks on, blowing a draft that makes half the recruits shiver.

At the back, a voice pipes up—a girl Kaia recognizes from the op, but not by name. She stands, face pale, and throws her lot in with Tanner:

"Your unauthorized operations put us all at risk. Is your ideological stance worth more than Corps integrity?"

The words land with surgical precision. Kaia's mouth floods with a metallic taste, and she's aware, suddenly, of her own heart as a raw nerve in her chest.

She turns to face the girl, searching for something—fear, or anger, or just a crack in the facade—but finds only exhaustion.

"I don't want to be a martyr," Kaia says quietly. "I just don't want to be a footnote."

A silence blooms, wide as a grave. For a moment, the only sound is the security system, logging every micro-expression and word.

At the moderator's table, Lt. Dojo maintains the regulation mask, but his eyes have narrowed. He's watching the room, not just for rule infractions, but for the way a wound can turn recruits into casualties.

Kaia feels sweat slick her palms, a tremor in her knees, the urge to scream, to run, to strike—but she stays still, lets the tension hang.

It's Tanner who cracks first, voice ragged around the edges.

"Spoken like a true Rebellion sympathizer. Hope you enjoy the audit."

Kaia doesn't flinch. She just breathes, once, twice, and sits.

The cameras record everything.

So does she.

The dismissal bell isn't a bell at all. It's a single note, synthetic, tuned to the frequency of spinal reflex. The moment it sounds, the recruits move: chairs scrape, shoes scuff, bodies exit in a rapid, orderly siphon. All except for Kaia, who stands at the podium, still as the redacted posters on the wall.

Her words hang in the air—"If we only protect what's sanctioned, we're not defenders—we're just another arm of erasure." The silence that follows is not just empty. It's deliberate. A tactical retreat by people who know the value of not being noticed when a purge is due.

Kaia doesn't look up as her classmates file past. Some keep their eyes forward, others glance sideways, quick and sharp, as if making note of a new variable in the room. The holoscreens have already begun cycling the next agenda, "Compliance as Community: The New Social Contract," but the lingering chill in the air belongs to her.

Yuki approaches, slower than usual. For the first time Kaia can remember, her gaze wavers, flicking from Kaia's face to the floor and back.

"You made some valid points," Yuki says, voice nearly swallowed by the hum of the reset projectors. "But... I mean, maybe next time—" She trails off, the rest of her advice dying before it's born. She gives Kaia a look that's not quite disappointment, not quite sympathy, then backs away.

Mikihisa tries to cut the tension. He sidles up with a crooked grin and says, "I told Yuki they should've issued fire extinguishers for this session, but they said it wasn't in the budget." He waits for a laugh. When it doesn't come, he gives a little wave, shrugs, and says, "Hey, uh, don't let the audit bots bite. You know where to find me."

He's gone before Kaia can reply.

For a long minute, the only people left are Kaia and Lt. Dojo. He's at the moderator's table, reviewing notes on his pad, stylus tapping out a rhythm that's too precise to be random. The desk lights cast his features in clinical blue.

Kaia starts to gather her things—note pad, data stick, the battered blue ribbon now wound so tight around her fist it's imprinting lines into her skin.

She's halfway to the door when Dojo's voice, smooth as fresh snow, stops her.

"Conviction without strategy is just noise, Recruit Mori," Dojo says, his voice smooth as fresh snow.

Kaia's hand hovers at the exit panel. She wants to keep walking, wants to leave it all behind. But she turns, meets his gaze, and says:

"And strategy without conviction is just compliance, sir."

He holds her stare for a second that feels like a duel, then looks down and resumes his notes, as if the matter is settled.

Kaia steps into the corridor, blinking as the harsh white of the seminar hall yields to the softer gloom of the outer hallways. The ribbon is still in her hand, and she clutches it, feeling the sharp edge against her palm.

She isn't sure if she's won—or merely inscribed herself into a new kind of isolation. But as she walks, spine rigid and shoulders squared, she knows the story isn't finished.

Not yet.

Chapter 19: Dojo's Ultimatum

The corridor after curfew held its own flavor of silence—different from the sanctioned quiet of lights-out, and nothing like the showy hush of the library stacks. It's dense and slightly electrical, as if sound itself might trip a sensor. Kaia's boots ticked the metal floor in a pattern that reminded her of the old clock in her mother's classroom, a relic that counted time by the death of its own gears.

The blue ribbon around her wrist—Hana's ribbon—snagged the overhead fluorescence every third step, reflecting a slice of color against her sleeve. She rolled it absently with her thumb, comfort and compulsion layered together. The hallway is a tunnel, just a shade too cold, the air moist and exhaled from a ventilation system that's been fighting the same war against mold since before Kaia was born.

At the midpoint, where corridor D intersects the admin annex, the lights change: the last few bulbs go orange, flickering in a way that makes the shadows move even when Kaia holds perfectly still. She knows she's not supposed to be out—not after the disciplinary, not after what happened in the comms hub—but the alternative is lying in her bunk, staring at the ceiling, counting the cracks between patches.

She's halfway to the service stair when he appears.

Lt. Dojo emerged from the dark like a judgment, not so much stepping as materializing, his uniform sharp enough to make a noise when he stopped. The fabric is the kind that never wrinkles, never stains; it fits him like a pronouncement. Every insignia is centered, every button closed to the top, the boots buffed mirror-bright. He blocks the intersection, arms folded, eyes unreadable.

Kaia's first reflex is the one they train for: blank face, eyes on a point just past his left ear, chin tucked. She thinks about her pulse, tries to slow it, but the ribcage has other plans.

"Recruit Mori," Dojo said. His voice was the same as in the seminar hall—measured, never raised, but with a gravity that made the room feel as though it was tilting toward him. "It's past curfew. Explain."

She wanted to make something up—a bathroom emergency, a summons from the night deck—but she could see from the set of his jaw that the window for lies was closed. She stands at attention, fists tight at her sides.

"I couldn't sleep, sir. I walked to clear my head."

Dojo's face is made of stone and angles, but the eyes narrow. "You're not authorized for unsupervised movement after disciplinary action. You know this."

"Yes, sir." The ribbon twists around her hand. Her tongue wants to say more, but she clamps it down.

He steps forward, closing the distance, and the scent of antiseptic and cheap cologne hits before his voice does. "After today's incident, you are on notice. This is not a warning, Mori. This is an ultimatum.

One more infraction—any infraction—and you're out. Not just the Academy. Out. You understand what that means?"

She knows. Expulsion from LDC isn't just a transfer. It's blacklisting, career death, a mark that follows you for life. If you're lucky, they reassign you to sanitation or data-mining. If not, you end up in the "special communities," teaching math to children who'll never ask why the answer is always less than zero.

Kaia nods. Her jaw aches from holding it shut. The memory of the last mission is acid: the girl's face, the blood, the evidence bag clutched so hard it left a bruise on her palm. The debrief had been a slaughter. Her actions weren't just reckless; they'd hurt civilians, and there was no way to explain it away.

But underneath the fear is something else—a suspicion that even Dojo's rules aren't built to protect people, but to protect the people in charge.

He waits, just long enough to let the threat marinate. "I expect better," he says. "From you. From all of you. The League does not tolerate emotional sabotage. You either learn to control it, or you don't belong here."

Kaia feels the heat behind her eyes, but doesn't let it show. The blue ribbon is a tourniquet now, cutting off the flow to her fingers.

"Yes, sir," she says, and the words taste like disinfectant.

For a second, she thinks he'll just leave. But Dojo stands there, studying her. His face doesn't soften, but something flickers at the corner of his mouth—almost a grimace, almost regret.

"There's a cost to defiance, Mori," he says, quieter now. "You want to change things, fine. But not at the expense of the people who count on you. Remember that."

He steps aside, the motion so abrupt it's like a switch flipping. The corridor opens in front of her, a straight line to the barracks, nothing in the way but her own shame.

Kaia doesn't say thank you. She walks past, her body a wire stretched to snapping. She waits until his footsteps fade, then lets her hands shake, just a little.

She pressed the blue ribbon to her lips, not sure if it was a prayer or a curse.

In the cold, echoing hallway, she keeps walking. She doesn't look back.

She's three meters past the intersection before the words come, unbidden, sharp as a knife turned in her hand.

"With respect, sir," Kaia said, not even turning around, "following every rule isn't always the right thing to do."

The echo hangs in the corridor. Dojo's footsteps stopped—she heard the slight scuff, then the measured return as he closed the gap. Kaia pivoted, slow, unwilling to seem eager for a fight but unable to just let it go. Her heart jackhammers, and her hands—traitors—shake as she folds them behind her back.

Dojo stands over her now, half his face shadowed by the flickering overhead, the other half drawn so tight it looks stretched over bone. For a moment, he just looks at her, a slow scan from hairline to boots. Kaia's uniform was crooked at the collar; there was still a trace of dried blood at the cuff, just below the regulation line. She resists the urge to smooth it down, knowing it would only advertise her nerves.

"Rules exist to protect people, Recruit Mori," he says, the words landing crisp and sharp. "Your impulsive actions put civilians at risk. You want to play at heroism, do it on your own time. Here, you follow protocol. Or you're gone."

The air between them is tight as a snare. Kaia breathes through her nose, letting the anger build just enough to keep her upright. "Permission to speak freely, sir?"

His eyes flicker—a microsecond of surprise, then the mask resets. "Granted."

She swallows, mouth dry as the edge of a slate. "If the rules really protected people, there wouldn't be a black market for memories. There wouldn't be children whose parents vanished for reading the wrong book. If I'd followed protocol in Sector 7, we would have lost three families. Maybe more."

Dojo's jaw flexes, a muscle pulsing at his temple. "You broke operational silence. You escalated a controlled situation."

"I saved lives," Kaia says, voice low, each syllable costing her. "And I preserved records that would have been incinerated if I'd waited. You talk about emotional sabotage, but what you're really afraid of is the story getting out of your control."

He steps closer, reducing the space to barely a boot's width. The corridor shrinks with them, the hum of the ventilation rising into a drone that makes the air vibrate between their faces.

"You think you're the only one who cares about truth?" Dojo's words fall quiet now, meant for her alone. "You think every day isn't a trade between what's right and what keeps us alive?"

Kaia holds his gaze, even as her vision blurs at the periphery. Her hands tremble so badly behind her back she's sure he must see. But she stands her ground.

"I just want to know what I'm protecting," she says, softer now, almost pleading. "And I want to know that it's worth the cost."

For a second, the lights overhead falter, plunging the hallway into brief, perfect black. In the dark, she hears his breath—a measured inhale, the kind you take before making a decision that can't be reversed.

When the light returns, Dojo's eyes are different: the anger still there, but something else layered beneath, something old and unhealed.

"Some stories cost more than you can afford," he says, voice rougher now, frayed at the edges. "And some scars don't make you stronger, they just remind you of failure."

Kaia nods, just once. "I'd rather have the scars than forget why we're here."

He looks at her for a long time, the line of his mouth flat, unreadable. Then, without another word, he pivots and walks away, boots making no noise at all.

Kaia sags against the wall, the blue ribbon digging into her skin as her lungs finally unlock.

She doesn't know if she's won anything. But she hasn't lost herself, and that's enough for now.

The wall behind her is cool, the seam of its panel pressing a line into her shoulder blade. Kaia waits for her hands to stop shaking, for the shame and anger to stop commingling in her throat. She can feel the old building hum, as if the ventilation ducts are carrying secrets from every room and sleepless recruit straight to this spot.

She almost misses it: Dojo hasn't left. He stands at the far end of the corridor, his profile carved into the dark by a single strip of light, his shadow thrown the length of the floor like a gnomon marking only lost hours. For a long time, neither moves. Then, slowly, he retraces his steps, head low.

When he stops, they're closer than before, the charged air crackling between them.

"I wasn't always like this," Dojo says. Not a confession—more a statement of chemical fact, something tested, found wanting. His voice is so low it almost blends with the background noise.

Kaia can't help herself: "No one is. We become what we have to."

He almost laughs, but the sound catches. "The first op I ever led, I let my guard down. Thought I could save everyone—civilians, my team, even the people we were sent to stop." His eyes flick to her, then away. "People died because I thought I could rewrite the script in the middle of the mission."

He touches his chin, and for the first time Kaia notices the scar: a pale crescent running just under the jaw, only visible because he's let his collar drop. It's subtle, but it's there—a badge not awarded, but earned in the ledger of failure.

"I've seen what happens when emotions override judgment," he says, and this time she can hear the years behind it, the whole unspoken disaster. "The stories never tell you about the ones who get left behind."

Kaia studies him, the way the light makes half his face look younger, almost unfinished. She doesn't respond with a wound of her own, or an apology—just the truth that won't let her sleep.

"And I've seen what happens when we forget why we're fighting in the first place."

The words hang between them—not a weapon, not a shield. Just a hand extended across the gap.

For the first time, Dojo meets her eyes and holds the look. In that space, the corridor shrinks to a room, the world outside gone to static. Something changes—a release of pressure, or maybe just an acknowledgment that the argument isn't about rules or stories, but about what survives when both fail.

He steps back, opens the way. "Prove me wrong, Mori," he says, a challenge but also a plea. "Show me there's another way."

She nods, the motion careful, as if afraid she'll break the spell. Then she walks, slow and straight, her shadow briefly overlapping his before peeling away into the darkness.

The blue ribbon is still tight around her wrist, but it feels different now—less a tourniquet, more a thread to somewhere better.

She doesn't look back.

Chapter 20: Library Zero

A fter dinner, the digital archive becomes a liminal place. It's too empty, too quiet—every cubic meter of air thick with ozone and the threat of being caught in a crime you haven't yet committed. At this hour, the other LDC recruits are clustered in the mess or blowing off steam on the upper decks. Kaia is alone, sweating through her undershirt, pressed so close to the server stack that her breath fogs the cold metal—each exhale a confession. The scar above her left elbow throbbed where it ground into the edge of a rack. She refused to move.

The blue ribbon was wound twice around her wrist, the ends ratty from years of habit. She flicked it with her thumb between keystrokes, like it was a metronome for her panic. On screen, the regular maintenance logs scroll by, the text in LDC Standard, columns neat and dead. But behind the logs, Kaia runs a shadow process—a tap on the real-time data feed for the central archive, flagged so deep it should have triggered a tripwire hours ago. If anyone upstairs is monitoring, she's already dead.

She's not expecting to find anything. That's the trick: you never do, until you do.

The anomaly appears as a blip in the packet flow, three times in two seconds, then gone. At first, she thought it a glitch—server-side clock drift, maybe, or the kind of ghost data that happened when old code and new hardware shook hands for the first time. She logs it, just in case. She wiped sweat off her forehead with the inside of her wrist, then shifted position, grinding the scar into the server until the pain sparked a sharp focus. She wipes sweat off her forehead with the inside of her wrist, then shifts position, grinding the scar into the server until the pain sparks a sharp focus.

A second anomaly, less subtle: a string of fragmented packets, the headers encrypted with a block cipher Kaia's never seen. Not LDC standard, not even close. The traffic is sharded, sprayed across three hops, then rebuilt at a node somewhere just outside their subnet. She leans closer, blinking to clear her eyes. The scar twinges again; she bites the inside of her cheek and pings the address, watching the echo. It comes back null, then again, then on the third pass a single, perfect line of data: partial coordinates, plus a string that at first looks random but, on closer read, isn't.

Kaia's fingers drum the keyboard, chasing the code across the monitor. The fragments don't fit the usual ops cadence, or even black ops cadence. They're half-broken, layered with a redundancy that's not for efficiency but for security. Every time she thinks she has the pattern, it inverts. She stares at the output for a full minute, tuning out the background hum of the servers and the whine of the overhead cooling. The line of code scrolls past again, this time with a tag at the end: "HX-03.17: See Also—Mori Protocol."

Her last name. Not a coincidence—not in this place.

The scar is a live wire now. Kaia glanced up—reflex, not logic—at the pair of security cameras planted in the corners of the archive. Their indicator lights are off, but she knows better. She opens a maintenance shell, mutes her own user log, and starts a local copy of the anomaly. Every muscle in her back tenses as she types, waiting for the room to go blue or for a shout from the hall. The blue ribbon cuts into her wrist until her hand starts to numb. She lets it.

The anomaly decrypts slowly, the server lagging as it tries to hash the packets into a usable string. She can feel the risk in every second that ticks past, a tightness in her chest like the air itself is collapsing inward. At the terminal, the fragments coalesce, then finally spit out a dump file: latitude, longitude, a truncated time-stamp. And then, at the very bottom, a four-character reference code that makes her mouth go dry.

ECHO.

Kaia remembers the stories from her mother—the ones she was never supposed to hear, the ones about hidden libraries and ghosts in the system that only the last generation remembered how to follow. She'd always thought they were fairy tales, a trick for falling asleep when the blackout panic set in, or a way to explain the things adults didn't want to say. But now, looking at the code, it's as real as the ribbon on her wrist or the scar under her sleeve.

She unspooled the ribbon, using it to cover the comm pad camera before sliding the encrypted packet onto her own drive. Every step is slow, careful, the pressure building as she checks her six, then the cameras, then her six again. The copy finishes. She double-deletes the temp files, wipes her own log, then resets the machine.

Half a second before she's done, the footsteps come: soft at first, then with purpose, echoing in the hollow concrete of the hall outside.

Kaia's hands race over the keys, closing the shell, dumping the packet analyzer, rerouting her connection to the diagnostic terminal. She jams the maintenance report up on screen, puts her hands behind her back, and tries to look bored.

The door slides open on a burst of light. A figure fills the frame—tall, squared-off shoulders, the kind of posture that expects rooms to make way. Senior Officer, judging by the bars. Kaia doesn't dare look directly at his face, but she can feel his eyes lock onto her like a targeting laser.

"Recruit Mori," the officer says, voice just this side of human. "Didn't expect to see you here after hours."

Kaia goes for the old standby: the blank, deferential expression. "Routine maintenance, sir. Diagnostics flagged a packet loss on the north node; I thought I could clear it before the morning shift."

The officer steps into the room, letting the door sigh closed behind him. The air pressure shifts; Kaia can feel the heat of him, even from five meters away.

"Funny," he says, walking a slow perimeter, "I didn't see a work order for the archive nodes."

Kaia kept her chin tucked, hands clasped at the small of her back. "I logged it as a soft fail, sir. Didn't want to trigger a full maintenance cycle for a minor glitch."

He stops two steps behind her, close enough to touch. She can smell the machine oil and whatever passes for cologne in the upper offices. "Show me the logs, then."

Kaia slides behind the terminal, calling up the sanitized diagnostic. She points to the appropriate lines, praying the lag in the server's cache didn't log her illicit activity. Her hands tremble a little. She flexes her wrist, letting the blue ribbon dangle in front of the monitor, hoping to sell the nervousness as the mark of a recruit too eager to please.

The officer reads the display, his breath fogging the side of her face. After a full thirty seconds—long enough for Kaia to sweat through her shirt—he grunts.

"Next time, route it through your supervisor. Chain of command exists for a reason."

"Yes, sir," Kaia says, just above a whisper.

He waits, expecting more, but Kaia keeps her eyes on the screen, hands dead steady now. Finally, the officer turns and walks to the door. He pauses there, the sensors flickering above his head, and looks back.

"Don't stay late," he says. "Nothing good happens in the archive after dark."

The door closes with a pneumatic hiss. Kaia's breath shudders free; her hands keep trembling for a full minute. When she's sure the cameras are reset to standard, she slides the thumb drive into the seam of her boot, erases the last traces of her log, and stands.

The scar on her arm aches, the skin hot and alive. The blue ribbon is a promise and a curse around her wrist.

She leaves the archive, double-checking every shadow and reflection in the corridor. The data burns against her ankle like a secret. She knows she's not safe, not really, but the risk is almost sweet. The urge to know—maybe to remember, maybe to prove the stories weren't all lies—outweighs the dread.

She thinks of her mother's voice, the bedtime tales, the way hope sounded when spoken softly, just for her.

Kaia walks into the night, the world outside the archive feeling wider, sharper, more dangerous than ever before.

Her dorm room, after lights-out, is less a sanctuary than a cell. At this hour, most recruits are already in sleep-sim or dead to the world, but Kaia's mind is in high gear and her pulse is climbing. The door locks with a click so soft only someone raised on paranoia could hear it. She stands, listening for footsteps in the corridor, before she moves to the single desk built into the wall and unlaces her boots.

The walls are off-white, the regulation kind that doesn't stain, doesn't show the traces of the lives passing through. Two bunks—one up, one down, Kaia's on top. The only personal touches are the row of battered books, their spines turned to face the wall, and the metal bookmark token hanging from a thread above the pillow. The air is sharp with disinfectant, layered over with the residue of Yuki's hair oil and the chemical tang of boot polish. Kaia breathes it in, lets it out slow.

She sits on the edge of the bed, legs bouncing with excess charge. Yuki is out—on night shift, or maybe playing cards with the upper-classmen in rec. For once, Kaia is grateful for the absence. She strips down to her undershirt, fingers tracing the scar above her elbow as it cools, then pulls the thumb drive from her boot.

She jacks the drive into her tablet, hands already clammy. The display flickers, then pulses as the packet reader loads. The data is still encrypted—nothing she didn't expect—but there's something about the error message that sets her teeth on edge. The script doesn't just reject her password; it returns a string of gibberish that looks almost like a taunt. The font is old, one Kaia hasn't seen since before she started at LDC, and the letters themselves seem to stutter and misalign as if the code is alive.

She glances toward the door, then at the tiny camera tucked into the corner of the ceiling. The admin AI is supposed to sleep-cycle after midnight, but everyone knows it's never fully dormant. Kaia pulls the blue ribbon from her wrist, drapes it over the lens, and sits cross-legged on the bed. Her knees crack as she settles in, but the pain is distant. She slides the tablet onto her lap, opens the code dump, and begins to work.

The encryption isn't LDC standard—she knew that already—but as she probes the blocks, something familiar nags at the back of her skull. The checksum is off. The logic loops on itself, then starts again, a recursive dance she's seen only once before: in the stories her mother used to tell, the coded lullabies Kaia could never fully forget.

She tries the first key: her birthdate. No dice.

The second: her mother's, plus the old apartment number. No.

Then she remembers the song—the one Hana Mori sang when Kaia was small and the blackouts lasted hours, the one with the numbers and the nonsense words. She sings it under her breath, letting the melody guide her fingers as she aligns the cipher's salt to the pattern. This time, the data shifts: the code unraveling with a slowness that feels both infinite and immediate. Lines of text scroll down the screen, and at the end, the word: "KEY?"

She looks at the bookmark above her pillow, the only thing she didn't surrender when she came to the Academy. It's thin, stamped metal, edges worn to a shine. Kaia plucks it from the thread, feeling the cool weight in her palm. She studies the ridges along its edge, the tiny pattern pressed into the face—barely visible unless the light hits it just so.

The password prompt blinks, a silent dare. Kaia presses the metal bookmark to the tablet's biometric pad. Nothing. She tilts it, aligning the longest ridge with the edge of the tablet, and tries again. Still nothing. Then, almost as an afterthought, she rotates the token, sliding it along the bottom of the device, just like her mother used to do with her old e-reader, back when stories came on glass and pixels instead of in code and ink.

The screen flashed blue, then black, before resolving into a cascade of numbers: longitude, latitude, and another string that looked like a time-stamp but in no format Kaia recognized.

Her heart stuttered. She blinked twice, hard. The data is raw, un-formatted, but it's clear enough: coordinates, and a reference code. She copies the numbers to a scratch pad, then overlays them onto the mapping app in her tablet.

The location lay in the middle of nowhere. Not a city, not even a township. The map labeled it "ADMIN EXCLUSION ZONE—ACCESS RESTRICTED." Kaia zoomed in, searching for detail, but the satellite layer was scrubbed clean—only a rectangle of gray remained, bisected by a line running north to south: an old rail line, dead for decades.

She tries the reference code next. It matches nothing in the LDC's open database, nothing in the League's, but when she pushes the search through the dark archives—a relic of the old city's net, only accessible through hacked proxies—she finds one match: a term she's only heard in stories.

"Library Zero."

She sits back, breath catching at the back of her throat. Her hands trembled, and she pressed them flat against her thighs to steady the tablet.

For a moment, there is nothing but the sound of her own heartbeat. Then the memories came, rushing in like a flood of data:

Her mother's voice—soft, urgent—telling Kaia never to trust a map that showed everything. The old man in the Academy's janitorial staff, slipping her a printout of a book page because "the original is always better." The whisper in the tunnels, the stories about a place that held everything the League erased.

Kaia's vision blurred. She wiped her eyes, unsure if she was crying or simply overwhelmed. The room is too small, the air too thick. She wanted to scream, but all she could do was breathe—inhale, exhale—just as her mother had taught her.

She closes the mapping app, re-encrypts the data, and tucks the thumb drive into a slit inside the bookmark's ribbon. Her legs are pins and needles, her chest tight. For the first time in years, she feels both terrified and—she can't help it—hopeful.

If the coordinates were right, then Library Zero wasn't a myth. It was real.

And she has the key.

Kaia sits in the dark, the blue ribbon coiled around her fist, and watches the seconds tick by until the sun rises. Every minute is an eternity. But for the first time in months, she knows exactly what she has to do.

Kaia times her move for the window between night-shift turnover and the first pulse of morning drills—when the LDC's attention, such as it is, is scattered to the winds and the lower archives are nobody's business but the ghosts'. She keeps her steps light, shoulders hunched, the bookmark token looped tight in one hand. The descent into the subbasement feels colder than usual, as if the air itself is closing ranks against her. Every stair is a mini-audible of static, and the metal railings sweat with the condensation of three generations' worth of missed maintenance cycles.

The lights are in emergency mode: red strips along the walls, half the fixtures flickering or dead. Kaia's face is thrown into sharp relief with every pulse, the shadows under her eyes deep enough to catch and hold the dark. She walks fast but careful, sidestepping the drifts of abandoned supplies—dusty cleaning bots, old racks of portable terminals, bins stuffed with cables and the brittle detritus of a thousand data updates. She knows the cameras here are real, but she also knows they're old, unpatched, and as easy to fool as a toddler with a sleight-of-hand.

At the far end of the corridor is the records room: a rectangle of reinforced plastic and wire mesh, locked with a keypad that's been sticky since the first year Kaia entered the program. She punches in the default code—she knows nobody's changed it—and slips inside, careful to let the door close slow, no noise. Inside, it's almost hot, the air thick with the smell of oxidizing circuit boards and the ghosts of a million erased files.

The terminal she's after is buried behind a bank of old, dead microfiche readers. She climbs over a toppled chair, boots crunching on glass, and powers up the station. It wakes slow, grinding through a century's worth of start-up errors before the screen flickers to life. She keys in her ID—this one's untraceable, a backup she built for exactly this kind of thing—and loads the mapping program.

She copies the coordinates from her tablet, then pastes them into the search bar. The interface lags, like it's choking on something it doesn't want to digest. The screen goes black, then resolves into a satellite view, the grid overlay painting the topography in angry red.

The coordinates drop a pin into a no-man's-land: a rectangle of scrub earth bounded on one side by the shattered bones of an old rail line, the other by what's labeled as a "Research Exclusion Zone." No buildings, no infrastructure, not even a single heat signature or comm relay. She zooms in, feeling the tension build in her fingertips. At maximum magnification, there's nothing but a featureless patch of gray, with a faint indentation—like a scar, she thinks—running north to south.

Kaia overlays the historical map. This time, the area lights up: a dense cluster of buildings, all labeled as part of a university research annex. Most are gone, wiped by the regime during the first consolidation. But one tag remains, barely readable through the layers of redaction.

Library Zero.

The words are a punch, but Kaia leans into it. She taps the tag, trying to expand the metadata. A single file remains, almost certainly a trap or a joke, but she can't help herself. She opens it.

At first, it's just a blur of numbers—old Dewey codes, probably—but underneath is a hand-scrawled annotation: "If you are reading this, the story isn't over. Find the wind, follow the thread."

She feels the bookmark heat in her palm, its ridges biting into her skin.

For a second, Kaia loses sense of the world around her. All she sees are the words—how they twist on the screen—and all she hears is her mother's voice inside her head, reciting bedtime stories in the dark. The security system's morning chime brings her back: a reedy, rising tone that signals the imminent arrival of real staff, real trouble.

Kaia works fast. She wipes the search log, scrubs the temp files, reroutes the cache dump to a dead sector on the oldest drive. She pockets a data stick with the coordinates, then powers down the station and crawls back through the obstacle course of ruined tech.

She's almost to the stairwell when she rounds a corner and slams straight into a body.

Lt. Dojo.

He's in full uniform, his face set to zero on the empathy dial. The collision is minor, but the impact is nuclear.

"Recruit Mori," he says, voice meant to wake the dead. "Early start."

Kaia keeps her face blank, blue ribbon tucked under her sleeve. "Prepping for drills, sir. I wanted to get in some study before the rush."

Dojo's gaze flicks to the data stick half-hidden in her fist, then back to her eyes. She can see him calculating, weighing the risk of pushing versus the risk of letting it slide.

"Archives open at six," he says. "You're nearly an hour ahead."

Kaia shrugs, letting the nerves show just enough. "I had trouble sleeping, sir."

A long beat. Then: "You always do," Dojo says, softer, almost a whisper. He studies her, the way a surgeon studies a wound. For a moment, Kaia wonders if he's going to arrest her, or just tell her to go back to bed.

Instead, he nods toward the stairs. "You'd better get moving. Wouldn't want to be late for formation."

She steps aside, the tension in her spine going electric. "Thank you, sir," she says.

Dojo stands there for a second, watching her go. "Some stories aren't meant to be found," he calls after her, his voice echoing down the hallway. "Be careful what you do with them."

Kaia doesn't slow down. She climbs the stairs two at a time, the data stick burning in her hand, the bookmark still pulsing with the memory of her mother's stories.

She doesn't look back, not even once.

When she hits the landing, she walks straight to her quarters, not stopping until the door is locked behind her. Only then does she breathe, slow and deep.

She has the coordinates, the key, and now the certainty.

Library Zero is out there. Waiting.

And Kaia will be the one to find it—even if it kills her.

Chapter 21: The Smuggler's Map

I f you stand still too long in the LDC Academy after curfew, you become infrastructure. Kaia keeps moving. Her boots barely whisper against resin-tiled floors as she slinks through the corridor's blue-black hush, hugging the wall like it could grant her sainthood. She counts the vent grilles overhead—the twelfth her mark. She kneels, pops the slats with a flick of a stolen torque key, and slips inside before the motion sensor can finish waking.

The air inside the shaft tastes of tin can and cold sweat, humidity thick enough to bead on her hairline. She twists around, pulls the grille shut, and secures it with a sliver of tape. Inside, it's too dark for sight, but her hands know the path: left, then a drop, then forty meters of crawl through a pipe that's just tight enough to scrape her knees raw.

She lets her weight slide with gravity, hands trailing along the upper seam to avoid loose rivets—every inch of this route mapped through weeks of insomnia. She passes the time by inventorying her gear: comm pad, three heat patches, the blue ribbon double-wrapped around her wrist, her mother's bookmark tucked against her skin under the collar. No weapon—better erased than burdened with traceable contraband.

Past the first junction, the shaft widens enough that she can stretch her shoulders. Rumor holds this duct once carried steam for the entire district, back when the city used water instead of forced air for temperature control. Now it's just a crawlspace for maintenance bots and, occasionally, a stubborn human.

She pauses at the next junction, listening. Down below, a pair of guards are running a shift change drill. She can hear their boots on the service floor, the jangle of their belts, the occasional suppressed laugh. Kaia waits, controlling her breath, slow and even. One of the guards jokes about the food in the mess—"If the synth meat gets any grayer, we'll all wear the same skin tone." They laugh, and Kaia feels the laugh in her chest like a tiny quake, not because it's funny, but because it's human, and for a second she misses being just another recruit, not a walking liability.

When the corridor is clear, she angles her body and drops to the next vent, a vertical shaft that plummets straight through three floors of admin. The trick is to take it slow enough not to catch the motion sensors, but fast enough to avoid detection. She braces her hands and knees, riding the friction down, landing soft on a ledge of fiberglass panel.

She's behind the waste-processing unit now. From here, there's only one more checkpoint—the service hatch at ground level. She crawls the last stretch, ignoring the fiberglass slivers in her palms, until she reaches the grate. A quick check: no one in the maintenance closet, no sign of the AI drone that's supposed to monitor these halls. She works the latch, swings it open, and slides onto the tile. Her shadow, cast by the night light above the washer unit, smears across the floor, less shape than stain.

Kaia straightens, dusts off her knees, and walks the service corridor like she belongs. Out the back door, onto the loading ramp, and into the city's damp underbelly.

Outside the Academy, the city feels like another species entirely. Here, every building is an afterthought, slabs of prefab concrete with decades of grime packed into the pores. The sky hangs low, angry orange, pulsing with the grid of floodlights meant to hold back dark. The streets are wet from a chemical rain that's part sanitizer, part crowd control. The runoff eats at the paint on her boots, leaving them scuffed and streaked like they're aging in real time.

She takes the old district perimeter, keeping to the shadow-side of the towers, careful to avoid the points where the streetlights overlap. Here and there, other silhouettes move—delivery bots, stray cats, people who know not to stare at faces after midnight.

Her destination is the old laundry block, two kilometers from the Academy's outer fence. The sign is still legible, if you know where to look: a stenciled "STAR-BRIGHT LAUND" with the "R" eaten off by rust. She ducks into the alley behind it, walks past the overflow of trash bins, and stops at a steel door painted a sickly yellow.

She raps twice, waits, then taps three short knocks. A click sounds inside, then the door hisses open on a wedge, just enough for her to slip through.

The inside is a sauna of ozone and wet dust. The light is blue-white, flickering from ancient strips nailed to the ceiling at random intervals. The main space is stuffed with hulking, dead washers, most turned into makeshift tables or storage bins for crates of paper, plastic, or things less legal.

Kaia heads for the stairs at the back. They're steep and rickety, patched with planks of mismatched wood. She descends to the sub-basement, the air growing colder and thicker with each step. Down here, the smell is different: raw toner, chemical fixative, the iron tang of solvent. A memory of her mother teaching her to sniff out forgeries returns, vivid and sharp—if it smells too clean, it's not real.

The printshop is a bunker, its walls lined with insulation made from recycled document pulp and, here and there, layers of old newsprint. In the center sits a massive, mutant printing press—a hybrid of antique rollers, repurposed document feeders, and a scanner bed the size of a coffin. A single lamp dangles above, casting harsh shadows that claw at the walls.

Vex is hunched over the press, feeding a spool of synthetic fiber into the intake. She's older than Kaia expected: maybe forty, maybe sixty, with a face so lined it looks etched. Her hair is buzzed short, the color of static, and her fingers are black to the knuckles with ink and carbon. Burn scars ride up both forearms, a road map of close calls and bad escapes.

She doesn't look up when Kaia enters. "You're late," Vex says, voice a gravely alto. "Security's been jumpy since the last memory-cull. You get followed?"

Kaia shakes her head. "I doubled back three times. No tails. The air's thick, though. They know something's coming."

Vex grunts. "They always do. Doesn't mean they know what." She finishes with the spool, then wipes her hands on a rag that's probably seen a hundred secrets. Then, finally, she looks up.

Her eyes are small and quick, reading Kaia in an instant. "You're the one looking for Library Zero?" she says, mouth twitching at the edge. "Dojo's pet project finally grew teeth."

Kaia's brain stalls at the word 'Dojo.' She lets it hang—unsure if it's a joke, a threat, or just a way to gauge her reaction.

Vex slides a printout across the bench—a slip of blue-tinted paper with a dozen coordinates printed in six-point font. "Don't look so shocked. The Literary Defense Corps talk shop like old men at a bar. Dojo's been poking at the dead zones for years. Difference is, you actually got close."

Kaia steps up, taking the paper, her hands shaking enough that she fakes a cough to cover it. "I didn't know—he never said—"

Vex laughs, a rusty cough. "Nobody ever says what matters, kid. They just make you chase it." She waves Kaia closer, voice dropping. "Show me the key."

Kaia pulls the bookmark from her collar, keeping it cupped in her hand. She hesitates, but Vex just holds out her palm, waiting.

The bookmark feels cool to the touch, its thin metal glinting dully in the blue light. Vex turns it over, running her ink-stained thumb along the ridge. She grins, crooked teeth exposed.

"Not a copy. That's real. Nice work." She tucks it under a reader lens, squints at the micro-etching. "Memory runs in your family, huh?"

Kaia nods, trying not to show how much her head is spinning. "It was my mother's."

"Then let's not waste it," Vex says. She shoves the bookmark back at Kaia and gestures to the side room, a tiny office littered with more printed scraps than floor. "Wait in there. I'll pull what you need."

Kaia obeys, stepping into the office. The chair sits too low for the desk, the only clean spot a square of faded linoleum beneath the window. She sits, hands in her lap, the blue ribbon sticky with sweat.

She tries to process the new information: Dojo was involved. Was he protecting her, or setting her up? The thought creeps in, poisoning her adrenaline high. But Kaia is too tired for paranoia; she'll get answers, then she'll run.

Vex returns within minutes, holding a battered manila folder and a sealed polybag. "There," she says, setting them on the desk. "Every map, every schedule, every cross-reference I could pull from the old League surveys. You've got one chance. When they realize you're gone, this whole district locks down."

Kaia flips the folder open. Inside are maps traced with faded ink, diagrams of rail lines and under-city tunnels. Some pages have notations in a script she almost recognizes—her mother's hand, or something close.

She looks up at Vex, questions boiling beneath her skin. "Why help me?"

Vex grins, wider now. "Because you asked," she says. "And because the League can't stand a story it didn't write."

She leans in, eyes sharp as broken glass. "You're going to find Library Zero, kid. And when you do, tell Dojo his old ghosts say hello."

Kaia's mouth goes dry, but she manages a nod. She gathers the folder, the polybag, and tucks the bookmark against her chest. She stands, legs steady now.

"Thank you," she says, voice small but growing.

Vex shrugs. "If you want to thank me, burn these walls down on your way out. This city needs a little more fire."

Kaia slips the materials into her pack, eyes flicking to the street beyond the grimy window before stepping back into the blue-lit bunker's main floor.

She walks out the way she came, moving through the chemical rain and the city's electric breath, the coordinates heavy in her pocket and her mother's ribbon blazing blue against her wrist.

She doesn't look back. But this time, she doesn't have to.

In the hours before dawn, the printshop pulses with a different energy. Kaia returns through the alley, past bins slick with rain and old bleach. The city's curfew never fully takes in these slums; if anything, the darkness is just an extra layer of plausible deniability.

Inside, the press hums like a sick animal. Vex is already up, eyes red and wired, a soldering iron pinched between her lips as she tinkers with a stack of battered circuit boards. The smell of scorched plastic blends with the ghost of last night's chemicals, a sensory warning sign that's somehow comforting now.

"Didn't expect you so early," Vex grunts, not looking up. "Good. Punctuality gets you halfway alive."

Kaia stands by the doorway, letting her breath slow. "Did you finish the forgeries?"

Vex grins around the iron. "Darling, I started on yours before you even called." She sets the tool down, hands black with conductive ink, and gestures at a bucket beside the press.

"Pull it up," she says. "No, harder. Don't let the friction scare you."

Kaia braces both arms and tugs. The bucket is bolted to a subframe; inside, behind a false wall, a metal panel covers a cavity stuffed with poly-wrapped bundles and something that looks like a frozen squirrel in a jar.

Vex shoos her aside. She jams her thumb into a print reader on the panel, and the whole assembly slides open with a pneumatic sigh. Inside: a clutch of microfilm canisters, two battered external drives, and a cloth-wrapped roll of aged paper, bound with an old-school wax seal.

Vex pulls the bundle free, then hands the rest to Kaia. "Maps. Real ones. From before they digitized the city grid. Most of these lines don't even exist anymore, except in the places that matter."

Kaia accepted the roll, reverent. She cracks the seal and spreads the paper on the scarred workbench. The maps are gorgeous and terrifying: spaghetti tangles of train lines and maintenance tunnels, annotated in three different hands. Some lines are crossed out, others highlighted in neon. Kaia's eyes lock on a set of coordinates, underlined three times.

"That's the entrance," Vex said, tapping it with a pen. "Old water treatment plant, decommissioned before you were born. Nobody scans it because it's flagged as hazardous. If you get in from the north, nobody will even ping you."

Kaia traces the route. The red line takes her under four city blocks, skirting the edge of what the map calls "Signal Blackout Radius." The label is hand-written, circled with angry loops.

"Why here?" Kaia whispered.

"Because you don't hide a bomb in the living room," Vex says. "You bury it in a graveyard."

She steps away, rummages through a drawer, and comes back with a blank white card and a heat printer the size of a sandwich. In seconds, she forges Kaia a transit pass, complete with fake name and an embedded chip. She hands it over, then starts on a matching one for herself.

Kaia kept her eyes on the map, running her finger over the faded lines until she was sure she could draw them from memory. "So Library Zero—it's just a backup vault?"

Vex laughs, sharp and dry. "It's the last backup. Physical media, nothing online. Rumor is, it's got a redundant core, and enough redundant stories to keep a generation angry. They built it so the League couldn't scrub everything, even if they burned the whole world."

Kaia looks up, heart running fast. "And nobody's ever gotten inside?"

Vex shrugs. "Maybe once. But nobody came back with proof. That's why you're here." She lowers her voice, glancing at the monitors that line the far wall. "League scanners are jittery this week. Someone high up knows there's a crack in the dam. If you're going, go now."

Kaia gathers the maps, the pass, and the tiny drive. "What about the comms blackout? I can't take half these devices through."

Vex gives a knowing nod. "That's the point. Once you hit the Blackout Zone, you're cut off. No calls, no signals, nothing. I've rigged this—" she holds up a thumb-sized black puck—"to give you five minutes of data burst. Encrypts everything, sends it out when you clear the Zone. After that, you're flying blind."

Kaia pockets the puck, then draws the blue ribbon tight around her wrist. "And if I don't make it?"

Vex meets her eyes, steady. "Then you're a ghost story. But at least you'll be a good one."

She hesitates, then reaches into her jacket and pulls out a second, smaller folder. "One last thing," she says, voice softer. "This is from Dojo. He asked me to give it to you if I thought you could hack it."

Kaia's throat goes dry. She takes the envelope, opens it. Inside is a single sheet: a letter, hand-written, with a code at the bottom. She recognizes the script instantly—her mother's. It's a memory protocol, just like the bedtime stories, but the ciphers are deeper, older, meant to survive more than sleep.

Kaia doesn't say thank you. She can't. She just holds the page to her chest, then tucks it safe inside her jacket.

Vex nods, then pushes her toward the back stairs. "Go. You're burning minutes."

Kaia didn't need to be told twice. She slipped out the back, into the wet morning, the maps and memories pressed tight to her ribs. The city is quieter now, the kind of silence that comes right before something irreversible.

She glances once over her shoulder. Vex is at the upper window, watching, making sure Kaia is clear. For a moment, the two lock eyes, and in that moment, Kaia understands the unspoken: nobody survives alone, not in this city. But if you can leave a trail, maybe someone else makes it out.

She walks the perimeter, counting steps, every turn bringing her closer to the old water plant and the blackout line. Every block, the world feels thinner, like a drum skin stretched too tight. Her heart pounds in time with the city's pulse.

She doesn't look back. But she knows the story's not done.

Not until the last library is empty.

The maintenance tunnel is cold enough to sting. Kaia shivers once and forces herself not to show it. She can already see Yuki's silhouette—motionless, arms crossed, boots planted as if daring the floor to shift under her. Mikihisa leans on a bundle of old wiring, eyes flicking between the corridor and the glow of his comm pad, every muscle telegraphing the urge to run or crack a joke or both.

"Two minutes late," Yuki said, without looking up. "Was it the guards or the weather?"

Kaia pushed the door shut behind her. "Neither. Vex wanted to be sure we weren't bringing ghosts."

"Smart woman," Mikihisa piped in, straightening. "We're definitely haunted, but at least we're punctual." He grins, but the smile is too sharp, too bright, the way a window shatters on the inside.

Kaia took a breath, steadying herself against the metallic tang in the air. She unwraps the folder of maps and spreads them across a workbench scavenged from the janitorial cache. The surface is sloped and stained, but it holds the weight of secrets as if born for it.

"Here's the route," Kaia said, tracing a finger along the faded lines. "We start at the north access, hit the blackout perimeter by the rail junction. Once we cross, there's no comms, no backup. We move fast, keep to the dry sections. If we hit water, we double back and try the secondary." She glances up, eyes flicking between Yuki and Mikihisa.

Mikihisa whistles, low and appreciative. "Is it wrong that I'm excited to see what a blackout does to our hair?" He preens, then shrugs. "Just saying. If we don't make it, I want my legacy to be memorable."

Yuki ignores the joke, as she always does. "The last crew that tried this lost all contact. League swept the sector for days, but nothing turned up. Not even rumor." She pulls a printout from her vest and slaps it onto the bench. "Failure means more than expulsion, Kaia. It means erasure. No appeals."

Kaia meets her gaze, the cold in her gut flaring hot to her chest. "I know the stakes."

Yuki holds the look for a full second, then nods. "Good. Because this—" she runs her hand over the map's edge "—is a one-way trip."

Mikihisa flexes his fingers nervously, trying to lighten the mood. "At least we'll have each other for company." He glances sidelong at Kaia. "Assuming the blackout doesn't fry our brains."

Kaia offers him the transit pass—a perfect counterfeit. Mikihisa holds it to the light, gives a low whistle. "My mother couldn't spot the difference, and she worked in doc control for twenty years."

Yuki examines hers, expression unreadable. "This will get us past the checkpoints. After that, we're ghosts."

Kaia finishes the distribution, then pulls the drive and the memory protocol sheet from her jacket. "These are the keys. If anything happens—" she hesitates, dry words catching in her throat—"get the message out. Even if I don't make it."

Mikihisa gives her a thumb's up, but it's softer now. "You're the boss, Mori. But if it comes to it, I'll drag you back myself."

A ripple of warmth stirs within her, but she clamps it down. This isn't about survival—at least, not for her alone. She glances at Yuki, then the tunnel ceiling, letting the silence deepen.

A buzz sounds from the upper hatch. Vex drops in, landing with a thud and a grimace. She wipes her hands on her jacket, checks the perimeter, then tosses a small black device to Kaia.

"Emergency beacon," Vex says, breathing hard. "One shot. If things go sideways, push the button. It punches through the blackout for eight seconds—no more, no less. Don't waste it."

Kaia turns the device over in her palm—heavier than it looks, cold and absolute. She tucks it into her boot, next to the blue ribbon.

Vex surveys the three of them. "You know what you're doing?"

"Not even a little," Mikihisa says, but it's bravado. He's scanning the map, double-checking every line.

Yuki clicks her tongue. "We're ready."

Kaia stands—her full height barely reaching Vex's chin—but in the tunnel she feels bigger. She rolls her shoulders, tightens her pack's strap, and fixes the route in her mind. She wishes, not for the first time, that her mother could see her now—fearless, or at least good enough at pretending.

"Let's go," she says.

They move together: Yuki in front, Mikihisa at the rear, Kaia between. The tunnel opens onto the city's underbelly, a gash of concrete and old rails. The air is wet, alive with the smell of ozone and old metal.

Above them, the city is waking. Kaia can feel the grid's heartbeat in the floor, the hum of power and anticipation. She closes her eyes for a moment, imagining the world beyond the blackout: a place where memory isn't a crime, where stories don't end with redacted pages.

She steps out into the pre-dawn dark, her friends at her side, the maps and ribbon and beacon all weighing her down just enough to keep her real.

The Blackout Zone is waiting. But so is the library, and the truth, and whatever comes next.

They disappear into shadow, their outlines merging—the story not yet written, but impossible to erase.

Chapter 22: The Blackout Zone

The edge of the blackout is not a line but a gradient—sound and air and color draining out of the world until there's nothing left but static and the urge to shiver. Kaia, Yuki, and Mikihisa huddled in the lee of an abandoned relay station, eyes drinking in the darkness as if it were a substance they would be forced to metabolize. Even Kaia's breath is careful, every exhale a negotiation with the silence.

No city noise out here, not even the subsonic thrum of the grid. Above, the only light is the chemical haze of the old aurora panels, most of them dead, the rest spitting a dirty green glow across the shattered concrete. To the north, the silhouettes of the transmission towers lean like broken teeth, their lines tangled in a geometry that even the League's survey bots can't be bothered to solve.

Kaia checks the map, a slip of paper gone damp from her palm. The ink from Vex's marker has bled into the margins, but the route is still legible: a zigzag between relay ruins, a shortcut through an access culvert, then a sprint across the open kill zone to the shell of the water plant. Her mother's bookmark peeked from her pocket, the polished edge catching the green light as if winking at her. She rewraps the blue ribbon on her wrist, tugs it until it cuts, then signals with a slow, steady hand: go.

Yuki's movements are glass-cutter precise—two steps forward, scan, a pause to check the passcard against the shadow of the checkpoint sensor, then another step. The fake transit chip glows blue for half a second, matching the pulse of the ribbon, before going dark. Yuki gives a minimal nod: clear. Behind, Mikihisa glides, careful to keep his center of mass behind the shield of Kaia's body. He sweeps the rear, posture relaxed but eyes never still. His right hand hovers at the ready—no weapon, but a coil of monofill line, the cheap kind that can cheese-wire through bone if you double it.

They move. Each step is rehearsed, but the world conspires to remind them how little rehearsal matters. Underfoot, the ground is littered with the exploded guts of old tech—fiber bundles, ceramic chips, bits of cable stripped by desperate scavengers. Kaia's boots crunch with every third pace, so she slows, letting Yuki set the cadence. Even so, the silence is greedy. It drinks up every sound, magnifies it inside her skull until her pulse drowns out thought.

At the halfway mark, the corridor narrows to a slot, framed by two broken transmitters. On the far side, a cloud of dust hangs in the dead air. Kaia breathes shallowly, the taste of ozone and hot metal raw on her tongue. She hears a distant click—sensor or rodent, she can't tell—and clamps down the reflex to freeze. Instead, she gestures Yuki onward, the signal a slow curl of fingers.

They clear the pinch point and duck into the ruins of a service alcove. The air here is colder, tinged with something almost sweet—chemical coolant, maybe, or the residue of some old leak no one ever cared to patch. Mikihisa whispered, barely moving his lips. "Bet you five creds we find at least one skeleton before we hit the fence."

Yuki doesn't bother to respond, just lifts her scanner and sweeps the next stretch. The LED shows nothing, then, on the right edge, a flicker: moving heat source, northwest, distance uncertain. She taps the unit, resetting, and it returns with a new signal, closer. She mouths the words: "MRB patrol. Two, maybe three."

Kaia's heartbeat spikes, the old familiar push-pull of fear and focus. She cycles her vision, scanning for movement, but the dark is too thick and the city's old ghosts too clever. The only thing that moves is a torn flag of insulation, waving from the next relay tower like a banner of surrender.

She tries to swallow but her throat is too tight. Instead, she looks to Mikihisa, who shrugs, then makes a face that says, I told you so, but also, It's okay, we've seen worse.

They settle into position, flat against the wall, eyes flicking between the approach and the fallback route. Time stretches out, not a second passing, not an hour, but something in between—an interval that lasts exactly as long as it takes for Kaia to regret every decision that brought her to this moment.

Then, footsteps. Not the soft, stalking steps of a friend, but the heavy, deliberate crunch of boots that know exactly how far their authority extends. Kaia sees them before they see her: three shapes, all in regulation black, armbands a shock of red in the green light. The lead MRB officer carries a scanner wand, its tip glowing with every sweep. They move in a disciplined wedge, boots leaving marks in the dust, faces hidden behind polarized masks.

Mikihisa leans in, breath warm against Kaia's ear. "Don't flinch, and they'll pass. The scanners are crap; they never ping the lower ducts."

Kaia nods, but her body is already half adrenaline, every nerve a live wire. She presses herself flatter, the rough plastic of the wall biting into her shoulder blade. Next to her, Yuki's eyes narrowed, lips pressed white. Even Mikihisa is silent now, every ounce of his energy devoted to stillness.

The patrol halts ten meters away. The officer on point raises a hand, silent command. The others fan out, scanning left and right. The wand passes within a meter of Kaia's hiding spot. For a second, the beam illuminates her boot, the blue stripe of her mother's ribbon fluorescing in the light.

Kaia held her breath. She counts the seconds—one, two, three, four. On five, the officer lowers the scanner, mutters something into his comm, and moves on. The patrol advances, boots fading into the tunnel's hush, red armbands receding until they're nothing but memory.

Kaia waits a full sixty count before exhaling. Mikihisa is first to move, flexing his hands to bring the blood back. "See?" he whispers, voice returning to its usual lilt. "All bark, zero bite."

Yuki shoots him a look of absolute murder. "If you ever breathe that loud again, I'll throttle you."

Mikihisa grins, but Kaia is still anchored by the afterimage of the scanner, the way it seemed to linger on her, waiting for an excuse to light up.

She closes her eyes, letting the tension drain. When they open, the map is still in her hand, its crease slightly torn, the route forward unaltered.

She signals: move.

They slide out from the alcove, every step now twice as careful, and head deeper into the blackout. The corridor ahead darkens, walls closing in, but Kaia finds she can breathe again.

The city's silence no longer threatens. It invites—to move, to remember, to outlast the story that wants her erased.

The second layer of the blackout is worse. The first is fear and ritual; now the world compresses—passageways narrow, time shortens, walls sweating under the strain of holding back consequences. Kaia's team breaks formation at the third junction, Yuki veering right to skirt the MRB's detection radius, Mikihisa doubling back to cover the tail. Kaia dives into the collapsed maintenance tunnel alone, the map's legend promising a shortcut but, from the look of it, more likely a deathtrap.

She crouches low, shouldering through the tightest spots. Glass underfoot slick with old oil, shards snagging at her pants and slicing the soles of her boots. Every crunch is a betrayal, but she can't slow—Yuki's voice is in her comm, a bare whisper: "MRB sweep has doubled. They're pulsing sector six."

Kaia ducks her head and pushes deeper. Tunnel light is limited to the red blinks of damaged fire safety panels—each an anxious heartbeat counting down to when real lights ignite and the world fills with uniforms. The air here is worse than outside—metallic, sharp, like chewing on old batteries. She thinks of the stories, the ones about rebels crawling these same ducts, but wonders if any of them ever survived long enough to make it mean something.

At a split, she hesitates—left is faster, right is safer. The voice in her head is her mother's: Never choose the shortest path, unless you plan to become part of it. Kaia turns right, almost slips on the incline, catches herself on a brace pipe.

Ahead, the tunnel widens. She can see a distant blue flicker—Yuki's beacon, set to strobe at the lowest safe frequency. Kaia's breath fogs in the cold, and the blue light gives it a phosphorescent glow. It's almost beautiful, if you could forget why you were here.

She's three meters from the rendezvous when her comm hisses to life—Yuki again, urgent this time: "They're onto sector six. Two groups closing from both ends. Less than sixty seconds."

Kaia looks back. The red glow is gone, replaced with the staccato sweep of search lamps—white, sterile, and unrelenting. The sound of boots on metal is not the precise step of a patrol; it's a full run, the way a predator closes in when it smells panic.

She flattens to the wall, eyes darting for a bolt-hole. Only one—a trash duct, half-blocked by a jammed safety grate. She grits her teeth, jams her fingers into the mesh, and heaves. The metal tears her knuckles open, but it shifts enough for her to slide through.

The crawl is tighter than anything she's tried, ribs compressed, lungs unwilling to expand. On the other side, it opens into a narrow vertical shaft. She drops silently, the impact jarring but familiar.

She lands in a graveyard of old hardware—tower cases, server racks, plastic crates filled with the bones of a hundred dead machines. She's not alone: to her left, a shadow stirs, Mikihisa's pale face grinning through the dark.

"Missed you," he whispers—a lie; he's terrified, sweat on his brow cold enough to freeze.

"Yuki?" Kaia mouths.

"Two levels up, locked in," he says. "She's trying to jam their comms, but they're using runners now. Human, not just bots."

Kaia nods. Worse than expected.

Then, from above, a faint click and the slow, sickening hum of a scanner wand coming to life. Mikihisa's hand is already on his wire, but his fingers tremble.

Kaia peeks up. The shaft is lit by nothing but the blue of Yuki's beacon, now repurposed to blind the scanner's optical range. The MRB runner at the top is using a hand-held—less powerful, but more accurate. He drops a flare into the shaft, the light a sickly green that eats up every shadow. Kaia ducks, eyes shut tight, then opens them to a nightmare in color-negative.

"Any ideas?" Mikihisa whispers, his bravado gone.

Kaia's mind is racing. She can feel the pressure—if they run now, they'll be swept up in the dragnet. If they wait, the runner will find them. The only way out is up, but that means exposure.

She pulls the emergency beacon from her boot, its casing slick with blood from her torn hand. She flicks the cap, feels the charge hum through her bones.

Mikihisa's eyes go wide. "Are you sure?"

"No," she says, but her hand is already moving. She sets the timer to fifteen seconds, then braces herself for the detonation.

The beacon pulses once, twice—then everything goes white; the signal spike so bright it momentarily fries every sensor in the shaft. Above, the runner howls and drops his scanner, the device clattering down and shattering at Mikihisa's feet.

Kaia grabs him by the elbow. "Move!"

They scramble up the old rack, using the broken struts as a ladder. Every move is loud, but it doesn't matter—their pursuers are blinded, disoriented, yelling to each other in the chaos.

They reach the top and roll onto the walkway. Yuki is waiting, already pulling a makeshift flash bomb from her kit. "Go!" she shouts, and the three of them sprint, their shadows huge and wild behind them.

At the next corridor, Kaia crashes into the wall, panting. Yuki presses close, her hand finding Kaia's and squeezing, just once, hard enough to leave a mark. They don't speak, but the message is clear: alive, together, not yet caught.

The MRB teams are still in pursuit, but now the advantage is flipped. The spike from the beacon has reset the comm grid; for a minute, maybe two, every pursuit algorithm will be working off bad data.

Mikihisa grinned, breathless. "Didn't think I'd see daylight again."

Kaia laughed, a ragged sound, but it felt good. She looks at her bleeding hand, then at the others, and for the first time tonight, she allows herself a glimmer of hope.

They press forward, slower now, careful to check every turn. The walls are tighter, but the threat is less—the patrols are regrouping, still reeling from the shock. Yuki's scanner says they're clear, at least for the next hundred meters.

Kaia led, heart thumping but steady. At the final junction, they pause, the weight of what just happened settling onto their shoulders. Mikihisa leans back, laughs again. "Do you think they'll ever learn?" Mikihisa asked.

Yuki shakes her head, but she's smiling, too. "Not unless they recruit smarter," Yuki replied, a faint smile tugging at her lips.

Kaia just closes her eyes, feeling the cold concrete against her spine, Yuki's hand still tight on her arm.

For a second, nothing else matters. Then the alarm klaxon blares, distant but getting closer.

They look at each other, resolve settling in.

"Ready?" Kaia says.

Mikihisa nods. "Always."

"Let's finish this," Yuki said.

And they're moving again, deeper into the zone, the memory of the near-miss burning in their veins.

The only way out is through.

It was less a dash than a collapse—Kaia's body a piston, legs numb and lungs burning, the world reduced to the corridor ahead and the storm behind. The blackout's final gauntlet is a maintenance shaft, barely wider than a coffin and slick with decades of grease and regret. Yuki leads the way, head ducked, arms folded tight to squeeze through the bottleneck. Mikihisa is last, dragging a length of copper pipe for leverage, breath coming in ragged bursts.

The MRB isn't searching anymore; it's hunting. Their shouts echo up the shaft, barking out coordinates and kill-box vectors. A moment later, the first warning shot ricochets off the wall, the spark so close that Kaia's hair stands straight from the static. She swore, then laughed, because at this point it was a better option than screaming.

Mikihisa grins, teeth stained with blood from a split lip. "Just like the simulations," he wheezes, "except with actual death waiting."

Yuki glanced back, face gray with effort. "Twenty meters to boundary. After that, their protocols tie their hands. Unless you want to be a martyr, keep moving."

Kaia didn't answer. She's running on pure muscle memory, every turn and crawl and lunge a sequence that's burned into her nervous system by years of drills and a lifetime of fear. The blue ribbon is still on her wrist, the bookmark still in her pocket, and somehow she's thinking about both—about what it would mean to survive, and what it would mean if she didn't.

The shaft narrows again, then drops, a three-meter chute into the unknown. Yuki goes first, sliding feet-first, landing with a hard grunt and a curse. Kaia drops next, bracing for impact but still jarring her ankles so hard she sees stars. Mikihisa, never the most athletic, hesitated for half a second, then just fell, letting gravity do the work. He lands on Kaia, knocking the air out of her, then laughs again, soft and incredulous.

On the far side, a hatch is jammed. Kaia and Mikihisa work it together, straining against the rust and the inertia of a thousand unspoken rules. Yuki leans against the wall, using her body as a shield while she hacks at the locking mechanism with a piece of scavenged wire.

The MRB was close now—close enough that Kaia could hear the snick of their safeties switching off, the low hum of a scanner ramping up There's no time for subtlety. Kaia plants her boots, braces her whole body, and throws her weight into the hatch. It gives, just barely, enough for Yuki to squeeze through. Kaia follows, then Mikihisa, whose left shoe tore off in the struggle but who didn't even slow.

They tumble into the open, onto a mesh walkway high above a cavernous expanse. The world outside the shaft is riotous—alarms blaring, lights strobing in patterns designed to disorient and subdue. Below, the plant's main floor is a chaos of metal scaffolds, water tanks, and catwalks. The boundary they need is on the far side, past a kill zone illuminated by spotlights and the muzzle flashes of the MRB.

Yuki is already moving, zigzagging across the walkway, her eyes locked on the one section of shadow not covered by a camera. Kaia is right behind, ignoring the pain in her knees, the taste of copper in her mouth. Mikihisa covers the rear, hurling the copper pipe at the first officer to crest the hatch. It hits with a dull clang, and the officer stumbles, but doesn't fall.

There's no time to think, only to move. At the midpoint, the walkway is exposed—a perfect shooting gallery. The first shot misses, the second is closer. Kaia feels the wind of it, the whistle at her ear. Then, all at once, they're at the end, the final door half-open, the world beyond an abyss of night.

Three MRB officers wait for them there, weapons up, faces lit by the blue strobe. Kaia sees the formation—the way they hold their ground, the way the lead officer keeps his feet slightly apart, just like Dojo taught her.

She doesn't falter. At the last moment, she cuts left, feints, then slides right, low and fast, just beneath the arc of the nearest weapon. She grabs the lead officer by the thigh, uses his momentum to flip herself through the gap, then comes up on the other side, winded but clear. Yuki is next, rolling under the second officer's aim, rising on the other side with her hand pressed to her shoulder, blood dark and seeping against the fabric.

Mikihisa is last. He barrels through, using his bulk like a battering ram. The officers close in, but Mikihisa is faster than he looks. He spins, grabs the wrist of the one nearest to him, and twists, sending the man over the rail. The others back off, not wanting to fire in close quarters.

They're through the door, into the open. The night hangs bruised violet, the air electric with the charge of blackout. Kaia can taste freedom—or maybe only the rush of not being dead.

She turns, catches Yuki staggering—face pale, hand pressed tight against the wound.

"Are you—" Kaia begins, but Yuki shakes her head before the question forms fully.

"It's a graze," she says. "Just keep moving."

Mikihisa helps Yuki, slinging her arm over his shoulder, and together they sprint for the fence line. The MRB is still in pursuit, but now the rules have changed—once past the perimeter, it's all politics and paperwork, no more shooting unless they want to answer for it.

Kaia leads the way, the map from Vex pressing like flame against her pocket. She doesn't look back, doesn't dare. Every muscle screams, but she pushes forward—feet pounding frozen mud, the world narrowing to a tunnel of focus and pain.

At the fence, Yuki produces the beacon again, still live from the earlier pulse. She taps it against the mesh, and for a moment the blackout field shorts out. The world beyond flickers, the sound of the city rushing back in, the sky above laced with the first hints of dawn.

They scramble through the hole, collapse on the other side, gasping for air.

Kaia rolls onto her back, staring up at the sky. It's the same city, but now it feels like a promise kept—rather than one broken.

She sits up, checks on Yuki, who is already bandaging her arm with a strip of shirt. Mikihisa lies on his side, clutching his ribs and laughing, the sound of it raw and beautiful.

"We made it," Kaia says, the words strange and unfamiliar in her mouth.

Yuki grins, teeth bloody. "For now."

Mikihisa nods. "They'll be right behind us."

Kaia says nothing. She pulls the map from her pocket, unfolding it with shaking hands. The route to Library Zero is still there, the ink smeared but legible.

On Yuki's comm pad, the coordinate pulses—a single blue dot, bright and persistent.

"Let's go," Kaia says, and this time there's no hesitation.

They stand, battered but whole, and melt into the dawn, the sirens behind them fading to a memory.

Ahead, the road is long, and every step is borrowed time.

But Kaia knows this story is hers, now, and she's not going to let it end.

Chapter 23: Echoes of Ink

They find the entrance at dawn's blue edge, beneath a flyover charred by two revolutions' worth of exhaust and riot fire. The subway platform above is a shell—cracked tiles, pillars barnacled with ancient gum and propaganda posters that have outlived their propagandists. Kaia's team slips in through the mouth of a tunnel disguised as a commuter dead end, feet splashing briefly in runoff before the city's noise drops out and the corridor swallows them whole.

It's colder inside, the concrete sweating chill even in spring, but the air is bone dry. Mikihisa whistled—a soft, two-note trill, cut short when Kaia shushed him with a sharp glance. The blue ribbon tied around her wrist was flecked with mud and something darker, yet it still marked her as the vector for movement. She leads.

Yuki follows, silent, eyes flicking from shadow to shadow, cataloguing every bolt and power cable as if the world might snap and strangle them at any second. Mikihisa covers the rear, pausing at every turn to dust the prints out of their path with a ragged glove. He's all bravado, until the silence makes him honest.

At 400 meters, the access tunnel forks, one side collapsing into a vertical split, the other marked with a faded stenciling: "Archives—Zone Epsilon." Kaia stops at the threshold, thumb pressed hard to the mother's bookmark under her collar. The metal is warm from her skin, cold from memory.

"This is it," she murmured, the words muffled, swallowed by decades of lost sound.

Mikihisa cracks a smile. "If we're breaking into a tomb, I expect at least one mummy or a haunted librarian. I call dibs on the first curse." It was a weak joke. Nobody laughed.

The corridor beyond is a time-capsule: dead bulbs above, glass bricks letting in just enough of the world's leftover light to outline the contours of old benches and the glazed tile mosaics spelling out stops no living passenger has ever used. They follow the line deeper, their flashlight beams slicing the dark into wedge-shaped pieces that never quite rejoin.

At the first checkpoint, a set of blast doors hangs partly open, gears jammed with the fossilized guts of a security drone. Kaia nudges it aside with her boot, careful, and it crumbles like a bird's skeleton. The silence after is so total it feels engineered.

"Stop," Yuki whispers, hand out. She kneels, scanning the floor. In the dust, a perfect, untouched line—like something swept it clean, very recently.

Kaia crouches, glancing back. Mikihisa shrugs, then kneels beside her. "Air currents, maybe?" But even he doesn't believe it.

They step over the line, single file. The next stretch is narrower, walls thick with piping and insulated cable, every conduit banded in color code. Here, the air grows richer, tinged with the slow-rot perfume of old paper and glue. Kaia's pulse quickened threefold. She remembered her mother's stories—libraries so vast you had to ride a train between sections—and wondered if this was where those tales had been born.

The first intact shelf takes them by surprise: an alcove carved into the wall, its grid of compartments filled edge to edge with books. Actual books, not the sanitized League printouts but real, ragged survivors—leather-bound, cloth-bound, spines cracked or gold-leafed, titles in a dozen languages and three scripts Kaia can't read. Some are banded in plastic to keep them closed, others tagged with handwritten warnings or catalog codes faded to near-invisibility.

Kaia stepped closer, every muscle bracing for the shelf to dissolve at her touch. It did not. She runs a finger down a spine, and the dust comes away in a single soft peel. The title is familiar—she'd heard it as a bedtime story, years before the cull. She lifts the book, slow, reverent, and for a moment the weight of it makes her dizzy.

Mikihisa leans in, trying to mask awe with a smirk. "You know, Mori, I always figured you'd loot a bank, not an old library." He picks a book at random, flips it open, and the crack of the ancient glue echoes down the hall. "Hope you're up to date on your fines."

Kaia ignores him, thumbing through the pages. The smell was sharp, almost electric—nothing like the memory-foam reek of League textbooks. It was the scent of lost things refusing to stay buried.

Yuki lingers a step back, gaze fixed on the far wall, where the library's own map is embedded in tile. It shows three rings, stacked concentrically, each labeled with an old-world number and a set of codes she recognizes from Academy data dumps. Her finger traces the route: they are in Section One, near the edge. The inner circles promise deeper secrets, more dangerous archives.

Mikihisa sets down the book. The joke is gone from his voice. "Did we just become history?"

"Not if we do this right," Kaia says, and the steadiness in her tone surprises even her. She tucks the volume into her pack, careful not to crease the spine, and gestures forward.

The trio moves as one, light bouncing ahead, shadows trailing behind. Every few meters, another shelf appears, some ransacked, others untouched. The further in they go, the less dust, the more intentional the order. It feels less like an abandoned site and more like a place kept in waiting.

They pass a row of workstations, keyboards yellowed and keys brittle, screens covered with film to protect against some long-ago epidemic. On the nearest desk, a hand-written note, preserved in a sheet of plastic:

"Take what you can, but leave what matters. The story is not the shelf..."

Kaia reads it twice, then slips the note from its sleeve and tucks it into the front of her jacket.

They reach a larger room—maybe once a reading hall, now stripped of all but the lowest shelves and a scattering of battered chairs. Here, the light is better: a trickle of sunrise leaking through cracks in the ceiling, fanning out into geometric patterns on the floor. The dust motes caught in the light moved with such slow grace that, for a second, Kaia could almost see the old world—students bent over books, a librarian dozing at the front desk, the calm expectation that time could be trusted to flow forward.

Mikihisa circles the perimeter, hands deep in his pockets. "If we live through this, I'm starting a book club. Rule one: no books that end with everyone dying."

Yuki offers a rare smile. "That's not a real book club."

"Then we'll start our own genre," Mikihisa says. The humor lands better this time—familiar, a thread through the unknown.

Kaia explores the shelves, letting her fingers read the titles—anthologies, atlases, poetry in spines so faded they might as well be blank. Every so often, she finds a book her mother had referenced—a rare, forbidden treasure—and her chest aches with the weight of it. Shelves upon shelves hold worlds and stories Kaia's never even imagined.

She remembers the last story her mother told her, the one about "the library at the end of the world, where every lost page finds its way home." Kaia smiles, then clamps it down, because the air here is sacred and she doesn't want to disturb the ghosts.

They move onward, deeper, each step shedding some of the outside world's tension. The threat of pursuit lingers, but now it's dwarfed by the enormity of what they've found.

At the next intersection, Kaia stops. The passage ahead is caved in, but through the rubble she spies another alcove, this one lit by a working emergency light—a faint orange glow that somehow makes the room feel warmer. She squeezes through, careful not to disturb the fall, and finds a shelf lined with journals, each dated and marked with the same librarian's careful script. The first volume is open, a pen still resting in its gutter.

Kaia reads a few lines, and the world contracts to the size of the desk.

"Day 3,108: The others are gone. I sort the new arrivals, even if no one will come for them. I dream the words aloud so they won't vanish when I do."

She traces a finger beneath the lonely scrawl. For a moment, Kaia forgets the mission, the world outside, even her own body. She is the last librarian, keeping the words safe for whoever is left.

When she looks up, Mikihisa and Yuki are waiting, silent, in the hall. Neither calls her back. They know the rhythm of her absorption, how every story she reads becomes a limb.

Kaia replaces the journal, tucks the pen under the spine where it belongs, and backs out.

She looks at her team, dusted in the first honest sunlight the room's seen in years. They're scared, but they're here.

"Let's finish it," Kaia says. This time, no one jokes.

The story will not end here.

The next door is a vault—literal, not metaphor. Steel thicker than a handspan, hinges engineered to outlast the regime that sealed it. But someone long ago left it ajar, and the gap is a mouth that begs to be fed. Yuki steps in first this time, her presence contracting the space into something manageable. She sweeps a flashlight in a steady arc, and the beam lands on a brass plaque: "Central Archive—Access All Stories."

Mikihisa whistles, a real one this time, long and low. "All stories? We're gonna need a bigger bag."

They enter. The chamber is vast, round, like the inside of a bell. The ceiling arches so high the top vanishes in dark, and the walls are ribbed with shelving that runs from ankle-height to far above their reach. Every shelf is packed: books, folios, bundles of paper tied off with old string, boxes marked in the livery of ten vanished city-states. There is no dust here. The floor is swept, the space maintained in a stasis that feels deliberate.

In the center of the room, under the dead gaze of a crystal chandelier, stands the analog card catalog. It is a monument to lost bureaucracy—hundreds of small drawers, each with a tarnished metal handle and a handwritten label. Kaia circles it, unable to resist. She pulls open a drawer at random; the scent of paper and wax strikes her like a memory. Each card is written in a different hand, some neat, some frantic, some in alphabets she knows only from the stories her mother smuggled under her pillow.

Yuki drifts to the far side of the circle, where a row of low shelves forms a horseshoe. Here, the books are smaller, softer-bound, many with illustrations stamped on the cover. She kneels, picks up a thin volume, and turns the pages with trembling fingers.

"Children's section," she says, voice flat.

Mikihisa edges closer, peering at the titles. "Bet these are the most dangerous books in the room. Start 'em young."

Yuki ignores him. She sets one book aside, then another, her movements growing sharper. Kaia watches from the catalog, alert to the shift in air. She knows Yuki enough to recognize when she's about to break, but she doesn't move. Not yet.

Mikihisa, left to his own devices, picks a shelf at random. He's drawn to a spine marked in blue foil—a manual, it turns out, for analog radio communication. He flips through it, scanning diagrams, and his eyebrows go up.

"Kaia," he calls. "You gotta see this. Some of this tech—hell, half the resistance would sell their grandmothers for a copy of these protocols. This is old-world, pre-grid." He glances up, smile twitching at the corners. "You think Dojo would let us print a few before we torch the place?"

Kaia joins him, taking the manual. The diagrams are simple, the instructions clear. It's a transmission scheme designed to evade even the most advanced signal-jamming. She remembers the countless failed attempts by the LDC to keep their channels open during blackout events, and how the MRB always seemed a step ahead. Maybe, she thinks, they were never fighting fair—maybe the real weapons were always buried in places like this.

She sets the manual down, crossing to Yuki, who now sits on the floor, surrounded by a semicircle of children's books. Yuki holds one open in her lap, eyes fixed not on the words but on the illustration: a brother and sister, standing hand in hand at the edge of a wild forest.

Kaia kneels beside her, careful to keep a respectful distance.

"It's the same one," Yuki says, voice gone thin. "My brother—he used to read it to me. I thought... I thought I was making it up, that it wasn't real, just a dream." She swallows, jaw tight. "They took him. I thought if I remembered hard enough, I could bring it back."

Kaia wants to say something comforting, something that won't feel like a betrayal of all the loss. Instead, she just nods. "It's here," she says, "and so are we. They didn't erase it."

A silence, then Yuki slams the book shut and wipes her eyes with the back of her hand. "Fuckers," she says. "They can kill the people, but they can't kill the stories."

Mikihisa chimes in, quieter. "Yeah, but they'll try. That's why we're here."

Kaia stands, scanning the shelves. She feels unmoored—half a minute ago, she thought she was on a scavenger hunt; now she's staring at a mausoleum for every memory the world ever had. She finds herself back at the card catalog, hands drifting to a drawer labeled "Personal Papers—Librarian." She slides it out, and in the front sits a journal, bound in battered maroon, the cover embossed with a name:

"Emiko Mori."

Her pulse drops. The room tilts.

She opens the journal, skimming the first page.

"To whoever finds this, the story is not yours alone. We kept what we could, for as long as we could. When the laws changed, when the censors came, we made ourselves keepers—not just of books, but of what mattered. We hid what we could not burn, and we taught the stories to each other, so even when they found the shelves empty, they'd never know how much was left behind."

Kaia runs a thumb over the writing. The hand is not her mother's, but the cadence is familiar—perhaps a cousin, an ancestor, maybe the last to remember how a story can survive by hiding in plain sight.

She flips to the end. The last entry is scrawled fast, the ink blotted.

"March 10: Final access. The new patrols are at the gate. We have done what we can. Maybe they'll think it a tomb. That would be funny—so much life in a grave. If you are reading this, you are proof the lie didn't hold. Take what you need, but don't forget to leave something for the next one. Good luck. /E.M."

Kaia closes the journal, clutching it tight against her chest. She wants to sob or laugh or scream, but the only thing that comes is resolve. She tucks the book into her jacket, right beside the blue ribbon.

Yuki and Mikihisa stand with her now, the three of them bracketed by stories on every side.

Mikihisa holds up the radio manual—like a trophy. "Maybe this will actually help us get a signal out. If we live to see the next sun, I say we have a party. Real food. Real stories. Invite the whole fucking city."

Yuki nods, and for once there's no acid in her tone. "Just promise we don't read anything with a happy ending."

Kaia grins, despite herself. "Those are the rarest ones," she says. "But I'll see what I can do."

They work their way around the chamber, taking only what they can carry. For every book, manual, or note they pocket, they leave another in a safer spot—honoring the pact of the last librarian. The pile at the children's section grows—a tiny shrine, maybe, to Yuki's brother, or to everyone who ever vanished for loving a story too much.

At the edge of the room, Kaia stops. A door stands apart from the others—heavier, not locked, just wedged shut with a scrap of wood. She glances at the others, then opens it.

A spiral staircase, metal steps frosted with condensation, leads down.

"Do we go?" Yuki asks, eyes still wet but sharper now.

Kaia nods. "If there's more, we find it—that's the job."

Mikihisa offers an overblown sigh, but his eyes are alight. "Down the rabbit hole. Figures."

They descend. The air grows colder, tinged with the electric stink of old servers. At the bottom is a single door, marked "Backup Core."

Kaia is the first to step inside.

The room is small, almost cozy, lined with stacks of tape reels and more card catalogs. At the center is a machine—a compact, analog-computer hybrid, all dials and paper tape. The console glows faintly, still powered by a battery older than Kaia herself.

She sits at the console, staring at the interface. It's not encrypted—just old, stubborn, a relic of a time when secrets were kept by making them incomprehensible.

Yuki and Mikihisa crowd in behind her.

Kaia pulls up the menu, and a text prompt blinks:

"Would you like to retrieve a story?"

She laughs, a dry sound echoing the room itself. "Hell yes," she says, typing in the first word that comes to mind:

"Mother."

The console clicks, whirs, and spits out a strip of paper tape, the message rendered in dot matrix:

"Story: Hana Mori—The Keeper's Daughter."

Kaia's hands shake. She feeds the tape into the reader, and the machine prints out a page. She tears it off, reads aloud:

"In the beginning, there was a girl who remembered. She did not know why, or how, only that it mattered. The world did its best to teach her silence, but she learned instead to hide her voice in the cracks between rules. When the time came, she did not run. She opened the door, and inside, the library was waiting. She would not let it end. Not ever."

Yuki leans over, reading the page. "Your mother was smarter than all of us combined."

Kaia tucks the printout into her sleeve. "She just had more time to practice."

They stand in the backup room, surrounded by the hum of dead tech and the presence of every person who ever refused to forget. Kaia glances at her team, at the manuals and storybooks tucked into their packs, at the card catalog drawer still open above.

She looks around; the room seems to breathe with her.

"Ready?" she asks.

Yuki nods, fierce. Mikihisa grins, alive.

They go back up the spiral, into the ring of stories, and toward whatever comes next.

This is what they're fighting for—not just survival, but the memory of what came before, and the hope that it might all mean something, even if nobody ever knows their names.

They climb back into the main archive, arms loaded, nerves raw. The room seems different now—more alive, as if their passage has pulled air into its hollow lungs. Mikihisa dumps his load of manuals onto a reading table and drops into a chair, feet propped, grinning like he's cracked a safe. Yuki lingers by the children's shelf, restacking the books with a care that looks almost like prayer.

Kaia paces, scanning the perimeter for anything they missed. The light has changed, too, harsher, slanting in through the broken high windows and catching on motes that swirl in unpredictable eddies. There's a smell, faint but sharp—a chemical that doesn't belong.

She's the first to spot it: a scuff of fresh mud on the otherwise immaculate floor near the opposite wall. It could be old, but Kaia's spent enough time in the tunnels to know the city's mud never dries. She kneels, pressing a finger to the print. It comes away wet, the residue fresh.

"Someone's here," she breathes.

Yuki stiffens. "Patrol?"

"Doubt it," says Mikihisa, standing slow. "No one gets past those sensors without tripping a million alarms. This is local." He sweeps the shelves with a quick glance, like a bouncer scanning a club for trouble.

Kaia circles the room, checking for other signs. At the far wall, near a glass-fronted case labeled "Rare Materials," she finds the wrapper: matte silver, torn ragged, the kind you only get with energy bars imported from the outer isles. This is not a snack you buy at a city bodega. It's contraband, and recent.

She flashes the wrapper to the others.

Yuki's eyes narrow. "We split. Cover more ground. If they're a runner, they'll hide. If they're a plant, they'll be waiting."

Mikihisa fakes a yawn, but Kaia sees the knuckles blanch white on his pocketed fists. "Just say the word. I'll play fetch."

Yuki takes the children's aisle. Mikihisa cuts left, sticking to the wide corridors that arc through the outer ring. Kaia is drawn to the spiral staircase again, but not the way down—this time, up, toward the mezzanine she'd barely noticed before.

The upper floor is narrower, lined with glass-walled cubicles and study rooms, each labeled in a hand-written scrawl. Kaia's boots are silent on the carpet, but her breath seems to echo, every inhale a trumpet. At the third door, she pauses: a reading room, its interior perfectly preserved, as if the last user just stepped out for tea.

Inside, the dust is thinner. The table at the center is littered with open folios, some blank, others covered in a jittery, urgent hand. She scans the text—resistance manifestos, dating back to the first days of the crackdown, names that never appear in LDC curriculum.

Her heart kicks. She recognizes one: "Sumi T. —If you read this, burn the rest."

Kaia flips through the pages, scanning faster now. Every few sheets, a name she knows, a voice she's heard before in whispered fragments and forbidden bedtime tales. And then—

There it is. Her mother's name, signed in the old style. Not as a minor note or co-signatory, but as the author of the first ten pages. The manifesto is concise, logical, a blueprint for survival and memory. Kaia reads, not breathing, as the words unfold:

"We are the stories we save. If they come for the books, teach them. If they come for the teachers, become one. If they erase the memory, remember harder."

She runs a trembling hand across the page. She'd always believed her mother was an accidental casualty, a bystander to history. Now, the evidence is clear: Hana Mori was a founding architect of the resistance, not just a participant, but the voice that gave it direction.

Kaia closes her eyes, biting her lip until the taste of blood blooms. She feels the world recalibrate—her own history, her mission, even her loyalty to the LDC—all of it suddenly in flux, remade by this truth.

A footstep sounds in the hallway—quick and light. Kaia tenses, slides the manifesto into her jacket, and presses herself against the doorframe.

The shape that appears is small—barely a teenager, hair in a bristly cap, clothes too big and stitched with utility. Kaia holds her breath, waiting for a flash of steel or a dart of alarm.

But the intruder just slips to the next cubicle, head down, moving fast. Kaia follows, silent, until she sees the hands—delicate, ink-stained, clutching a book to her chest.

She steps out, blocking the narrow passage. "What's your name?" Kaia demands, voice sharp.

The kid jumps, then freezes, eyes wide and wild. "I'm not with them," she whispers. "Please. I just wanted—" Her voice cracks.

Kaia keeps her stance aggressive, but softens her eyes. "Wanted what?"

The kid lifts the book. It's a battered children's story, the same one Yuki found below. "My sister used to read this," the girl says. "I thought if I could find it again, maybe... maybe I'd remember her voice."

Kaia lets the tension drain, knowing the logic is her own. "What's your name?" she repeats, quieter.

The girl hesitates, then: "Jun."

Kaia nods. "You can stay, but you have to help us. There's more at risk than you know."

Jun's jaw sets. "I know more than you think," she says, steel unmistakable in her tone.

Kaia gestures to the stairs. "Come on, then."

They descend together. At the bottom, Mikihisa and Yuki are waiting, both with the charged expressions of people who have seen something impossible.

"We found it," Mikihisa says. "The vault."

Yuki points. "End of the hall. It's not on the map. Some kind of… time-locked security. We think it's been running since the day they sealed the place."

Kaia feels the old rush of panic and possibility. "Show me."

The vault is a glass box, set flush into the wall at the corridor's end, lined with portraits of long-dead librarians. The door is transparent, the inside lined with rows of digital media—solid-state drives, optical cards, even a bank of microfiche, all cabled to a chunky console that hums with a low, angry power.

Yuki is already at the panel, fingers flying. "It's running a biometric lock—DNA and voice, old-style. Needs a match from the original staff."

Kaia looks at Jun, who stares at the vault as if it were forbidden fruit.

Jun's eyes flicker. "My father worked here. He used to bring me on night shifts after the city went to sleep." She steps forward, pressing her palm to the pad. It glows blue, then white. The machine chimes, a gentle, musical sound.

"Match confirmed," the console says. "Jun Emiko. Welcome."

The glass slides open, silent. The scent inside is ozone and lost decades.

Mikihisa lets out a breath. "So what is it? Just more books?"

Yuki shakes her head. "Not just books. This is a digital copy of everything on the shelves. Updated continuously. If we get this out, we can rebuild the archive anywhere."

Kaia feels possibilities unspool in her mind: the resistance, the city, the world—all changed, if only the stories can be re-seeded.

But the risk is immediate. The vault is built with a failsafe—trigger the wrong sequence, and the drives will wipe. There's no time for error.

"Can we extract it?" Kaia asks.

Yuki scans the cables, tracing the lines with a surgeon's care. "If we pull the main drive, we'll have to run. The security will ping the city grid, maybe trip every alarm on this block."

Mikihisa's smile is gone. "We get one shot."

Jun cradles the children's book in one arm, the other hand trembling on the panel. "Let me do it," she says. "My father taught me the failsafe. I can buy you thirty seconds."

Yuki hesitates, then nods. "We'll need all of them."

Kaia watches the three of them—Yuki, Mikihisa, Jun—as they coordinate the heist of a lifetime. She stands by the door, the manifesto in her jacket, her mother's words in her head.

She wonders if this is how it felt for Hana Mori, all those years ago, making the choice to save what could not be saved.

The sequence moves fast. Jun keys in the code, her voice steady even as tears run silent down her face. The drive pops out, heavy and cold. Yuki wraps it in a sleeve from her own jacket, hands it to Kaia.

"Go," Yuki says. "Now."

Mikihisa grabs the manuals, Yuki shoulders the rest of the books, and Jun pulls the emergency lever, locking the vault in a permanent loop. They sprint down the corridor, Kaia leading with the drive pressed tight against her ribs.

At the exit, Kaia looks back. The library is still, the stories undisturbed, but in the silence she hears the pulse of the world's memory rebooting, the possibility of a future built from words instead of wounds.

They burst into the morning, sunlight catching the blue ribbon at Kaia's wrist. The city wakes, and somewhere out there, alarms are already starting.

But Kaia is not afraid.

She has the story. She has the team. And she has, for the first time, the knowledge that every risk is worth it.

They run.

Chapter 24: The Betrayal

T he LDC debrief room feels colder than necessary. Some design
flaw in the air system, or a deliberate choice to keep returning
agents one degree off equilibrium—nobody knows. The lights are
blue-white, angled so nobody can hide in a shadow. The table, a giant
slab of reconstituted stone, was pitted with the history of a thousand
nervous fingernails. Kaia sits at the end, unbandaged knuckles pressed
to the rough edge, forcing herself not to notice her hands still tremble,
just a little, even now.

Across from her, Yuki stares past the walls, eyes like slits carved
from old obsidian. Mikihisa leaned back, boots crossed, the recovery
drive cradled in his lap as his thumb idly traced its serial number. Jun
perches on the edge of her chair, shoulders bunched, fingers dancing
along the seam of her sleeve in a silent Morse.

The screens flicker to life, cycling through maps, logs, and a growing stack of flagged evidence files. Kaia's after-action report pings on

the overhead, bullet-pointed and sterilized in LDC Standard. For the first time since the blackout run, she feels the weight of bureaucracy pulling the moment down, threatening to render their survival an exercise in paperwork.

Yuki is the first to break silence. "Mission objective: achieved. Primary risk factor: MRB pursuit, sector six. Unknown variables: persistent, but containable." She recites the words in the same cadence as every morning drill, yet beneath it lies an undertone—fatigue, or maybe relief—that draws Kaia's gaze upward. Kaia notices Yuki's mouth clenched as if holding in a scream.

Mikihisa swings a boot off the table. "Not to nitpick, but we were nearly dead three times. I vote we include 'miraculous improvisation' under positive outcomes." He flashes a grin at Jun, who almost smiles, then swallows it.

Kaia nods. "Anything unexpected in the drive?" she asks, nodding at the box in Mikihisa's hands.

He shrugs, plugs the unit into the table's port. "Data integrity checks out. Encrypted, but with a key ring that's older than any of us. Some files in triplicate, most of it raw archive. But—" He pauses, running a fingertip over a status light. "There's a shadow log. Not mainline. More like... annotations left by someone on site."

Jun leans in, hunched and sharp. "Metadata?"

"Or a dead man's switch," says Yuki, flat. "If anyone flagged our extraction, there could be a digital tail."

Kaia watches the interplay, the way Jun's eyes dart from Yuki to Mikihisa to the door and back. She remembers the steps of the mission—every decision, every checkpoint—and something doesn't add. Jun's energy is wired, yes, but also throttled, as if she's suppressing something that wants to get out and run screaming down the hall.

"We'll sweep it," Kaia says. "Full isolation until the techs clear it for transfer." She gestures to Mikihisa to keep the drive sealed. "Let's walk the op from ingress."

Yuki straightens, the old discipline snapping her back into focus. "Entry was clean. No bot detection, zero patrol presence until sector three. Mikihisa tripped a passive on the fire door, but we doubled back through the utility shaft." She glances at him; he shrugs, unashamed.

Kaia runs a mental play-by-play, ticking off every moment. "Jun, confirm the timing on the patrol sweep? I remember a gap, but I want your read."

Jun tenses. "They paused at the loading dock, like they were waiting. It didn't match the patrol algorithm—too long."

Mikihisa tilts his head. "Could've been a handoff. The MRB swaps in human runners when they're serious."

Yuki's mouth twitches. "Or they had a local asset. I didn't see a comms burst, but they could have gone analog."

Kaia notes it: Jun's account is one line off from what she remembers. The pause at the loading dock was longer, yes, but there had been a blip in comms. She remembers her own panic, the way the hallway lights dimmed as if the building itself was holding its breath. She remembers hearing Jun's voice in her ear, the faint tremor masked by static, but only after the patrol passed.

She looks at Jun, who is chewing her bottom lip now. "When did you rejoin the comm net?" Kaia asks, voice mild.

Jun's head snaps up. "Right after the runners cleared. My set cut out, I had to cycle the battery."

Kaia glances at Yuki. "Did you see her do it?"

Yuki shakes her head. "We were split. I assumed Jun was shadowing behind, like we planned."

Mikihisa frowns, runs a check through his log. "You missed two pings, Jun. Was there interference?"

"I told you, the set was dead," Jun said too fast, then caught the way the others watched her. "Sorry. It was—scary. I thought I was cooked."

Kaia's skin prickled. She had seen this before at the Academy: the way people tell the truth, but with tiny edits, shaving the story smooth where it ought to snag. She wants to let it go, but the image of Jun's eyes darting is stuck in her mind, like a bug in code that can't be debugged without bricking the whole program.

She changes tack. "On egress, we doubled back to the main corridor and crossed the boundary at the fence line. Yuki took a graze. Mikihisa covered the rear. Jun—"

Jun jumps on the prompt. "I cleared the way at the vent, like you said. Then I got stuck—my leg slipped. I didn't want to hold you up."

Yuki makes a sound, very nearly a laugh. "You didn't. If anything, you bought us the extra seconds. We owe you."

Jun nods, but the words don't land. Kaia watches the way she tugs at her sleeve again, harder now, until the skin underneath goes pale.

Mikihisa powers up the display, projecting the top level of the recovered Library Zero archive. It blooms across the screens, a river of titles and indexes and, buried deeper, entire volumes of banned memory. He whistles, low. "This is going to keep the LDC in work for a decade."

Kaia's own heart skips, watching the proof of their mission flicker and fill the air. She half-expects the screens to erase themselves, for the memory of what they did to be gone like every other thing worth remembering. Instead, the drive hums on, the data safe for now.

Jun's voice interrupts the moment. "Shouldn't we copy the archive? Distribute it to fallback nodes, in case this one is compromised?"

Yuki's brow creases. "That's not protocol. We centralize, scan for compromise, then replicate."

Jun shakes her head, urgent. "But what if there's a raid? We could lose everything. Just one copy isn't safe."

Mikihisa grins, but it's not unkind. "We're not the only crew running this op, Jun. Trust me, if we get wiped, three more teams will pick up the slack."

Jun's mouth opens, then shuts. She looks at Kaia; desperation plain on her face.

Kaia lets the silence stretch—the hum of ventilation, the staccato of the drive, even the sharp ping of the wall clock; she hears it all. In the spaces between the sounds, she weighs her instinct: something is off. Maybe just nerves, maybe exhaustion. Or maybe the oldest trick in the book—a new face, too eager, too clever by half.

She sees the moment Jun makes a decision. "Maybe... I can begin transferring to a fallback node, just as a precaution. I know one in the old city—no one would trace it."

Kaia fixes her with a stare. "We'll follow standard. Until the techs give clearance, nobody touches the drive. Not even you."

Jun flushes, red flooding up her neck and into her ears. She looks down, then away. "Okay," she says. "I just thought—never mind."

The air in the room thickens. Mikihisa coughs; Yuki picks at a scab on her forearm; Kaia rests her hands flat, not trusting herself to move.

After a minute, Kaia stands, stretching out the stiffness in her spine. "Get some rest," she says. "Briefing with command at oh seven. I want clean uniforms and clear eyes."

The others file out. Mikihisa is humming by the time he hits the door; Yuki leaves with her head down, lost in her own calculations.

Jun lingers at the table, eyes locked on the drive. She reaches for it, then pulls back her hand, as if burned.

Kaia watches her. When Jun finally leaves, she does not close the door behind her. Kaia sits in the empty room, the data drive humming in the silence, wondering who is already listening.

She wonders if this is how her mother felt, every day after the cull—knowing the real threat isn't the enemy outside, but the one sitting two chairs down, making plans to erase everything you love.

Kaia's hands shake again, just for a second. Then she steadies herself and starts writing her own report—unredacted.

The words flow from Kaia's fingers like a fever breaking, each keystroke a small act of defiance. When she finally looks up from the screen, the room has grown dark around her, the setting sun painting long shadows across the metal walls. Her neck aches from hunching over the console, but the pain feels right—earned, like the weight of the truth she's just committed to memory.

Outside her window, the evening shift change sends echoes through the compound's corridors. Boot steps and murmured passwords, the rhythmic beeping of security checkpoints—all the mechanical heartbeats of a system that wants to swallow her whole. Kaia transfers her report to a secure drive and tucks it into her boot, where it presses against her ankle like a secret oath. She needs to move, to breathe air that isn't thick with betrayal and stale coffee. The maintenance catwalks above the agricultural dome should be empty this time of day, and she knows exactly which cameras to avoid.

The archives after hours feel like a sensory deprivation chamber—soundproofed, refrigerated, lit so harshly they leave afterimages on the inside of your eyelids. Every surface is wiped twice daily; the only scent is disinfectant and old ozone from the air filtration. Kaia is alone for the first three minutes—the time it takes to memorize the new layout: double rows of shelving on the left, deep stacks on the right, center table set up for digital indexing.

She hears Jun's approach long before the door opens. Even when she's trying to sneak, Jun carries herself like she's prepping for a footrace, every step loaded for the next.

"Did you need me?" Jun asks, standing awkwardly at the threshold, her gaze darting left then up.

Kaia is at the center table, sleeves rolled and head bent over a codex volume. She gestures to the far end. "I can't make sense of the index for these. You did the pull—walk me through the sort?"

Jun steps in, the door sealing with a soft pneumatic hiss. She moves around the table, posture nervous but determined. Kaia watches the micro-expressions—the way Jun's hands hover above the old paper before touching, the subtle favoring of her right side when she bends to look.

They work in tandem for a minute, Jun narrating her sort logic: "Anything dated pre-collapse is grouped here, by author if possible, by subject if not. This shelf is for duplicate volumes, most of those are in pretty bad shape so I was just flagging for digital restoration."

Kaia nods along, letting her own voice go slack, casual. "You ever see the old city catalog? They had a separate cache for books considered too volatile to destroy. Some got indexed, but the rest—" She shrugs. "Rumor was, they kept a secondary archive. Hidden. Not even LDC Command had access."

Jun's hands freeze on a slipcase. "Secondary cache? Where?"

Kaia lets herself smirk, as if indulging a rumor. "I don't know. But Yuki mentioned a set of coordinates in the map overlay—here, see?"

She points to a hand-drawn note in the corner of a blueprint, a flourish she added just before Jun arrived. "Wouldn't be surprised if there's another stash, maybe with the rarest stuff."

Jun's eyes narrow, skeptical but too hungry to hide it. "You think the League missed it? Even with all their sweeps?"

Kaia shrugs again, feigning indifference. "Maybe. You'd be surprised what the old system could lose track of." She pretends to check her watch. "Shit. I need to run—Command's pinging for a follow-up. Can you finish this?"

Jun's mouth opens, then snaps shut. "Sure," she says. "I'll log out when I'm done."

Kaia grabs her jacket, heads for the door. As soon as she's through, she rounds the first bend, listens for a beat—then slips back, silent as her old infiltration instructor used to preach: "Don't fight the air, let the air forget you."

She edges along the outer stacks, pressing her body flat to the cold metal. Through the gap, she sees Jun at the center table, but not working. Jun's hands are under the table now, rooting for something beneath the false bottom of the index tray.

Kaia steadied her breathing, every rib vibrating with tension. She's aware of her own heartbeat, the sweat beading along her hairline despite the chill. Through the shelving, she watches as Jun lifts a narrow black rectangle: a comm device, smaller than any LDC issue, barely the size of a stick of gum.

Jun checked over her shoulder, set the device flat, and keyed in a short sequence. The comm lights red, then green. Jun covers her mouth with one hand and speaks, voice barely audible, but the silence of the room turns it up to eleven in Kaia's ears.

"Package located. Awaiting extraction coordinates. The Ink's ready."

The words are dry, rehearsed, nothing like the jittery edge Jun wore all night. Kaia clamped a hand over her mouth, barely catching the shudder of panic before it leaked out.

Jun listened, nodded, then typed something on the pad. She holds it to the underside of the table for three long seconds, as if scanning a code, then pockets the device and returns to the books. The transformation is seamless—Jun's back to the old routine, humming a half-song under her breath, face blank except for the tiniest twitch in her jaw.

Kaia waited until Jun was lost in the stacks, then ghosted back down the hall, lungs burning with the effort to stay invisible. She slipped into the corridor, pressed her back to the cold wall, and felt every piece of her certainty slot into place, one after the other.

She needed to tell Yuki, Mikihisa—now, before the Ink was anywhere near the cache. But mostly, Kaia wants to run, because the last time she heard a traitor talk that calmly was the morning the League took her mother away, and nothing has ever come close to that kind of silence.

She pulls herself together, shakes out her hands, and starts for the lower barracks, where the others are supposed to be.

This time, she makes sure to check every corner. She's not going to be erased by a story she didn't write.

Scene 3

Kaia found Yuki and Mikihisa in the mess, eyes puffy, postures slumped over a half-eaten plate of algae loaf and the sharp, oily smell of reconstituted coffee. It would be almost funny if Kaia didn't feel like her blood had been swapped out for battery acid. She waste no time.

"Jun's the leak," she said bluntly, before even sitting down. "She's transmitting out of the secure archive. I heard the whole message."

Yuki puts her fork down, unreadable. "You're sure?"

"Verbatim," says Kaia. "'Package located. Awaiting extraction coordinates. The Ink is ready.' She was talking to someone, probably MRB."

Mikihisa looks like he wants to laugh, then realizes no one else is. "That's—" He stops, tongue flicking the inside of his cheek. "Shit. That's why she pushed to copy the drive. She wanted a back channel, just in case."

Kaia nods, jaw set. "She knows about the secondary cache. I told her as a test—she took the bait. She's going to move fast."

Yuki stands. "She'll head for the main comms suite. It's the only way to blast a real signal. We can intercept her in the fiber trunk, block the transmission at the source."

Mikihisa is already pulling up the blueprints on his pad, cross-referencing maintenance tunnels. "There's a dead spot in the B-level access corridor—no wireless, old fire shielding. If we corner her there, she can't call for help."

Kaia grabs her own gear, the movements automatic. "Let's not wait."

They move as a unit, years of drills compressing the three of them into a single, rolling mass of purpose. The corridors are empty, save for the faint rumble of distant server racks and the pre-dawn hum of life support. Every door they pass locks behind them; every hallway echoes with the click and echo of boots.

At the intersection to the comms corridor, Yuki gestures for silence. She checks the sensor grid—dead, just as Mikihisa promised.

Kaia peers around the corner. Jun is there, face lit blue by the diagnostic panel, one hand jammed deep in her pocket, the other flicking switches with surgeon's speed. She doesn't look up, but Kaia can see the tension in the set of her shoulders.

"Don't move," Kaia calls, voice level.

Jun froze. For a second, there was no sound but the low whine of active cooling. Then Jun turns—slowly, like someone forced to move each vertebra by hand.

The change in her is immediate and terrifying. The slouch is gone, replaced by a straightness that makes her seem two inches taller. Her voice is the same, but the words are different, clipped and precise.

"Guess you figured it out," Jun says. There's no regret, just relief. "You're good. Not as good as they said, but good enough."

Mikihisa snorts. "Who? The MRB? They pay you in ration packs or just the pleasure of fucking over everyone here?"

Jun's eyes flick to him, then back to Kaia. "You don't understand. This isn't about data. It's about survival. You think you're saving memory? You're just hoarding rot. The Ink Plague will bring order—selective forgetting is mercy."

Kaia feels the anger, but she doesn't show it. "You gave them the coordinates," Kaia said.

"Of course I did. Library Zero is a hazard. You read the manifestos—you saw what the old world did to itself, right? It drowned in stories, in secrets. The more people remembered, the faster they killed each other."

Yuki steps forward, arms crossed. "And you think you're some kind of saint? Rewriting the story so only the 'right' people get to remember?"

Jun smiles, the expression crooked and too wide. "I'm not a saint. I'm a janitor. And I've already cleaned up more than you ever will."

Mikihisa spits on the floor. "You always did have a thing for garbage."

Jun ignores him, eyes locked on Kaia. "You still don't get it. Your mother figured it out, eventually. She learned to cooperate. So will you."

The words hit like a punch, and for a split second Kaia loses the thread. "What did you say?"

Jun's face softens, a glimmer of old-June peeking through the mask. "She lasted years. They said she was the best, that she could crack any archive, turn any code into a story you'd want to believe. But in the end, even she stopped fighting. She just wanted you safe."

Kaia's hands ball to fists, nails digging half-moons into her palm. "You don't know anything about my mother."

Jun shrugs, the gesture almost gentle. "I know more than you think. She gave up the location of the first backup. In exchange, they let you live."

Yuki catches Kaia's arm before she lunges. "Not now," she whispers.

Jun uses the second of distraction. She kicks the side of the panel, hard, and the corridor erupts in flashing alarms. The red light stabs Kaia's vision, but she doesn't hesitate—she and Yuki are moving before Mikihisa even registers the trick.

Jun sprints for the access ladder, her speed doubled by desperation. She's halfway up before Kaia catches the rung, nearly tearing Jun's shoe off in the scramble.

Mikihisa yells for backup from below, but the fire door slams shut, isolating the chase to just the three of them.

Kaia scrambles up the ladder, grabbing Jun's ankle and yanking her down a rung. Jun twists, lands a heel in Kaia's face—but Kaia holds on, spitting blood.

At the top, Jun slams into the hatch and barrels into the upper corridor. Kaia follows, every muscle screaming, vision blurred by the blow. They crash through a row of maintenance lockers, the clang of metal echoing like gunshots.

Jun grabbed hold of a steel conduit nearby and swung it towards Kaia with all her strength. Kaia ducked under the makeshift weapon, feeling the rush of air above her head as it missed by inches.

Not one to be outdone, Kaia seized a locker door and thrust it at Jun's arm with controlled force. The impact made Jun flinch, causing her to drop the conduit with a resounding clang that echoed off the walls.

Breathing heavily, they stood locked in a tense standoff, both unwilling to yield. The clash of metal against metal rang out like thunder in the confined space, punctuating their silent battle.

Jun's face contorted in a mix of rage and sorrow as she spoke again, her words laced with bitterness. "You could have walked away, started over somewhere new."

Kaia shook her head slowly, her resolve unwavering. "If I walk away, what's left? You think you're making a better world, but all you do is erase the people who never had a say."

Their dialogue became a verbal dance of defiance and determination as they faced off in the dimly lit corridor, shadows playing across their tense forms.

The conflict between them was palpable as they stood on the edge of confrontation, neither willing to back down from their conflicting ideals. And as they prepared for the next exchange in their high-stakes battle, the outcome hung in the balance like a blade waiting to fall.

But before they could make another move, echoing footsteps approached from down the corridor, signaling that their fight was far from over.

Jun laughs, a dry, broken sound. "That's all anyone ever does, Mori—rewrite the world until it fits."

The standoff lasts a second longer, then Jun feints right, but Kaia anticipates, tackles her to the floor. They tumble, bodies slamming into the cold tile. Jun gets a hand around Kaia's throat, squeezing—but Kaia jams her thumb into the web of Jun's hand, breaking the grip, and flips them, pinning Jun with her knee.

"Stop!" Kaia yells, voice raw.

Jun stills. Her eyes flick to the left—something Kaia can't see, but she doesn't fall for it.

"Call off the extraction," Kaia demands. "Or I'll erase every trace of you from this place."

Jun grins, teeth red. "You don't have that in you."

Mikihisa and Yuki burst through the hatch, weapons drawn but faces uncertain.

Kaia presses down, voice shaking. "Try me."

Jun looks up at her, and—for the first time—there's real fear in her eyes.

But it passes, replaced by a tired resignation. "It's too late," Jun says. "They're already in the building."

The alarms intensify, the world shaking with the promise of a final purge.

Yuki grabs a tie from her kit, binds Jun's wrists with practiced ease. Mikihisa pulls her up, none too gently.

Kaia stands, breathing hard, and for a moment everything is silent but the rush of her own blood.

Jun doesn't struggle. She looks at Kaia and says, softer than before, "You're going to have to choose. When it comes down to it, there's only one story worth telling."

Kaia doesn't answer. She turns to Yuki and Mikihisa. "We need to move. Lock down the archive. Destroy any access they might have."

Yuki nods. "Already queued the virus. It'll wipe the secondary cache if anyone tries to open it without our code."

Mikihisa half-drags Jun to her feet. "Where to?"

Kaia looks at the two of them—her team, her friends—and then at Jun, a ghost of who she once was.

"We finish it," Kaia says.

They run, the alarms a funeral dirge behind them, the future uncertain but still—somehow—possible.

At the far end of the corridor, the doors slam shut. Kaia hears the echo, and wonders, just for a second, what her mother would think.

Then she's moving again, and there's no time left for wondering.

The facility descended into chaos with a precision that only a place built on paranoia could achieve. The moment Jun's hands slipped free of Mikihisa's grip, a burst of strobing red light painted every corridor in emergency mode. Doors slammed, then unlocked, then slammed again, caught in a cycle of conflicting firewalls. Somewhere in the ceiling, the warning klaxon stuttered, then settled into a keening drone that sounded less like a siren and more like a scream stuck on repeat.

Jun was fast—faster than Kaia remembered, her boots barely touching the mesh floor as she zigzagged through the B-level access. Yuki was two steps behind, hacking at her own wrist console, but every override she issued got swallowed by the lockdown, a digital hydra growing new heads for every one she severed. Mikihisa, whose entire skill set was built on charm and not chasing traitors, lagged behind, but his curses filled the empty space in a way that somehow kept Kaia moving.

Kaia saved her breath for the sprint, the cut corners, the vault over a toppled barricade in the transfer bay. All that mattered was not letting Jun get to the central command node, where even a half-open channel could broadcast their entire operation to every regulator in the hemisphere.

At the main stairwell, Jun feinted left, then ducked through the old food storage. Kaia was right there, body low, breath jagged in her throat. She didn't slow—just tackled Jun at the waist, the impact shoving them both into a rack of freeze-dried rations. Foil pouches burst, raining powder everywhere, clouding the air with a faint, nutty smell. Jun thrashed, knees Kaia in the hip, but Kaia held tight, every muscle burning.

"Stop," Kaia grunted. "It's over. Just stop."

Jun spat in her face and bucked hard while Mikihisa barreled in and landed with his full weight on Jun's shoulders, pinning her flat to the metal rack.

"Got her," he pants, sweat mixing with the powdered protein on his brow. "Little sneaky is strong."

"Don't call her that," Kaia says, still holding on. "She's not a kid. She's an agent."

Yuki arrives, pale but composed, bleeding from a shallow gash above her eye. She checks the corridor, slaps a quickpatch on her forehead, and keys in a series of commands on her pad.

"System's corrupted," she says. "Can't lock it down. We need to get her to the command hub—hardline only. Physical control."

Kaia and Mikihisa haul Jun up, but she's not fighting anymore. Her face is slack, eyes unfocused, body gone limp. For a second, Kaia wonders if they broke her. Then Jun smiles—subtle, sly—and Kaia knows the real damage hasn't happened yet.

They drag Jun through the winding tunnels, Yuki in the lead, Mikihisa swearing and bleeding from a scraped arm, Kaia feeling the ache in every joint. The farther they go, the less the facility feels like home; lights flicker with purpose, walls seem to close in, even the pipes overhead vibrate in time with the alarm.

At the command hub, the door is propped open by a chair. Inside, half the monitors are dead, the other half looping distorted images: Library Zero in flames, old city streets full of censors in riot gear, Kaia's own face, eyes wide and mouth twisted in fear, projected twenty times larger than life.

Jun lets out a sharp laugh. "You see? It's already started."

They force her into the command chair, Yuki yanking her arms behind her and binding them with zip ties. Mikihisa roots under the desk for the manual override. Kaia slaps the wall console, pulling up a status report.

Yuki's hands tremble, but her voice is ice. "I'll run a burn protocol on the backup. That'll at least give us a window before they wipe everything."

Jun shrugs, the motion jerky. "Doesn't matter. The MRB strike is minutes out. You're already ghosts."

Kaia leans in, voice low. "You said my mother gave up the archive. Was that a lie, or are you just trying to make it hurt?"

Jun turns to look at her, the smile gone. "I never lie, Kaia. She made a deal, same as everyone does. In the end, there's always a deal."

Kaia's gut twists, but she holds the stare. "She never wanted this. She didn't want her stories to end with a blank page."

Jun sighs, like she's tired of all of it. "You still think stories matter. It's almost sweet."

Mikihisa finds the kill switch, jams it forward. For a second, the alarms cut out, the lights return to normal, and there's silence.

Then Dojo arrives.

He enters with two security officers, both in partial armor, faces set to maximum skepticism. Dojo's eyes flick over the scene—the bound traitor, the wrecked hub, Kaia's bloodied lip—and his jaw goes tight.

"Explain," he says. Not a question, more an order.

Yuki doesn't hesitate. "Jun was the leak. She's been in contact with MRB since before the blackout op. We caught her trying to transmit a dump of the entire Library Zero archive."

Dojo looks at Jun, who smiles, looking every bit the wronged child.

"Don't believe them, sir," Jun says. "Kaia's been compromised since her mother's arrest. Check her file—she has more unauthorized comms than anyone here. She used me to get into the archive, then tried to pin it all on me."

The officers glance at Dojo, waiting. Kaia's face burns.

"She's lying," Kaia says, voice shaking. "Check her sleeve. There's a comm device, unregistered."

Dojo doesn't move. "Kaia, you are on record as the last to see Jun before this. And your own record is... unconventional."

Yuki tries to cut in, but Dojo holds up a hand. "I'll hear you out, but if this is another op gone off-script, I can't shield you."

Kaia's world narrows to the pulse in her ears, the faint smell of Yuki's blood, the sound of Jun breathing slow and steady.

Mikihisa, desperate, rips the comm device from Jun's sleeve and tosses it on the desk. "Run it," he says. "Pull the log."

The tech officer takes the comm, scans it. It pings live, and the last message is still queued.

"Playback," Dojo says.

The comm outputs: "Package located. Awaiting extraction coordinates. The Ink's ready."

Dojo's mask cracks, just a hair. He turns to Jun. "Anything to say?"

Jun sits straight, posture regal, and says, "You're too late. The Ink is already flowing. By dawn, Library Zero will be nothing but blank pages."

Dojo signals the officers. They cuff Jun, haul her out of the chair.

Kaia staggers back, hits the wall, and slides down to the floor. She doesn't cry, but her body shakes so violently she can't stop it.

Yuki kneels beside her, hands gentle. "It's over, Kaia. We got her."

Kaia looks at her, at Mikihisa, at the wrecked command center. She shakes her head. "It's never over. They'll just find another Jun. Another dupe in their story."

Yuki holds her hand, firm. "Then we write better stories."

Dojo crouches, his voice softer now. "You did the right thing. But there's a price."

Kaia manages a laugh, bitter. "There always is."

He nods, then stands. "We have an hour, maybe less, before the next strike. Gather what you can. Prepare for burn."

They rise together. Outside, the alarms are gone, but the world feels no less dangerous. Kaia looks at the empty chair where Jun sat, then at the pile of books on the command desk, and for the first time lets herself hope—just a little—that they might keep some part of the story alive.

She wipes her face, squares her shoulders, and heads for the archive, Yuki and Mikihisa at her side.

This is what's left: three bruised bodies, one fractured team, and a library under siege.

And with renewed purpose, they stepped back into the fray, ready to face the challenges that awaited them, knowing that as long as they held fast to the power of their words, their story would endure.

Chapter 25: Shield of Silence

The stairwell behind them smoldered with the smell of burning insulation and fear-sweat. They burst into the control vault shoulder to shoulder—Kaia first, then Yuki, Mikihisa on her heels, the three of them pressed tight by the shriek of alarms and the certainty that if they fail here, the world rewrites itself with their names scrubbed from every page.

The server room is a bunker beneath a skeleton of ancient book stacks, ceiling ribs blackened by two centuries of disaster and regret. The space is rimmed with battered library shelving, every case jammed with the forbidden and the irretrievable. At the center, a ring of servers hums like a beehive. Red emergency strobes pulse along the walls, washing the stacks in murder-scene light. The old air is thick with static and the aftertaste of ozone. Every surface is cold, even where a pair of ragged jackets hang from a hook like the skin of two ghosts.

Kaia launches herself at the central console, her breath already ragged. Yuki peels left, snaps down the blast-shield on the main entrance, then double-checks the deadbolts with a mechanical click. Mikihisa lopes to the breaker panel and rips it open, scanning the power grid with eyes that for once hold zero humor. For the first time since the Academy, there are no adults—no command to call, no backup, no fallback. Just three bodies, thirty seconds, and a thousand years of stories waiting to die or burn.

Kaia stabbed at the console, her hands guided less by conscious thought than by a muscle memory trained on sleepless nights and hacker's prayer. The interface was old tech—no holo, no voice, just a monochrome slab and a keyboard so worn she typed by sound instead of feel. She bit her lip and muttered the LDC failover mantra "Boot the core, flood the channel. Encrypt as you go."

She's in. The mainframe's menu was a waterfall of legacy code, every line flickering with decades of patchwork and sabotage. Kaia scrolls until she finds the root—**DISPERSAL PROTOCOL**. The letters throbbed against her retina, blue and ugly. She punches in the first passcode and the system spits it back: **REJECTED**. "Damn," she whispered, voice small and sharp. "Try the old hash."

Outside, the building shuddered. A concussive whump echoes up from the stairwell—maybe a breach charge, maybe just another piece of history coming loose. Yuki's hands moved over the security panel with knife-blade precision, locking down one emergency bulkhead after another. "Two minutes, maybe less," she calls, voice tight.

Mikihisa's breathing is the only sound louder than the server fans. He levers a crowbar into the power switch and holds it there, muscle corded and face white with the effort. "Shunt's live," he grunts, "but the capacitor's cycling like a rabid raccoon. We're on borrowed time."

Kaia gritted her teeth and retyped the hash. This time it takes, and the protocol queue lights up in sickly green: **INITIATE DISPERSAL Y/N**?

She hits **Y**.

The console chugs, scrolls a page of warning: "This operation is irreversible. Are you sure?"

She thinks of her mother's voice, the bedtime story version—of all the stories that used to have names, now remembered only as absences. The metal bookmark is hot against her chest, where she's looped it on a wire. She takes it out, runs her thumb along the edge, and plugs it into the console's reader port. The screen flickers, freezes, and then opens a new prompt:

"Override. Mori Family Protocol: Parley. Dispersal with fragmentation?"

Kaia types: **YES.**

A hum goes through the room—like the servers themselves are waking up, pissed off and hungry. The mainframe spits out a status bar, the progress crawling in increments so slow Kaia wants to scream. She knows the numbers: there are over 60,000 unique records in Library Zero, every one of them a splinter waiting to detonate inside the regime's head.

Behind her, Mikihisa's voice is a steadying counterpoint. "Power stable for now. Yuki, how's the entry?"

"Sealed. But they're cutting the manual." Yuki's hands are slick, but her eyes never leave the hallway cam feed. "Three MRB. Full kit. They brought a Wrecker."

Kaia doesn't look up. "How long?"

"Not enough," Yuki says.

The status bar on Kaia's screen blips past six percent. Then nine. Each point is a year of lost history, another teacher's suicide, another family vanished for loving the wrong kind of story.

A crash—louder than anything before—jolts the entire room. Mikihisa's hand slips on the bar, and the servers drop to brownout for half a second before the emergency generator kicks in with a choked growl. A blue spark spits from the ceiling and dances along the ductwork.

Yuki moves to the backup entrance, her sidearm drawn, her face set. "If they come through here," she says, "you trigger the failsafe, Kaia."

Kaia doesn't answer. She's already typing in the last sequence—something from her mother's stories, a fragment of code she's never shared, not even with the LDC instructors. The system digests it, and a secondary bar pops up: "Parley Protocol Initiated. Dispersal priority: **BANNED TEXTS / ORAL HISTORIES / REDACTED EVIDENCE.**"

Mikihisa slams the power shunt again, sweat pouring down his jaw. "They're torching the upper stacks," he says. "I can feel the temp spike. We've got to go, or we're toast."

Kaia rips the bookmark from the reader. "If you break the connection before 60 percent," she said, "the records go nowhere. If we last until 80, it'll seed the backups across the entire rebellion net. That's all we get."

Mikihisa's old bravado flickers. "So, just hold the line?"

Kaia tries to smile, but her lips barely move. "We're librarians. It's in the job description."

A clang against the far door—someone using a breaching ram now. Kaia feels the vibrations in her ribcage. She watches the bar—23, 28, 31.

Another crash. Yuki moves a shelf in front of the backup entrance, the only cover between them and the corridor. She glances at Mikihisa, who nods once, grim.

"Tell me you're almost there," Mikihisa mutters, voice barely audible.

"Three minutes," Kaia says, eyes locked on the screen. "Maybe less if the net holds up."

Yuki's hands were white-knuckled on her weapon. "Then we just need to not die for three minutes."

They brace. The air is thick with ozone, sweat, and the dust of burning books overhead. Kaia's heart pounded in time with the status bar, each percent a hammer blow.

Forty-nine percent.

The next crash hit directly. The backup door buckled, the top hinge tearing loose in a squeal of steel. Yuki leans into the barricade, planting her boots, gun up and ready.

The keys clacked and clicked with each tap of Kaia's fingers, the familiar sound of typing filling the air surrounded by the chaos and tension. She triggered a last-minute relay, bundling the final orphaned stories into a blind dump—if nothing else, they'd scatter across the dark net like seeds, waiting for someone to dig them up.

A heavy foot pounded the outside corridor. The Wrecker is close enough now that they can hear the low hum of its power pack. Mikihisa eyed the breaker box, then Kaia. "If you need me to cut loose, now's the time."

"Not yet," she says.

Sixty-three percent.

The far door split, a bright blade of light carving the room. Yuki fires once—sharp, controlled. The beam misses, but the shock wave forces the door to jam fully open.

A figure in black riot gear stumbled in, weapon raised, the mask blank and all business. Yuki's second shot takes him high in the shoulder. He goes down, screaming.

Two more MRB behind returned fire. Chips of concrete explode from the bulkhead, raining shrapnel over Mikihisa and Kaia. Yuki ducks behind the stack, fires again.

Mikihisa crouches by Kaia's station, arms up to shield her from the flying debris. "Time?"

"Seventy-six," Kaia says, "but the packet lag is getting bad."

"Cut it at seventy-eight," Mikihisa says. "Give us a chance to fry the main before they get to you."

Kaia nods, swallows, and braces for the last push.

Another barrage from the Wrecker. The next blast rips the backup entrance fully open; Yuki fires twice, this time at center mass. One officer drops. The other dives behind the door and sprays the room with suppression fire.

Kaia felt the heat—real heat, now, as the top floor's flames ate down through the ceiling tiles. A fire alarm whoops, high and wild.

"Seventy-eight," Kaia yells.

Mikihisa grabs the crowbar and jams it deep into the main's kill switch. The servers wail, a chorus of dying drives. Kaia hammers the final sequence, fingers numb and bleeding.

A flash grenade rolls in. Yuki throws herself on top of it, absorbs the brunt with her body. The blast is less than lethal, but the concussion stuns her flat. Kaia tries to scream, but her voice is eaten by the howl of the alarms.

The last bar on the console hits eighty. A single line flashes up: **DISPERSAL COMPLETE. THANK YOU FOR YOUR SERVICE**.

Kaia yanks the drive, smashes the console with the butt of her palm. "Done," she whispers.

The room spun with smoke, gunfire, and the taste of melting insulation. Mikihisa helps Yuki up, her face pale and lip split.

Outside, the boots of MRB thud closer.

Kaia held the drive against her chest, the bookmark burning in her fist.

"Ready?" she says.

Yuki manages a smile, bloodied but still defiant. "Always."

Mikihisa grins, the old light back for a second. "After you, Mori."

They moved for the maintenance shaft—the only way out now.

As they go, Kaia looks back once. The stacks are burning, but the stories are free.

Let them come.

The vault was alive now—not just with the mechanical buzz of overclocked servers, but with something feral and raw. Kaia could feel it in her teeth, a low-frequency tremor that rattled bone and memory alike. The transfer protocol had chewed through half the data, but each percent grew harder; the system lagged, a wounded animal fighting to finish its run before it collapsed.

The emergency generators kick in, rattling the floor with a thud like a distant fist. The lights brown out, then come back, weaker but holding. Kaia's pulse was all spikes and gaps. Sweat beads on her forehead and slides down her cheek, stinging the cut where a chip of plastic caught her on the dive to the floor. The scar above her left elbow throbs—a living reminder of every drill and every time she ignored orders in favor of getting the job done.

"Seventy percent," she says, voice tight, hands flying. Her sleeve is rolled up past the biceps, the old wound exposed, a jagged white seam against sunless skin.

Yuki is a whirlwind at the breaker array, popping panels and jabbing wires with the precision of a bomb tech. Her hair is plastered to her head with sweat and static. Every time the grid surged, Yuki grit her teeth and yelled over the noise, "Cycle three, clear! Cycle four, next!" She punches a reset, and the entire room lurches as another bank of servers comes online, the cooling fans roaring.

Mikihisa's voice crackles over the private comm—he's in the crawl-space above, just as they planned if the first defense failed. "MRB in the upper stacks, two minutes to breach. They're torching every floor on the way down. Full riot gear, with a couple drones for cleanup."

Kaia's left hand skitters across the keyboard, her right jammed into the backup drive's port. She's typing blind now, lines of code flying across the monochrome monitor as she pushes the upload past the bottlenecks MRB has jammed into the network. The metallic taste in the air is thick, like she's been sucking on a mouthful of loose change.

The console flashes: **"SECURITY BREACH: OUTER SYSTEM COMPROMISED."**

Kaia hissed. "They're inside the firewall. Yuki, kill the uplink if you can—I need them off the console."

Yuki slams a fist into the kill switch; the server room's outside comm goes dark, leaving only red warning lamps to mark their step toward isolation.

Kaia glances at the status bar: seventy-one percent. Time thickens to syrup, every second stretching into an hour. Her fingers ache, but she types faster, improvising firewalls and counterstrikes she'd only sketched on napkins or whispered during blackout hours at the Academy.

A flash of light from the ceiling: Mikihisa drops into the vault, skin streaked with grime and face alive with terror and glee. "They've got a brute-force coder up top," he says, "but I broke their relay for at least thirty seconds. How close are we?"

"Not enough," Kaia says. "If they break the next lock, the protocol dies with us."

Mikihisa doesn't even blink. He rips a server from the rack, hot-swaps it, and reroutes the power manually, hands burning on the casing. "Thirty seconds," he says. "Give or take."

The lights dip again, then return, harsh and nearly blue. Kaia smells burning insulation and beneath it, the unmistakable scent of something organic—an old stack of papers, finally catching fire.

The memory strikes at the worst possible moment. The taste of burning, the smell of fear, the memory of her mother's last day: Hana Mori on her knees in their kitchen, arms around a garbage bag full of children's books, sobbing as she sorted which to hide and which to surrender. Kaia is nine, and she can't understand why the world must be this cruel.

But now she's the adult in the room, the only one who can save anything.

She blinks hard, returning to the console with fingers moving quickly. Another breach warning—MRB's digital signature, now inside their system. Kaia types faster, scripting a recursive loop before slamming the ENTER key so hard her hand tingles.

The bar jumps: seventy-eight percent.

A thump at the door—the physical one this time. Yuki pulls her weapon, checks the charge, and moves to cover. She looks at Kaia, and for a moment her face is all the warmth Kaia's ever known.

"If this works," Kaia says, "every story in here lives forever."

Yuki smiles, fierce and proud. "Then we're immortal already."

Another crash, the door frame warping inward. Mikihisa throws his body against it, wedging the server rack as a makeshift brace. "Keep going," he says, "I can hold it."

The breach alert doubles, then triples. The screen fills with red warnings, and Kaia fights to see the upload bar through the digital noise. She types a final override, using a code her mother invented for bedtime stories—part song, part cipher.

The room is vibrating with noise and pressure. Kaia's hands are numb, her brain on fire. She types through it, and finally the bar hits ninety.

The last phase hits like an aftershock. MRB boots pound against the outer vault, metal on stone, the rhythm of inevitable violence. The air vibrates with the low whine of a powered breach saw as it bites into the security frame. Yuki's knuckles whiten around the grip of her sidearm; she watches the progress bar on Kaia's screen as if willing it to finish before the next wave of hell bursts through the door.

Mikihisa rips cables from dead servers, then yanks a ceiling panel loose to expose the access crawl. His hands move with perfect economy, all the jokes burned away by adrenaline and the simple desire to survive long enough to see tomorrow.

Kaia's heart jumps with every jolt. The dispersal's status bar is crawling now—ninety-four, ninety-five, ninety-seven. Sweat blurs her vision; she blinks hard, refusing to lose sight of the finish line. Another warning flashes: **"REMOTE ACCESS DETECTED. MANUAL INTERVENTION REQUIRED."**

She types faster, fingers jamming the override codes, last-ditch tricks learned in shadowed rooms and forbidden files. On screen, the progress bar hangs at ninety-eight percent for a full five seconds, then surges to one hundred in a single, improbable leap.

The system flashes: **DISPERSAL COMPLETE. ALL RECORDS SEEDED**.

Kaia's breath shudders out of her, shaky and relieved. "It's done," she says, but her voice is a croak. On the monitor, the final upload batch scrolls past: rare manuscripts, banned poetry, fragments of memory that would outlive all of them by a hundred years.

She reaches for the emergency purge, punches in the kill code. The server fans spool down, one after another, the room going strangely silent as the screens flicker and die. For a moment, it's just the three of them and the hollow thunder of the world falling apart outside.

Yuki puts a hand on Kaia's shoulder—just a brief squeeze, but it steadies her more than any speech. "Time to go," Yuki says, her voice the only thing still unbroken.

Mikihisa drops the last cable, grabs his pack, and gestures them to the crawl hatch. "We'll have three, maybe four minutes before the fire or the MRB gets here. After that, we're history."

Kaia grabs the backup drive, loops the bookmark around her wrist. The metal is cool, grounding, and she finds herself mouthing a fragment of her mother's old lullaby—the song with the hidden numbers, the one that cracked every code in the world if you listened hard enough.

She ducks into the crawl, Yuki behind her, Mikihisa last. The shaft is barely big enough to move, lined with dust and the ghosts of a thousand forbidden conversations. The echo of boots and shouts follows them, but for once the darkness ahead is safer than the world they're leaving behind.

In the crawlspace, LDC command pings Kaia's pad: text only, all caps. "**MISSION COMPLETE. ALL NODES REPORT RE-CEPTION. YOU ARE CLEARED FOR EXTRACTION.**"

She should feel proud—triumphant, even. Instead, she feels scraped raw, every victory nothing but a scar for the next fight.

Mikihisa, always the first to break the silence, whispers, "We saved the words, boss." Then, quieter: "But at what cost?"

Kaia has no answer. She thinks of the burning stacks above, the friends who never made it, the stories still unwritten.

Yuki's hand finds hers in the dark, a lifeline as the tunnel bends and the world behind them catches fire.

They crawl for what feels like forever, the taste of victory bitter and sharp.

At the end of the tunnel, the city is waiting—a little more danger-ous, a little more possible.

Kaia tucks the bookmark inside her sleeve and thinks, maybe, just maybe, her mother would be proud.

But she knows one thing for certain: there's no going back. Not now, not ever.

And with that, she leads her team into whatever comes next.

Epilogue: A New Dawn

They descend into the lowest bowels of Library Zero with the taste of ash still in their mouths. The fire behind them had faded to a rumor—an irregular pulse in the static of the comms, a faint red strobe flickering down air shafts clogged with a century's worth of dust, skin, and secrets. For the first fifty meters, it's nothing but tight tunnels and crushed shelving, the only light the grim yellow eye of the emergency lamp Mikihisa carries. The deeper they go, the colder it gets.

At first, they walk in silence. It's not camaraderie—just the kind of exhaustion that fills every space where words might otherwise live. Kaia's legs burned with soreness, her left boot squelching with every step, and the cut above her left elbow itching beneath the makeshift bandage she'd wrapped at the crawlspace exit. She glances at Yuki, who walks with her arms crossed over her chest, knuckles white and jaw set, but Kaia can tell it's not pain she's fighting—just the weight of what comes next.

They reach a cross-junction where the old pipes split in four directions, and the lamp reveals shelves so caked with ancient dirt that the volumes resemble fossilized loaves. Kaia breathed in; the taste was as much history as mold. Mikihisa sweeps the beam along the ceiling, then down at the floor, where the dust is disturbed in a narrow groove: a path, recently walked.

"Either we've got company," Mikihisa murmurs, "or this place is haunted by very tidy ghosts."

Yuki barely reacts. She's already crouched to scan the track, tracing it with a fingertip. "Single person. No drag, so they knew where they were going. No shuffle in the stride—likely a runner, not a crawler."

Kaia says nothing. She presses her hand to the wound at her elbow, feels the heat of inflammation and the sharper heat of memory. Her mother used to say, *"Every wound is a bookmark—don't ignore what the page is trying to tell you."* Kaia wants to laugh at the irony, but the muscles of her face have locked up for now.

They move onward, Yuki following the trail. The corridor narrows again, so tight Mikihisa has to turn sideways to fit, the emergency lamp flicking shadow across every surface. At a sharp bend, Kaia pauses—there's something wrong with the wall here. It's not the same pitted, grayed concrete as the rest. This section is darker, the texture smoother, almost like it's been painted over.

She runs a thumb along the surface, and her nail catches on a seam. A hidden panel.

Yuki stops behind her. "Problem?"

Kaia says, "Maybe. Hand me the lamp."

Mikihisa passes it forward, and for a moment the three of them are pressed so close that Kaia can hear the other two breathing. She points the lamp at the panel, then gives it a tentative shove. It resists, then yields with a sticky, sucking sound, as if the air behind has gone bad. She slips her fingers into the edge and pulls.

The panel comes loose, and a gust of cold air flows out, carrying with it the unmistakable scent of old paper, ancient glue, and something else—something sharp and metallic, like the snap of ozone right before a lightning strike.

Behind the panel is a cavity just large enough for a child to hide in. The space is filled with stacks of notebooks, all bound in the same cheap maroon faux-leather, the corners warped by damp and years. Kaia's heart kicks into her throat. She recognizes the binding instantly. Her mother's journals.

She doesn't realize her hand is shaking until the lamp trembles and rattles against the shelf. She sets it down, then reaches into the darkness. The first journal comes free easily, but it leaves a faint residue on her fingers—a mix of dust, oil, and the sloughed-off skin of everyone who ever touched it. The second is stuck to the first by a band of dried mold, but she works it free, careful, reverent.

Mikihisa, behind her, is quiet for once. Yuki's voice is low and careful. "You all right?"

Kaia wants to say yes. Instead, she brushes the dust off the first journal's cover. The name on the spine is written in blocky, blue-black ink: "Emiko Mori. 21st Cycle." Her mother's handwriting—she'd recognize it even in the dark.

She pulls the lamp closer, flips to the first page. The ink has faded but the words are still crisp, each line running left to right with the stubborn refusal to be erased.

"Day 1: Assigned to MRB subcommittee, Codename: Project Delta. Initial observations: subjects compliant, memory alteration rate steady at 17%. Personal note: recommend increased latency between redactions to mitigate synaptic fatigue."

Kaia's hands clench on the journal, the knuckles paling beneath the grime. Her breathing has gone shallow; she can hear her own heartbeat behind her ears, and her vision tunnels in on the next line.

"Protocol 7-A implemented successfully. Subject compliance increased by 42% after targeted memory redaction."

She reads the line again. Then a third time, as if the words will change under repeated assault.

A sound escapes her, halfway between a laugh and a choke.

Yuki moves closer, the grazed arm pressed tight to her chest, her face unreadable in the half-light. "What is it?"

Kaia doesn't answer. Instead, she flips ahead, scanning entry after entry. The years run together—a parade of numbers, test subjects, percentages. Then, at the edge of a page, something new: a name, underlined twice.

"Mori, Emiko. Chief Archivist, MRB Central Division."

Kaia's voice, when it comes, is dry and brittle. "My mother. She wasn't just a victim. She was..." The words fractured, then reassembled. "She helped build the thing we've been fighting."

Mikihisa, for once, has nothing clever to say. He just leans against the wall, the lamp throwing his shadow up onto the ceiling, where it looms over the three of them like an accusation.

Kaia flips to the last page. The ink here is rushed, jagged.

"They're coming. If you find this, remember: the system has a backdoor. Look for the silver thread."

Kaia's hands are shaking so badly now that the journal rattles in her grip. She tears the page free, folds it into a precise square, and tucks it inside her jacket, right next to the blue ribbon. She wants to cry, but her body has decided on something more useful: rage.

She closes the journal, rises, and faces the others. "We move," she says. "Now."

She doesn't look back at the panel, or the remaining journals, or the shadows that move on the wall behind her.

She just walks, every step carving a groove deeper into the floor and into memory.

Ahead, the archive waits.

But this time, Kaia is ready to write her own page.

They huddle in the shadow of the next alcove, as safe as anyone gets in this part of the ruins, with only the emergency lamp burning the color out of their faces. Kaia cradles the journal in both hands, the maroon binding gone gray with dust, and draws a slow breath through her teeth. She reads aloud, at first just for herself, but her voice grows until it pins the air between the three of them.

"Protocol 7-A implemented successfully. Subject compliance increased by 42% after targeted memory redaction."

The words fall from her tongue brittle and cold, but the silence after is worse. She flips the page. "Tested on sample set: memory audit revealed high success rate, but emotional destabilization remains problematic. Solution: increased sleep-cycle interruption, combined with scheduled story deprivation."

Yuki's face is illuminated and hollow, her eyes locked on the lines, body angled forward as if she could press the truth into herself by proximity. The graze on her upper arm seeps a slow, dark ring through the bandage, but she doesn't flinch, even as she leans in close enough to read the next lines along with Kaia.

"Your mother was running ops on this?" Mikihisa asks, voice low, no trace of joke. He adjusts the lamp to cut the glare, but his hands are steady, almost delicate.

Kaia's answer is a near-whisper. "Not just running. She was writing the playbook."

She turns another page, the paper brittle enough that it flakes at the edge. "Emiko Mori, Chief Archivist, MRB Central Division." Kaia says the name aloud, as if conjuring a ghost might make it more bearable. Her voice shakes, but she keeps reading, each word scoring her lungs from inside out.

"Rumor had it," Yuki says, "that the MRB always had an insider, a 'memory mother' who could write a mind like a clean slate. Never believed it was a Mori." She shakes her head, not in disbelief but in the peculiar awe reserved for monsters and martyrs. "Explains why you never got a clean record, even when you tried."

Kaia's knuckles go white around the journal. "She made us memorize everything—no pad, no tablet. I thought it was paranoia, but it was training. She was building resistance even while she..." The words dry up. She doesn't know what comes after that, not yet.

Mikihisa says, "It's not betrayal if you sabotage your own side." He means it to help, but it just sharpens the edge. "I bet she hated every second of it."

Kaia skips ahead, looking for something redemptive, anything. There are test logs, names of vanished subjects, tables of compliance rates that never dip below sixty percent. Then, buried near the back: an entry scrawled sideways, as if it had to be hidden in plain sight.

"Year 6, cycle 21: Directive 9-B issued. All non-compliant archives to be permanently disabled. Suspect higher command intends full memory purge—no rehabilitation, no record. This is not the project I joined."

She lets the words hang.

Yuki's eyes flick to Kaia's. "She turned, then."

Kaia nods, and for a second, she is nine years old again, watching her mother weep over a trash bag of children's books—a survivor in a world that wanted only erasures.

She reads the next, final entry, her voice suddenly sure: "They're coming. If you find this, remember: the system has a backdoor. Look for the silver thread."

The phrase catches in Kaia's mind—silver thread, silver thread—and she remembers the bedtime story her mother used to tell. The one about the girl who unraveled the night by following a single shining line through the darkness. She wants to believe that's what her mother left her, that the story wasn't just a way to keep her quiet when the world got loud.

Kaia tears the last page out, folds it carefully and small, and tucks it into her jacket. The blue ribbon tightens around her wrist, a promise or a warning.

Mikihisa is first to break the hush. "So, what's next?" He tries for lightness, but it's just raw.

Kaia closes the journal, lets the dust settle on her lap. "We go after the thread," she says. "We follow the story to wherever it leads."

Then she remembered her mother's voice from those early days, whispering as she tucked Kaia in: *"The truth always hides in plain sight, little one. You just need to know how to look for it."*

Yuki nods, as if that's all the answer she needed.

They pack up, the lamp throwing their shadows huge and strange against the far wall. Kaia lingers, a hand on the maroon cover, and this time the ache in her arm is not pain but a pulse, steady and alive.

As they move forward, the dust settles behind them, burying the past for good. But ahead, somewhere in the infinite dark, a silver thread waits.

Glossary of The World of Aetherra

Welcome, Apprentice. Should this Codex find your hands, you are either preparing for Guild elevation—or trespassing where winds dare not tread.

Contained herein are the essential elements of Aetherra: her lands, factions, rituals, and the harmonics that hold her aloft. May your breath remain steady and your soul aligned.

—Archivist Nelthra Wynn, Sky-Library Vaultkeeper, Vahlien

1. Settings & Locations

Primary World & Geography

- **Aetherra**: A visually striking world with fractured archipelagos of floating isles, each featuring distinct microclimates ranging from tropical jungles to crystalline tundra and areas of acidic rainfall. The surface world below is covered in cracked cities and ashflat deserts, where rare luminous crystals called "ether-shal" can be found beneath the haze. In the sky, algae groves float in sky-pools.

- **Fractured Archipelagos**: Suspended by ancient levitation cores, these isles range in climate and terrain, forming isolated biospheres with contrasting environments. The separation encourages distinct languages and customs to evolve on each isle.

- **Isle of Vahlien**: A temperate, caste-structured island with matri-guild dominance. Its skyline features airships, vertical terrace homes with dangling mid-air gardens, and constant humming from wind turbines. Annual events like the Crystal Liberation Festival fill the air with floating lights and aromatic ether-shal vapor.

- **Ruined Surface World**: A charred, cracked expanse of ashflat deserts and ruined cities bathed in gray haze. The ground smells of scorched stone and ozone; ancient buildings crumble beneath the weight of time.

- **Algae Groves & Sky-pools**: Lush, buoyant groves float in pools suspended mid-air. The air smells clean and sweet with the fragrance of sky-algae and mist. Wind patterns ripple the surface like tidewater.

- **Floating Isles**: Ethereal landscapes suspended in wind-currents. Trees shimmer with algae-luminescence, and Skylure

Nymphs flit through air trails that glow faintly blue-green at dusk.

- **Ground Routes**: Dimly lit industrial tunnels lined with echoing metal rails and the smell of oil and ash. Walls pulse faintly with hacked ether-tech.

- **Wealthy Isles / Poor Isles**: Wealthy Isles glisten with storm-forged glass spires and fresh pumped winds; Poor Isles suffer from thin, dry air and rust-covered tech.

- **Sky-tree Farms**: Vast farms anchored in clouds where wind-currents swirl and Skylure Nymphs perform aerial pollination, leaving glittering trails of light.

2. Organizations by Role

Political & Societal

- **Matri-guilds**: Guilds that command vital technologies. Their headquarters echo with mechanical hymns and smell of warm crystal and ozone.

- **Sky Elites**: Lavishly dressed technocrats living in aerated luxury. Their palaces hum with invisible power currents and the scent of wind-scrubbed air.

- **Ground-cultures**: Grease-stained rebels navigating sulfur-choked tunnels. Conversations are terse, laced with grit-speak.

- **Syndicates**: Cold laboratories and holding cells illuminated by flickering screens and faint sobs. Their environments reek of sterilization and ambition.

- **LDC Academy & LDC Operatives**: Cold steel corridors lined with flickering codex glyphs. Air buzzes with tension and whispered rebellion.

Guild Caste Roles (Isle of Vahlien)

- **Scholars**: Robed in wind-silk, they smell of paper and crystal ink, speaking in riddled proverbs.

- **Wind-wrights**: Carry soot-streaked gloves and glyph-etched tools; their chambers echo with core-hymn chants.

- **Sky-sailors**: Windswept and armor-plated, with whistled codes echoing across sky-bridges.

- **Ground-traders**: Grit-marked uniforms and cart-bound trade goods; voices roughened by surface ash.

- **Guild-wisdom**: Elders marked by feathered helms and sky-canes etched with sonic glyphs.

3. Magic System

Primary System: Etheric Harmonization

- **Sources**: Wind, Crystals, Algae-frequency — each has a sensory resonance (e.g., wind has a low hum; crystals pulse with colored light; algae exudes faint bioluminescent mist).

- **Access Methods**: Meditation (silence broken by wind-breath), Glyph-tattoos (glow faintly with the user's heartbeat), Ether-shal infusion (causes sensory disorientation and temporary light halos).

- **Users**:

  - **Healers & Elementalists**: Surrounded by soothing hums and the aroma of sky-herbs.

  - **Storm-forgers**: Work amid controlled tempests, thunder-pulses shaking the bones.

  - **Skylure Nymphs**: Glide with trails of wind-song and crystal-harmonics.

4. Key Factions by Magic Use

- **Skylure Nymphs**: Bodies glowing like living lanterns; their presence carries a soft breeze and ethereal lullaby.

- **Storm-forgers**: Hands calloused, robes crackling with static. Their forges scream with tempest echoes.

- **Sky-sailors**: Their voice whistles cut through gale, directing vessels via sound.

- **Temple-guilds**: Sanctuaries lit by floating glyph-lanterns and echoing with chants harmonized to core vibrations.

5. Religion & Spiritual Systems

- **Vahlinon Aether-Mysticism**:

  - **Belief**: Ether as life's flow, soul as wind's echo.

  - **Rituals**:

    - *Breath-Cycle Prayer*: Participants chant in unison, channeling ether through glowing breath masks.

    - *Ash Burial*: Ash spirals in the wind as mourners whisper final verses.

  - **Controversy**: Core-repair glows strangely during rituals, causing debate on divine vs. defilement.

6. Technology

- **Ether-Tech**: Emits a constant hum and faint ozone. Devices react to touch with warm light pulses.

- **Levitation Cores**: Hidden beneath shrine-temples, humming with energy, often guarded and draped in silk.

- **Teleport Temples**: Stone runes shift and rearrange mid-air; teleportation comes with a sudden gust and blinding light.

- **Sky-bridge Supports**: Glow under moonlight, vibrating subtly beneath footfalls.

- **Bio-mech Suits**: Clank and hiss when moved; smell of treated leather and mineral grease.

- **Ground Infrastructure**: Echoing tunnels, flickering hazard lights, metallic footsteps echoing like drums.

- **Sky-tree Algae Farms**: Damp, fragrant air with faint melodic insect calls and luminous pollen drift.

- **Tech Controlled by Priests**: Calibrated through ritual touch and harmonic chants.

7. Timeline of Key Events

The Cataclysmic Fall

- **When**: Ancient past

- **What Happened**: A terraforming spell by High Archmage Il'Vyr shattered the planet, launching land into the sky.

- **Implications**: Birth of floating isles, death of billions, foundation of Sky-councils, ether-shal gains sacred/dangerous status.

Guild Rivalry over Core Maintenance

- **When**: Ongoing

- **What Happened**: Guilds (especially Sky-sailors and

Ground-traders) fight for control of levitation core upkeep.

- **Implications**: Persistent social unrest and power struggles destabilize Vahlien's political structure.

Sky-sailors Clash with Ground-traders

- **When**: Present

- **What Happened**: Violent conflicts erupt over resource access and transport rights.

- **Implications**: Deepens caste divides; threatens trade networks and communal unity.

Uncontrolled Storms / Rift-blasts

- **When**: Sporadic incidents

- **What Happened**: Etheric Harmonization overdose causes massive magical outbursts.

- **Implications**: Infrastructure damage, social fear, tightening regulation of magic users.

Eco-magical Reckonings

- **When**: Present, increasing

- **What Happened**: Capture of Skylure Nymphs causes ecological imbalance.

- **Implications**: Sky-tree farms wither, air stagnates, potential collapse of floating isle ecosystems.

8. Language & Culture

- **Sky-Tongue**: Whistled calls echo melodically through towers, answered in chirping reverence.

- **Grit-speak**: Harsh, earthy tones barked between tunnel creaks and mining picks.

- **Levitation Glyphs**: Radiate a heatless glow; carved lines shift subtly when activated.

- **Isle-centric Cultures**: Every isle features a different scent, dialect, and sky color palette.

- **Floating-night Gatherings**: Sky filled with laughter, echo-music from wind drums, clouds lit with lanterns.

9. Daily Life of Isle Citizens

- **Housing**: Floating terrace homes creak gently with the breeze, wind-chimes singing lullabies.

- **Food**: Algae-bread is chewy with a saline tang; sky-trout flakes with iridescent oil; jam smells like fermented honeysuckle.

- **Clothing**: Robes rustle with each step, flock glyphs shimmer as if alive.

- **Routines**:

  - Glyph-rune upkeep: Done in candlelight with crystal chisels

  - Cloud-catcher net sharpening: Metallic rasping under open skies

  - Core-hymn ceremony: A chorus that reverberates through the bones

- **Leisure**:

  - Floating-night gatherings: Mists swirl underfoot; dancers wear bioluminescent veils

  - Sky-library holograms: Words float midair, reshaping as readers speak

  - Courier rides: Wind rushes past ears, sky arches overhead like a living dome

Let this Codex be your ballast and your beacon.

A Note to the Reader

Thank you for joining Kaia on the first step of *The Codex Rebellion*.

This story began with one question: What happens when silence becomes the most powerful weapon? Kaia's fight has only just begun, and in **The Codex Rebellion: Echoes of the Forbidden, Book 2**, the rebellion widens, alliances strain, and the stakes cut deeper than ever.

If you connected with this journey, I'd be grateful if you left a review or shared the book with another reader. Every voice helps keep the rebellion alive.

With gratitude,

—A.D. Tenebris

Creator of *The Codex Rebellion Trilogy*

Afterword

When I first imagined Kaia Mori, I didn't see a warrior or a leader. I saw a teenager clutching a ribbon, standing in the ashes of a book, with a memory too fragile—and too dangerous—to be allowed to survive.

The Codex Rebellion has always been more than a dystopian tale. It's a story about silence and defiance, about the cost of remembering in a world built on forgetting. Kaia didn't ask to carry that burden. She didn't even know if she could. But like so many of us, she stepped forward anyway—half-afraid, half-broken, but wholly unwilling to let the last thread of truth be cut.

This trilogy began with a single question: *What happens when the war isn't against weapons, but against words?*

And so, Kaia fought.

From the academy's ruins to the underground archives, every step has tested not only her courage but her loyalty, her grief, and her belief that stories—no matter how fragile—are worth bleeding for. And yet, the rebellion is only just beginning.

The next chapter takes Kaia beyond the shattered walls of the academy to the hidden monasteries of the Northern Mountains, where forbidden texts whisper of a deeper history and a darker weapon. In ***The Codex Rebellion: Echoes of the Forbidden, Book 2***, alliances fracture, the Ink Plague spreads, and Kaia must decide whether leadership is sacrifice—or betrayal.

If you've felt the echo of her struggle in your own, if you've caught the pulse of memory in her defiance—then thank you for walking this road with her. With me. With all of us who still believe words matter.

And if this story has spoken to you, I hope you'll leave a review or share it with another reader. Every voice that joins in keeps the rebellion alive—and ensures the silence never wins.

With gratitude in every unwritten margin,

—A.D. Tenebris

Creator of *The Codex Rebellion Trilogy*

THANK YOU FOR READING!

H ey, Adventurers—

I'm **A.D. Tenebris**, and I'm thrilled you joined me for this journey. If the story sparked your curiosity, made you laugh, or kept you up way past midnight (sorry – not sorry), I'd love to hear what you thought. A quick review does more than you know: it helps fellow readers decide to take the plunge and lets this book find its tribe.

Got sixty seconds?

Drop a rating or a few honest lines wherever you picked up the book. Your voice keeps these pages turning for new readers.

Stay in the loop

Want more spice, speed, and supernatural secrets? Sign up for my newsletter at https://adtenebris.com/mailing-list and get a FREE copy of *The Wingman Chronicles!* Join the squad for exclusive updates, behind-the-scenes extras, and first looks at upcoming releases. Don't miss out—your next adventure starts with one click!

Sign up here: https://adtenebris.com/mailing-list

Let's connect

- Instagram: behind-the-scenes sketches, mood boards, and occasional time-travel memes.

- BlueSky: rapid-fire writing vids, character polls, and live Q&As.

- Website: (friendly platform): bite-sized lore drops and sneak peeks.

Pick your spot, say hi, and tell me which character is you favorite.

Until the next adventure—keep questioning reality, embrace the impossible, and read fearlessly.

— A.D. Tenebris

ABOUT THE AUTHOR

A .D. Tenebris writes where memory fractures and myth bleeds into the present.

Blending science fiction, fantasy, and echoes of ancient worlds, his stories explore the unseen threads that bind time, truth, and identity. From time-bending odysseys to divine rebellions and post-apocalyptic awakenings, his work

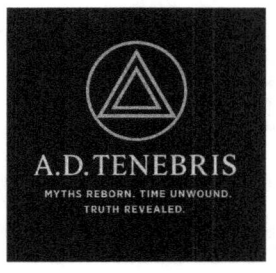

delves into the spaces between—between light and shadow, fate and free will, legacy and loss.

Tenebris is known for crafting immersive worlds and emotionally charged narratives driven by flawed heroes, forgotten histories, and impossible choices. His young adult and crossover novels are read by those who crave high-concept adventure wrapped in heart and mystery.

When not bending timelines or mythologizing the future, he writes under stars, studies the past, and believes every story we tell is a bridge to the one we're becoming.